The Witches and Wizards of Ozz
Deep Impact

By J. Lew

www.jlew-books.com

Dedication

To those who have fought and are fighting the good fight, and all who endure to the end.

Table of Contents

Introduction

She runs through the woods, pushing through tall weeds and bushes, running into trees, and being blinded by the darkness and the tears flowing from her eyes. Her master teleported her to the old burned-out ruins for training, and now she is running for her life. Unaware of her location or any way home, she runs to elude the darkness that follows her in silence through the woods. All she can do is run, run as far away as she possibly can. She stumbles over vines, tree roots, fallen branches, and other things she cannot see, for the night is pitch black. It is a moonless, cold, wet night, and the cold blows through her like an open window. The woods are as quiet as she has ever known, and she pauses to gather her thoughts and whispers, "What am I doing? Where can I run so that they can not find me? Oh, for heaven's sake. What was I thinking? I have a family, a good husband, and my child." The woods crackled, and the wind freezes the tears on her face, but there was nothing more chilling than what she had just witnessed.

"Run," she says to herself. "Run, damn you."

All the while, something is watching her, following her from the shadows of darkness. Minutes feel like hours as she succumbs to her delusions, stopping to laugh or cry and then turning again to the darkness. She leans against a tree, pleading, "Let me be, I beg of you. Please, just let me be!"

She turns, slipping away from the tree to run again, and releases a blood-curdling scream.

Two weeks passed, and on Wednesday, March 12, 1692, a tired, broken, and weary LeAnne Hempstead was dragged down the courthouse steps following a lengthy trial. The magistrates did not feel there was any need to read her sentence to the townspeople, who stood by waiting for what would come next. Women in the township threw stones at her and called her a witch. The word *witch* echoed through the crowd, and soon the masses began to chant, "Stone the witch, stone the witch." No one had mercy for the poor woman, not any of the townspeople who watched, and indeed, none who were stoning her.

LeAnne noticed one lone retarded woman weeping, standing away from the crowd and shielding her face from the horrible sight. LeAnne was one of the few women who paid attention to her and allowed her to play with her daughter. LeAnne's precious little daughter died only a week before from what many believed was a high fever; soon, rumor spread, and the townspeople began to talk. The townspeople were convinced that a dark and sinister shadow hid among them. LeAnne, accused of being a witch – accused of her daughter's death! During her trial, each time she tried to stand and speak on her behalf, she fell to the courthouse floor like a person with epilepsy. The townspeople believed it was the work of her wizard master or specter to keep her from revealing his identity and hideout.

After the trial, LeAnne's husband watched helplessly as his wife curled up on the steps, pleading for her life. She was slowly dying from her wounds. The Magistrates said she and her wizard master met in the woods to conjure up spells against the township. After her death, the sheriff and his deputies searched the woods for the wizard, but their search proved fruitless.

Because of this, my aunt and uncle insist I stay out of the woods. They are spiritually disturbed by Mrs. Hempstead's stoning, and I often find them whispering and then changing the subject each time I walk into the room. We often pray for Mr. Hempstead, who left the township before his wife's burial. "You murdered her; you bury her," he told the townspeople. Then he packed up the few belongings he still had and left the Williams River Township for good. Sunday worship was never the same after that; the murmurs and the pointing gave way to fear and distrust, and it didn't take long for the church to be divided. Now I go to my room afraid, not for myself, but for my Aunt and Uncle, because they are afraid of something they will not speak of. Their fears are my fears, and all I can think about is this thing they say is hiding among us. I stand at my bedroom door, trying to listen to what they are saying, straining my ears until I can no longer bear it, at which point I walk right out of my room to make them stop. Even after they go to bed, I kneel outside their door and listen.

I often pray and recite Psalm 23: "The LORD is my shepherd; I shall not want. He maketh me to lie down in green pastures: he leadeth me beside the still waters. He restoreth my soul: he leadeth me in the paths of righteousness for his name's sake. Yea, though I walk through the valley of the shadow of death, I will fear no evil: for thou art with me; thy rod and thy staff they comfort me. Thou preparest a table before me in the presence of mine enemies: thou anointest my head with oil; my cup runneth over. Surely goodness and mercy shall follow me all the days of my life: and I will dwell in the house of the LORD forever."

At night I rest upon my bed, thinking of my parents, whom I have no memory of. My aunt tells me I am much like the two of them, but more like my mother, who would roam the woods like a wild roe deer as a child. I love running through the woods and jumping over old man Kirts's fence just to frustrate him. Aunt Liz tells me my mother would have run along with me until she married my father. Now, my life is filled with worry for my aunt and uncle. We hear each week that others were dragged from their homes in the early morning, just before daybreak. My aunt and uncle repeatedly warn me, "Stay out of the woods. It's for your own good." It seems more annoying to me now than a warning.

These days I try to write in my journal as much as possible, but this morning I awoke from a dream that wouldn't escape my mind. I was standing by the edge of the fence between two farms, and suddenly a horrible thing grabbed me by the arm. I screamed, awoke, and could not fall asleep because of my dream. It is now early morning, and I am writing about what I saw in my dreams. Even writing about it in my journal frightens me. This dream has put me on edge, and with all the talk going on about witches, I believe I should tear the page right from my journal and throw it into the fire, lest someone reads it, in which case I would be dragged from our home and torn from the loving arms of my aunt and uncle. It's best for all of us that I never mention this dream to anyone.

It's been a month, and I continue to dream of this most hideous thing that knows my name and calls out to me. It seems I am running from it, but I am not going anywhere, just running and crying as she calls my name.

When I awake, I fear that I am vexed by this dream and dare not tell a single soul, alive or dead. I pray every night before I go to bed, hoping never to dream of this dream again. I drift in and out of sleep, afraid of my dreams. Thinking about it makes me tremble as I lie awake, and I cry myself to sleep.

This week has been good for me; I have not had that horrible dream that keeps me awake at night. I hear my uncle and aunt talking in their room, and to my aunt's frustration, she mentions a woman's name, but I cannot hear her clearly. I do, however, hear the word *wicked,* and my aunt pleads that we leave this place before it's too late. I run quietly into my room, trying to go through the names of the people in our township, and then the woman's name becomes clear to me: *Elmira*... Elmira Pembroke. I don't know her very well outside of Sunday worship, but come to think of it, I don't like the way her son looks at me. The way he watches me makes me bristle with fear.

It's been months now, and I can't get her name out of my head. The word *wicked* seems to coincide with my dreams. It reminds me of a quote from a play by William Shakespeare that was read to me when I was a little girl: "By the pricking of my thumbs, something wicked this way comes." Oh, how I fear this thing, and now I believe it's closer to us than we think. Only the Lord can help us now.

Chapter 1
Seeds of Vengeance

Who could have known that it would go so far? Why was this happening, and why were so many people being taken away to their deaths? My aunt and uncle tell me to stay on the farm; they say I must not venture out.

"Please stay out of the woods, child; I don't know why you don't listen." Aunt Liz scolds. "The woods are dangerous, and we don't want you hurt. You're not ten years old anymore; playing in the woods is what children do. Now, you are seventeen, and you will soon be eighteen. You're a young woman. You should be thinking of marriage!"

"Marriage!" Dorothy exclaims. "Oh my God, to whom? There isn't one person in this entire township whom I'd marry."

"Dorothy Adams, you can't stay single all your life." Aunt Liz sighs, shaking her head. "You have to grow up sooner or later."

"I hope it's later rather than sooner," Dorothy mumbles.

"What's that, child?" asks Aunt Liz.

"Nothing, Aunt Liz," replies Dorothy.

Clarence turns to his wife and pokes her. "Ask her about that young lad, Horus Hunter," he says. "She's always talking to him, right?"

"Dorothy, what's wrong with that handsome boy, Horus?" Aunt Liz smiles. "You fancy him, don't you?"

"Horus?" Dorothy's eyes widen. "Aunt Liz! You're joking, of course. Listen to his name, Horse or Horus – I would not know which name to use! He's so far from handsome, and he looks like a horse. No, he looks like the other end of the horse."

She, Aunt Liz, and Uncle Clarence laugh at her joke.

"Well, what about his brother, Adam?" asks Aunt Liz. "Now, you can't say he's not handsome."

"Well, that ugly Sarah Washington has her hooks in him," says Dorothy. "If you so much as look at him, she'll grab him and whisk him off in a different direction. I can't imagine what it's like with all those girls in the same house; you know, they always argue over one thing or another. They're not even friends with each other, let alone with other people."

Dorothy looks exasperated.

"Oh, I think I know what that's like," Clarence interjects.

Both Elizabeth and Dorothy shoot him a glaring look.

"Don't you have some wood to cut?" asks Aunt Liz. "The barn needs mending, and the fence too, while you're at it."

He raises both arms in a gesture of surrender and says, "See what I mean?"

Once Clarence is gone, Elizabeth calls Dorothy to the table, motioning for her to sit down.

"Come here, child. You know that your uncle and I can't have children and that you are the joy of our life." Aunt Liz grabs Dorothy's hand. "Marriage is a good thing; you have responsibilities, and besides … we want grandchildren. Your uncle and I aren't getting any younger, you know. When your parents died, we raised you as our own. I'm afraid we've spoiled you, child. Don't be afraid of life, Dorothy. You have to embrace it."

Elizabeth squeezes Dorothy's hand and pleads with her, her eyes downcast and sorrowful. "Listen," She says in a low voice. "The other day, your uncle talked to Avery Kirts, and he said he's willing to sell us a piece of his farm," she continues. "He'd sell it for you."

"Aunt Liz, I'm not afraid," Dorothy explains. "I just want to travel to different parts of this new world. All this is okay, but it's not what I want. They say it's warmer down south and even better for growing crops. It's better for everything," she continues, lost in her daydream.

"Child, when we left England, all we could talk about was this new world and all it had to offer." Aunt Liz's voice is firm. "You sound just like your mother. She couldn't wait to get here and was just as headstrong as you are now."

Aunt Liz stares up at the ceiling, lost in a daydream of her own. "Oh, your mother was a beautiful woman; she was. We were so excited when she and I got on that ship with our family. But once the voyage began, the two of us stayed on the deck... sick as ever, we were. We leaned over that ship's side until nothing was left in us. At times the water was so rough that people's things and even some people were rolling across that ship like wine barrels. But we were determined to get here, grow crops, and have children."

Dorothy stares intently at her aunt.

"I tell you, Dorothy, at times, life here is just as hard as it was crossing the ocean. Beatrice was a dreamer, just like you are. She would only see the world her way. Our mother died two years after we settled here. And then all the work fell on me because I was the oldest. Beatrice was twelve years younger than I, so she would spend her days running through the woods and jumping fences like a wild roe. Even after Clarence and I were married, someone had to maintain this farm. When Poppa took sick, we took care of him until he died. The hard winters and the hard living – that's all we have. No matter where you go, life has a way of making things hard. Your mother knew this when she grew up and had to take on her responsibilities as a wife."

Aunt Liz pats Dorothy's hands, then clutches them in her own. "It's time to grow up, Dorothy." She looks her in the eyes. "You're more beautiful than your mother, and someday soon, you'll make some man a very lucky husband. Now, your uncle likes that Horse or Horus fellow, but I think he looks more like a jackass if you ask me."

Dorothy and her aunt enjoy a good laugh.

"Oh, Aunt Liz, I know I'm all grown up now, but the men here aren't the men of your day," Dorothy explains. "These men like their corn drinks and ale, and the boys my age are lazy. They're always talking about growing cotton or tobacco on a plantation somewhere, with blacks as their slaves, and they talk about sneaking into Old Man Bowe's barn and drinking toddies by the cupful." She rolls her eyes. "I hear what happens when those men get drunk."

"Now Dorothy, I've warned you not to get caught up in all that gossip," admonishes Aunt Liz. "You keep yourself busy, and you won't have time for all that nonsense." Elizabeth leans back in her chair, looking around to ensure no one else is listening. "While we are on the subject, tell me, who got the black eye this time?"

"Well, if you want to know, it was Mrs. Trevor," says Dorothy. "She's always a mess."

Elizabeth puts her hand to her mouth and whispers, "Well, this must be the third time this month."

Dorothy smirks. "Seems to me, Aunt Liz, you've had some spare time on your hands."

"Well, I wouldn't call it spare time." Aunt Liz looks Dorothy right in the eyes. "You run along now and ensure fresh hay is in the barn."

As Dorothy leaves the room, Elizabeth mutters, "I thought for sure she was going to say, Mrs. Bowe."

Dorothy, hearing her aunt, tilts her head slightly to one side. "I would have, but I figured you already knew about her." Elizabeth will have no more to do with this conversation. "If you don't go on and get your chores done, I don't know what I'll do to you," she says. "You, child, have ears like a mole has senses."

Out in the barn, Dorothy replaces the old hay in the stalls while her Uncle mends some loose boards. The old mare is peaceful and moving around nervously in her stall.

"Dorothy," her Uncle calls out. "You be careful around her. She's been a little nervous this morning. I can't tell why, so you let me get the hay for her stall. She'll get it as soon as she settles down."

"You would think both horses would be nervous, but it's just old Peaceful today," Dorothy notes.

"Yes, it's like she knows something that no one else knows. You make sure all your other chores here are taken care of," says Clarence.

"Uncle, do you think the Carolinas are a good place to grow crops? They say it's nice there." States Dorothy.

"Well, Dorothy, I know that some places are better than others, but it's all in what you make of it. No matter where you go, it'll all be the same if you're taking hardships along with you. You have to approach life, and land, as it comes to you and figure out how to work it as you go. We never know what life will throw at us."

Clarence takes a seat on the stool while Dorothy ponders his words. "You take old Abraham Kirts, for example. He lost his family and became a mean, bitter old bugger. Before the old colony was attacked and burned down, I heard he was a good man willing to help anyone in need. After he helped build this colony, it seemed no one wanted anything to do with him. No one really talked about him, and maybe it was with good reason, I don't know. When his children grew up, I know they hopped on the first ship back to England. But Avery, his youngest son, endured his father's hardness and stayed here. And now he owns the largest farm around."

"And he's really nice," Dorothy pointed out.

"The point I'm getting to is this," continues Clarence. "You can be a miserable person and make everyone else miserable as well as your own. As sure as the sun rises, those people will catch the first boat out of your life, and you'll never see them again. You should always pray that the Good Lord help you move past your hardships and you can bring up your family lovingly to help them do the same for their families. It's not easy losing the people you love, but you have to look around you. You have to see that other people in your life need that same love you are extending to the ones who have died." Clarence stands up, gripping a wooden hay rake while Dorothy listens.

He sighs. "When Elizabeth lost her sister, she was hurting for a while, but she found comfort in prayer, and eventually, she moved on. She had you and did all she could to make your life enjoyable. You are the child she never had, and on top of that, you are the spitting image of Beatrice. You remind her of her sister. So you see, all we want is what's best for you."

"I know that, Uncle," Dorothy says warmly.

"I'm sure she told you about the piece of land Avery Kirts has offered us. It would be for you." He said.

Dorothy leans against one of the beams in the stall, considering what it would be like to spend the rest of her life on the farm. In a relaxed tone, she says, "Yes, I guess it would be nice to take over that land. Did he say which part?"

"Sure did." Clarence steps out of the barn and points toward Kirts' property. "It's this piece that's right next to ours. Now, it's only four acres, mind you, but I'm sure your husband will build a really nice house for the family when you get married. It'll give your little ones enough room to run free, just as your mother used to do, and like you who still do. I'm sure you remember when Mr. Kirts would chase you across the field when you were younger."

Dorothy laughs. "I wouldn't call it a chase, exactly."

"Well," Uncle says, "I have to say, he would be pretty angry at us for letting you jump his fence. He didn't like you running loose around his farm like you owned the place." He chuckles as he imitates Mr. Kirts waving his rake in the air like a whip. "He'd storm over to our house like a madman giving me and your aunt an earful." Still waving his arms,

Clarence mimics, "That girl of yours needs the whip. You'll never see any of my children so disobedient."

"His fingers were waving, and his arms were flaring about, spitting mad he would be, spitting mad indeed. Your aunt would be so afraid for you. She would cry and say, 'If he ever catches Dorothy, he'd use the whip on her for sure.' Mr. Kurts was never one to spare the rod, mind you."

Dorothy, her arms still draped over the post, mumbles, "Well, that's why he never saw his children again."

"Maybe so," he says in a more somber tone, "but it is time for you to grow up. You have your whole life ahead of you. Time waits for no one; you're a young lady today, but tomorrow you'll be an older woman wishing you'd done things differently. We all have certain regrets in life, but we don't regret our entire lives. You get busy and finish up; you have the cows to feed after this."

Dorothy sighs and finishes the horses' stalls. She walks lazily across the back of the farm, thinking, *a month has passed, and I have not gone into the woods, just as I was told.* Dorothy looks at the forest, tempted to jump the fence. *I should go just a few feet into the woods to see why Peaceful is so nervous. There are days when Sam, our younger horse, is nervous too.* She runs back to the barn door, where she hears the horses stomping about inside. When Dorothy peers in, there is nothing to be found, so she runs to the edge of the farm right at the wood line and crouches down on her knees. She hides in the tall grass to watch and listen for a while. *I can't see or hear anything, not even breaking twigs on the ground.* Dorothy slips between the rails of the fence, curious about what she'll find. Deeper and deeper, she ventures into the woods but doesn't see or hear anything. She sits quietly, thinking, *Nothing, and I have no idea what I'm looking for. If it were a wild animal, I would see tracks; but I see nothing that would make me believe it's an animal. With all this talk about witches, I'd better be careful what I say. I must be careful in these woods, especially if I want to discover who or what makes our poor animals so nervous.* Dorothy sighs. *I cannot imagine what it could be.*

Daily, her Uncle reminds her, "Be careful of wild animals; they may be close enough for the old mare and Sam to smell. They can hear far better than humans, smell things, and sense danger where we can't. Keep your eyes open when you move about the farm."

All Dorothy can do is say, "Yes, Uncle. I'm always watchful. I have great eyesight, and I'm very aware of my wooded surroundings. I know these woods better than I know my own bedroom." She rolls her eyes as she walks away.

Dorothy walks back into the barn and talks to the horses as though they understand her.

"I'm going to find out what is in those woods if it's the last thing I do," she says. "I've checked behind the farm all the way to the town and seen nothing amiss." Scratching behind the old mare's ears, she continues, "I wonder what my mother was like. They said you were there when they died on that cold day. Oh, I wish you could talk! You could tell me what happened. You could tell me why my parents unhitched you and the old steed from the buggy. What did you see? What did you hear? And why did you leave them alone in that terrible storm?"

Dorothy walks away, looking out the back door of the barn. "I have so many questions and no one to answer them," she says to herself. And then, her Aunt Liz calls her to help prepare supper. Dorothy walks out of the barn and runs into the house to help her aunt.

"Aunt Liz, what was my father like?" asks Dorothy. "Everyone is always talking about my mother, but no one ever talks about my father. Do I resemble him at all?"

"Yes, you do," replies Aunt Liz. "You are beautiful like your mother, but you have your father's eyebrows, and you are a lot stronger than your mother; your uncle and I have noticed your strength, which I believe you got from your father as well. In a way, you got your wit from him too." She pauses. "Mind you, your mother was pretty intelligent, but your father had a keen sense about him."

Dorothy smiles and tries to picture what her father looks like.

"When he was here, he would help your uncle around the farm. I tell you, he could really use that ax. When you were young, he would try to show you how to use it and the bow he made for you. That bow was taller than you were, but you looked so cute when he showed you how to shoot it. Oh, Beatrice would throw a fit when she saw him. She would tell him, 'Axs and bows are not tools for a proper lady.' She would bring you in and tell you, 'never use an ax, for it's a man's tool.' She'd say."

Dorothy has a big grin on her face. "Did I ever try to use it?"

"Oh yes, I would watch you go out with a stick and beat on that old chopping stump like your father was beside you. He taught you how to use the bow and arrow the same way the Indians taught him. You remind me so much of him when you would go off into the woods with that bow. You'd stay in those woods for hours, but I never worried. I knew you were just like your parents; your mother, who hopped fences and ran through those woods like a deer, and your huntsman father. No, I never worried about you in there."

"Oh, I wish I could remember those days," Dorothy says in a dream state.

"He could shoot a musket, shoot an arrow, and throw that ax. I watched you grow into a beautiful young woman, wild, but a beautiful young woman nevertheless," Aunt Liz expounds.

After supper, Dorothy helps her Aunt Liz clear the table and wash the dishes. She goes to bed contemplating who she wants to be like the most, her loving mother or her huntsman father. She often thought of her father's merchant work, travel to different towns, and his knack for meeting new people. That evening, Dorothy finds solace in the thought that she is like both her parents rolled up into one.

Dorothy is skilled with the bow and arrow, but she worries that her ability to use the ax might mean she will have to work, so she trains with the ax secretly and only ventures into the woods with the bow to hunt.

I'll keep exploring the woods, she thinks. *And I will learn how to become a warrior princess.*

The winter season is upon the family, and they are storing and salting food for the winter. Uncle is drying meats and fish while Aunt Liz is shelving preserves.

Dorothy appreciates wintertime. She likes how she can see through the trees when they have dropped their leaves. The snow will soon reveal the tracks of the animals nearby.

The following day, she peers out at the Kirts's farm from the barn. She sees it is looking a little worn. It must be because his father's heavy hand is no longer over him. He doesn't seem to do as much on the farm anymore. Dorothy wanders around the barn, speaking to herself.

"I'm kind of looking forward to getting the four acres he promised me," she states. "I hope I won't have to be married to get the land. I guess I will have to pray that I can take possession of it without giving my hand in marriage. I really don't like to think of marriage right now."

She approaches Sam's stall. "What do you think, Sam? Are you ready to be in the stall with a young mare? Then again, you are a male, so I doubt you'd mind at all. I just don't think it's fair. Why couldn't he have said that the land would simply be a gift for my eighteenth birthday? That's just next month."

"Dorothy!" Her aunt calls.

Dorothy steps outside the barn and waves to her aunt. "I'm here, Aunt Liz."

"It's time to start supper." Her Aunt shouts from the back door.

Dorothy turns and closes the barn door and then casts the stick she uses to scratch behind Sam's ear to the ground. She makes her way toward the house to help with the cooking.

"Aunt Liz, why didn't we ever see the Kirts' in church?" She asks.

"Dorothy, there's a lot of people on farms and in the town, but not all of them go to church for one reason or another. It could be that Mr. Kirts couldn't find it in his heart to ask God to help him overcome the loss of his children. I believe he lost faith in God and felt he no longer needed him. So he kept his son out of the church."

"That's really sad," Dorothy replies. "It's like Uncle said, 'everything we do has a *deep impact* on others."

"That's right, he couldn't see past his losses , and neither could he see everyone else he still had around him." Aunt Liz says.

"Was his wife as bitter as he was?" asks Dorothy.

"Well, she was just as miserable because her husband made things that way," says Aunt Liz. "No one really knows what happened at the old settlement, for we can only go by the stories passed down over the years. My parents purchased this property from one of the surviving families, and my father didn't know why they sold it. I don't even think he bothered asking. We noticed how terribly he treated those poor kids. They really had it bad growing up on that farm.

"That is so sad," Dorothy says.

"Yes, you're right," Aunt Liz agrees. "I would pray every day that the Lord would give that old man a kinder heart. Maybe the kids wouldn't have had it so bad. The two eldest left there so fast they only took the clothes on their backs. I believe the oldest son went to work somewhere in Boston, saved up enough money, and paid for his and his sister's passage back to England."

"I think your prayers missed Mr. Kirts and landed on his son Avery. He and his father are like night and day." Dorothy's tone is somber. She leans against the table, resting her chin on her hands.

"Well, that's often the case, Dorothy. The kinder and gentler heart often falls on the next generation."

"Maybe it's because they want their children to have better lives than they did growing up," Dorothy considers.

Clarence walks in, having overheard their conversation. "Smells good," he remarks. "What are we having for supper?"

"Lamb stew," Dorothy announces.

Clarence nods. "Well, I had better get cleaned up." He says, and Dorothy hurriedly runs to the water basin to pour water over his hands as he washes up.

"Is it possible for those who don't seem to worship the Lord to enter into heaven?" asks Dorothy.

"Well," Clarence replies, drying his hands, "Dorothy, only God knows a man's heart. He and only He will determine who is worthy to enter into His kingdom. Of whom are you speaking?"

"I was thinking of Mr. Avery," admits Dorothy. "He seems to be a very nice and generous man. It would seem terribly wrong if he could not enter into God's kingdom."

"Sit down, Dorothy," says Clarence. "There's a lot to learn, and I'm going to tell you about two things that you should try and understand. First of all, I believe the Kirts family was a very religious family, at least before the Indians raided the old settlement. True, he became a very bitter man, but I know that his children never lost their faith in God. Through it all, they endured their situation until they left the farm, so you see, the children never wavered. I believe this is why Avery is so kind and generous. You don't have to worship indoors; God's outdoors are also made for worship."

"So whenever I'm in the woods, and I kneel down and pray for our family, it's just the Lord and me," Dorothy interjects.

"Absolutely," says Clarence. "And secondly, there are those eleventh-hour believers."

"Eleventh hour?" Dorothy raises an eyebrow.

"Yes, the eleventh hour. Look at the parable of the man who hired other men to work in his vineyard. The owner of that vineyard went out in the morning and in the afternoon to hire those who wanted to work, and then in the eleventh hour, he found others standing idle and told them to go and work on his vineyard. At the end of the day, the ones he found in the eleventh hour were paid first, and then he paid all the others who worked throughout the day. God is forever searching for those who are willing to believe, even in the eleventh hour of their lives. That's why only God determines who is worthy of entering into His kingdom."

Dorothy grins, content with her uncle's explanation.

"Well, Dorothy, let's get the food on the table." Aunt Liz says. Dorothy obeys, and Uncle blesses the food. He thanks the Lord for his family and all that the Lord has given them. Between spoonfuls, Dorothy mentions the possibility of living in the South and seeing the whole world while the family eats their supper. They also talk about the things the day brought forth. After supper, Dorothy prays for the Kirts family, and she thanks the Lord for the wisdom He has bestowed upon her uncle.

Early in the morning, they are awakened by the sounds of horses, shouting, and muskets being fired. They sleep lightly because of the disturbances in order to get up quickly should these sounds lead to danger.

Uncle says, "Dorothy, do not go outside the house; we'll all stay put." This time the commotion is coming from the Kirts's house. They keep the lanterns out to keep the house dark while the Sheriff and his men ride by on their horses.

"Oh my God," says Elizabeth. "That poor man and his wife have kept to themselves."

"Quiet!" orders Clarence in a hushed tone. "Elizabeth, please!"

"Once the commotion has died down, and the Sheriff and his men have passed the farm," Uncle reminds them, "We'll remain quiet for a while, and I'll go over and check on young Mr. Kirts and his wife. I'll need to get dressed."

Aunt Liz begs him, "Wait until sunrise."

When dawn breaks, Mr. Adam Hunter, who owns the farm to the east of Dorothy, visits the Kirts's farm with Clarence. They discover the house has been ransacked and find Avery Kirts and his wife, Anna, on the floor, dead. Both have been shot, and Avery more than once. As far as they can see, Mrs. Kirts was shot closer to the door, while Avery was shot closer to the fireplace.

"They must have tried to drag Anna out the door," Adam reasons.

"Yes, and Avery here must have taken his musket and shot one of the deputies. Also, given the amount of blood on the wall, someone else must have been shot."

"He likely shot a couple of the deputies, and then the other deputies shot him," Clarence deduces. *Good for Avery,* he thinks to himself. Then he ponders, "They fought for what was right. I wonder who the lucky deputies were!"

"Or Sheriff," Adam mentions. He and Clarence glare at each other, unsettled.

"It is tragic that such a nice couple has fallen victim to these witch hunts. This man and his wife stayed away from the church, the town, and its people. What in the name of heaven were Keith and his men doing here? Why this poor couple? Lord Almighty, what is going on? Do you think this has anything to do with these ungodly trials?

Adam shrugs.

"I need a seat." Clarence sighs. Resting his arms on his knees and staring at the mess of this needless loss of life, he whispers, "This is just unbelievable. Now we are all as nervous as our animals."

Adam speaks quietly to Clarence. "Do you think she's a witch?"

"Who...Elmira?" Clarence whispers back.

They glance at each other and then around the room as though someone has just walked in on them. "No, Clarence," Adam whispers. "They would only come here if they claimed young Mrs. Kirts was a witch."

Clarence raises his hands in disbelief. "I don't know what to think anymore. I do know that someone will be claiming this property in a few days, and I'll bet it will be a member of the Pembroke family or at least one of their friends," he remarks.

"Yes, it seems that a lot of property is being taken, and this is the best farm in the entire colony, or at least it used to be. Avery wasn't much on upkeep." Adam has examined the house and finds it in desperate need of repair. He continues. "I know that Wyndham Washington is talking about leaving. He's all packed up and ready to move on. He has a house full of girls, and since the girls are the ones being targeted, he wants to protect his family by leaving this township."

Clarence shakes his head and says quietly, "I don't much blame him for that."

Adam, whose hands are resting assuredly on his hips, peeks through the rooms and says, "Well, after seeing all this, I'm seriously thinking of doing the same. You may want to leave here yourself; you don't want to be sorry you didn't leave later down the road." Clarence stares at Adam, frustrated by his hurtful comment. Elizabeth has been asking him to leave ever since Leanne Hempstead was stoned. Clarence wants to defend his choice to stay, but he cannot find the words.

Adam says, "Mary and I have been trying to figure these things out, but we can't make sense of it all."

"There is no sense in chaos," says Clarence, "just a lot of what you see here, senseless murder. You have the townspeople accused of witchery, but they have no hard evidence to prove it. Then they go and seize the property. I don't know what you see, Adam, but I don't see any sense."

Adam's hands are still on his hips. He says, "I'd rather give up the farm and leave it to the devil than end up like this poor fellow and his wife, victims of the devil."

"Where would you go?" asks Clarence.

"Well, there's Virginia, the Carolinas, Florida," Adam considers his options. "They say those lands are bountiful."

"It sounds like you've been talking to Dorothy," says Clarence. "That's all she talks about these days."

The men laugh.

"Well, seeing this sad sight has helped me make up my mind," says Adam. "I'm taking the missus and the children and leaving."

"There's nothing more to see here." Clarence is ready to leave the Kirts's property. "I guess we can take this poor fellow and his wife and bury them. It's the least we can do. I'll go and hitch Sam up to the buggy, and we'll bury them next to Avery's father."

"A little respect, Clarence," Adam says firmly. "Those kids lived with that man's harsh hands in this world. You don't really think they would want to be buried next to him for the rest of eternity, do you?"

"No, I suppose you're right," Clarence replies. "It's too bad we don't know where he buried his mother. We could have buried them there."

"We'll find a decent place for them, old friend," says Adam, his tone comforting.

After they leave the house and close the door, a shadow travels across the room to the fireplace and hovers over Avery's body. A tear falls upon his face while the shadow of a hand caresses his cheek.

From then on, Clarence, Elizabeth, and Dorothy spent most of their time in church praying for the accused and their families. The townspeople pass one another in silence, meekly waving but distrustful of one another. There is no love anymore, only fear of the other, and people keep their eyes open for the others who travel there as well. Adam Hunter follows through on his promise and relocates his family to Florida a week later. The township and the farms grow smaller as the trials go on. Dorothy begs her uncle to follow Mr. Hunter's example and move. Clarence keeps repeating that things will get better and that all will return to how it was before the trials. Elizabeth and Dorothy pray that he is right, and they desperately hope things will get better. Often, Dorothy overhears her aunt Liz asking her uncle whether he thinks leaving would help.

"Clarence, this is not the work of God," Elizabeth says, her voice trembling. "I know some say it is, but this is the devil's work. Maybe Dorothy is right. Right now, the Carolinas sound pretty good to me." She swallows. "Clarence, I'm afraid. Did you hear that they dragged Lucy James right out of her home? And when Charles tried to save her, they beat him and threw him in jail along with her! We can't just stay here and hope things will get better."

Elizabeth tries to get through to Clarence, hoping he will understand. She wants nothing more than to leave and start anew somewhere else. Clarence sits at the table, his head in his hands, and says nothing. Although they attend services like they always have, it would never be the same for the family. They would only sit in silence. When the Reverend stands to deliver his message, he is careful about what he says to his divided congregation.

Dorothy turns to her aunt, whispering, and asks, "If we trust in the Lord and have done nothing amiss, why are we being so careful? Why are we so afraid?"

"Hold your tongue, Dorothy," whispers her aunt. "This is neither the time nor the place."

All the fire and spirit in the church have long since gone out. Everyone is trying to protect their family and property. As hard as Dorothy tries, for the life of herself, she cannot figure out how this all started. She doesn't understand the accusations, for she has never seen any signs of witchcraft. No, Dorothy can only trace it back to the death of the Hempstead's' daughter, for which they'd blamed on Mrs. Hempstead. Or perhaps it began with the drifter wandering through the township. Dorothy believes their daughter got the fever from the harsh winter. Many people were sick in the township, and others were buried because of it. Many of the houses were in desperate need of maintenance; they were good for the spring, summer, and fall but not for the cold winters. When the townspeople searched the woods for the strange man that drifted in, they found no signs of him. Talk among the elders suggests that the drifter was a warlock of some kind, a wizard, or a demon. Many have come through the township over the years and left, but no one was ever accused of witchcraft. Why now? Why here? And why, of all things, were the members of the church involved and those who owned good property? There had to be another reason.

Clarence tells Dorothy that she's too young to worry about this.

"Really, now you think I am too young!" She shouts silently.

Before he told her, "You need to grow up and get married."

In an attempt to reason with herself, Dorothy believes they are simply trying to protect her, but she still has to worry for them. Her uncle Clarence and her aunt Liz always talk amongst themselves, and when she enters the room, they either change the subject or act as if they'd been doing something else all along. Dorothy's worries are felt deep down inside, for she can sense something near but does not know how to focus. She can see they are even more worried for her, so she prays that this will not become a part of their daily lives.

Early the following day, a rooster on a neighboring farm begins to crow before sunrise. It isn't long after there is a heavy knocking at the door of their home. Men from the outside are shouting, "Open the door, witch!" One of the men kicks the door open, and before Dorothy and her aunt and uncle can react, they force their way through the house, pushing Clarence to the floor and holding a musket to his head. They carry swords and lances and use their torches to light their way to Elizabeth while she hurries to get dressed. They grab Elizabeth by the hair, yell at her, and call her a witch. Two men grab Dorothy by the shoulders, trying to throw her to the floor and struggling to hold her down.

"She is much stronger than she appears." One of the men says.

Pushing their way to the front door, they drag Elizabeth from the house as she screams for her life.

Chapter 2
Days of Regret

Days of torture and hours are spent in the courtroom. It is like a bad dream from which one cannot awaken. The accusations come one after another, nightmare after nightmare. During the trials, Dorothy is not allowed to visit her aunt. She pleads with her uncle to take her with him but does not prevail. She screams at him, begging him to take her to see her aunt Liz. It has been two days since they dragged Elizabeth Lester from the house. On the third day, Dorothy's Uncle gives in and allows her to accompany him to the jail. He tells her not to ask too many questions because his wife is weak and tired. When Dorothy sees her aunt Liz in the jail cell, she nearly screams, holding her hands to her mouth. There is a stool that Elizabeth sits on, with nowhere to sleep but the floor. The walls are stained, hay is strewn across the floor, and it is in much worse condition than the hay in the horses' stalls. The smell is terrible, and her Aunt looks exhausted, just as her Uncle had warned her.

He reminds her again, "Remember Dorothy, do not ask too many questions."

Dorothy sits in silence on the floor, watching her aunt cry. She is horrified by what she sees.

Elizabeth speaks in a weak voice. "It's like the day Jesus died," she says. "Many accused him, but none of it was true. Still, that didn't stop them from hanging him on the cross. I fear I shall suffer the same fate."

Her clothes are torn and tattered by those who have tortured her. All she can do is cry and Dorothy with her. Elizabeth tries to hide her hands, but it is clear that they are bloodstained. Her fingernails are gone on her right hand; she has bruises on her wrists and ankles from where they laid her on a board and stretched her until she lost consciousness. She is so tired and wounded that she can barely hold her head up to speak. One of the deputies stays with Dorothy and her uncle the entire time.

"Keep your hands away from the bars, and don't get too close." He warns."

They have no choice but to speak to Elizabeth between the bars of her cell. All the while, Clarence weeps throughout the visit. He apologized for not being able to do more for her in her time of need. The words of Adam Hunter are played over and over in his mind, *'You may want to leave here yourself; you don't want to be sorry you didn't leave later down the road.'*

Dorothy and Clarence can only use their words to comfort Aunt Liz, but nothing they say means much to her anymore.

Elizabeth holds her head up to speak to her husband, "Take Dorothy home, and make sure to keep your promise to me!"

"I will, my love," Clarence weeps. "I will."

"Keep your promise Clarence, you hear me?" Aunt Liz's voice is weak but stern. "Keep your promise!"

Dorothy and Clarence leave her in the hands of the murderous villains, for they have no choice but to do so. Dorothy glances into another cell where a woman is weeping in the corner of her cell. She lies on the floor, sobbing uncontrollably. Dorothy cannot see her face, nor does she recognize the woman. Her hair is matted, and patches of her hair are missing, making Dorothy's stomach churn.

The following day, Clarence insists she stays behind. The farm is as quiet as it has ever been. Before he leaves, he warns her, "Stay out of the woods, and do not allow anyone into the house."

Dorothy thinks, *if we couldn't stop them as a family, how can I ever stop them on my own?*

He repeatedly warns her, reminding her that he only allowed her to go with him because she'd begged him incessantly. Now that Dorothy has seen that horrible place, she never wants to look at it again. She does most of the chores around the farm now. She chops wood because it is cold, and the house must be kept warm. Dorothy also tends to the animals and keeps the house in order. When her uncle returns from town, she asks about her Aunt Liz, whose answer is always the same.

"She's a little worse for wear, but things will be okay. When this is all over, my Elizabeth will be back with us, and we'll be a family again," he says weakly. "Just wait and see."

He puts up a brave façade, but it is clear that Clarence is hurting just as much as she. Dorothy remembers what her aunt Liz said from her cell: "*I fear I shall suffer the same fate.*"

Tears and prayers are all that remain. Her uncle does not know it, but Dorothy has begun to sneak out in the night and take the shortcut through the woods to see her aunt Liz. The night before Elizabeth's sentence, Clarence did not say a word upon his return home. He did not eat, nor did he warm himself by the fire. He went straight to his room, and Dorothy could hear him praying aloud, asking "Why?" repeatedly.

Dorothy realizes that it is unlikely her aunt Liz will ever come home. She puts on her warmest cloak and runs through the woods into town. Dorothy cannot see her beloved aunt near the jail wall, but she can hear her, and the other woman is weeping bitterly. The two women recite Psalm 23 together in an attempt to control their sobbing.

Dorothy recently found out that they hung the lady's husband two days ago when she overheard her uncle's conversation with Mr. William Downer. Although she wants to call out to her aunt, she knows she cannot see her, so she stands listening to her and the other woman praying and weeping aloud. She left the jail before she thought her uncle would come looking for her in her room. Dorothy hurries as fast as she can through the darkness, pausing every few yards. It's as if someone is in the woods with her. She strains to see in the darkness. Masking her breath from the cold with her mittens and the hood of her cloak. Dorothy sees nothing but shadows a few yards ahead of her. Those shadows seemed to disappear each time she thought she heard something. Dorothy pauses just long enough to let whatever it is, or whomever it is, disappear in the woods just north of the barn and south of the township. She wouldn't dare travel the roads; after all, she'd been warned time and again never to go out at night.

The road makes one large loop around the farms before it straightens out for about a mile to the town, right along the wood line. There are only two farms with families still living on them, and those people seem to have barred themselves inside their homes. As far as Dorothy and her uncle Clarence know, no one has claimed the Kirts' farm. The woods are much faster than going to town on the road. Dorothy has only to cross the road twice to get to the woods on the other side of the jailhouse near the other houses in town. Dorothy has taken this route many times before, and she knows these woods very well. This night is different because Dorothy is not alone. She ran faster and faster until she saw it – a silhouette of a person! This is a different kind of person, she observes. When most people run, their heads bob up and down, but this person moves as though riding on wheels. It is too quiet to be traveling on wheels, and there is no noise. This person moves with ease through the woods without breaking any branches. Dorothy sits there watching it until she sees nothing more. She waits a little longer, making sure this strange shadow does not hear her running through the snow or breaking branches. Her heart is pounding in her chest, and she cannot wait to get back to the farm. When Dorothy arrives home, she eases the door open that her uncle recently repaired. He is still in prayer when she slips inside. He's quieter and weaker than before. Still, Dorothy does not want to interrupt him. She leaves some cheese and bread on the table, just in case he gets hungry. Dorothy can only pray that her aunt and the other woman find mercy. Her heart is racing so fast that it is hard to breathe. She can only wonder what they are going to do to her Aunt Liz and the other woman.

It seems this started years ago, but it has only been a few months. There are rumors of women in other colonies being tried as witches. The accused are often destitute women, the homeless, and the elderly. In the Williams River Township, many have been dragged from their homes and thrown into prison by the Sheriff, his undersheriff, and their deputies. The word around town is that the undersheriff is shirking his duties by pretending to be ill while the others are falsely accusing the colonists of witchcraft. When these women deny they are witches, they are tortured in the most gruesome manner and forced to confess. The Sheriff and his deputies push sharp pieces of wood under their nails, tying them down on boards and stretching them, and sometimes throwing them into the river to see if they will float. If any of these women manage to float, the townspeople believe they are witches, while those who sink end up drowning in the frigid water, while the Sheriff and his deputies do nothing to save them.

Conspiracy, jealousy, greed, and superstition are major factors that led to all these accusations. Dorothy often wonders, *What if someone saw what I saw in the woods south of the township? What if Mrs. Hempstead had seen something, and all this was just to cover it up?* All the townspeople are asking themselves what-if questions these days, but it seems that no one wants an answer to their questions. This hatred fuels parents to use their young daughters in court to pretend they are under the control of the accused. This gives the magistrates reason to accuse their victims as witches falsely. Uncle tells Dorothy watching the accusers smile to themselves makes him angry, not to mention sick to his stomach, but there is nothing he can do. Dorothy's one visit to see her aunt Liz with her uncle was more than she could bear to see from the inside. Her nightly visits do not help much; it hurts more to hear her aunt cry and makes her want to know more about what is happening. The question is, who or what was in the woods, and why? Was it the warlock they could not find? Questions, questions, and no answers.

Dorothy was told not to worry about these things, but surely seeing her family destroyed warranted some kind of worry! It seems as though no one dared oppose this dreadful system – Ms. Pembroke especially, or the Sheriff, her son, and the Undersheriff who is his best friend from their youth. To oppose them would warrant a visit from the High Sheriff and his henchmen.

To Dorothy's knowledge, her aunt and uncle did not have anything to say about the witch hunt, at least not in public and surely not to anyone in town. The few people Uncle trusted have already left this place. Dorothy and her aunt Liz had begged Clarence to flee the township, and now her Uncle is filled with regret. At night, Dorothy can hear him in his room, praying for the Lord to forgive him for not having decided to leave. Often, he weeps bitterly. He clearly blames himself for trying to hold out for better times. Dorothy does not want to see her aunt Liz while she's wasting away in a cell with only scraps to eat, and she dares not think of the things they are doing to her to make her confess.

Dorothy knows it will be a long while before things improve – that is, if they improve.

She asks herself. "Will Aunt Elizabeth ever be allowed home?" Despite her uncle's optimism, Dorothy knows deep down that she is not coming back. The accused never came back. And besides, her uncle isn't a big man; he is thin, frail, gray-haired, and balding. His hair grows grayer by the day, and his no longer caring for himself has become more apparent. She prayed the night before, and between quiet fits of sobbing, she prayed all night until morning. Before he leaves for the morning, he tells her, "The jailhouse is no place for a young lady."

He looks Dorothy straight in the eyes, gripping her arms, and says, "You are the spitting image of your mother." And then he squeezed her hands and kissed her on the cheek as though he would never see her again. Then he turns and slips out of the door while he weeps. Dorothy watched him get onto the old buggy he had not unhitched the day before. She watched him ride slowly toward town, and after a few minutes, she grabbed her cloak and slipped out to see her aunt one last time. Dorothy runs through the woods behind the farm. She did not care whether anyone was in the woods with her, and she certainly didn't care about making noise.

When she arrives in town, Dorothy hides behind the houses and small farms, careful not to be seen. Crowds flock outside the courthouse, waiting to see what will happen to the two women inside. Carefully, Dorothy walks behind the jail. She cannot see her aunt Liz, nor can she hear her or the other woman. The jail is in the back of the courthouse; Dorothy wonders if they've already been taken to the courtroom. She waits a while before she walks between the jail and another building, where she sees out into the courtyard. There are two posts, with fetters and chains attached to the middle and top. Dorothy was never allowed to attend the events here, and her uncle and Aunt Liz never had the urge to observe any of the whippings or burnings, so she did not know what to expect. When she sees the post, Dorothy thinks of what her uncle has always said – that perhaps things will get better soon. Maybe there is a chance they will let her aunt go. If hey whip her, she will be free, and Dorothy can care for her aunt Liz while she heals. At least she would have her back. Finally, she hopes her aunt is coming home, and they can all be a family again. But then she hears the musings of the crowd, and soon she sees her Uncle Clarence walking behind the deputies, who are escorting her aunt to the post. She watches them push her Uncle away as he struggles to get close to his wife, pleading for mercy. Dorothy's heart pounds, and she begins to cry as she watches the two people she loves most so afraid. The deputies chains Elizabeth with her back to the post, which is too much for Dorothy to bear. To her horror, she sees stacks of wood and hay piled around the post to which her aunt is chained. Two of the deputies pushed branches and hay in the gap used to walk her and the other woman to the post, while others held their muskets in her Uncle Clarence's face as they continued to pile the wood around Aunt Liz.

They read the charges aloud to the crowd.

"The crimes for witchcraft of Mrs. Elizabeth Lester and Mrs. Lucy James share the death sentence by burning."

Dorothy can hardly hold her peace, and she covers her mouth with both hands, releasing a silent scream from the depths of her core. She walks out toward the crowd in a daze, but no one sees her, for everyone is watching the deputy use his torch to set fire to the wood and hay around her aunt Elizabeth. Dorothy observes her aunt's face from behind the crowd. She can see her poor aunt is too tired to plead for her life. No, Elizabeth simply closes her eyes while the deputies toy with the fire around her. Aunt Liz does not say anything to Clarence until she sees the pile of wood catching fire around her. At this time, Dorothy hears her aunt tell Clarence that she loves him and that he must keep his promise to her. The crowd watches the wood catch fire right in front of Elizabeth, and she begins to scream. Dorothy runs through the crowd and pushes her way toward her Uncle, screaming that he must do something.

Dorothy cries, "You have to do something to save her! Please help her. You know she's no witch."

Her uncle holds her back, and the two watch Elizabeth burn. Dorothy screams as loud and for as long as she can, covering her ears to drown out the screams of her aunt Liz and the other woman, Lucy James. Then the Sheriff walks over and grabs Dorothy from her uncle's arms. She faints right then and there.

"Leave her be, and let me take her home where she belongs," Clarence begs of Keith, the Sheriff.

Keith looks over his shoulders at his mother. His mother nods and Keith releases Dorothy to him.

Her uncle carries her to the buggy and sets Dorothy down, trying to comfort her. The Sheriff walks over to his mother, who whispers to him, "This is better than I thought. The little tramp can see what I have in store for her too."

When she turns to walk away, she looks back at him and says, "You know what you have to do."

The Sheriff looks down at his feet and sighs. "Yes, Mother," he replies.

Later that night, visitors arrive at the farm. They call out to Clarence.

"Mr. Lester, why don't you come out of the house?" Keith demands.

Trevor, one of the deputies, warns, "If you don't, we'll have to come in as we did on our last visit,"

When Clarence steps out and stands before them, the Sheriff warns him.

"Mr. Lester, I consider myself a reasonable man, so I'm giving you a chance to leave this farm on your own."

"This is all I have left," pleads Clarence. "Where am I to go?"

"Mr. Lester, you can leave this farm or hand over the witch you are hiding inside," Keith says cruelly.

"She's no more a witch than my Elizabeth," Clarence retorts. "You should let us be. Let us grieve in peace." Clarence shakes his fist at Keith.

Two new young deputies, Dorothy's age, James Snider and Douglass Hess, dismount their horses, walk over to Clarence and grab him by the arms to hold him steady.

"Don't make this any harder on yourself, Mr. Lester," says Keith. "Leave here immediately and save what's left of your family."

Before he can protest any further, Deputy Trevor walks up to him with his staff, thrusting it into Clarence's stomach and ribs.

Keith orders him to stop. "Mr. Trevor, I believe Mr. Lester got the message."

The two deputies allow Clarence to drop to his knees. He collapses facedown into the dirt.

"You have three days to get off this property," Keith snarls.

Clarence knows that Dorothy is in no condition to move, and it is clear now that his condition is worse. He is relieved he has three days to make a decision.

"Three days, Mr. Lester, or we'll be back to take the farm and your niece!" Trevor shouts. He laughs, and then he, the deputies, and the Sheriff ride away.

Clarence tries to get up, but he is in too much pain. He lies on the ground for what seems like hours. Once he sits up, he notices a buggy driving through the gate to the house. When it reaches him, he can see that it is one of his trusted friends. George Thopham, who has come to ask about Dorothy.

"Clarence, for Pete's sake, what happened?" George shouts, hurrying to get down from the buggy.

"Well, if you can get me into the house, I would really appreciate it," says Clarence.

"It's a good thing Mrs. Thopham, and I came by," remarks George helping Clarence into the house.

"I don't know…" Clarence winces in pain. "I don't know how long I was out there, but I had a visit from the Sheriff and his men. They told me I had three days to leave, or they'll be back to take the farm and Dorothy. I fear this is not over for us." Clarence grimaces with each breath, more painful than the last.

"We have to get you to the town to see the doctor, " George advises.

"Not before we get Dorothy out of this house," says Clarence. "I just don't know where to go. I have no place to take her."

"Mr. Lester, where's Dorothy?" Gloria Thopham asks.

"She's in her room." He points to her bedroom across from where he's sitting.

Gloria enters the room and finds Dorothy conscious but with a high fever. "George," She calls. "We have to get them both to the doc."

"Yes, mother, let me get Clarence in the wagon first, and then I'll come back for Dorothy." Mr. Thopham is shouting while he helps his friend into the buggy.

"George, we have no place to go!" Clarence says, trembling.

"My friend, you let me worry about that. There's a house left for me to tend to; you can stay there. We'll talk about it later. Right now, we have to get the two of you to doc's place."

When Dorothy awakens, she finds herself in a strange bed and a strange room she does not recognize. Clarence is sitting next to the bed caring for her. She can see that he has been terribly beaten, but she is not feeling well enough to ask what happened.

"You have a fever, and you need to rest."

Dorothy asks, "Is it over?"

"It has been four days since Elizabeth died," He informs her.

"I hate them all," murmurs Dorothy. She pushes the wet cloth off her forehead, rolls over, closes her eyes, and falls fast asleep.

Another week goes by before Dorothy is ready to face those that murdered so many in the township. She sits up in her bed, taking note of the drafty room. She stands, grabs her blanket, and drapes it across her shoulders.

The room is no bigger than a closet. Dorothy stands in the doorway, staring at her frail uncle as he sleeps in his chair by the fireplace. Slowly, she steps into a small room by the fireplace and sees another space she believes is his bedroom.

"Three rooms, only three rooms," Dorothy whispers.

The house is very drafty and cold, and Dorothy can see outside through some of the boards of the walls. Tears fall as she looks around and remembers all they had and what she and Uncle have been reduced to. *Why are we here? Why did we come to this place?* She wonders.

Uncle wakes up to find Dorothy standing behind the table to the right of the fireplace.

"Hello, Uncle." She greets.

"Dorothy, you're awake! Come and bring a chair, and warm yourself by the fire."

"Thank you, Uncle," says Dorothy, wiping the tears from her face. "It's so cold in here."

"I'm afraid this was the best I could do with such short notice," he replies.

"What are we doing here? Why aren't we at the farm?" Dorothy asks.

Clarence gazes up at the ceiling and then down at his lap. He sighs. "The day your aunt Liz died, the Sheriff and his men paid us a visit," he explains. "They told me I had three days to leave the farm. I wouldn't have known what to do if it weren't for George and Gloria Thopham. By the grace of God, they came by that very night. The next day he moved as much as he could before they took the farm. This house was placed in George's care when the owner moved out. So here we are."

Dorothy cries even harder. Not only has she lost her aunt, but now they've lost the farm too.

"What happened to Peaceful and Sam?" she asks. "Did we lose them as well as the cows and chickens?"

"No, there is a small stable in the back." He replies

"Oh, I feel a little better," admits Dorothy, her tone much calmer. "That means we didn't lose everything." She pauses. "I notice your bruises. Are you okay?"

"I've been a lot better, thank you." He replies.

"What happened?" She asks.

"That damned Trevor fellow did a number on my ribs, but Doc said I will be as fit as a fiddle in a few months. I'm terribly afraid there isn't much to eat, and I've never been much with making food in pots and pans."

Dorothy laughs and leans over to hug her uncle. When she does, Clarence winces from the pain.

"Oh, Uncle, I am so very sorry," says Dorothy. "You are hurting more than you've let on. Tell me the truth – have you seen Doc, or haven't you?"

"I really have seen him," says Clarence. "He was here just yesterday to check on the two of us. I'm afraid we are both under his care, and Mrs. Thopham has been a great help herself."

Dorothy looks at Uncle the same way her Aunt Liz did when she knew he wasn't taking care of himself.

"You know, you're looking at me much like your aunt used to," he says.

Dorothy sinks back into her chair and sighs. "Uncle?" she asks.

"Yes?" He replies.

"What's going on?" Dorothy asks.

"The same thing that has been going on, I'm sorry to say." He says.

"Do you think this will end soon?" She asks.

"Lord, I sure hope so," He replies. "Just this week, the Sheriff and his henchmen met George and Glenda Evans walking by the river. They accused Mrs. Evans of being a witch. For some reason, the Sheriff's best friend, Charles Langram, wasn't there when the Sheriff and his men rode up to our farm, nor was he there the day they rode up on the Evans'." He sighs again, leaning back in his seat.

"From what I was told, this is what happened on that day."

George and Glenda asked, "What's the meaning of this, Sheriff?"

"We have a witness who says they saw your wife in the woods behind the town, wearing some kind of witch dress," explained Keith.

George cut him off. "That's a lie," he said. "You sure you don't want to stop by the house a little later under cover of darkness to do your mother's murderous deeds? And since when do you go around murdering innocent folk in the middle of the day, you filthy…"

Before he could finish, young Deputy Williams punched George in the face. George punched Deputy Williams in return knocking him to the ground, and then the others began to beat George to the ground. Deputy Trevor grabbed the Evans's two-year-old daughter right from the arms of Mrs. Evens. He threw the child into the freezing water, and Glenda screamed at him, following him and grabbing Deputy Trevor's staff from his hand. She came at him from behind, and Glenda punched him across the nose when he turned around to take it back. When he reared back, she took a step forward and hit him across the mouth with his staff, knocking most of his teeth out of his mouth. Deputy Trevor nearly fell backward into the river himself. When he screamed, Deputy James ran over, grabbed Glenda by her right shoulder, turned her around, and punched her with his right fist. Glenda fell into the river, still clutching Deputy Trevor's staff, and the currents dragged her down just like her helpless child. Trevor, holding his mouth, had to be helped up from his knees off the river's edge. They dragged George to jail behind their horses. Later that day, Deputy Trevor lied to the magistrates.

"I swear it was an accident," he said. "I was just trying to take the child to arrest Mrs. Evans, and in her resistance and struggle, the child fell into the river."

Clarence finishes, and Dorothy holds her hand to her mouth. He continues.

"Mrs. Evans gave Deputy Trevor such a good wallop that I wished I'd been there to see it," He laughs. "Sadly, they only found the baby's body, but there's still no sign of Glenda. I tell you that Trevor fellow had a few things to cry for. First, the teeth he lost, and second the staff he was so proud of that Mrs. Evans took it with her to her death. And lastly, he was bested by a woman."

Clarence sighs, a big smile on his face, and Dorothy smiles, being comforted that someone fought back.

"Oh, that would have been something to see," says Clarence.

"Aunt Liz once told me that Mrs. Evans has always been a fighter," says Dorothy. "She was never one to hold her tongue either."

Dorothy stands up and grabs a wooden spoon from the table, turning it around and holding it like it's a club. "Just the thought of it sounds so refreshing. Just one swing! I wish he'd fallen into the river also."

She slumps back into her chair. "Tell me more, Uncle."

"Well, I don't think the men will ever let him forget it," says Clarence, still laughing. "Not that he'd ever be able to do so alone. Every time he tries to chew meat or look at his reflection, he'll be reminded of it. These days, you can hardly understand a thing he says. I believe that man cried more for that blasted stick than he did for losing his teeth!" Clarence sighs and leans his head against the back of the chair, looking up with his eyes closed.

"They say that George was beaten so badly when they hung him that they had to fasten him to a chair to tie the rope around his neck. They had to hang him and the chair on that sad day. Wasn't much to hang, I was told." Uncle's voice is grim. "George was near death before they put him in the chair."

Uncle holds his face in his hands and sobs. "You know, those murdering bastards never even blinked an eye at the terrible deed done to baby Victoria. That animal threw her in the water, and not a single word was ever spoken on her behalf. She was just a wee little baby, a baby…" Clarence weeps harder.

Dorothy can only cry with him, thinking of her days with baby Victoria.

Clarence composes himself, for he wants to talk because doing so helps him move on.

"If that confounded stick is the only thing that animal values, then I'm pleased to hear that Deputy Trevor lost it. He used it with pleasure the night they showed up at our farm, so good for Mrs. Evans."

As the days pass, Clarence talks more about how he and Dorothy will have to leave before things worsen. He often complains of his pains which gives Dorothy great concern for her uncle. He looks a little worse for wear as each day passes. Clarence and Dorothy have no choice but to live in the old house that Mr. and Mrs. Dane left behind when the trials began; they were good friends of the Hempstead's. The house is damp and drafty. Mr. Dane did not build his house particularly well, so Clarence and Dorothy walk around with blankets around their shoulders most days. Very little wood is left to burn, so Dorothy ventures out to collect fallen branches and drag them back to the old shelter for chopping. Things are not getting any better for the people in the township; Ms. Pembroke and her son are coercing the townspeople and the surrounding farms like beasts poised to strike at any moment. The scriptures are true concerning the devil and his followers:

"They are like roaring lions, seeking whom they can devour." These people are as wicked as the wicked in the scripture that reads, "Her princes in the midst thereof are like wolves ravening the prey, to shed blood, and to destroy souls, to get dishonest gain."

Life has no meaning to these people at all. Dorothy thanks God, knowing that the wicked will one day cease to trouble the rest of the world. Life has become difficult now, and many are afraid to talk to those who have had family members tried for witchcraft. As the days pass, Dorothy can only hope that her Uncle gets better as the weather improves. He has his good days and bad days. Sometimes he has trouble breathing or complains of back and chest pains. On the good days, he gets around and does a little more for their temporary shelter.

"We'll be better off when we leave this place," he tells Dorothy. "Things will be better; you'll see."

Dorothy has begun sneaking over to the old farm to see the only other place she's ever called home – until now. She's relieved to see it from her hiding place in the woods. She can see the stable where Peaceful and Sam once lived; now, they are kept in a quaint little stall their friend and neighbor built for the horses. There wasn't much that Clarence and Mr. Thopham could get from the farm, so they left most of their possessions behind. It was a sad moment, especially with Aunt Liz gone. Just the thought of the accusers living in the houses of the people they've murdered transforms Dorothy's sadness into anger. Now that her family no longer lives on the farm – the farm that her aunt and uncle worked so hard to keep makes Dorothy aware of the grim reality that life can change at any moment. She doesn't know why she thought of this, but she realizes that she will no longer receive the four acres that were promised to her by Mr. Avery Kirts. She glances at the Kirts's farm and sees some sort of activity there. Someone has moved in, and Dorothy can already see that the new residents have been there long enough to make the improvements Mr. Avery neglected. Servants tend the farm, meaning whoever moved in is greatly influenced. This can only mean one person: Ms. Elmira Pembroke. Seeing this, Dorothy hurries out of the woods to get back to town. She has to pick up the chores that Aunt Liz used to do, and because of how weak her uncle has become, she's also taken over most of his chores. She knows now the life of a child is a blessing. Until now, Dorothy did not see how hard her uncle and aunt really had it. Doing the work of one is more than enough, but the work of two people is more than Dorothy thinks she can bear. She can only imagine how much harder it would be if they lived back on the farm. *Well,* she thinks to herself. *Now it belongs to the High Sheriff and his wife, and now Amanda has the burden of all those chores.*

Dorothy often walks through the township in a complete daze, wondering how so many people went along with this madness. Innocent people are dying, and for what? Houses their accusers did not build, the land they did not till. Seeing these things only makes her angrier. Dorothy would easily hate them openly, but Aunt Liz would not approve of that. Nonetheless, Dorothy hates them all. That night at the dinner table, Uncle tells her how lucky she is to be alive.

"If you had kept up with that confounded racket, they would have taken you also," he says, waving his finger at her.

Dorothy gives him the coldest look she can. Her mouth opens, and as she takes a deep breath and exhales, she utters a low hissing sound, her teeth closed tight together. Uncle stares at her in fear, and Dorothy tightens her eyes and whispers, turning her head to him and tilting it slightly to the left, "I hate them all." She stands slowly from the table, shoves the food to the floor, and says, "It may have been better if they had taken me and thrown me in the fire with Aunt Liz."

Clarence gathers himself. Pounding his fist down on the table, he yells, "THAT'S ENOUGH!"

This startles Dorothy, for she has never heard her gentle uncle raise his voice like that before. Anyone passing outside the old shelter could have heard him.

"What choice did I have? I did everything I could to protect my family," sobs Clarence. "They wanted everything we had, but I wouldn't give in to them." His fist pressed tightly. "Then they took my Elizabeth." He pauses and takes a deep breath. "They took everything I had. And now I'm trying to keep my promise to my Elizabeth. I promised that I would not let them take you too. She told me to escape this town and never come back, but I couldn't just leave her here. She didn't want you to see her die like that, and there was no one I could trust to keep you. I had no choice! And I told you to stay put, but you stole out anyway. Why did you disobey me?" The rage in his face is fearful, drool falling from his mouth. Clarence weeps on. "You think I didn't want to jump in that fire and die with her?" pointing to the fireplace as if it were the post Elizabeth was chained to. "I had to protect you!" He turns away from Dorothy, leaning against the table with his right hand and gesturing with his left hand. He takes another heaving breath and continues.

"When they came to take the farm from us, they told me I could give up the farm or...or you." He turns to look Dorothy in the face. "Either way, I was going to lose both you and the farm." Wiping his face, he changes the subject and says, "One of the Sheriff's men stopped by earlier today and warned me that you had better keep off the Pembrokes' property. They'll arrest you if they catch you there again. Is that what you want?"

"No, Uncle," says Dorothy.

In a low voice, he says, "I gave them nothing!" He turns his back to Dorothy and says in a quieter voice, "You get this mess cleaned up, and be off to bed." He then walks to his room sobbing, closing the door behind him.

Dorothy takes another deep breath, cleans up her mess, and runs to her room. She has no choice but to look at things differently now. Being older, she's expected to do more around the house at eighteen. She has learned how to cut wood for food and warmth, for Clarence's ailments will not allow him to use the ax. He hasn't said anything, but Dorothy believes that Deputy Trevor's staff may have broken Uncle's fragile ribs. She doesn't know what to do aside from doing as many of the chores as she can manage without complaining.

As she lies on her bed, she can't help but wonder who was in the woods. Her mind runs wild. *What were they doing out there? How did they know that I was off to see the old farm? How did they know I was there? I was careful not to reveal myself. All my life, I've run and hidden in those woods; I know every inch of them, and I know no one could see me. Who is it that saw me, and I not them? Is there someone else who knows these woods as well as I do? I know the creatures and the trees aren't revealing my hiding place. What am I missing? What have I done differently?*

As the days pass, Dorothy cares more and more for her Uncle. She is still doing most of the work, but Clarence fares no better than before. Dorothy is worried now because he's so weak and frail. She prays that she can nurse him back to health so they can leave that unholy place. The cold and drafty house is not helping matters, so Dorothy does what she can to keep it as warm as possible. Their neighbor Mr. Thopham comes by every day to help as much as possible. He shows Dorothy how to fill the gaps between the boards of the house, so Dorothy spends her days mixing mud with tree moss and thatch. The two of them work most of the day mixing and filling the gaps in the boards. It seems to work, and the house has begun to retain more of the heat from the fireplace, allowing less of the cold air in. Dorothy is grateful for the help of Mr. Thopham, as she fears this house will be the death of her Uncle. Dorothy does all she can to help around the house so that she and her uncle can leave their captures and never return to what she calls a den of witches.

Chapter 3
Eyes See You

Months have passed, and everyone is trying to start anew — Everyone but those families who have lost their loved ones. Most of the townsfolk have gone. Between the harsh winters and the Pembrokes, death or relocation would welcome a great relief. Everyone knows the Pembrokes' (specifically Ms. Pembroke) is behind the witch hunts. And nothing happens unless Ms. Pembroke says so. She goes through her son Keith, the High Sheriff, whenever she wants something. At this time, the witch hunts have ended, and the imprisoning, the killings, and the takings of property have all but stopped. Everyone is going about their business as if nothing has happened. Clarence warns Dorothy to stop going by the old farm.

"They don't like it when you show up there," He says.

Dorothy tries to explain how careful she's been. "I hide in the woods behind the old mare's barn, so there's no way they would know that I am there."

"You should never go back, in hiding or otherwise," warns her Uncle. "Somehow, they know when you are there."

These days, Dorothy doesn't go back for the memories. She goes for the hunt instead. She believes no one knows these woods better than she does.

Clarence won't hear any of it. "It's too dangerous for you there," he says. "They know, Dorothy. They know."

His words echo in Dorothy's mind; *they know.* She believes that Uncle knows more than what he is telling her. He's hiding something. From how they went about things before they dragged Aunt Liz to jail, Dorothy knows they were hiding things from her. Clarence rarely leaves his room now, and he's eating less than ever. Dorothy can see his life wasting away. These days, she finds herself alone in the old shelter. Food is scarce, so she goes off into the woods with the new bow that Mr. Thopham handcrafted for her for small game hunting. One morning, he came by to visit Clarence, and when they finished talking, he told Dorothy he'd brought something for her. It was her old bow, the one her father made for her when she was two years old.

"I found it the day after we took you and Clarence to the doc," explained Mr. Thopham. "Mrs. Thopham and I grabbed as much as possible because the Sheriff did not wait three days before he and his wife moved in."

He'd modeled the new bow after her father's. The new one is stronger and harder to pull.

"You will get used to it as it wears a bit," Mr. Thopham explains.

Dorothy found it harder to use at first, but after three weeks, her aim improved as she continued to sharpen her hunting skills.

A couple of months from now, another winter will have come to an end. Dorothy wants to try and get her Uncle out of the drafty old house so he can breathe in the fresh air. It's been more than a year since Aunt Liz died, and Dorothy longs to leave this 'evil place.' These days, she feels as though all eyes are on her. Somehow she feels their presence, but she cannot see them, yet they know when Dorothy is in the woods.

She tries not to think about it, but it is always on her mind. She often walks around thinking of what she and Uncle will do when they leave the Williams River Township. *Where will we go?* She thinks.

One afternoon she took a lazy walk and found herself by the fence of the Hunters' old farm and their old farm. She laid her right arm across the beam, resting her foot on the bottom rail. She wanted to determine whether she was visible from the front of the farm. As she stared at the old barn where she used to play until supper, a cold breeze swept through her, and then Dorothy saw shadows in the woods behind the old barn. That feeling of being watched returned to haunt her again, giving her shivers. It was not yet dark, and Dorothy was not sure whether her eyes were playing tricks on her or not. She felt she was being watched from every direction, but she did not sense how close Ms. Pembroke was until she stood right behind her from the side of the Hunters' fence. Ms. Pembroke grabbed Dorothy by the left arm, jerking her around to face her. Dorothy screamed and covered her mouth with her free hand, and Ms. Pembroke continued to hold on. Her grip is strong.

"Your time is coming, Dorothy Adams," she said.

"You're hurting me," pleaded Dorothy. "Please let me go."

"You little pretty," said Ms. Pembroke. "I've been waiting a long time for this."

"Please let me go. I'm not on your property." Dorothy pleads.

Ignoring Dorothy's pleas, Ms. Pembroke said, "If it had not been for you, my son would still be alive."

"Your son Keith is alive, and he and his wife are living there on our farm," Dorothy explained.

Ms. Pembroke yelled, "Don't you dare act like you don't remember my son; you're responsible for his death."

"I do not know what you are talking about!" screamed Dorothy. "You're hurting me!"

Ms. Pembroke cried, "My son was not supposed to be on the ice, but you took him out there to play, and he fell through the ice and drowned, and you… you didn't even get your pretty little shoes wet. But I swore I'd get you, you and your whole family. You killed my son!" Then she slaps Dorothy across her face.

Dorothy screamed loud and long and pleaded, "Let me go!"

"I can't do anything to you now, but the time will come," the old woman shouted.

Dorothy held her free arm to her face, hoping that the mean old woman wouldn't strike her again, and then she watched in horror as Ms. Pembroke's face changed, her voice became raspier, and her eyes went pitch black and lifeless. Dorothy screams, even more, twisting her arm from Ms. Pembroke's grip, and runs away.

"I'll get you yet, Dorothy Adams! I'll get you yet."

Her fingers curled like long narrow claws, and her twisted mouth and teeth were unlike anything Dorothy had ever seen before in a human. *What is she?* Dorothy wondered. The woman's eyes had become black as coal. In all her rage, not even she knew of the transformation that had taken place. She was no longer Mrs. Elmira Pembroke but something else. And then, just as fast as she transformed, she quickly recovered, looking at Dorothy with her fist held tight. She stepped towards Dorothy, still smiling as she rubbed her hands together.

"You can't hide from me, Dorothy Adams," she yelled. "I'll know where you are no matter where you go, no matter where you hide, for the woods aren't thick enough to cover you. Even the trees will tell on you. So run and hide, Dorothy Adams, and I will find you, and when I do, I'll kill you…"

Dorothy swallowed hard, wiping tears from her face, and said, "When that day comes, I'll be waiting, and I promise you this: I won't be the weakling you see today."

Ms. Pembroke stepped towards Dorothy, seemingly ready to transform again. But Dorothy did not wait for her to get into full stride; she turned and ran as fast as possible, too afraid to look behind her, running and hearing her loud laugh. She cut through the woods when she got on the far side around the bend, behind the old Hunters' farm. She did not stop until she reached the house, back to her uncle. She repented, "I'll never go back, I'll never go back."

Clarence is sitting in front of the fire when Dorothy bursts through the door, crying from her experience. She rests her head in his lap and repeats, "I'll never go back."

"Back at the farm again, Dorothy?" He asks.

"I only took a walk and found myself at the fence of the old Hunters' farm. My intention was not to stop there. I did not realize I had gone so far or that it was so late, and it got a little dark and frightful out on the road."

He brushes Dorothy's hair with his hand and says, "Things will get better when we leave."

Those words are like gold to Dorothy. The day they leave cannot come fast enough. But Clarence is tired. He sits softly in his chair, with his niece perched quietly by his side. He looks down at her and smiles.

"Uncle?" asks Dorothy.

"Yes, Dorothy?" He answers.

"Did the Pembrokes have another son other than Keith?"

Clarence's eyes open wide, and he sits up in his chair. "Why do you ask?"

"Because I heard someone mention it," replies Dorothy.

"Well, you don't need to be bothered with townsfolk talk." He brushes Dorothy's hair and continues to warm himself in his blanket.

"They say that I was responsible for his death."

Clarence sits farther forward in his chair. "There's no truth to that." He shouts.

"Then tell me the truth." She demanded.

For a long while, he stares at Dorothy. "Well, you're old enough to know now," he sighs and slumps back into the chair. "When you were three, your mother let you play at the edge of the ice pond with her and her friends close by. Not everyone had come out because it was a little early in the day." He takes a deep breath and sighs again, sitting with his eyes closed.

"Little Thomas was five, and his older brother Keith was twelve. A young lad named Nathan James, who was six, was on the ice with you. The two of you were playing on the ice pond before Keith and Thomas arrived, pulling a little sleigh. Everyone knew that Keith was jealous of his brother. Thomas was a strapping young lad, while Keith was sickly. He was a little crippled in his left leg, as you know, and he hated it. When the accident happened, you were sitting on an old fallen tree on the side of the ice, closest to your mother and Mrs. Lucy James. They were talking while the four of you played. Thomas and Nathan, Lucy James's oldest son, were using the Pembrokes' old sleigh while Keith pushed them. Gregory and Elmira trusted Keith to watch over his little brother.

"There was a patch of thin ice on the far side of the pond that joins the river; everybody knew it stayed thin there, even after the pond froze over. This time, when Keith pushed the boys, he pushed them right onto the thin ice, and the two young lads fell through. Keith never said a word, of course. He just stood by quietly while everybody tried to save those two boys. Keith ran home to get his parents to get their help. He must have told them he went to gather some wood while you, Thomas, and Nathan played on the ice. Mrs. Pembroke blamed you because, in her mind, you were the only one who survived that day on the ice."

Dorothy swallows, horrified.

Clarence continues, "Keith told his mother and the townspeople that he had just gotten there when they fell through the ice. Your mother and Mrs. James told them they were watching their own children when Keith and Thomas came out and started playing on their sleigh. Elmira was so distraught that she refused to listen to anything anyone had to say. I believe her husband Gregory was a little skeptical when he saw the sleigh that should have been used for gathering wood was underwater. But for the sake of his wife, he went along with her."

"She's a mean old woman." Dorothy calmed down.

"You don't know the half of it. Anyway, no matter how often your mother told Sheriff Williams that Keith was the one pushing the sleigh, no one listened because others sided with the Pembrokes. It did not matter that Lucy James was just hurt as the Pembrokes over the loss of her son. They blamed your mother and Mrs. James for Thomas's death.

Keith knew where the ice was thin, but he pushed the boys in that direction anyway." Uncle explained.

"They should have blamed themselves for not being there themselves."

"Unfortunately, that was not the case. I believed then, and I believe now, that Keith was a very wicked lad and is now a very wicked man. The Pembrokes became bitter after that. We did not see much of them outside the church. They sat on one side, and we sat on the other. The townspeople were split from that day on."

Clarence leans forward in his chair and says, "We didn't find their bodies until spring the following year when the lake and river thawed. We found them still holding onto each other between some branches that had fallen in before the freeze. I fear that Mrs. Lucy James and your aunt were Elmira's seeds of vengeance victims from so long ago."

Dorothy sits up straight, holding her mouth. "Was the other lady in jail, Mrs. James? The one with Aunt Liz."

"Yes," Uncle said. "I can't prove any of this, but your aunt and I believe this to be true. I'm sure that if Sheriff Williams were alive today, he would have put two and two together, and none of this would have happened. Seeing that Keith is the Sheriff now, we never had a snowflake's chance in hell of preventing this."

Uncle is crying again, but he continues to tell Dorothy everything he can remember. He tells her about the time her mother and father died. Dorothy sat quietly, not saying a word.

"When you were four, your parents visited the James family. The best we figured was that they were caught in a bad winter storm. When they left, only a little snow fell; the sky was clear, and there was hardly any wind. They were gone about half past the hour of three, and soon it began to snow hard. The wind picked up into a gale-like blizzard. Elizabeth and I hoped they would be okay and remain at the James's house until the storm passed. Our worse fears were realized when both horses returned to the farm without the buggy or your parents. We could only guess the storm was so bad that they couldn't continue in the buggy. We found the buggy near the wood line off the road, so we figured they must have tried to ride the horses back. Maybe they were thrown from the horses and lost their way, or maybe they were turned around in the storm. We found them three days later, on the other side of the township, about a half-mile past the fork in the road.

"They went past the township?" Dorothy says, gasping.

"Yes, they were walking in the wrong direction; they would have never found their way back in the direction they were going. Your father was alive but gravely ill, and your mother had already passed. We buried your mother that November; the next month, we buried your father. Your aunt and I always thought it was a strange storm. It lasted through the night but was only bad on one side of the colony and ended just as fast as it began. We knew that after your parents died, Mrs. Elmira Pembroke would one day come after you to get her revenge. On the anniversary of her son's death, the storm took your parents." Now he worries that they will somehow suffer the same fate.

Dorothy wonders, *Could a witch create storms?*

"She's a mean and vindictive woman, so you stay as far away from her as you can! Do you hear me, Dorothy? I can only pray the Good Lord blesses us to leave this place in the late spring or summer before she gets another chance."

"I will, uncle." The image of Elmira is fresh in her mind.

It was late in the evening when he finished telling her all she needed to know at that time, so Clarence and Dorothy retreated to their bedrooms. Dorothy can hardly sleep; she tosses and turns, thinking, *I saw her change. I saw her face change lizard green, and her hands were like the talons of a hawk, only longer. Her teeth were sharp like pike fish's, and she grew taller. What does all this mean? Will it happen again? I wonder if someone saw the shadows in the woods as I did and found out who Ms. Pembroke is or what she really is. She's the witch, and she has been for years. How powerful of a witch is she? Can she control the weather? Can anyone stop her?*

Dorothy ponders these things all night. Then she understood her dream that she had told no one about, and she sat up in her bed, whispering to herself, "The dream, I was standing by the edge of the fence between two farms, and suddenly a horrible thing grabbed me by my arm." Dorothy remembered and fell back to her bed, "Oh my God," she said, trembling. "In my dream, I screamed when this hideous thing knew my name and called out to me. I was running from it, but I was not going anywhere, just running and crying as she called my name." Now she even feared the darkness of her room, and she wanted desperately to leave the township. They have to go soon. She can only pray that her uncle will recover quickly.

In the morning, Dorothy goes about her regular chores of cleaning the house and cutting wood. She prepares her Uncle's breakfast when he comes out of his room.

"Morning, Uncle," greets Dorothy. "How was your night?"

"As well as can be expected," he replied. "Tossed and turned a bit. And you?"

"About the same, I guess. I was thinking about leaving here. I could not sleep because of it. Oh, Uncle, when will we leave this unholy place?"

"Dorothy, I only wish I knew. I hope I'll get better to help you more, but I just can't now. We'll plan to leave, but I fear they are watching you. That makes things harder. I don't know what they are planning, but it's like they are holding us here." He said.

"Why?" asks Dorothy. "Wouldn't it be better for them if we left? We don't have anything else for them. They took Aunt Liz and our farm. Now there's nothing else to take."

"They can take you, Dorothy," says Clarence. "They can take you. Our graves may be our only way out of here."

"Don't say that, Uncle. You don't really mean that. You said everything would get better for us, but how can it get better if we stay here? Aunt Liz would not have wanted us to stay here. You can't just give up on her like this. Uncle, please, let's get out of here. I'm afraid." Dorothy pleaded.

Dorothy runs to her room crying. This makes Clarence sit up and remember Elizabeth's pleadings. He tries to stand up, but he is too weak. He looks down at his hands and speaks to himself in disappointment.

"Never have you been this idle and useless." He berates himself.

He pushes his food aside and looks around at the house, remembering how unkempt Avery Kirts's house was before he and his wife were murdered. Then Clarence gathers the strength, gets up from his chair, and walks outside, taking deep breaths while looking around. He looks over toward the Thophams' and walks to their house.

"Good morning, George." He waves.

"Well, well, well. Do my eyes deceive me? What's gotten you out of the house this fine morning?" George replies.

"George, I fear I have lost all hope," says Clarence.

"Well, Clarence, what do you plan on doing to change that?" George asks.

"I don't rightly know yet, but that's why I'm here," Clarence replies.

"Well, let's go inside and talk about it," suggests George, wrapping his arms around Clarence.

Mr. Thopham is a big man, about six foot five, and these days he weighs over three hundred pounds. After discussing partnering in a business, George says, "Clarence, I'll do the hunting, and you can do the salting, and together we can serve the township with our cured meats. Spring is upon us, and I have a place I spied where the wild animals go for their water. I've been watching for a while now. They are there more regularly these days. I tell you, I saw the biggest buck the other day, I wanted to shoot it, but I guess I'm getting a little clumsy and spooked it instead. I tell you, that buck will be salted by month's end."

"Well, George," Clarence says, "I have an idea for some spices that will make him the best salted meat anyone has ever tasted. You bring him here, and we'll turn him into cured heaven. The other day Dorothy noticed some digging by the back of the house and some closer to the wood line. That means there is some boar around."

"Yes, she's right, Clarence," says George. "I've seen quite a few tracks around the water's edge too. This is going to be a blessed hunting season. I'll start about a week from today, and that will give us enough time to build a small smoker back in the woods. I got myself a hand cart I built that will carry a good-sized kill. I'm getting too old to pack anything over my shoulders out of those woods. I'm not the man I used to be; I have to work smarter these days."

They both laugh, thinking of their younger days. "Young bucks we were, Clarence," says George, grabbing a handful of belly fat. "I had more chest and less of this. There are times I can't even see my feet."

"Yes," says Clarence, "there was a time I had to suck in my stomach to see my ribs, and now that's all I see. If you want to know how many ribs we men have, just ask me." They continue to laugh.

"I haven't laughed so much in months," Clarence adds.

"It's good to see you are doing better and out of that house," George commends. The two men stare at the embers in the fireplace. George looks over at Clarence as he wipes away a tear.

"Everything is going to be just fine," says George. "Old boy, you must believe that."

"I'm sorry," says Clarence. "I just pray I'll be more helpful to you than I have been for Dorothy. She's been working awfully hard taking care of me and that drafty old house."

"She'll be very proud of you, Clarence. I know this may be easier for me to say, but you have to move on. It's what Elizabeth would have wanted."

Clarence does not say a word. He sits thinking about what he has become since the death of Elizabeth.

"Every time I look into the fire, I can see her," Clarence says, "not so much in pain anymore, but it's like she's just staring at me. I find myself sitting there in front of the fireplace for hours on end, wondering if I could have done more, fought back or something."

"Well, Clarence, I believe that could have left you burning right there with her. You have to accept the fact that you could not have done anything more than what you did." George comforts him.

"Yes, I do realize that. I never told you or anyone this, but Elizabeth and Dorothy pleaded with me to leave after young Kirts, and his wife was murdered. Adam Hunter even advised me to do what he and Mr. Washington considered at the time; leaving this ungodly place. He told me to leave so that I would not regret it later. I believe my Elizabeth is staring at me because I should have left, and then she would not have died the way she did." Clarence says, looking into the fire.

"Maybe you see Elizabeth staring back at you because you had not kept the promises she asked of you before she died," George says gravely.

Clarence has that blank look on his face again; all this time, he's been staring; he's forgotten that she asked him to take care of Dorothy. He remembers his promise to her from back when Elizabeth demanded him to keep his promise to her.

"Promise me that no matter what happens, you will find a way out and leave this godforsaken place. Take Dorothy as far away as possible. Elmira will surely seek her out as she did me. She'll stop at nothing; she wants to destroy our family until nothing remains of it. She's a scorned woman Clarence, and she'll never forgive us for Keith or her son Thomas. Take Dorothy far away, and swear never to return. Remember, I'll love you to my death. I can only pray that the Good Lord will shield the two of you until you have gone far from here." Elizebeth warns Clarence from her jail cell.

Clarence thanks George again, saying, "I'll be waiting for the first deer, hog, or fowl you bring in. I'll be ready to butcher and salt whatever you set before me."

"Until then," says George. And then they stand up and shake hands. Clarence walks to the door and stops in his tracks.

"I'll be ready, George." He promises.

"I know you will, my good friend," George replies.

As he walks back to his house, he thinks of that wicked Keith. *I knew the day he was born into this world; he'd be the death of us.*

Chapter 4
Steal Away In the Night

After Dorothy's encounter with Elmira, she saw the woods she played in differently. She could not look at them as she did as a child; as an adult, she had to look at her new world from a different perspective. When the witches are watching her, she begins to notice that they are all Elmira's friends, and they follow Dorothy everywhere she travels in town. No matter where she went, they were watching. They were as cold as Elmira and did whatever she told them. It was mid-winter of 1694, and spring was just around the corner. Dorothy could not wait until the day she and her uncle would leave the Williams River Township. It was something they kept to themselves. Clarence traded some of their old furniture for a raggedy buggy; it wasn't much, but it would be enough. Everyone is glad to see him up and about, and so is Dorothy. He still looks frail and pale but moves around a bit more these days. Maybe the thought of leaving motivated him or the business he started with Mr. Thopham. All Dorothy knows is that they are both happier.

For the same reason, she does not care if the witches watch her anymore, for she knows she will soon leave it all behind. She can only hope they cannot read her mind. The thought sickens Dorothy, but then she pulls herself together.

If they had been able to read my mind, they would have done something already. She thought.

She often imagines herself walking by the river and finding the staff Mrs. Evans took to her grave. God rest her soul. She thinks of using it to knock Ms. Pembroke's teeth out. But knowing her, she would probably catch it in her mouth, use her nasty fangs, and whittle it down to a finger-sized stick. And then she'd find herself thinking of running again. As always, her thoughts run away with her. Dorothy sees the witch Ambrose (she calls them all witches now), and this cuts her daydream short. It is as if she has just appeared behind the neighbor's house.

"Good morning Miss Adams." Greets Ambrose.

Dorothy returns the greeting, but she says nothing more. Her heart pounds heavily from within, and she cannot believe how afraid she is. Ambrose appears when Dorothy thinks about giving her master a good old-fashioned whipping or hitting her in the mouth with a stick. Dorothy holds her breath, her head down, and walks faster to the house. It is as if they want her to know they are watching. She opens the door to go inside and then sees that Ambrose is still watching.

"Oh, that's just great...she's looking at me looking at her." She pouts.

Dorothy closes the door in a hurry, leaning against it to protect herself. She watches Ambrose through a space between the curtain and the window. Then she looks down the other side of the street to see if anyone else is taking her place. Once she is sure there is no one else, Dorothy walks out of the door and goes around the back, where Clarence is salting the meats. Mr. Thopham built a small smokehouse and a prep area for Clarence to carry out his part of the business. Clarence is salting deer meat and some wild hog. Mr. Thopham hunts the deer, and Clarence salts it for their families and business. He has been salting meats for nearly three months now. Dorothy brings him fresh water to wash with, for their new business is very messy and smells as well. Clarence and Mr. Thopham butcher the meats away from the back of the house in the woods. Then he and Dorothy take the flesh and put them on a cart, push it to the house and hang them in the smokehouse just a few feet away. The excess skin and bones attract dangerous animals, so they dispose of the remains deeper into the woods. This way, their work is away from the town but not too close to the house.

Sometimes Dorothy is more afraid when she doesn't see Elmira's witches.

I would rather keep them with me to know exactly where they are. She thinks

Today witch Ambrose spoke to me again, but I tried not to let the situation startle me as much. I don't jump anymore when they speak, for I think they enjoy catching me off guard. She thinks, *are they just waiting for me to return to the farm? That would never happen unless the queen witch Elmira and her murderous son were dead.*

But these thoughts don't do Dorothy much good. She has things to do; she must go to the creek to gather more water for her uncle. As she walks through the woods toward the creek, she stops and looks around, pretending to admire the birds singing. The real reason she stopped was that she could feel someone following her. Somehow, she knew they were there. She cannot hear or see them but can sense them, watching as if they are there by her side. She has trained herself to hear and notice things in the woods that do not belong. Dorothy chops wood with more aggression to build her strength, carrying water in two buckets instead of one to strengthen her arms and legs. Sometimes she runs through the woods with the buckets. She promised that old witch she would be ready for her the next time they met. Dorothy has mapped the woods in her mind, and now she notices something is out of place every time, but she cannot see it. She carries a staff with her because she knows Mrs. Evans has the right idea, using the staff to knock the hell out of the enemy.

Dorothy does physical training in her room when her Uncle is out of the house. And now, she has decided the next step is to sharpen her skills as a huntsman so she can begin to hunt small game better with the bow Mr. Thopham made for her. She has been practicing secretly with the staff, for she wants those witches to know she won't go down without a fight. The sleeves of Dorothy's dress hide her build; her arms and thighs are firmer than ever, and she feels a lot more confident with the ax and the staff.

There was a time when she wouldn't have known they were there, but now there is something that stirs inside of her when they show up on the streets. She gets the same feeling while fetching water for her uncle in the woods. At least Dorothy knows how they knew she was in the woods at their old farm. She did not notice it when she saw the shadow the day the old hag grabbed her from behind. Now Dorothy goes about her business as though she's afraid, timid even, and this is what she wants them to think. She prays the Lord will send her to a place where she can learn to train and fight like a soldier. She wants to use weapons to defend herself and her uncle. Until then, Dorothy must work with what she knows, all in the privacy of her and Clarence's adopted home.

Early spring is here, and Clarence is eating more and feeling much better. His strength is slowly returning, but he's still thin and fragile. Clarence and Dorothy have enjoyed many nights of Mrs. Thopham's dinners. They often talk, although Mrs. Thopham avoids the subject of Dorothy's mother and her aunt Liz. When she talks to Mrs. Thopham, it's like talking to Aunt Liz. The kindhearted woman goes on and on about how she had already married and given birth to two children by the time she was my age. Of course, the last thing on Dorothy's mind is marriage. Every once in a while, Mr. Thopham tells her that she will make a beautiful bride for some lucky fellow someday, which makes Dorothy feel awkward. She smiles at the gesture anyway. During those times of the conversation, Clarence notices Dorothy's discomfort and complains of some ailment, and they leave. On the walk back to the house, he lets her know the Thophams mean well and only want the best for her. She let him know she understands.

One warm spring evening, George Thopham drops by the house and notifies Clarence that he's heard Keith is planning a rather large feast at the old farm.

"Are you and the wife thinking of going?" Clarence asks.

"I could never do that, knowing how they obtained the farm," George expresses. "Haven't been to the farm since you and Dorothy moved here. And his mother, Ms. Pembroke, moved into the Kirts's place. Not to bring up a sore subject, but why do you think they wanted the Kirts's farm?"

"Not really sure," says Clarence. "All I know is that it's the largest farm in the colony next to our old farm. I did wonder the same thing for a while, but I figured the reason was greed. Young Avery had offered to give Dorothy four acres on the side next to mine."

"He was nothing like his father, was he?" George states.

"Oh no, I tell you," replies Clarence. "There were times Mr. Kirts would storm over to our farm after chasing Dorothy off his property and just give us an earful; he would. He had Elizabeth so upset and worried when he left that she wouldn't let Dorothy out of the house for days. Said he would give her the whip if he ever catches her again."

George laughs and says, "Catch her? Kind of like a turtle chasing a deer."

Clarence laughs. "Yes, Dorothy did say it wasn't much of a chase. He'd take a few steps and wave his fist. Then he'd hitch up his buggy and come a-hollering with the buggy whip in hand."

They both sit in silence for a couple of minutes.

"Still can't find a reason, huh?" George asks.

"The only thing I can think of is the old colony," Clarence says. "I don't think anyone has gone there since the Indians burned it down. It must be overgrown with weeds and trees by now! It's been over forty years, and there are no other survivors but the young Kirts' who took a ship back to England. No one ever dared ask where the old place was with Old Man Kirts' behavior."

"Clarence, do you think the old settlement has anything to do with all this?"

"Don't really know George, but got me thinking, who would watch Dorothy when she went back to visit the farm? They wanted her to stop going for a reason. I remember my father saying that Old Man Kirts said the old settlement was cursed. He said people had seen things there, but he never said what. Everyone just thought he was using superstition to keep people away. He buried many of his friends and family there, you know." Clarence Said.

"You know, Clarence, I don't believe in witches and warlocks any more than I do vampires and werewolves, which the folks used to talk about in England," says George. "It's all a bunch of nonsense. If you ask me, I think you have a few rotten apples in the bunch. They got greedy, and things got out of control."

"That could be, George, but something is happening on all those farms, and it's not superstition. Whatever it is, it kept the old mare and Sam pretty nervous. Something is in those woods – werewolf, vampire, witch, warlock, I don't know, but it's there. It used to scare me too. I would be mending a fence at the tree line and could not see it, but I could tell that something was watching me, and it made the hairs stand at the back of my neck. I would not let Dorothy walk the horses because the closer they got to the back of the Kirts's farm, the more nervous they became. If they ever got spooked while Dorothy was walking them, they could have hurt her, and I would never have forgiven myself."

"It sounds like you know more than what you're letting on, Old Friend," George said, staring at Clarence.

"I'm just saying I could tell something was there," says Clarence firmly. "I knew it, the horses knew it, and I believe Dorothy seen it too. If you want to keep a secret, you hide things. Sooner or later, someone will stumble across the old settlement and see what's there. So, if you really want to keep it a secret, you take over the farms and control the area."

"Clarence," George continues, "do you have something to say? I'm your friend, and there's no one here but the two of us."

Clarence looks at him and says, "Are you sure?"

George leans over in his chair, staring back at Clarence with a puzzled look. "Are you trying to make me a believer of spooks and specters?"

George rubs his hands over his mouth and pulls down on his beard, scanning the room without moving his head. "You're beginning to scare me, Clarence."

"I'm not trying to scare you, George," Clarence says. "Just saying that if there were demons in the days of our Lord Jesus, what makes you think they don't exist in our time? The Devil is forever empowering those who are willing to worship him. The scriptures read that the Devil waited until Jesus was hungry and had not eaten for forty days and forty nights before he tempted him. He tempted him to turn stone into bread, cast himself off the top of the temple, and offered him power and riches. That's how the devil works; he waits until we are at our weakest and most vulnerable point in life, and then he tempts us with the promise of the things we want most. Like Christ, many have resisted his temptations, while others welcome him with nervous arms."

"You're right to say nervous arms, Clarence. No man or woman would be crazy enough to welcome him with open arms." George expounds.

"George, the problem with some people is they don't read the scriptures as they should. If they did, they would know that when the Devil left Jesus and after the angels tended to his needs, they would understand he only fled for a season. The devil is persistent; he'll always come back to tempt you. He looks for the weaknesses in you and tries to exploit them."

George asks, "What of you?"

Clarence does not answer right away. "Like Job, he has inflicted great pain and suffering upon me. He searches for not only weakness but also strength. He's found in me weakness only; I have no strength left in me. I aided him by doing nothing."

George asks for Clarence's forgiveness. "I meant no harm in that."

"I understand," Clarence says.

George sits and waits for Clarence to get to his point. After a moment of silence, Clarence speaks.

"I used to see things in the woods, George. I could not explain it, but I saw something I will never forget."

"What was it, old friend?" George as with genuine interest.

"Years ago, I went out to hunt for meat in the woods behind the Kirts' farm; It was a long search, and I was late looking for a deer I shot. When I caught up with it, it had run behind Old Man Kirts's farm for nearly a half-mile on the other side before it fell. I was getting ready to drag it back to the farm when I saw Mrs. Kirts walking through the woods, but it was more like floating. It scared me so badly that I relieved myself right then and there. I just froze and did not move for what seemed like hours. I'm not a strong man, George. All I could think of were Elizabeth and Beatrice."

George sat silent.

"Do you remember how Mrs. Kirts's life was after her son and daughter left for England? She was bitter. Her husband made life a living hell for that whole family, and she lived that life in hell with her son Avery. Avery turned out to be a good Christian man, and Keith was the devil. Often, I had to discourage Dorothy from going into the woods behind that farm. You know children today, you can't tell them anything. I found that when you tell them not to do a certain thing, they will do that thing because that's what they do. Until the recent warnings, I did not know she was returning to the farm. But when she did the last time, something scared her so badly that I feared they would come after her. While she was growing up on the farm, I knew she would never venture too far beyond *their* farm. She would go to his farm just at the tree line, then climb the Kirts's fence to ruffle his feathers. It was all a game for her."

George laughs.

"No matter how much I scolded her, I knew she would do it again, so I watched how far she went into the woods and saw that it was just a few paces beyond his fence. I never hunted behind their farm after that; I drew a line in my mind and said that if I ever shoot a deer and it goes that way on the other side of that line, I will just say, 'Good luck to you.' I thought things would change for Mrs. Kirts after Old Man Kirts's death, but she stayed in that house all the same. I can only believe that after Avery married, he and his wife took care of her until her death."

"That's true," George said.

"Now, we helped bury Mr. Kirts, but I only knew of Mrs. Kirts's death after she was dead and buried. I believe whatever I saw in the woods that day was just something playing tricks on my mind, but I kept an eye on that farm. They said she wanted to be buried with her children on the old settlement, not far from where I found the deer, but I was only about a half-mile past the west side of his farm. A mile on the other side of their farm, there is nothing but more woods. It had to be farther than a mile, maybe no less than two, and no more than four or five."

"You sure?" George ask.

"I don't know, George. I did not even see a trail, so if the old settlement is out there somewhere, it's farther than what I know. I have hunted back there as far as two miles on the west side of that farm with Avery, Dorothy's father. Avery Kirts knew where it was because he buried her there, but I never wanted to know, and he never bothered to volunteer that information. Now I wonder if she was ever buried at all. Could she and Elmira have joined forces?"

"Pardon me, Clarence, but today Mrs. Kirts would be near a hundred years old, if not older."

"I suppose you're right, but maybe the devil has raised another devil in its place. No one really knew Mrs. Kirts, for she always kept to herself. We always thought she feared her husband, but after I saw her in the woods, I believed otherwise. She's a mother, and no one can ever know what she was going through her mind when her children were buried after the Indian raid."

George clears his throat. "Well, whatever she went through, she hid it well."

Clarence glances up. "I believed that too. You can hide many things from outsiders but can't hide everything from your children."

"I'm afraid they took their secret to England and Avery to his grave," says George.

"Right," Clarence Agrees.

"My good friend, that's great stuff for conspiracies." George is starting to believe that these things may be true. This frightens him, so he changes the subject. He clears his throat.

"Before I forget, one of Keith's henchmen requested that I sell him some of our salted meats for that feast. Do we have enough stored? Do we have enough in store to sell to Keith for his feast?"

Clarence replies, "Yes, we have enough in store." He pauses. "George, why didn't they ask me?"

George speaks candidly. "Would you?"

Clarence chuckles. "Perhaps not," he says. "I suppose he believes it's less likely to be poisoned if he gets it from you. He's almost a smart man." His eyes twinkle when he says this last bit, but George appears worried.

"Don't worry, my friend," says Clarence. "I'll take a bite of all I give you if that will ease your mind."

"No," replies George, "that won't be necessary… Would it, Clarence?"

Clarence grabs his arm and says, "God will deal with them in due time; I won't have to lift a finger against that man or his mother. Come, and we'll give him a couple bushels' worth."

As they weigh the meats, Clarence thinks, *this is our chance, for tomorrow is Friday, and everyone will be at the feast. For three days, they will be occupied, which will give us a good start.*

When Clarence returns home, he says to Dorothy, "Tonight, we will pack up the old cart for the journey and keep the load light."

The old cart has undergone a few changes. Clarence uses it to make his salted meat deliveries around town, which requires him to keep the buggy all that much sturdier. Four heavy wheels, springs, and a firmer bed with strong wood replaced the broken boards that originally made the cart unsafe. George worked on the cart over the past months. He added a cover over the back to protect the meat from the rain. The seat is not meant for long rides, so Dorothy hastily sewed some old rags of dresses and blankets into makeshift pillows and supplies. An old dress is now a seat cushion for the long ride, and another has become a bed. This way, one can sleep while the other drives the cart wagon. Clarence and Dorothy will store dry goods like fish, fowl, nuts, cheese, and bread for their journey to New York. They can only hope to find fresh milk on the way there.

George sees them packing some of their things, so he walks to the house and asks, "Going to visit family?"

"I thought it would be a good time to visit relatives east of here in New York. I haven't seen them in years," says Clarence.

George retorts, "Kind of sudden! You're packing a little light, for that's a good long ride to New York."

"We don't require much. We will get supplies in other townships on the way."

"When are you leaving?" George asks.

"Tomorrow," says Clarence wearily. "We weren't invited to the feast, so tomorrow will be soon enough. We'll see you by late summer."

"Godspeed to you and Dorothy. We'll see you then." George bids him goodbye.

They shake hands, and George retreats home. He turns around and says to Clarence, "I'll take care of the house and business until your return."

"Thank you," nods Clarence. "You're a good man, George."

When George arrives home, he suggests a trip to Martha to visit their children. "I believe it will be a good thing if we visit our family over the weekend. It's only a half-day ride, and if we leave at sunrise, we'll be there by mid-afternoon."

Martha is in good spirits. "This will be a welcome change for the two of us," she says. "It will be good to see our children, Thomas and Amy, and the grandchildren too."

While his wife goes on excitedly about what to take, George finds comfort in the fact that he truly has no answer for anyone who asks about Clarence and Dorothy's whereabouts. If anyone does ask, he can honestly answer with a clueless expression.

When Clarence and Dorothy finish packing the buggy, they go inside to clean up a bit.

"We are going to leave at first light," says Clarence. "At least that's what we want our neighbors to think. I figure when the night falls, the witches will all be in the woods, doing whatever witches do."

The night is cloudy and moonless, with no stars to be seen.

This 20th day of May 1694 could not have come soon enough; Dorothy's heart was beating out of her chest. She and her uncle can barely see what they are doing when they step outside to leave. Clarence puts cloth rags around Sam and Peaceful's hooves to quiet their steps. He and Dorothy walk them gently out of town before they climb into the buggy. Getting out of town isn't too difficult, seeing how the pair only passed a few houses on their way to the road. Dorothy and Clarence travel in the same direction Dorothy's parents went when they lost their way in the storm.

Maybe this is fate, she thinks. Dorothy often thinks about how they got so far out without running into any of the houses or townsfolk. Had they already visited their friends, or had they gotten close enough to the house and thought they still had farther to go?

As she and Clarence leave, Dorothy can see how easy it would be to get lost when visibility is poor.

It's really dark without the moon. She thinks.

When Dorothy thinks about how frightening the snowstorm must have been for her mother and father, tears fall from her eyes. They must have lost all hope of finding their way home. Dorothy can only pray that if she and Uncle get lost, it will be far better than staying back in Witchville. She does not look back toward the township, no, not once. But Dorothy remembers Ms. Pembroke's warnings: *"You can never hide from me. I'll find you and kill you, Dorothy Adams."* The thought of the horrible transformation Dorothy witnessed has haunted her mind ever since it took place. That is a story she will never tell her uncle.

Once they are close to the fork in the road, Clarence says, "We will avoid some of the larger townships so that we don't attract too much attention. The townspeople there can't tell the witches what they did not see. The witches would certainly visit Leominster and Harvard. It'll make our days longer in the wagon without these stops, but we'll do well to avoid them just the same."

Dorothy agrees; she is there for the ride. This is the first time in her life that she has left home, and she will not be at all homesick for the occasion. In her heart, she says goodbye to Aunt Elizabeth and good riddance to the Williams River Township. After they pass the fork in the road going east, Uncle lights two lamps, and he and Dorothy place them on the sides of the buggy. This gives them a little light to get through the night.

Chapter 5
Elmira, Queen of the Witches

That night Elmira is frustrated and not sure how things are going. Her son is throwing a big feast at his farm. Everyone will be about, and kids will be scurrying around in the woods at the back of the barn. Not the best timing for her stupid lame son, as she often mocks him.

"I think he deliberately did this to annoy me," whines Elmira. "I must talk to Amanda immediately and find out how many of his idiot deputies and their families to expect. I'm sure he invited the entire township, no doubt."

Elmira wants to have more of a say in things. She wants to make sure that all her girls are in the right places to prevent any of them from going where they shouldn't. She has her trusted servants spread the word that there will be a meeting tonight at her farm. Elmira lives with her sister Mary on the farm she runs with the servants' help. Her husband died when Keith was thirteen, a year after her youngest son Thomas's death. In an unfortunate accident, while riding his horse, it was spooked, reared, and threw him to the ground. His injury caused him to lose all movement in his body, and he died the following week.

Now Elmira can do as she pleases in her house, and she doesn't have to worry about being revealed by anyone she does not trust. She often thought of her husband as weak and intimidated by that old windbag sheriff Lester Williams. Her anger over her son's death often brought her heavy hand and harsh words down on her son Keith when he was younger. Keith endured these times in silence, doing what he was told and nothing more, simply waiting... waiting patiently for his time to come. Elmira's sister is also a witch and lives on the farm with her. She lived with her in her old house, so she did not have to worry about anyone going into Thomas's room, which she had kept private all these years. It was in Thomas's room at the old house they lived in when Elmira's change occurred for the first time. After Thomas's death, she vowed there would not be a single Adams left in this world. She kept her grandmother's mirror in his room. The day they found Thomas and Nathan James's bodies, she stood in the mirror late that night, seething over Thomas's death. Then, she saw something move behind her in the mirror, frightening her. She looked behind her and saw nothing, so she stood there staring into the room's darkness. Elmira turned slowly, trying to keep her eyes on the room, but when she looked in the mirror, something was looking at her that frightened her so severely that she fainted. When she awoke, it was already morning. Elmira did not remember going to bed, nor did she remember leaving the room. At breakfast, she looked over at her sister, who was eating cut apples and oats.

"Keith," Elmira said, "Cut your mother some apples."

"Yes, Mother." Keith obeyed.

"I don't have the stomach to eat anything heavy this morning," Elmira said.

"I guess you had a long night," Mary said.

Elmira looked at her sister, whose mind had never fully developed. Mary is mentally retarded, and many people in the colony call her simple-minded and stupid.

"What?" Elmira said.

"You crying in your private room, but it's okay, Mira," said Mary. "I cry too. I don't like it when he leaves; he okay, though."

"I don't like it when you talk like that. Thomas is dead; you hear me!" Elmira shouted.

Mary lowered her head. "Yes, Mira."

Elmira stood from her chair and walked around the table to reassure her sister. "I don't mean to yell at you. I love you and would never hurt you. Come, and we'll finish these apples and nuts, and we'll go and visit with friends."

Elmira cleaned up after Mary, and they left to visit their friends. She wondered what she saw in the mirror and why she couldn't remember anything after that. That night she stood before the mirror and figured she'd do her best to remember what happened. It was about midnight when she saw the figure cross behind her; this made her shriek and her body tense. She steadied herself in the mirror without looking back. Then she heard it:

"What do you want?" it said in a low, hollow voice that seemed to echo in her ears. She wasn't sure who or what was talking to her, so she ran to the door and opened it, expecting Mary to be there. She peered out into the hall, but no one was there. She slowly closed the door, using the light in the hallway to scan the room. Then she walked back to the mirror, folding her arms, not knowing what to expect.

"What do you want?" it asks again.

Elmira did not know whether to run or scream, so she just stood there shaking and shivering like she was standing in the cold rain.

"Who are you?" she asked in a frightened voice. She swayed from side to side, holding one hand to her heart and the other to her dress.

It asked again, "What do you want?"

"I'm not sure what you are asking of me," Elmira said.

And then a blurred image began to form in the mirror. She stared at it for a minute, and then it became clear to her. It was Thomas.

For the fourth time, it asked again, "What do you want?"

By then, she was no longer afraid when the image disappeared. She was angry and even angrier when she saw flashes of her failed love affairs with the men of her past. They'd all gone on to marry other women and live successful lives.

In a low voice, she said, "I want them all dead. I want the power to do whatever I damn well please." Raising her voice, she continued, "Give me what I want; you give me what I want!"

"You already have what you want," the voice continued, "but you have only to look deep within yourself to find it."

More images appear and disappear in the mirror, images of her useless husband and her idiot son, Keith. Rage began to brew, and she screamed as the images came and went until she punched the mirror and shattered it. When she awoke the next morning, she noticed there were no bruises on her left hand from breaking the mirror. She told her husband that she wasn't feeling well and that he would have to help Mary and Keith fix breakfast. While her family was eating, she rested in bed and began to wonder how Mary heard her but not her husband or Keith. She wondered whether it was all a dream until she looked under the washbasin. There, lying right on the floor, was Thomas's nightshirt. She went over, picked it up, and clutched it to her chest, weeping. She could hear Keith knocking at the door; with her teeth tight, she opened it, still holding the nightshirt.

"Are you okay, Mother? I heard you crying." He said.

Elmira dropped her arm to her side as she gave him an unloving look. Keith looked down and saw the nightshirt that had belonged to Thomas, then back up at her, and they stared at each other for a few seconds until Elmira slammed the door as though he hadn't been standing there at all. Once the house was empty, Mary came to her.

"All gone now, Mira. Can we go and visit our friends?"

"You go on; I'm tired," said Elmira. "Get Keith, and tell him to take you."

When Elmira peered out the window, she saw Mary stumbling about and asking Keith to take her to their friends. Elmira hurried back into the room to clean up the broken glass, but she found it all intact. She then turned to latch the door and walked over to touch it. She stretched out her hand to do so, but before she could, two eyes and a mouth full of teeth opened wide and slowly emerged from the mirror. She screamed as loud as she could, but no sound would come out. She fell to the floor, crawling, backing away from it as fast as she could, but it came toward her at equal speed. When she could go no farther, she found her back pressed against the door as she reached for the knob. Breathing heavily with tears falling from her eyes, they were face to face. She tried to turn her head, but it only stared at her.

"I can give you what you want, but I warn you, this is a powerful thing," it said, "and vengeance is an even greater, deadlier power. You give yourself to me, and I'll give myself to you, and together we'll rule this place. I will give you knowledge. I will give you the ability to go anywhere you want in time; I'll give you riches untold and control of the elements, and all I ask in return is that you give yourself to me."

This being had the face of a dragon with the mane of a lion. Elmira did not know how to answer. Soon it backed off a little to make her feel at ease. And then its features began to change, and it was no longer just the head of a beast; now, it was forming a body. It had the face and body of a woman. It walked over to the window and stared outside with its back to Elmira. Somehow Elmira thought she recognized who it was. She stood up and slowly walked towards the window to get a better look at the thing. Full of deception and guile, it had changed to an image she knew well.

"Aunt Agnes?" She calls.

It spoke in a quiet voice. "They disowned me, and I was not allowed to come here to the new world with the rest of the family. They left me in that village, where my only company was a wandering band of gypsies. I'm sure you've forgotten all I taught you as a child, but I want you to know that you come from a long line of hypocrites. My father told me that it was best I stayed in England and that he would send for me when they got to Holland. After five years, I'd all but lost hope. I wanted desperately to come to the new colonies."

Elmira listened to every word it said without interrupting a single time. It continued, "Your grandfather separated my sister and me. He said your mother had a better chance because she was married, had you and your sister Victoria, and was pregnant with her third child Amos. It took ten years of waiting and hoping before I realized I would never leave. One night, soldiers came to our village, killing the men, beating the boys, and raping the women and young girls. They left us for dead, and I swore I would somehow get even with them all. I wanted to get even with Father the most for leaving me behind. I have always loved you, Elmira. I can teach you everything you need to know. I've been watching you, knowing what they took from you.

"Everything." Elmira whispers.

"Your father was no different than your grandfather; they tell us who to marry and who not to marry. They take away our freedom, our joy, our men, and the life we could have had if it wasn't for their constant meddling in our affairs. I was left to live a hellish life in England because I refused to marry some pompous tart. He said I was too wild and no different than the gypsies who roamed the land. It's time, Elmira; it's time that we take back what's owed to us."

Elmira stood listening to all that her mother's sister had to say. The figure told her what she wanted to hear and promised to give her everything she asked for and more. She'd been a young girl when she left the village. She remembered the trip to Holland and then the long trip to the New World. Until today, she had forgotten about her aunt Agnes. Then she thought about how her father had forbidden her from marrying the man she loved and about the punishment she endured being with a child without a husband. When the man she loved left, she was labeled a disgrace to the family and then scorned by the man she loved when he returned and married another woman, Beatrice,

Elizabeth Lester's younger sister. Her own marriage was in vain, and it was a disaster for her. The only one she loved was her son Thomas, and he was taken from her.

"What do I have to do?" Elmira asked.

It turned and looked at her, smiling, and caressed her face.

Fourteen years later, she owns the largest farm in the colony. She could use the feast as a reason to gather her witches and allow her and the others to meet without suspicion. As they come together, she lets them know of the new spells and how she can now give them the power to teleport themselves from place to place without her doing it all for them.

She tells them, "Tonight, I'll summon up the spirits so you can remain young and avail the beauty of your youth while appearing as you truly are to their families and neighbors."

Elmira has taught them all different kinds of spells and incantations over the years, showing them the importance of frequent practice so they can strengthen their bond as witches and bind their gifts.

Tonight is different; *tonight is just the beginning of many beautiful nights to come.* She thinks.

Elmira praises the witches who have been with her over the years. She welcomes the newest members and expresses gratitude for the work that has been carried out. Mrs. Unity Bowe is the newest member at twenty-five years of age; she's only been with them for three months, and she is one of Winthrop Trevor's sisters eager to learn. She married the son of a merchant who wants nothing to do with the family business, although he has been looking for ways to exploit it for his own selfish gain. He wants to be a farmer, grow cotton, and leave for Virginia. He isn't the best of husbands, nor is he the best businessman; he often beats Unity to keep her under control, and he believes her place is at home rather than in the homes of all these gossipers like that old nag Elmira Pembroke. He tries to convince his friends that cotton is the crop of the future – of *his* future. Unity once believed in his dreams, but years have passed, and they have nothing to show for it. If he could raise money to buy property and slaves in Virginia, he could pay his friends back after two years.

"A few slaves and a good whip, and you could make a fortune." He says.

His friends always encourage him, but a penny between them has never been produced. After one toddy too many, he takes his frustrations out on Unity and the children, Abraham and Gwenavear. Unity wants nothing more than to control her own life and do what Elmira promised they could do. As the months go by, she reluctantly does the chores and takes care of the children. She knows it would be much easier to leave John Bowe and his dreams behind if it weren't for the children. Elmira likes Unity because she's a fast learner, and her situation makes her a good candidate for the type of witch she is looking for. Elmira always tells her to have patience and reminds her that time is on her side.

That night, they all drink from the same bowl Elmira has prepared. Elmira teleported them to the old settlement beyond the Kirts's farm, about six miles west of the property. The settlement had the main building and twelve houses for the settlers when it was built. Around the settlement were many large posts that had been cut from the trees, standing upright to form a solid wall. Now all that remains are scorched ruins. Trees have grown where some of the houses used to be over the last forty years. The entire compound is overrun with vegetation, although stones in the middle of the settlement are laid to form a large fire pit. The old widow, Mrs. Kirts trains Elmira there; now, it's where they train Elmira's followers.

Mrs. Kirts and the other women hated their husbands and the other men at the old settlement. If the men had kept their promise to the Indians, the women and children who died would still be alive today, and her own children who survived and remained would not have hated their father and run off to England. She would often visit her children's graves against her husband's wishes. She blamed God for not protecting her family and leaving her with a miserable bastard of a husband. One day she stayed too long at the gravesite while her husband was at the main port in Boston securing goods for the family. From her buggy, she did not know what direction her farm was in and began to panic when she saw a strange figure standing over the graves. She got down from the buggy, picked up a stick, and asked, "Who are you?"

The voice replied, "A friend."

She stopped, not recognizing the voice as any friend she knew. When she came near, he called out, "Mother."

"Winston," she said, walking closer but still clutching the stick.

When she reached him, he said, "Do not look at my face. It's horribly burned."

She grabbed his arm to turn him around, but he positioned his head away from her. She dropped the stick and told him that her love for him saw past the scars he bore. Slowly, she cupped his face to see him.

"Oh my god, how is this possible?" She says.

Winston looked at her and told her what had happened to him during the raid that night.

"I was trying to run and get little Anne Worthington out of her house, which was burning down. When I reached her, she was already dead. I tried to get out, but the front door was fully engulfed in flames. There was no other way out, so I panicked and ran through it, but my hair and shirt caught on fire. There was a hole in the wall from the fire where a tree fell through it, so I ran off until I reached the river and jumped in. The currents took me farther into the woods, and I didn't know what to do the next morning when I saw my reflection. I thought everyone was dead, so I went farther west, away from everyone. I did not want anyone to see me. When I returned to the old settlement, I saw the graves and knew there were survivors."

"We often wondered what happened to you," She said. "We thought the Indians had captured you."

"No, I just wandered off through the woods, surviving the only way I knew how," he replied.

She asked, "Did you know of the farm?"

"I often came by and stood at the edge of the woods. I never came any closer, though." He said.

"Why not?" She asks.

"I blamed Father and the other men for what they did; because of them, I am as I am." He angrily said. "Besides, Father would not have had someone as hideous as me. He would have disowned me because of my condition."

It was not hard to convert her after that, for Mrs. Kirts wanted the power to control her life and get back at her husband. After a year, Winston told her that he could not train her any further and that someone else would be there to continue as her mentor.

"I belong to another and must do the will of my master," he explained. "My scars remain, but I can hide them by transforming myself back to the days before the raid. When my master found me, I was in great pain, and she took me in and healed me. I cannot go any farther, and I want you to understand." He said.

Mrs. Kirts caressed his face and watched him vanish. She allowed her husband to live out his miserable life. She believed the hell he was living in his mind was better suited for him than anything else he would get if she killed him. She still had one son with her, and nothing else mattered. She wanted to show him what she was, but after many years and the death of her husband, she thought it better to leave things as they were. She made Avery promise that when she died, he would not bury her next to her husband but where her family and friends had died at the old settlement. On the day of her perceived death, she asks him to take her to the old settlement so that she can see it one last time. Of course, Avery wanted to return to where his father would beat him for going.

He agreed. In his mid-thirties, he loved his mother and would not have her buried near his father. When they arrived at the old settlement, he began to reminisce about the days when he and his siblings would ride off with the horses and play around when their father was out on business. They laughed as he talked about those times.

"When your father would ask your older brother and sister where they came from, they would confess that they were here, at the old settlement. Boy, did he ever punish them well?" She said, reminiscing.

Then Avery asked the big question. "Why did all this happen?"

She looked into the clouds and began to cry, and then in anger, she said, "Stupidity. I can't think of anything else but stupidity and ignorance. You were born after all this happened; a young Indian boy was caught in the woods with one of the young girls, Abigail Williams, one of the daughters of our founder. They brought the girl and the young Indian back here to the settlement. Oh my, was that young boy ever afraid, and so was Abigail Williams. I guess another Indian saw them taken away and told some of the tribespeople."

"Is that when they attacked?" He asks.

"No, we had an okay relationship with the tribe then, so the chief asked if he could take the boy back. He said they would punish him according to their law, but the men and Mr. Williams lied to the chief. They explained that he had to stand trial here first, and then he would be released to the chief the next day. They said he would never be allowed to return or see another white girl again. The chief did not want to leave the boy, but they wanted to keep the peace and agreed to return the next day to retrieve him."

Avery asked, "Did the boy rape the girl?"

"No," his mother replied. "They were in love, but her father would not have some Indian savage in his family. They held a trial that same day and decided that the Indian boy had defiled the young Williams girl. They wanted to teach him a lesson and ordered all the young women to come to the courtyard and watch. They told the young women that no decent white woman would ever be allowed mix with these savages. When they brought him to the courtyard, they acted like he was free to go, but one of the men shot him in the back while he ran for the gate. Abigail was taken home and beaten in private by her father."

Avery asked, "Who shot the Indian, and what did they tell the chief?"

Mrs. Kirts sighed. "Your father shot him, and they did not tell the chief a thing. Apparently, some of his young Indian friends were sitting on that hill and watching." She pointed to the hill above the settlement. "They saw him walking toward the gate and came down to meet him. After your father shot him, the men went after the others. Then they returned to their tribe and told the chief, who showed up that night very angry. He demanded to know what had happened. Your father and the other men started shouting at the chief and the small group of Indians, demanding that he and the rest of his savages leave the colony immediately. They took the boy's body back with them, and nothing happened for the next three days. We all thought that was the end of it, and the men began to go about their business as usual. They went out into the woods to hunt and caught fish in the river. It wasn't until the third night that the Indians attacked the settlement and began to burn it down. The attack lasted all night, for they would stop and repeatedly start in a different place, so nobody knew what direction they were coming from. The next day, more than half the colony was dead. Most of the women and children died in their homes; they couldn't escape the flames. All they had to do was let him go and let his own people punish him. Your father hated the Indians; he always referred to them as heathens, savages, and pagans. We were invading their home and lands, and they accepted us. The problem was - we didn't accept them."

She took a deep breath and sighed, falling to her knees at the graves of her friends and children.

She told him, "All this made me as tired as the night it happened. We got no sleep. The Indians stopped just long enough for us to close our eyes, and then they attacked again."

"Mother, let me take you back home," Avery suggests.

"No, my son, I'm fine. This is a place of rest and so peaceful here." She said.

"I'm going to look around a bit, Mother." He kissed her cheek and wandered off. Every once in a while, he would look back to see if she was okay. Behind one of the old scorched houses, he carried a doll his sister had lost when they were children.

He shouted, "Guess what I just found?" Avery dropped the doll and ran to the grave where she'd kneeled. She was dead, and he began to weep. When Avery woke up the next day, he did not remember much of the day before, nor did he remember burying his mother. He looked over at the mantle, saw the doll he'd found at the site, and began to weep even more. His wife told him he was carrying the doll when he arrived home. She told him his mother died with the people she loved and missed. She said that his mother is with those people now, which she'd always wanted. He looked at her and promised he would never return to the old settlement again.

The night before Elmira brought the witches to the old settlement to talk about Keith's festival at the farm, Ann Kirts came to Elmira with a heavy heart.

"The time has come for me to die," she said. "I have nothing left to live for, and you will never see me again after this night. You, Elmira, have been chosen to lead the witches, but I leave you with a warning; to trust no one. When you lead others, you should never stop learning. Grow in strength, Elmira, and fare thee well." She stepped toward the flames that filled the pit.

"I'll tell you this," she warned,

"There will come a time when a new Dorothy shall be dropped upon a strange world. There she shall rise above her watchers in courage and valor. Beware of the waters of that world, for it will be the fall of the old. Guard well your heart, for the blight will see it part."

Elmira asked, "What does that mean?"

In a weak voice, she said, "Beware, Elmira. Beware." Then she walked into the flames, her clothes caught on fire, and she began screaming. Elmira screamed too, wanting to stop her, but she took a step back and just stood by looking on as she did when Elizabeth had burned. She wept for her old mentor, unable to believe she'd wanted to die that way.

"Why?" she asked herself.

But then she considered what she'd said: *"I have nothing left to live for."*

Avery was dead, and Elmira knew how much she'd loved her son. When Elmira had her son killed, Ann Kirts knew then that her apprentice would soon become the master. She knew then that she no longer had anything to live for. She wept over her son's body when Clarence and Adam left her home, and then she watched Clarence and Adam bury her son and daughter-in-law far away from her husband. She wept bitterly and decided she would no longer appear to Elmira or the other witches; she found herself standing at graves in two different places, cursing her husband. After Elmira stood there for a while, watching Ann Kirts burn without remorse for having killed her son, she could only think about what that old battle-ax had said about Dorothy before she stepped into the flames.

"A new Dorothy, says she," Elmira murmured to herself. "Now that's a sobering thought. I hope she won't mind if I take care of the old Dorothy first, and then I'll take care of this new version in due time." She screamed in laughter and vanished from the old settlement.

Elmira and the other witches gather in a circle around the pit, chanting and summoning the spirits of the night. Elmira reveals her power; she transforms into the youthful woman of her late teens. Oh, how the others long to do this. Their beauty has long since passed. Some of them can only long for youthfulness; if they only had the power, they would have the beauty they never possessed. But Elmira does not want to reveal her true self to her newest members. In the early months of 1692, she revealed her true self to one of her newest members, LeAnne Hempstead. When LeAnne saw her transform, she was so frightened that she fled from the old settlement in the cold dark of the night. LeAnne tried to tell her husband, but no one believed her story. Mary Grace, Elmira's retarded sister, Alexandra Schmidt, and LeAnne Hempstead were the only three with her that night, for all the others were at home. Mary didn't want LeAnne to know that she was a witch. She did not want her to keep her daughter from her. Fourteen years later, Elmira and Mary's powers have grown immensely. Mary is a follower; she has never been one to lead the pack. She just wanted to be of a sane mind. And Elmira had wanted to extend the sisterhood by recruiting LeAnne.

She had been training her for only a couple of months before revealing herself. She transformed into the foul witch she truly is – and when Leanne watched in horror as Elmira's face took the greenish scaly color of a lizard, her nose flattened, her hair grew longer and stiffer, and her arms slimmed down – well, LeAnne could not believe it. Elmira's hands began to curve, and her nails grew like the talons of a large bird of prey while her feet became even longer and narrower. Her teeth sharpened, and her eyes were as black as burnt coal; her voice was hollow and raspy, yet strong and clear. After LeAnne witnessed this, she was afraid, and even more, she feared that she would look like Elmira. LeAnne was a young and beautiful woman Elmira secretly admired for her beauty. Elmira tries to talk to LeAnne and convince her of all the wealth she can have and the freedom, but LeAnne begins to threaten to go to the Sheriff.

When she saw she could not control LeAnne, Elmira placed a horrible sickness upon her daughter. She wanted to let her know how powerful she was. She tried to talk to LeAnne again but still would not listen. She blamed the child's death on LeAnne and the wanderer who had drifted into the township. This led Elmira to devise a plan to exact her revenge on the others and their friends, whom she blamed for her son's death. And she wanted nothing more than to get rid of this treacherous witch. She could not allow LeAnne and her husband to destroy everything she'd worked so hard for, so before LeAnne could accuse her, she'd accused LeAnne of witchcraft. She produced clothes LeAnne would change into at Elmira's house during training, and then she accused her of associating with the warlock who had drifted in. She told everyone that God had punished her by causing the sickness to come upon her young child. LeAnne's trial took a week, and her sentence – was death by stoning. They dragged her out of the courthouse by her hair as she screamed. It was apparent to Elmira that she did not need the power of a witch to get rid of her enemies, only the power of persuasion. Elmira, her followers, and the whole witch's sisterhood waited for LeAnne to be dragged from the courthouse. When LeAnne was dragged from the courthouse, they stoned her at the bottom of the steps. Her husband Henry moved out of the township and left for Harvard the following day, taking only the clothes he possessed.

Elmira felt her power over the other witches. She felt that she could do anything. Strange eyes were seen hovering above her, but the others were so entrenched in their power and enthralled in their chanting that they were not afraid – or they'd simply failed to notice. With every word, Elmira felt power and strength.

She spoke with all her might. "This drink will give us the power of immortality. It will give us the strength of ten men and the power to go wherever we want at any time and place." Her voice became raspier with every word. She was holding onto the outward beauty of her past, but her inward ugliness began to show as she continued.

"We have the power, and we have the strength." And while she spoke, flames engulfed both her hands. "We have the ability to control all the elements. Let us draw from the spirits and bask in our powers, glory, and all the wonders we now possess."

Then Mary began to demonstrate her power by revealing the beauty and innocence of her youth. She stretched her arms out from her side, levitating off the ground and causing a heavy fog to spread and cover the settlement and the surrounding woods. The witches began to scream excitedly, and the entire settlement was in an uproar. At this, Elmira took notice; she had never before seen Mary demonstrate her powers in such a way; yet, she was proud of her sister's capabilities. They ended their night by levitating around the fire. Elmira was proud of her own wicked powers and filled with self-glory. This was clear in her cold black eyes, lifeless heart, and the fact that she had all the witches encircling her while she levitated above them, just above the flames. The others chanted praises to her, and she basked in her glory as she thought, *I have to keep an eye on this - sister of mine, now that I've seen her powers revealed.* Then she thought of the warnings that she should trust no one.

Oh, she's good, all these years holding back as a simple-minded fool. What other little trifling tricks is she hiding up her sleeves?

Mary looked up at Elmira and smiled. "Good for you, Mary Grace," Elmira said. "Good for you."

Elmira's lust for power went far beyond what she initially desired. It would soon consume her mind, body, and soul. She felt her power was greater than anyone else's, including the power of her master... at least for now. She was strong and powerful, and nothing on earth could get in her way. Unknown to Elmira, Mary had been changed long ago, long before Elmira and even before the birth of Thomas.

Chapter 6
The Winds of Change

Keith welcomes his guests on Friday morning, the first day of the three-day festival.

"Welcome, welcome one and all." He stands on the podium he has built as a platform for politicians. "I want you to enjoy yourselves, and feel free to enjoy the food, the Ale, the games, the music, and the friendship. Enjoy the fellowship of the Williams River Township." Keith raises a toast to the new and hopefully annual festival and the idea of a bigger and better colony. Elmira looks at him with guile.

"This crippled fool has been more of a blunder than a help." Nonetheless, she puts on her best face to mingle with some of the more affluent guests.

One of the magistrates asks, "How are things going on the farm?

"Things are getting better. Unlike his father, the younger Kirts wasn't the best with farm maintenance."

"Yes, I do remember that old bugger." The magistrate rubs his arms and looks down at the ground. "I do remember falling victim to that damn whip of his. Cantankerous old bastard carried that whip everywhere he went on the farm and here in town. I felt pity for young Kirts, that poor fellow. His father was a very harsh man.

"I believe many of us remember him well." She remanences.

"I really can't blame his children for running back to England the way they did. When I heard the news that young Kirts killed his wife and one of the deputies and wounded another, I thought it was so tragic." Winfred said.

Mr. Winfred Gaines is one of the only magistrates Elmira admires. He was a comfort to her when her husband died.

"Now that all the riffraff have been weeded out, maybe this township can grow." He says.

"Well, not quite," says Elmira. "I believe there may be a few of them left."

She smiles at Mr. Gaines and sips her tea. "Well, Mr. Gaines, I know you have plans to help grow the town, but we still have to contend with that insufferable Monroe and his two idiot friends."

"I'm afraid so, Ms. Pembroke," says Mr. Gaines. "He believes that cotton is the best product to bring the winds of change to this colony. There are times when I believe he's right, but then I think of the harsh winters and the bad soil we tread upon, and his ideas make no sense at all."

"I agree. But I do believe the soil of my farm will do well to grow flax," comments Elmira.

"So much can come from a simple plant," Gaines adds. "Its oils and seeds will bring a handsome price to the market, and the plant can be spun into yarn and weaved into a cloth that will yield equal gains. It will indeed do well, and I believe a mill is the best solution to grow this town. However, I have brought other things to the table, only to be rebuffed by my opposition."

"I want to hear what Monroe has to bring to the table other than cotton," states Elmira.

"I believe he's holding an audience now," Gaines speaks mockingly. "Shall we proceed and give him our undivided attention?" Elmira says.

They both laugh and approach the platform Keith has built for the debates. Keith thought he would give the Mayor the stand first, as he is often known as the grandstander, the orator of the people.

Elmira looks up at the platform.

"Just a fat ass bag of hot air." She mutters, "Today, he looks like a little fat Leprechaun all dressed up in red." She mutters.

Monroe wears a white shirt with a ruffled collar and sleeves, a red vest with a matching overcoat, red trousers, white stockings, and black buckled shoes. He wears a new French wig and a red feathered hat. He allows the applause to last a long while before he waves his hands to quiet the crowd.

"To my esteemed colleagues and the proud people of the Williams River Township, I bring you tithing of great joy and with gladness of heart," he says. "Please, lend me your ears for the moment. My esteemed colleagues and I believe the township should purchase land to grow tobacco and cotton. This will bring great wealth to this township."

Many townspeople groan at the announcement.

"Yes, I know you are aware that the land here is far too harsh to grow tobacco and cotton," Monroe continues. "Still, tobacco and cotton grow in the land just south of here…in Virginia."

Now the majority of the audience is grumbling and exchanging worried glances. "Has Monroe gone mad?" Someone in the crowd asks, "Why Virginia?"

"My friends," continues Monroe, holding his right hand over his heart. He points to the ground with his index finger on the opposite hand. "Stomp the ground with your feet. It isn't the kind of fertile ground for the profits we seek, nor can we achieve the benefits we desire trying to grow it here for this great township. We need fertile land, and Virginia is the place to achieve this."

Holding the top post with both hands leaning forward toward the crowd, he says, "How many more years must we invest in the failure of crops that bear no fruits for all our hard labor?" He pumps his fist into the air, clutching his vest with his left hand. "I propose we grow these crops on lands where our money will serve us better. Why should we pour out our hard-earned pence and sweat only to see failure in the end? Let someone else sweat and toil, and let them labor as we have all these years. Let them carry the burden, and let us bring forth the fruits of our labor in the growth of this great township. Together we can build the Williams River Township, making it as great as we all deserve. Today we celebrate the rebirth of this township, so raise your mugs with me." Someone hands Monroe a mug. "Raise your mugs with me and watch the future unfold for our children and our children's children as they grow with the greatness of this township."

Monroe continues for another thirty minutes of babbling, as Elmira calls it. Someone in the crowd shouts, "Let them work," and the rest of the crowd shouts the same. Chanting erupts for a few minutes. Monroe is pleased with how the crowd has responded; he and his two cohorts, Jameston and Eagleton, drink from their mugs and raise them to keep the crowd going for as long as possible. Monroe steps off the platform holding the lapels of his vest as if he just saved the world. Keith walks over to Mr. Gaines and his mother, who is standing and watching the little fat Leprechaun bask in his glory. Mr. Gaines will soon speak to the people about his vision for the township.

"How do you get behind something like that?" Keith asks.

"Tomorrow, the drink will have worn off, and the last thing they'll remember is what I have to say. Today will be a mere blur in the minds of many," replies Mr. Gaines.

He and Elmira start walking to the tables where the food is served. Gaines turns to look back at Keith. Keith's head is down, and he is smiling deeply.

"Come, young Grace," beckons Gaines. "Your feast has only just started, and the people want to enjoy it with their host."

Keith points at Mr. Gaines. Shaking his finger, he says, "You sly devil, you."

"Wisdom, young Grace, and patience," says Gaines. "I must now go and congratulate Monroe on his most…what should I call it – his most heartfelt speech yet?"

As they reach the table, Monroe is greeted as though he has just found the cure for the plague.

Mr. Gaines greets him and shakes his hand. "Marvelous speech, my good fellow. It seems you have the whole township eating from the palm of your hand."

"Mere formalities, Mr. Gaines," sneers Monroe. "I'm sure you'll do almost as well."

Monroe leaves to mingle with more of his constituents. He passes Elmira and Keith like they do not exist.

Elmira comments on how well Keith built the podium.

"You did a great job with that beam, son. I was hoping he'd have made a mad dash to the ground when he leaned forward with both hands on the banister."

They all laugh. Mr. Gaines adds, "I can imagine him looking like a beached walrus while he rolls on the ground trying to lift himself up. I can see him cursing the banister for not supporting his rather large stature."

At the end of the day, Elmira remarks on how well the start of the event has gone.

"Keith, you outdid yourself today," she praises. "Let's hope the rest of the weekend goes just as well."

It's not often Keith hears something positive from his mother. Most of the things she says to him begin with the words "You bumbling idiot" or some other disarming comment. He thanks her gladly with a big smile and tells her, "I will do my best to make it so."

Keith tries hard to please his mother, and he is most willing to do anything she asks of him to make her happy, but it's rarely ever enough. Try hard as he may; he struggles to please her. But today, he and his wife Amanda retreat on a high note.

The next morning, Keith is up early to ensure everything goes well. He talks to the servants and volunteers, reminding himself that he should not overdo the event. In his mother's eye, overdoing something is just as bad as underdoing it, so he does his best to focus on what is out of place. Monroe does not bother to grace the grounds, thinking there is nothing Winfred Gaines could say to steer the people away from tobacco and cotton. Besides, he would hate to watch Mr. Gaines in a feeble attempt to out-speak him on any platform. Monroe sends his good wishes to Keith and his wife regarding the festival's first day and asks for their forgiveness, for he must be on his way to a small township not far from there.

As Mr. Gaines approaches the podium in a white shirt, blue vest, and matching overcoat, with blue trousers, white stockings, black-buckled shoes, and a British wig and black hat, he is greeted with applause. Not quite willing to quiet the crowd, Winfred lets the clapping go on for as long as he can while looking at Monroe's two accomplices, acknowledging that he is just as esteemed as Monroe. Removing both hands from his vest pockets, he waves to the crowd. The masses are eager to hear what he has to say.

"My fellow townsmen, I come humbly as a servant to the township, looking out into our future in the hopes that we can draw from our past experiences with knowledge," says Gaines. "Knowledge that as a township we can rely on ourselves will build on the foundation laid down by the blood, sweat, and tears of our forefathers." With both hands in his vest pockets, he turns from left to right and speaks to the people. "I propose that we townspeople grow the things we know will grow here on our soil. We will build a mill here in the Williams River Township, a mill that will use the resources with which our Lord has blessed us. We will grow flax and import cotton, and we will raise our own sheep for wool. All these are needed to spin yarn and sell it to textile mills in other townships and larger cities. These mills will weave fine materials that we can proudly say originated from the Williams River Township."

A roar of approval comes from the crowd. Gaines raises his hands to quiet the crowd.

"Let's build taverns for our visiting families, friends, and neighbors, and let's build a great market where we can sell our products. I propose that we build on what we know and are already doing, but we do it on a grander scale. Let us use the gifts of craftsmanship and the talents bestowed upon us."

The townspeople like what they hear and respond by shouting, "Yes!" They shake their heads in agreement and poke one another as a gesture of fellowship.

Gaines continues, "We, the people of the Williams River Township, will control our own destiny and growth. Our children will look back and know that it was their parents and their parents' parents who forged ahead to make this great township a better place for them and that it will be up to them to forge on and make it an even better place for their children."

Gains pauses for a moment to pull his audience in as he walks to the end of the platform.

"My fellow townspeople, let's build right here in our own great township and let's make it better for us today and for our children tomorrow. We will work together, sweat together, and earn honest gains for our tireless efforts to make this a township for our neighbors to envy. So, let us rise and stand on our own two feet and prepare this township for the new millennium. Let's not look to Virginia hoping that he who manages the plantation will remember us when the profits are making great gains in his favor. Cotton and tobacco are great sources of great wealth; I'll admit...but at what cost? And will it profit us in the end? From the birth of the Williams River Colony, we have relied on our hard work to make this township what it is today, and it will require the same tireless efforts to make it all it can be for our future."

Gaines's speech does not elicit shouting and chanting from the crowd, but it does get him a round of applause and happy townspeople. He raises a hand to quiet the crowd and calls the Reverend James Cribbage up to the podium. Gaines announces that he will come and bless this day's festival. Winfred wants to start early in the morning so he can speak to the people before the passing of the Ale. He wants clear minds and receptive hearts of the people so they can hear what he has to say. Besides Winfred's desire for Elmira, his heart yearns for the township's growth. He wants to do all he can to put the colony's past behind them. Magistrates Jeremiah Jameston and Quincy Eagleton look on as the townspeople offer a greater response to Winfred Gaines than they did to Monroe Wilson. There are less than two hundred people in the colony, and over the last two years, more than thirty-five percent have either moved away or died. Winfred Gaines believes that this is a time for healing and growth. Put the horrible past behind them and move on.

But Jeremiah Jameston and Quincy Eagleton move through the crowd to sway people to Monroe Wilson's side. Even though they do not entirely know Monroe's plans, they are not sold on the idea of tobacco and cotton grown in Virginia. They side with Monroe because they blame Elmira and her son, the Sheriff, for the deaths that plagued the Williams River Colony. To them, Winfred has sided with the devil. So, as they greet the men at the festival, they remind them that Winfred has sided with the people responsible for the witch hunts and theft of property and that neither Keith nor Elmira – and certainly not Gaines – has their best interest at heart. And at the same time, they push Monroe's proposal to grow tobacco and cotton in Virginia.

Charles Langram did not attend the festival on the first day, but he decided to bring his family on the second day, Saturday. He overhears what Jameston says to some of the men, and then he turns to face Jameston as he talks with his back to him. After shaking hands with one of the men, he turns to greet another.

"Oh! Young Langram, I did not see you standing here," says Jameston. "We were wondering whether you were going to attend the festival, but here you are, you and your family with you. Good morning, Mrs. Langram. I hope that you enjoy the festival."

"We look forward to it," Mrs. Langram replies.

"I believe they have a puppet show set up for the children; the good Sheriff has outdone himself, if I may say so myself," Jameston remarks.

Sarah Langram excuses herself and heads in the direction of the puppet show. Charles kneels to tell little Charles to mind his mother, and then he asks Kate, his eldest, to stay close by. He kisses them both and squeezes Sarah's hand. Then he turns to Jameston and looks over his shoulder, and sees that Quincy is just walking up to greet him.

Charles greets him as he steps up. "Gentlemen, I must protest the way you are conducting business here. You are standing here on the Sheriff's property and at the same time vilifying him and his family and your fellow colleague Mr. Gaines, whose sole purpose is to unite the people of this township."

Quincy interrupts. "You, of all people, know what we are saying is true," he says. "You pretend to be sick and cower in your bed while your friend, the Sheriff, and his henchmen go about murdering and stealing. If you don't have the stomach for it, maybe you should resign from your post."

"Mr. Eagleton, you'll do well to be careful of what you say," Charles responds angrily.

Jameston interrupts, "Gentleman, this is neither the time nor the place. Why don't we put our differences aside and enjoy the festival?" He looks at Charles and says, "Maybe another time, young Langram."

"Yes, another time," replies Charles, "but I warn the two of you – you'd had better remember the people here are not all on Monroe's side. While you're going around spreading ill will, you'd better damn well think about who it is you're talking to." Then he points at Eagleton. "Magistrate or no, I'll bloody your nose the next time you talk to me that way."

Charles turns and storms off. He knows that Quincy is right about his having excused himself on many occasions while Keith and the others paid visits to the families of the deceased and those who lost their property to their accusers. Nonetheless, he puts on his best face and joins Sarah and the children, who are now enjoying the puppet show.

Jameston and Eagleton look around and smile at those who greet them in passing. They think about what Charles has said. They do not have to say anything to each other; they know they may have already said something amiss to one of Elmira's friends. They do not know who their friends are and who are the foes of Monroe. Ambrose Smith, one of Elmira's witches and servants, is next to them. As Charles walks away, Ambrose finds Elmira and tells her what has just transpired between Charles Langram and the others, Jameston and Eagleton.

The day ends as well as the first, but Elmira is eager to end it all. One more day and the festival will be over. She is tired, and so are all the others. Keith is glad, and before the day ends, he announces that the festival will only be for half the day tomorrow.

Elmira walks over to him and says, "Your announcement for a short day tomorrow is well received. Thank you." She and Amanda leave for the house, and Keith nearly falls to the ground.

Two days and she has given me two good compliments, he thinks to himself. With his hands on his hips, he looks around as they walk away. He takes a deep breath and finds himself laughing aloud and shaking his head. "If this is a dream, I do not want to wake up." He charges.

Sunday comes and goes, and the day is half gone when the guests start to make their way home. Keith decides a visit to his friend's house is in order. When he arrives at Charles's home, he is all too ready to tell him the good news. Excited, Keith explains that his mother has complimented him two days in a row.

"Charles, I want you to pinch me because I can't remember if she has ever said a kind word to me." Keith expresses.

They laugh and talk about the times when they were young and hope for things to get better. Keith thanks Charles for always being there for him, bidding him goodnight before he heads home to Amanda.

After the long weekend has ended, Elmira sends Unity to keep an eye on Dorothy. Her watchers were ordered to keep an eye on the Sheriff and his band of idiots for the festival, and she wishes she had not let Dorothy and Clarence escape their watchful eyes. To her, Keith and his men seem to be getting more incompetent as the weeks pass. She knows that she needs to get as much information as possible. She needs to feel that she has complete control over the entire township and the surrounding farms, including her son Keith's farm.

When Unity sees that Dorothy isn't cutting wood or her uncle fussing about salting meets, she goes back and forth through the woods and then to the creek to see if Dorothy is fetching water for her uncle. She knows the exact route Dorothy takes several times a day. When she does not find her in the woods, she goes to the back of the house, looking for signs of them. She knocks at the back of the house to see if anyone comes around. She scans the area before turning and goes back to the front of the house, where she raises the door's latch. It opens, and Unity walks through the house and finds it empty; she then looks out a small window and sees old man Mr. Thopham working on his cart. She continues to search through the house, levitating with a strange feeling of euphoria about her. Seeing that no one is there, she twirls around the room with her arms outstretched like a child enjoying the freedom of youth. She glances out the window to ensure Mr. Thopham is still working on his cart. She looks at the things Dorothy has left in her room, running her fingers across the small dresser. When she is sure no one else is in the house, she slips outside and walks toward Mr. Thopham as he works. She watches Mr. Thopham work for a minute, standing behind him to see if he notices her presence.

Unity greets him. "Good morning, Mr. Thopham."

He turns around, startled. "Wonderful morning it is, Mrs. Bowe. How can I help you?"

"I walked over to the Lester's house because I wanted to purchase some salted and smoked meats, but I found no one there," she explains. "I tasted some of it over the weekend at Sheriff Grace's farm, and I just had to have some for myself."

George looks over her shoulder at his neighbor's house, puzzled. He scratches his head.

"Strange, I could have sworn I saw him earlier moving about." He says

Unity looks around and tells him, "Trust me, no one is there."

"Well, I'll have to take your word for it," says George. He looks at her with a raised brow and invites her onto his property. "I'll tell you what. I sold those meats to the Sheriff, and I believe we have more in storage."

He extends his hand to allow her entry.

"Oh, not to say yours isn't as tasty, but I heard that they came from his storage," says Unity.

"Same meats, same storage," George replies. "We're partners; I'm sure you know that. Anyway, I hunt, and he salts and smokes the meat. We both sell the meat to our neighbors. That smokehouse is where we keep everything. We'll just go through the fence there, and I'll get it for you."

Reluctantly, Unity follows Mr. Thopham to the storage. He opens the door to the smokehouse, where the meat is being dried and smoked.

"Wow, the two of you really do store a lot of salted meats." Unity looks surprised.

"Yes, we do," agrees George. "How much do you need?"

"Well, seeing as you have a lot, I'll talk to my husband and return with my basket," says Unity.

"Okay, that's fine with me. It's here when you need it." He says.

Turning to leave, she asks, "By the way, Mr. Thopham, do you happen to know where they are?"

"No, can't say I do. If they are not home, then I do remember Clarence saying this past winter that he had relatives in New York. Maybe he decided to take a trip to see them."

"Oh," Unity says, "they have family there!"

"I believe so," replies Mr. Thopham.

"Do you know when they left?" She asks.

"No, can't say I do. My wife and I left Friday morning at first light to see family northeast of here. We spent the whole weekend there and didn't get back until late yesterday evening. Figured I'd check on him this morning." He says this while looking at the house as if he's seen someone moving about; Unity turns to see what he's staring at.

"Do you know when they'll be back?" She asks.

"Well, Mrs. Bowe, we have a good partnership going here, so I should hope he would be back soon. If he's indeed gone, that is. Why are you so interested in their whereabouts?" He asks.

Unity says, "That's none of your business."

"Perhaps I should have told you the same," murmurs Mr. Thopham. She turns and looks at him with cold eyes and walks away. George watches her as she walks down the street, greeting others as she moves through the town. The whole time he keeps his eye on her walking away. He does not know what he is looking for, but he watches her anyway.

Unity turns and stares at George before she walks out of sight and uses her new powers to vanish from the side of the road and reappear on Elmira's farm. She reports to Elmira and tells her everything she saw and all that Mr. Thopham has told her. Elmira's face grows grim as she meditates on her thoughts. She remembers that Clarence's brother moved to New York after marriage. She isn't sure where in New York he lives. It could be west in New York or south near the harbor, but now is as good a time as any to see all the fuss about New York.

"Maybe it's time I pay New York a visit," says Elmira. "I'll have one of the servants take me there. Keith would never bother taking me; he's too puffed up in his role as Sheriff. Oh well, times are changing, and we have to adapt. The new century is upon us, and the townships and cities are growing; some are failing. More people are arriving in the New England states and moving to Massachusetts, Rhode Island, New York, and to that state... Virginia. The colonies are growing, and we have to grow with them. You may think about getting out and getting acquainted with these growing cities. They could get as big as some of the cities in England. You might find it...exciting."

"I might indeed," Unity says. "I might indeed. Is there anything else you need me to do? I have to get back to the house before I'm missed."

"No," Elmira replies. "You did well as usual."

Elmira contemplates Dorothy's journey. *My idiot son and his great ideas made it easy for them to sneak out of the town. My girls and I were preoccupied with the festival, and I did not post anyone to watch them. If it were me, I would have left as soon as possible. They probably waited for George and Martha to set off at first light, but they would have had to wait a long while not to overtake them on the road, being in a hurry. It's a short trip to the fork in the road, so they did not have to wait too long if they left early Friday morning; that gives them a three-day head start.*

You may have used my idiot son's feast to your advantage Dorothy, but I'm not my son. Elmira's thoughts run wild. She lies in bed and calls one of the servants into the room, explaining that she has a headache and will spend the morning in bed.

"Make sure I'm not disturbed," demands Elmira. "I'll call you when I need you."

"Yes, ma'am," replies the servant.

Once the servant has left the room, Elmira jumps up and points to the door to lock it silently. She levitates to the mirror to put her hair up, grabs her hooded cloak, and vanishes from her bedroom. Elmira reappears inside Dorothy's house. She enters Dorothy's bedroom and sees that she's left behind a few personal items. Clarence's area is the same. Staring out the window at George, Elmira sees him working on his cart. She goes about the house in anger, wondering how long she should give them to return.

"How long before I hunt you down, Dorothy Adams?" Elmira speaks through grinding teeth. "If you are indeed gone, my pretty, I will burn this house to the ground. Then I will find you, and I will kill you yet."

Elmira vanishes from the house and reappears at the edge of the woods near the fork in the road. "I depended on the girls to keep watch on you, Dorothy Adams, and soon I'll show you that I mean business. I'm going to hunt you and that weak and feeble uncle of yours down. The game's afoot." Elmira laughs and says, "Run, Dorothy Adams, run." She laughs aloud and disappears.

The magistrates, the Sheriff, and his men are interested in growing the township because too many people are leaving. The Sheriff and his men first met at the Undersheriff's small farm. It was just out at the edge of the town on the road to the larger farms, and it's less than four acres. The property has a small box house, a barn, and a stable in the back. Though it's not much to look at, Charles has done well to keep it up. He and Keith grew up together, and Charles was the only child Keith's mother would allow in the house – aside from Keith, that is. His parents were friends with the Pembrokes' after Thomas's death, and they grew even closer after Keith's father died. Unlike Keith, Charles did not like what went on during the trials. He went along with it, but his heart wasn't in it. He began to repent for all that he did and for knowing about the circumstances of Thomas's and James's child's deaths. Charles told Keith he was not feeling well that day they hung Mr. Evans in the chair. He just did not want to see another innocent person die because of the hatred Keith's mother had for the people she blamed for something Keith did. Charles and his wife often discuss moving away with their children. That night they both lie on the floor while Charles prays and asks the Lord for forgiveness.

"Lead us, O' Lord, in the path you have laid out for us," he says. "Be our strength, sword, and shield, and let me know what it is you would have me to do. We are your humble servants in the presence of great evil and lost in the darkness of it all. Please, Holy Father, show us the way out, and help me to transgress against you no more."

Charles feels his prayers are rambling on, so he and his wife weep together through the night. Neither one of them can sleep. Charles remembers the day he saw who was truly responsible when he was just ten years old, the moment it all happened. He never told Keith that he saw him push his brother and Nathan James onto the thin ice. He wanted to join them on the ice, but he had not finished his chores. He ran inside when he hurried through gathering and stacking the wood for the house.

"Mother!" he called.

"Yes, Dear?" She replies.

"May I go and play on the ice pond?" He asks.

"Yes, but don't be long. You'd better come home right away when I call you."

"Yes, Mother," he said from halfway out the door. "I will."

Before he reached the pond, Keith had already pushed the two boys onto the thin ice. He hid behind a tree and saw how Keith just stood there watching the young boys drown. He saw Keith run home after he'd watched them struggle to stay afloat. The ice water and the currents did not take long to pull the two young boys under and away from those who were trying to save them.

He lies in bed with his eyes closed tight, trying to put what he saw behind him, but each time he wakes in the night, the same scene plays over and over in his mind. In the morning, he decides it would be better to go out and finish his chores and work his thoughts away. Charles wants to tell Keith that he no longer has the desire to be his Undersheriff, but he doesn't know how to say it. For now, he insists that they change how they administer the law.

Charles is in the stable brushing his horse when Keith and his deputies arrive. He invites them over, and they stand in front of the stable, talking. Leaning against the top rail, Charles says, "We must get past the witch hunts if we want to grow. We have to be fair in our judgment. At present, lies, and deceit only serves to run people off. We're trying to get them to help us build this township into a thriving place, not drive it to its ruin. We have to pool our resources and go to the big cities and see what they are doing to attract newcomers."

The look on Keith's face is numb. He doesn't like what Charles has to say. He stands straight and tall. "Gentlemen, we should leave before Mr. Langram says something he'll regret," Keith says.

Keith has never called him Mr. Langram before. Perhaps he's known how he feels and simply kept it to himself because of their friendship. Keith and the deputies mount their horses and ride off. Keith turns to look back at Charles, but Charles is sitting on a small stool with his head in his hands, unwilling to make eye contact. Riding off, Keith knows that Charles is right, but he will not go against his mother – at least not for the time being. If he is to help build the town, he will have to do what his friend has requested: go to a bigger city and see what keeps that city thriving. It also means he'll have to take his mother to New York. This is something he's been putting off for more than a month now, meaning that he will have deal with her remarks about him and his deputies. He thinks it will be the worst possible time to go on the road with her, locked up with her for the entire trip. He would rather hide out in an outhouse in the summer heat for a whole week than be cooped up in a carriage with his mother for five minutes. The thought is enough to make him shiver. Later that night, Keith thinks about Charles, who is like his brother. *All this time, he's never told my parents that he saw me push my brother to his death. He's kept that to himself all these years. I know how to cheer him up – tell him I'm willing to go to New York with my mother; that'll make his day.* Keith finishes his drink and some salted meat and cheese and ends his night.

The next day, Keith rides out to Charles's farm alone to talk to him. Charles is out chopping wood.

"Make sure you cut enough for me," Keith says as he dismounts his horse. "My apologies, my good fellow, things got a little tense, and I thought it would be better if we allowed time to cool things off a bit. Anyway, I came here to tell you that I lay awake all night thinking of what you said about the big city. I have decided to travel to New York in the hopes of bringing back glad tithing. I think you made an excellent suggestion to look into what makes successful towns and cities thrive."

Charles says nothing.

"You know...this means I'll be traveling with my mother," explains Keith.

Keith's friend looks up at him as he chops his final log. "Oh my, that's a frightful thought. Do you plan on being drunk the whole time?"

They both laugh. "You better come in and have a spot of tea," says Charles. "I think this summer heat has you going batty."

As they walk into the house, Sarah greets Keith. Charles offers him a seat.

"Sarah, could you make us a cup of tea? Chopping that wood brings an awful thrust." Charles asks.

Keith speaks of reaching a consensus on how the law is administered. He looks up to the ceiling, draws in a long breath, and asks, "How do you think we should go about this?"

Charles looks at Keith and thinks about being careful regarding what he says.

"You know, just be fair about it," says Charles. "The newcomers are looking for a fresh start. They want to leave the persecutions on the other side of the ocean." He grabs Keith's knee and says, "A new start, old friend, that's what we all want. A new start."

"Of course we do," Keith replies. He accepts the tea from Sarah.

"So tell me, what am I to look for when I get there? New York, of course."

"Talk to the people there, go to the mills and find out about the log cutters and the spinners for wool, flax, and cotton. They'll bring in growth, and we won't have to work so hard and long on building the town. What are the new gadgets being used? How can we employ and train the people in our new town? Should we build an Inn for visiting friends, family, and those passing through? Inns and taverns are really big now. Look around and bring back some fresh new ideas."

Keith feels more comfortable now that the air is clear; he and Charles haven't lost their friendship and trust. The Sheriff finishes his tea and decides it is time to go to the magistrates and talk more about the town's growth. He and Charles walk out of the house together and discuss the future. They shake hands, and then Charles watches Keith ride away. Charles knows he will soon have to let Keith know he wants out. Even though he knows he wants to be a part of the town's growth, he thinks it is time to leave and start life anew with his family. He tries to think of ways he can leave without the wrath of Elmira coming down on him and his loved ones. He thinks long and hard about these thoughts. Charles considers how Clarence Lester and Dorothy Adams left the town without anyone noticing their departure. He and his family may have to leave the same way, especially if he tells Keith that he no longer wants to be his right-hand man. *Why even tell him?* He thinks. *Why tell him anything? Clarence and Dorothy didn't!*

Keith goes to the magistrates to inform them of his pending trip to New York. He tells them everything Charles has told him, only as if it were his idea. "I think this is a great idea, Sheriff," some say. But not everyone is sold.

"A big city brings big city problems." Mayor Wilson voices his opinion. "With all the trouble we have had – witches, lunatics shooting their wives and deputies – I don't see these problems going away anytime soon."

Keith looks at him and says, "If this town gets any smaller, we'll all be moving to cities like New York. There won't be anything left to call a town here."

The others agree with Keith and say that it is a worthwhile venture. One of the magistrates announces, "I will go with the delegation, and together we can bring back our views on what makes cities grow and what makes them fail. It is our duty to see that this town grow and that we stop the exodus of our citizens."

"Hear, hear." The others agree.

Things are heating up between the Mayor and Keith, so he bids the magistrates a good day and leaves them at the courthouse.

"Blind fool," Keith says angrily. "This is the best thing that could happen for this town, and that bumbling Monroe doesn't see it."

Meanwhile, Mayor Monroe Wilson makes his thoughts known regarding how he feels about Keith and his mother.

"Everything he says comes from the ass end of his mother, and that includes him," Monroe rants. "She has total control of this town, and she uses her crippled ass son to carry out her madness. I'll tell you, big city, big problems! Whenever I go to Boston or New York, I think it is a total madhouse."

The others allow him to vent. They know Monroe will have more fuel to burn if they say anything. Once he's finished, they all depart. As Winfred Gaines passes by on his way out the door, he stops and whispers to the Mayor. "You may be careful where you step." He says, and the Mayor looks at him with disdain.

Keith walks in with good news. Elmira is waiting inside Keith's house when he arrives home. Her unexpected visit isn't welcome, but Keith seizes the opportunity and lets her know what he, the magistrates, and the deputies have been discussing. He tells his mother everything the magistrates agree about town growth.

"That babbling Mayor Monroe Wilson will fight it to the end," says Keith. "He's going on and on about how big cities bring big problems." Keith takes a big swallow of rum and sighs aloud. "We are sending a delegation to New York. So Mother, fancy a trip?"

With a big smile on her face, she says, "Keith, I've been waiting a whole month for you to ask! Was this your idea?"

"Well, as much as I would like to take credit for it, I can't. It was Charles's idea."

Rubbing her chin and pointing, Elmira says, "Ah yes, Charles Langram. He has a good head on his shoulders, even if it is often turned in the opposite direction. Never mind where it came from, for it's a good idea indeed. Although I'm glad you told me this, I wish you had come to me first. It's better to hear good news before that council, and the Mayor gets it and perverts it with their horrid ideas. But that's not something I care to think about right now. So Keith, when do I pack my things?"

"We'll leave next Monday if that's alright with you."

"Marvelous, I'll have Jacob ready the carriage," says Elmira. "He'll drive us there. I have a new carriage that was built in Boston. It's really fancy, and it has windows and curtains that can be drawn to keep out most of the dust. Monroe won't be traveling with us, will he?"

"I'm not entirely sure," replies Keith. "He's always rejecting good ideas, but then he'll be the first to plant his flag when things go right." His tone is sarcastic.

"Never mind him; we'll make this a fun trip. It will be fun, just you, Amanda and me. We'll make this an adventure. I think a fortnight there in the Provence of New York will be plenty of time. Then we can come back and start building our new town."

Elmira leaves Keith's house in good spirits. Keith, on the other hand, sits with his mouth open. He holds an empty glass and does not know what to say. He has never seen his mother happy before. *Does this mean I will not have to deal with the insufferable insults?* He wonders.

For the rest of the evening, Keith is like the child he never was. He goes about the house whistling and humming. He can hardly wait for Monday. But in the back of his mind, he thinks the situation may be too good to be true. The thought makes the hair on the back of his neck stand up. "Get control, old boy. One day at a time."

Elmira is incensed at what Keith said of Mayor Monroe. "If he wants problems, I'll give him problems," she mutters. The next morning she takes a short trip to town and tells all her friends that she will be part of the delegation traveling to New York. When she drives up in her buggy, Winfred Gaines is walking toward the courthouse. Elmira stops her buggy and blocks his path.

"Afternoon, Ms. Pembroke," Winfred greets.

She returns the greeting. "Afternoon, Mr. Gaines."

"Fine day today," he says.

"Yes indeed," she replies. "How's Joan? I heard she wasn't feeling very well."

"Oh, just a touch of the fever," says Gaines. "Why, she's already fussing about in the house. She'll be glad to see you if you stop by."

"I may do just that, Mr. Gaines. By the way, Keith told me about the delegation that will be going to New York. Are you part of the party?"

"Why yes, most of us will be in attendance," he says.

"Will the Mayor also be in attendance?" Elmira asks.

Winfred glances down for a moment, sighs, and says, "It's likely he will be in attendance, Ms. Pembroke." He is reluctant to share this with her.

"I see." Elmira pauses. "Well, I'd best be going. Good day, Mr. Gaines."

While Elmira rides away, Winfred walks into the courthouse. It turns out Monroe was watching while he and Elmira spoke.

"You two looked quite the pair, Mr. Gaines," Monroe says mockingly. "Should I expect the Sheriff and his henchmen to stop by my home sometime in the near future?"

Winfred walks on without saying a word while Monroe stands at the door and watches Elmira riding off into the distance. Before he walks back into the courthouse, Elmira pulls on the reins to stop her horse, and then she turns in her seat and stares at Monroe for a couple of seconds before she turns around and uses her whip to get the horse moving again. As Monroe stands at the door, he dismisses the sight of Elmira and steps back inside the building.

It is time to prepare the carriage for their trip to New York. Keith and Amanda find Mr. Gaines already at Elmira's home with his luggage.

Odd, Keith thinks. *Mother must be in good spirits to have one of the councilmen with us. She often refers to them as babbling buffoons. Of course, he's the only one who has stood by her side all these years.*

Mr. Gaines helps Elmira into the carriage and then Amanda. Keith offers Mr. Gaines the next place, and then he climbs in last. The men sit facing the women.

"This is truly a nice carriage, Mother," says Keith. "I've never seen one like this before. It's really comfortable." He pats the seat and repeats, "It really is very comfortable."

Elmira simply smiles and says, "I know."

She knocks on the carriage floor to signal to Jacob and Elroy, her servants, that they are ready to go. As they pass through town with the curtains parted slightly on the ladies' side, magistrates Jameston, Eagleton, and Mayor Wilson are just getting ready to leave. They have not yet pulled away when Elmira's carriage passes them by. Monroe Wilson stands outside the coach and looks back at the carriage as it goes by. He can see Elmira and Amanda through the curtains. They use a coach that isn't as comfortable as Elmira's carriage. Nonetheless, she makes sure that Mayor Monroe sees her, not turning her head to acknowledge them as the men tip their hats.

"Pompous hag," Monroe mutters under his breath.

"Mayor Wilson, you need to remember that we are on a quest for goodwill and need not cast a dark cloud on our expedition before we leave the township," comments Jameston.

"Mr. Jameston, your comments are ill-advised, and I must protest that we should all be on our best behavior. I would have preferred to leave earlier. If we had already left, we would have kept that dark cloud behind us," says Monroe.

The other two simply look at each other, shaking their heads.

Eagleton whispers, "This is going to be a long trip."

"Indeed it is, Mr. Eagleton," Monroe responds.

Once they are well on their way, Elmira's carriage is rather quiet. Then Elmira breaks the silence.

"I know you are wondering why Mr. Gaines is here in our carriage and not in the coach with that Monroe gentleman." She says.

"Mother, this is your carriage," replies Keith, "and you have every right to invite whom you please to ride in it."

"Well, he's credited with most of the great ideas for the town thus far, so I thought it would be advantageous to know his thoughts on what we should look for when we get to New York. I'm sure his expertise will greatly benefit our town's future." Elmira turns her head to address Winfred. "What are we to look for when we get to New York, Mr. Gaines?"

"One of the ways we have never employed in the township is free marketing." He explains. "Oh, we've had individuals benefit their families through mercantilism, which only served England but not the township as a whole. Since we don't have the type of land needed to grow products for trade, such as tobacco and cotton, we have to rethink things altogether. On my last visit to Boston, I heard that Rhode Island had built a thriving textile mill. Building and financing this venture could set our town apart from those towns that are barely hanging on.

"Take your wife here, young Grace. She's been using this yarn to knit hats and gloves. What if we invested in a mill that spins wool, cotton, and flax into yarn? And, in turn, have it woven into cloth that we can sell to other developing colonies. We need to invest in our future. This opens up so many possibilities, like transportation, for instance. Of course, we would need to find a way to get these products to and from Boston, New York, and other ports. We must engage in trade that will help our town grow. Our commerce must be our strong suit."

"Wow, you have done your homework. I'm impressed," expresses Keith.

"Thank you, Sheriff," Gaines says.

"You're welcome," Keith replies.

"If only I can convince the others of this worthwhile endeavor. Understand we need the funding first. We can have the greatest intentions, but without sufficient funding, it all means nothing. That is why I'm on this expedition – purely to get funding for this venture. I'm afraid you're riding with a hopeless dreamer. But I am always open to suggestions." Gaines looks around at the others.

"I have always believed you have an uncanny wit about you that never ceases to amaze me. This is the reason why I invited Mr. Gaines to ride with us. I promise you that my son and I will do everything we can to help you secure the capital to help you move our town into the next century," says Elmira. "You've convinced me to offer up my own finances to help you build the mill if we fail to attract investors."

"That's mighty generous of you, Ms. Pembroke," Winfred says.

"Now, Mr. Gaines, I want to know if I help you fund this venture, what role can the Pembroke family look forward to?" Elmira looks at Winfred face-to-face.

"Well, Ms. Pembroke, securing the capital we need for this venture will require the utmost diplomacy, and I can't think of anyone else other than you to aid in this endeavor. As for your family's role in the mills, it will be nothing less than the top. Of course, I am expected to run the mills as president; it is what the other investors will expect of me, you know."

"Oh, I know very well what you mean. I believe we have a deal, Mr. Gaines," says Elmira.

"I believe we do, Ms. Pembroke," he replies.

Keith listens to this with great intentions. He asks, "Am I expected to remain Sheriff of the town?"

"No, Keith," Elmira interjects, "I expect you to serve as vice president of this venture. I'm sure Mr. Gaines will agree!"

"Why it makes perfect sense," says Winfred. "It will be my pleasure to introduce Mr. Grace as one of our venture's investors and vice president."

Keith cannot believe his luck. He looks at Elmira, beaming. "I will not fail you, Mother."

"I know, son, I know. By the way, you ought to promote Mr. Langram as your replacement. It upsets my stomach to think of Mr. Trevor as Sheriff."

"I agree with you," says Keith. "I'll do just that as soon as we return."

Keith is pleased; for now, Charles can administer his righteous laws as he sees fit, as long as they don't interfere with his mother or himself. This will surely make Charles's day when he hears the good news of his promotion.

Keith comments, "Monroe will be pleased to hear that."

"Oh, I'm sure he will!" Elmira exclaims.

In the coach, Monroe is still irritated that Elmira and her carriage are ahead of them.

"Did you notice that Winfred Gaines was in the carriage with that woman? Even with the curtains drawn, I knew he was in there. I know they have already devised plans to upstage us when they get to New

York. They're not the only ones who have come up with brilliant ideas to help our town without bankrupting it."

"I'm all ears, Monroe. Of course, that was apparent the day I was born. My mother would tell me she had to knit special hats just to cover my ears," Jameston jokingly says.

The coach erupts with laughter. "Mr. Jeremiah Jameston, I believe laughter is what we needed here very badly," says Quincy. "Good one, old boy."

"Monroe," Jameston asks. "What are these brilliant ideas you have to save our town?"

"A brilliant plan is afoot, my dear Mr. Jameston," says Monroe. "I know many in the township think of John Bowe as the town's idiot, but he has the right idea regarding cotton and tobacco. The man has been on key for years, and it seems I am the only one who thinks he's right. The South has proven that cotton and tobacco sell, and I don't see why we can't use God's good earth to grow it to our advantage."

"Well, our winters are longer than the days are short. The Hunter family tried tobacco before and found that the weather and hard ground would not support it. We're not sold on Virginia, so don't tell us that is one of your brilliant ideas," Mr. Eagleton says.

"Are you going to hear me out or just criticize?" Monroe groans.

Eagleton and Jameston sigh. "Say on, Mr. Wilson."

Monroe clears his throat. "As I said before I was so rudely interrupted – cotton and tobacco, gentlemen. We could finance Mr. Bowe's venture down in Virginia. He could be our foreman there, and he could run the plantation for us. I could oversee the venture as its president and be sure that our town profits from the products it invests in. These are products that can't be ignored."

"So, where are we looking to purchase this land in Virginia?" Asks Jameston.

"Have you heard of the James River?" Monroe asks.

"We have." They reply.

"Well, there are failed plantations and very prosperous ones," explains Monroe. "All we have to do is model our plantation after the successful ones, and I believe we can become very rich men." Monroe clears his throat once more. "Besides, we have already acquired about one hundred acres with a payment."

"What payment are you talking about, Mr. Monroe?" Eagleton demands. "We haven't authorized any such investment."

"Well, you need not worry about that, for it's already a done deal," says Monroe. "As the town's representatives for the people, you can make special trips to Virginia to ensure no investments are wasted. As for the town's morals," Monroe whispers, "or lack thereof..." he continues, "Since it's Virginia, slavery shouldn't be an issue. Besides, that retched hag has black servants on her farm. Riches untold can be made here, gentlemen; these colonies' future lies in these two products. We are about to embark on the 1700s. Our riches could put us all in carriages so we will not have to endure these insufferable coaches."

Jameston and Eagleton want to ask Monroe how he has appropriated the funds for this secret venture without the others' advice and counsel, but they simply agree that it has great promise.

"Cotton has been growing in the south since the mid-1500s," Monroe explains.

"Monroe, I believe you have a very promising proposition," says Mr. Eagleton. "I believe funding this venture is much more acceptable than financing two mills in such a small town."

"Well said, Mr. Eagleton, and thank you." Monroe comments.

"Okay," says Jeremiah. "But we still have to convince the townspeople that investing in Virginia has more promise than investing in mills for the township."

"Well, Eagleton, I believe that's where your influence comes in," says Monroe. "The majority of the people are on your side. Thanks to the Sheriff and that old hag, the people who believed in her plight initially are no longer so sure. You need to exploit that and win them over."

After spending a couple of nights in inns on their route, they finally make it to New York down by the harbor. Of course, Mayor Monroe made it clear that they would pass the inn where Elmira was staying and travel farther on. They also left earlier the next morning to ensure they stay ahead of her. This pleases the other two because a happy Monroe is much preferable to a cantankerous Monroe.

Chapter 7
The Price You'll Pay

In New York, Winfred Gaines suggests they lodge in one of the larger taverns. He wants to stay in one that can provide an atmosphere for the ladies. Upon their arrival, they find Monroe made it to the city the previous day. The tavern they check into has a separate parlor for ladies, and the food is plenty good as well. It is better than the food they ate on their route to New York. Winfred suggests that the ladies stay in a separate room from the men, which Elmira and Amanda do not mind. Doing so will give them the privacy they need to search for Dorothy and Clarence. It will also allow Elmira to find a way to rid herself of Monroe once and for all. Their rooms are adjacent to the men's, and the ladies find the warming pans a comfort at night, for there is still a chill in the air. They welcome the comfort of a bed as well. It is a great relief to be off the road. Even in a comfortable carriage, the ride was still hard.

Elmira has an idea. "I want to see if I can teleport myself from the room back to my house on the farm.

"Oh wow, that's a challenge." Said, Amanda.

"Well, I'm not sure if it will work because we've never done it before from so far away. I do not want to find myself somewhere between colonies or an unknown place. We'll start with small steps, teleporting to the last inn we stayed at the day before."

"Okay, but be careful," urges Amanda.

When she returns to the inn, Elmira familiarizes herself with the area. She then teleports herself inside one of the empty rooms and back to the wooded area behind the inn. From there, she returns to the tavern in New York. She tells Amanda to focus on the inn where they spent the night. Amanda vanishes and appears at the inn. At the same time, Elmira is watching from the wooded area just behind the inn. She watches Amanda, who seems to be dancing over her accomplishments. Amanda then teleports herself back to the tavern, where she finds Elmira waiting.

"Are you comfortable with going farther?" Elmira asks.

Amanda claps and tells her that she is ready to go. Elmira and Amanda do this several times to ensure they won't have any problems as long as they know where they are going. They are taking pride in what they have done so far before they end the night. Amanda and Elmira will meet with the men in the morning. Elmira waits until Amanda has fallen asleep to return to her house on the farm. Mary is waiting for her, and they both go back and forth to New York with Elmira's help.

Back at the colony, after a few trips, Mary asks, "Do you want to try flying?"

Elmira thinks of old tales of witches on brooms. "Let's go to the old settlement and anoint a couple of brooms and practice around the old place," she suggests.

For an hour, they try to use a broom to fly, but Elmira is too afraid to go high up in the air. She fears that if she were to fall off the broom, she would fall to her death. Mary looks at her and laughs out loud, grabbing her broom and repeating, "Fly, Elmira, fly."

Mary flies above the trees. She peers down at Elmira and flies back down to her. "Get on your broom and fly," she says. "If you fall, I will catch you."

Elmira looks at her sister with a questionable stare because it appears that Mary is more advanced than she has let on. She mounts her broom, and Mary grabs her hand and flies above the trees. They fly low for a few minutes before Mary takes her higher and higher. Elmira gasps as she looks down at the entire colony. She then looks around and sees the beauty of the land. She can only express how beautiful it is, even in the dark.

Then Mary asks, "Are you ready?"

Elmira looks at Mary for a second, and then off they go — faster than Elmira has ever been before. They fly to the port of New York in just half an hour. When they are back on the ground, Elmira is shaking.

"Wait until I catch my breath." She takes in a deep breath to unnerve herself. After a few minutes, she sees Mary staring at the ocean.

Elmira asks, "Are you okay?"

"Yes," Mary replies in a low tone. "I'm just thinking of how our parents crossed this ocean. Was it fun?"

Elmira says nothing.

"All I should remember is the colony, but for some reason, I remember crossing this same ocean and being very sick," Mary explains.

"You were not yet born." Elmira stares at Mary.

"I remember it all, Elmira. I remember being sick and not wanting to leave the deck of the ship. I remember it all."

"It's impossible for you to remember something you never experienced." Elmira expresses.

"I'm not sure how I know, but I know," protests Mary. "Maybe I remember because it's what Mother went through, and I'm seeing things from her perspective."

"You're not the same anymore, are you, Mary?" Elmira asks.

Mary smiles and says, "No, not anymore."

"Did this happen after you became a witch?" Elmira asks.

"Yes, that's when the change happened," Mary explains.

"I have a feeling you are not new to any of this. So how long have…" Mary cuts her off.

"I know what you want to know. And yes, I have been a witch for a long time now, since before Thomas was born. I met the master one night while I was playing around in Grandma Hadley's room after she died. I was looking in the mirror and holding one of her dresses up. The figure appeared to me as Grandma Hadley, and she played with me every day for a month. Then she asked me if I could keep a secret, even from you. She took me to the old settlement, where we played hide and seek. She always played hide and seek with me before she died. One day I was kneeling by the graves of the old settlers, and Mrs. Kirts knelt beside me and told me that her children were there. She said that I looked just like her daughter. She and Grandma Hadley would brush my hair and make me feel pretty.

"Then Grandma Hadley asked me, 'Do you want to be like everyone else? Would you like to be normal?' I told her yes. I did not even know what normal was. That was when they changed me. It felt so different and… liberated. I could think and understand things, and it was so exciting. I was so happy when it happened. I did not want to go back to being the simple-minded idiot I once was. I begged them not to change me back; I wanted to stay this way for the rest of my life. Soon Mrs. Kirts began to train me. She told me, 'You will have to learn to act as though you're still simple-minded.' I told her that was the easy part."

Elmira grabs her arm.

"I've been of a depraved mind all my life," continues Mary. "Grandma Hadley and Mother were the only ones who did not treat me with malice because I was a simple-minded retard, which was how many in the family saw me, and others too. I didn't mind it so much coming from others but not from those in my own family. That made it hurt more than ever. They think because you're simple-minded, you don't understand when you're being treated differently, but I did. I just learned to accept it. There was nothing I could do about it."

Elmira says, "I'm sorry. I tried to keep that from happening."

"Thank you, and I know. Father and Grandfather wanted to take me deep into the woods and leave me there, but Grandma Hadley and Mother fought. They refused to let them take me there."

"I never knew that," Elmira said angrily.

"It was done in secret. When Grandma Hadley and Mother died, you helped and protected me."

"And I'm still doing that." Says Elmira.

Still gazing off into the dark, Mary keeps her eyes on the water. "She came up and told me, 'I can take it all away from you. No longer will you have to be the idiot or the retard of the family, or the one everybody is ashamed of or wished you were dead because they no longer wanted to care for you.' She changed all that in one evening."

"So you learned to pretend to be simple-minded," Elmira says.

"You don't have to pretend when you've lived it all your life. It comes naturally."

"You fooled me," Elmira speaks with a hardened heart.

"Mrs. Kirts told me it wouldn't be long before you became a witch!"

"Oh, did she now?" Said Elmira.

"You were so hurt and angry at the world, but you've done well, Elmira. You just have to let go and experience the fullness of what you are. Control your anger and rage, and let yourself be free."

Elmira lets go of Mary and stare at her. She folds her arms. "You talk as though I've been your apprentice and not you mine," she says.

But Mary only smiles, caresses her sister's face, and says, "I'm not quite the simple-minded idiot anymore, that's all."

She keeps her gaze fixed on the ocean. "Look at that ocean, Elmira. Even in the dark, it holds a certain kind of beauty. I really enjoy flying over this land and looking at its wonders. I've flown all over this land, even toward the west. There are mountains, valleys, rivers, lakes, and waterfalls, and then there are the hot deserts. Kind of reminds me of life; you have the beauty and the ugly all wrapped up in one. You can't have one without the other."

"Did Mrs. Kirts warn you of some kind of pending fate you'll…" Mary puts her finger to her sister's mouth. "I try to keep the beauty of life before me and the ugly behind me." She turns and looks at Elmira. "Let's fly over the South, and you'll see some of the best of what this new world is. It's quiet and solitary there, and once you get used to it…"

Elmira grabs Mary's arm in a not-so-gentle way. "It sounds like you are regretting the decision you've made."

"Well, Elmira," Mary says calmly, "When you come out of a simple-minded world, and suddenly you have the understanding of an adult, you see things differently." Mary grabs Elmira's hand, pulls it from her arm, and then warns Elmira. "Be careful what you ask for. It may not be what you think you want."

"No, you be careful," Elmira retorts.

"Elmira, you've always had your wit about you. Me? I just wanted to be like everyone else." Mary sighs and says, "I guess it's late. I'll fly back to the farm, and you can go back to the tavern, and we'll meet again on the morrow."

Mary senses Elmira's anger. She kisses Elmira on the cheek, turns away, and flies off on her broom. Elmira simply vanishes and returns to her room. It is hard for her to take in this new information.

Elmira wonders, *how strong is Mary? Is she better than me*? Then she speaks aloud. "Oh, if she thinks she has played me the fool, I'll show her."

Now Elmira wonders whether she is truly the leader of the witches. Could it be Mary, her not-so-simple-minded sister?

In the morning, the ladies meet with the men for breakfast. Elmira asks, "What is on the agenda for the day?"

Winfred states, "We will meet up with the others and discuss our course of action."

"When do we talk to the investors?" Keith asks.

"That will be discussed tomorrow morning," replies Winfred. "We must have a solid plan if we want them to invest in our small colony. I believe the best action is for our delegation to meet with them alone."

"I see," says Elmira.

"I've taken the responsibility upon my shoulders to either bring good or bad tithing back to the township. There is always that chance the investors will think it a greater risk than they are willing to invest in," says Winfred.

"Why is it a greater risk?" asks Amanda. "It seems a mill is far more economical to invest in than an entire cotton plantation."

"True," says Winfred. "But I must admit, the failure of a mill is far greater than the failure of a cotton plantation. Not to mention, the profits of cotton far outweigh the profits of a textile mill."

They all sit quietly for a few seconds.

"That's why we are meeting here this morning," Winfred said. "We should discuss the benefits of what our town offers and what will make this a viable investment."

Keith asks Winfred, "What's required to run a mill?"

"First, we need water that flows through the town."

"We have that," Amanda interjects.

"Right," agrees Winfred. "Also, we'll need workers and then the spinners – at least twenty of them. We need the tools of the trade, and we also need raw materials. Now, as for cotton, we currently rely on England to supply it; and for wool, we'll need lots of sheep. We will also need flax that can be grown and harvested on our farms. The sheep can be purchased from the market in large quantities. I'm afraid these things will require a bit of hard labor."

Keith says, "I know a family back in the colony, the Alexander family, about twelve strong. They live in that small house just past Thophams' house. Before arriving in our township, they were sheep shearers. They can teach the young lads the trade, and we could have full production by next spring. I believe there's a parcel of land just outside town past the fork in the road. It's far enough out of the town and can be made suitable for a sheep farm. Once established, they'll have the help they need to run the farm."

"Well done, Keith. I trust you to meet with the family after we have secured the monies. Arrange for them to move on the property and get started on building it up for production." expresses Winfred.

"When do we meet with your esteemed colleagues?" Elmira asks.

"Speak of the devil; here they come at this moment," Amanda comments.

"Morning," Winfred says. "Gentlemen, please join us; we've been waiting for you. This morning's agenda is to discuss our plan of action for the colony." He invites them to the table.

Monroe is a fat man of about five feet four inches with a curly mustache and long thick bushy sideburns. He loves being the center of attention. Breathing heavily due to his rather large stature, Monroe clears his throat, which looks like a turkey's neck, and then takes a seat at the head of the long table.

"Morning, ladies and gentlemen; I believe in only one such solution for our town: to invest in Mr. Bowes's idea of cotton and tobacco."

Everyone at the table looks at him in shock and turns to one another.

He continues, "Now, I know we have all had a laugh or two at his expense, but I have been pondering the notion for quite some time now, and I think it's time to invest in this endeavor. Cotton is the future, and I believe we should invest now in a good piece of land in Virginia and get started. I hope you can see this as the best investment for our colony. We have depended on England for cotton for years, and I do not intend to depend on them for more years. We must think for ourselves, take advantage of this product, and not wait another day."

The table is quiet for a moment. Elmira speaks to break the silence. "I believe that's a grand idea, Mr. Wilson!"

"You… you think this is a grand plan I have?" Monroe's tone is one of great surprise.

"Yes, we discussed the idea of a town mill before your arrival. We can spin and weave your cotton into thread and ship it to England and other colonies as raw material."

Everyone stares at Elmira in shock, and then Winfred laughs aloud.

"She's right," he says. "Gentlemen, we've sat on opposite sides of the table with different opinions for the colony, but the answer to our prayers is right here in the middle."

Elmira speaks to Monroe. "Mills and cotton, Mr. Wilson. Quiet the pair, don't you think?"

Monroe clears his throat and says, "Quite the pair indeed, Ms. Pembroke."

Winfred begins to brief the others on how the mill should run, adding that they would like to start a sheep farm for the wool. He asks their opinion on the ideas presented. After much deliberation, they finish discussing their plans, omitting any talk of who will be president of these ventures. Once they have all agreed on a course of action, the ladies decide to go out and see New York. The men split up and talked to various esteemed gentlemen in the city.

"Where do you think Monroe is getting the funding to secure the plantation in Virginia?" Keith asks.

"Good question, Keith," says Winfred. "I'm not sure, but there are a few financiers in the city. Some of them are from the old Virginia

Company, and others are from the Massachusetts Bay Colony, so that could be any of them. I can only hope we successfully secure the funds for the mill. We need those spinners and the tools to work the cotton, wool, and let us not forget the flax."

"Who, if I may ask, are our investors?" Asks Keith.

"We have an appointment with members of the former Virginia Company. We've dragged our feet for so long, I have all but lost hope for our colony. But now these are exciting times, young Grace." says Winfred.

"Exciting times indeed, Mr. Gaines," Keith replies.

Around noon, Winfred and Keith enter an inn for their afternoon meal and drink. Two gentlemen who could be their investors are sitting with a group of men, enjoying a drink and having a good laugh. Winfred points them out to Keith.

"Our potential investors are enjoying an afternoon meal." Winfred points out.

"Why aren't we enjoying it with them?" Keith asks.

"It would be best not to rush over while they enjoy a drink," Winfred replies.

"Would it not be advantageous to talk now and get them to sign an agreement while they drink?" Keith asks.

"Young Grace, you have a lot to learn; don't be deceived by the watered-down drink," says Winfred. "Don't be in too big of a hurry where fools rush in, for it wouldn't be they who walk away with empty pockets. Many have signed away the farm, thinking they had the advantage, only to wake up with a bad headache and in servitude to their new masters. No, young Grace, we'll fill our stomachs with meats and bread and meet with them across the table with clear heads. Order your meal, and let's enjoy the day as it is."

Keith tells him, "Keith."

"Beg your pardon?" Mr. Gaines asks.

"You can call me Keith." He says.

"And you, Keith, can call me Mr. Gaines."

Keith glares at the smiling Mr. Gaines. Keith watches the investors as they eat and wonders whether they are eating with others like them. *Are they drinking their victims into signing over the farm?* He thinks.

While Keith and Winfred eat their lunch across town, Monroe and his two cohorts meet with their investors to purchase the resources for the Virginia land, slaves, tools, and other materials. Monroe has always been quite the diplomat and ever the charismatic gentleman. At the table that morning with Winfred and company, he told them he was not sold on mills.

Meeting with his investors over lunch, Monroe is confident of his chances of getting what he wants. "Cotton is the future." He says. "And I'm not about to let those buffoons waste the Township's funds with such foolishness."

"Now," Monroe bellows, "I wish to finish up this trip, head back to the township with my great news, and upstage Winfred Gaines and that vengeful hag Elmira."

He is quite verbal regarding his feelings and does not seem to care if others in the tavern appear to be whispering and looking his way. They have a good meal and wash it down with ale. His investors met with him on a previous visit to Boston, so this meeting is only to close the deal. Monroe stands to gain quite a lot in this deal. He met with Mr. John Bowe the night before they left for New York to let him know that he is finalizing his deal with investors Mr. Wayland and Mr. Eckhart of the former Virginia Company. John Bowe agreed to run the plantation with two of his friends, Mr. Tyler McClann, and Mr. Adam Flynn. After Monroe left John Bowe's home, Unity went to Elmira, informing her of Mr. Monroe Wilson's plans.

Monroe already had the plot of land, now they needed the finances to purchase and secure the slaves, tools, and materials to get started.

Meanwhile, Elmira and Amanda have transformed into a couple of young ladies sitting across the room where others have gathered for lunch, listening to Monroe boasting and bellowing over his accomplishments. Elmira sits like a lion, ready for the kill, with only Monroe in her sights. It seems to her that Monroe is long in his drink and in no way prepared to leave the tavern. Elmira and Amanda leave as the other ladies do, mingling and hiding among the ladies.

Later that evening, the ladies meet in the lobby with the men, and Elmira tells them how much she and Amanda enjoyed exploring the town. She informs them that they want to continue doing so the following day. Winfred and Keith also talk of their adventure, of how they visited one of the town's mills and wished they could compare the mills in Boston to those in New York.

"I believe we have an excellent chance of securing the finances for our mill, for there aren't many here in these parts, and even fewer as we venture west towards our township."

"How can you be so sure about this?" Elmira asks. "Our illustrious Mr. Wilson is a sly fox whom I'm sure will do all he can to ensure his plan is the only plan for the colony."

"Well, Elmira, I believe he's had a small change of heart now that he sees the mills and cotton go hand-in-hand. Yet… he is a real sly fox, and I would be deceiving myself if I said he's on our side. In the back of my mind, I believe he's out there, pulling the pin to the trap door we are standing on. Although, he's not the only one who has met with his investors in Boston, for I too have met with my investors, Mr. Dunlap and Mr. Turney, as a mere formality to close the deal."

"Why Mr. Gaines, you're the sly fox if I've never seen one before," Elmira admires.

"I have my days, Ms. Pembroke," says Winfred. "I believe in keeping my enemies close. I, too, love the chase – it's exhilarating." He turns to Keith. "Shall we retire to the smoking room, Keith?"

"We shall, Mr. Gaines."

The men tip their hats to the ladies, and the ladies retire to their room for the evening.

"We ladies must be ready for tomorrow's adventures," Elmira says, smiling.

"We can't wait," says Winfred.

They bid one another goodnight and go their separate ways. Elmira and Amanda leave for their room, and Elmira tells Amanda to remain there just in case Keith comes up. Elmira vanishes and meets with Mary and the other witches at her farm.

Back on the farm, Elmira asks, "Has Mary taught any of you how to fly on brooms yet?"

They all answer, "She has not." The others look at her with their arms folded.

"That sounds great, but I'm not sure if I like to be too high off the ground," complains Unity.

"I have problems levitating a few feet off the ground," says Premise.

"I prefer to think of where I want to go, and then poof, I'm there," Margaret says.

"Poof," Premise mocks, and they all laugh at Margaret.

"Well, it's the sound a soft dirt clog makes when it hits the ground," explains Margaret. "If none of you noticed, it looks like it just appears out of nowhere when the children throw it close to your feet. It scared me the first time they did it, but now I throw it at them when they are not looking."

"Interesting," Elmira says, "But we must learn how to fly on these brooms, ladies. So let's all go to the settlement and mount up."

Most of the witches are too afraid to fly higher than waist level so they won't get hurt if they fall. Eventually, they gain the confidence to fly over the farms east of the settlement.

While in flight, Unity asks, "What advantage does flying have over thinking of the place you want to be? It does not seem faster, but much slower."

Mary replies, "You have to know where you are going to just poof off to another place, but you don't have to know where you are going when you are flying. You only need to know how to fly, and you'll find where you need to be."

Unity and the others understand that both options have their advantages. Hours have passed, so they fly back to Elmira's farm. Once they've all gone home, Elmira thanks Mary for her advice.

"I really enjoyed flying," says Elmira.

"You should try to do it more and go faster like me," replies Mary. "I want to be as fast as lightning. One flash in the sky, and you could be back in New York. How about we try that when you return on the morrow?"

"You have my promise; we'll do just that," says Elmira. "Keep the girls on the brooms. It'll be a couple of nights before I return."

They kiss each other on the cheek, and Elmira vanishes.

Elmira and Amanda search for Clarence's brother for the next few days. They ask around in some of the more affluent areas of New York, but with no luck. Then they begin to look in the areas where the impoverished, the poor, and the unsavory hang out. They transform into a pauper state to blend in and gather information. In this place, they find the person they are looking for, someone whom Clarence's brother once employed.

"Me and my missus here used to do servant work for Mr. Morris Lester, but that's been more years than I can remember." He declares. "I believe the gentlemen and his wife left to Foreman, one of them sugar cane plantations in Barbados somewhere around 1686. If my memory serves me right, I hear things turned bad down there in '92, with the slave rebellion in all. Me prayers went out to them because they were nice folk. I hope he and the wife didn't get caught up in all that rebellion stuff."

"We sure hope not," agrees Elmira.

"You know, things have gotten a little desperate here too." The man goes on about his unemployment. "These be hard times for the lot of us here."

"We understand." Says Amanda.

"Have two people come by looking for the same man? They be a young lady around nineteen or twenty and an older gent in his mid-sixties." Asks Elmira.

The man asks, "Why all the questions about me, ex-employer? And who is the other two you're asking about?"

"The young lady and the older gentleman are all that's left of his family. They, too, went off to find a better life. We were indentured to them before they left. They promised my niece and me jobs if we could find our way here."

Rubbing his chin, he looks up at Elmira and Amanda. "Well, missus, they didn't come this way, but I'll keep an ear for you just the same. By the way, if you do find them, see about getting me on with you," he says. "I sure would like to be better than I am now."

"You have our word," Elmira promises. "When we find them, we'll let them know where to find you."

Elmira and Amanda turn and walk away, but the man waits until they are in the ally and follows them. With his knife in hand, he and his lady friend creep up behind them. Before they are close enough to jump them, Amanda turns around to face the man. Elmira keeps walking, and Amanda glances at the knife and pretends to be afraid.

"Your aunt, if that's who she is, was smart," he says. "She ran off and left you. Maybe you should have done the same."

He walks closer to her. Amanda keeps looking back as if she is expecting help.

"Please, sir, please don't hurt me," she pleads. "If you let me be on my way, I'll make sure you are rewarded for your mercy."

"Mercy, little lady…" he says with a snicker. "I can't even spell the word."

"Oh, how sad." Her voice changes to a deeper tone. "But that's okay. I can spell it for you." Her expression changes.

"What are you, some kind of retard or something?" He asks, waving his knife with a crooked smile.

"No, but I can show you - better than I can tell you." She says.

She begins her transformation from an impoverished woman to her youthful self. The man cannot believe what he sees, and the woman with him screams, "Witch!" She then turns and leaves him with Amanda.

Then Amanda begins to change again, her skin like a scaled lizard. She grows two feet taller, her arms become slender, long, and muscular; her hands become thin, and her nails are now like an eagle's talons. She looks at him with her head tilted to the left.

"You should have turned and run with your missus; better yet, you should not have come at all."

He turns his head slowly and finds himself alone. Amanda thrusts her left hand into his face, driving her long talons under his skin, squeezing his skull like soft fruit and slashing his body with the talons of her right hand. She swings down, left to right and right to left. He cannot scream or fight back, for both his feet are off the ground. When she is finished slashing him, Amanda holds him by the face with both hands and vanishes. They appear in the deep woods outside New York, and she tosses him across the wooded area, slamming his limp body against a large tree and breaking his back. He looks up in immense pain as she levitates toward him.

"You loathing bastard," she says. Then she swips down hard, her talons slicing right through his chin into his skull. The she vigorously shakes the brain matter and blood from her talons and vanishes.

Elmira waits on the lady as she turns the corner after her own transformation. She slaps her so hard that her large claws slice through her skull, killing her with a single blow. Before she falls to the ground, Elmira grabs her by her shoulders and vanishes. She reappears over the ocean, away from the ships in the harbor. She screams in sheer rage and snatches the woman's waist, digging her talons through her midsection, pulling her apart, and dropping her there. Both Elmira and Amanda believe there is nothing they cannot do after that; they feel nothing can hold them back and that they are invincible. They meet back at the tavern, convinced that Dorothy and Clarence could not find his brother. It may even be possible that they met with the likes of those two criminals and are dead, which infuriates Elmira. She also ponders the thought that someone else may have told them where to find his brother; if so, they may have left for Barbados. Elmira decides to deal with them later; now, she has her eyes on other prey.

The next morning, the men accompanied the ladies to some of the places they visited during the week. They go through the markets and venture out to the harbor to watch the ships. For most of the day, they enjoy riding in the carriage and taking in the sights of New York.

Elmira asks Winfred, "How did the meeting go with the investors?"

"Not as well as I thought," Winfred replies. "We secured some of the finances but did not get funding for the mills."

"Oh really!" She says with a raised brow.

"For some reason, they changed their minds. I suspect they met with Monroe about his cotton venture; that man is truly a sly fox. Nonetheless, I believe we can still build the mill with our personal finances and use the investors' monies we've secured to purchase the spinners and tools we need."

Elmira struggles to control her anger fidgeting in her seat as Winfred speaks.

"We have already acquired a fellow to build our spinners for us. Not only will he build them for us, but he's promised to build two extra. Your son is excellent at haggling. Now instead of ten, we'll get twelve."

"I'm glad to hear that." Elmira is still trying to calm herself.

"This fellow has a small shop in Boston," continues Winfred. "By the time we get the mill built, we should have the spinners around the same time, if not sooner. By the way, we also secured the finances to purchase three hundred heads of sheep. I say we are down but not out, Ms. Pembroke."

Amanda adds, "I expect our news will be a bit of a surprise to that weasel Monroe."

"Indeed, young Mrs. Grace, a shock to the old fox and his counterparts, whom I believe think they have secured all our investors."

"How did they know who our investors were?" asks Amanda.

"Well, Mrs. Grace, all these gentlemen know each other and have been making deals for many years. No doubt they realize that we are all here from the same small township, and they do not wish to invest their monies in two places. I would do the same. Like Monroe, most of these men are investing in tobacco and cotton, so the prospect of a mill is not as promising. I secured an investor Monroe does not know of, which is good enough for now. Look on the bright side of all this – Monroe may have done us a favor; our township is less indebted to these investors now."

"Well, I still think he dealt us a blow," says Amanda.

"Yes," says Keith, "but I believe the people of our township will be more apt to understand what they can see more than what they can't see, and that's a cotton plantation that may as well be in England as far as they are concerned. Not only will they see that our way is better, but we will be providing work for our people right there in the township." Keith turns to his mother. "I'm also proposing to build the mill large enough to create furniture as well. Not only will we provide jobs for the women and children, but our men as well."

"Mr. Gaines," Elmira calls, "it appears you are well-prepared for a good fight. You regroup well in the face of adversity. And it sounds like my son has become quite the businessman; I think he'll do well as your vice president."

"Yes, Ms. Pembroke," says Winfred. "He's a quick study, and I think with him in the mills and the sheep farm, we'll see production by next spring."

When Elmira sees the tavern Monroe frequents, she suggests, "With all this talk of business, we should stop here for a bite to eat."

The tavern is a well-kept business locale that provides a place to eat, a smoking room for the men, and a sitting room for the ladies. Elmira and Amanda pretend to be amazed at how nice it is. They comment on the lovely sitting room for the ladies. Of course, Winfred lets them know that he has eaten there once before on a different trip. They all sit down, order food and drinks, and discuss the new township. Around the time their food is brought to them, they notice Monroe walking in alone and meeting with a group of gentlemen.

"What a pompous group of windbags," says Elmira. "And where are Mr. Eagleton and Jameston?"

"Well, Mother, I'm sure they enjoy Monroe's company as much as we do, so maybe they decided to eat elsewhere," Keith says.

They laugh and eat. The group can hear Monroe boasting about his accomplishments, which they find annoying. When he looks over his shoulder across the room, he raises his glass to toast his success. Monroe sent Eagleton and Jameston back to the colony in the hopes of subverting the plans of his nemesis Mr. Gaines, and that hag and her son. Eagleton and Jameston are all too eager to go back and sway the colonists to their side.

Cotton is the buzzword around New York, and they have also caught cotton fever. They plan to spread the word loud and long, so by the time Winfred Gaines returns from his trip, it will be hard to sell his plans for the mill. Monroe thought it would be hard for Winfred to secure the finances for the mills since he secretly swayed the man's investors to finance his Virginia charter instead. Monroe is full of himself now, so much so that he doesn't care if Winfred and his party can hear him. His meeting with the gentlemen is short, and they bid him goodbye. Following their departure, he decides to invite himself to their table and sits next to Winfred. Once seated, he looks up at Elmira.

"My apologies. Do you mind if I sit?" Monroe asks.

Winfred gestures with his hand, as he has already taken the seat next to him. Monroe shuffles in his seat and begins to discuss his concerns regarding the mill.

"I know the mill means a lot to you, but the town needs a leg up, and as Mayor, it's my sworn duty to provide the means to do so," says Monroe. "But, I only learned of your brilliant plan when we met at your tavern the other morning. Am I to understand that you plan to use your personal wealth to build this mill of yours?"

"And you know of this by what means?" Elmira asks.

"Oh, come now, Ms. Pembroke, you'll find that there are no secrets in this town," Monroe brags.

"Oh really?" She responds.

"Well, I promise to do my part to help you succeed in this worthy endeavor. I will provide the cotton you need, but I must first satisfy my investors from England and the other colonies. That was the deal I must adhere to, and they expect me to stick to it." Says Monroe.

"Mr. Wilson, I'm sure you're doing what you believe is best for the Township, but since we are financing the new mill ourselves, it would stand to reason that we will be getting our cotton from an existing plantation," says Elmira. She continues, "Oh, and by the by, how long will it take to establish this plantation of yours? A year to three years or so?"

"Oh, I believe we can build it in less than three years, Ms. Pembroke," replies Monroe.

"And what do we do in the meantime?" asks Winfred.

"Well, Mr. Gaines, Rome wasn't built in a day," Monroe remarks.

"No, Mr. Wilson, it wasn't, but Rome wasn't built on Virginia cotton with the town idiot and his friends running the henhouse. That would be like sending them out to milk the cows and later checking on their progress, only to find them trying to milk the chickens." Winfred speaks sarcastically. Everyone at the table laughs at this prospect.

"Bravo, Mr. Gaines," says Elmira. "I'm sure the Mayor has a better plan than that than to let these men run the plantation all alone."

Monroe clears his throat. "Ms. Pembroke, you would be correct," he says. "I have already appointed two of the finest gentlemen to represent the colony for the plantation."

"Ah, I see," says Keith. "I believe that'll be Mr. Eagleton and Mr. Jameston. You wouldn't happen to know where they are right now, would you, Mayor? Say, on their way back to the Township?"

"I believe they are adults and can go wherever they please," Monroe shoots back.

"I suppose so," Keith replies.

"Well, I had better be off," says Monroe. "I have another meeting to attend. Better luck next time, my esteemed colleague. Remember, cotton is king right now, and we must get in while the getting is good."

Elmira watches him waddle from the table and out of the door.

"He does love to rub it in a bit, doesn't he!" says Winfred.

Elmira smiles and suggests that they finish their meal.

"Our investor who sponsored the spinners and sheep did not mention to Monroe that he did so," Elmira says. "Otherwise, Monroe would have mentioned that."

"Good for him," says Winfred. "It was a small investment, but it will pay off greatly for the township."

"We'll have to visit Boston on our way home," says Keith. "The gentleman building our spinners wants us to stop by and see what he has. He also told us of a small mill in operation there and would show us how it operates using his spinners and tools."

"Wonderful," says Elmira. "Son, I believe we should make plans to leave in the morning."

"That sounds like a splendid idea," Winfred says.

Later that evening, Elmira goes to her room without eating dinner. She insists that the rest of them go and dine without her.

"I'm not feeling well," she says. "It must have been something I ate."

She waits until the darkest hour of the night and vanishes from her room, reappearing in the shoddy part of town where she knows ladies of ill repute hang around. She appears as an older woman looking for her granddaughter. In her search, she says that she's found out her daughter is dying and wants the young girl – her granddaughter – to come home and say goodbye. Some of the men in the area point out a few of the women who fit her description, but they warn her it is possible she may have syphilis. Elmira expresses her sorrow over the news and walks away with a smile. She stands back in the shadows and observes three women, then picks the one who looks like she has the most promise. She talks to the young lady and informs her if she does this favor for her, she will be paid handsomely after the fact. When the young lady agrees to an amount, Elmira takes her to a tavern where she can clean herself up and put on a beautiful dress and fancy blue shoes. The young lady desires to keep the dress and shoes when she looks in the mirror.

"At the end of the night, you can keep everything I give you," Elmira promises.

She wants to kill Monroe for what he's done, but Elmira finds it far better this way. She is beginning to understand what Mary is talking about concerning her temper. She disguises herself as someone else and feels she has total control for the first time. She and the young lady walk to the tavern where she knows Monroe is eating. She tells the young lady that she has a friend already inside the tavern who will tell her what she needs to do and whom she is there to meet. When the young lady goes inside, Monroe spots her immediately. Elmira goes around the tavern and transforms into a young, fair but common redhead in a powder blue undress and black shoes. She sets her hair under her hat and goes in looking less desirable to men so as not to take anything away from the young lady.

She meets the young lady, points Monroe out, and says, "My boss wants to meet with you, and he would like to talk to you. He's going to stand and let you know when he's leaving, and then he'll wait for you to leave the tavern and follow you out to return to his room."

They sit at a table where she is sure Monroe will be watching.

"Make sure you keep a shy look about you," Elmira says. "He'll like that quality about you."

After half an hour has passed, Monroe is already making eye contact with the young lady and hoping that he can sway her to his room. Monroe is his usual self; he continues to hold a loud conversation with his companions at the table. When he is sure he has the young lady's attention, he gets up to leave, then hesitates at the table. He hopes she will get up from her table and leave before he does. She goes out the door and waits just outside when she passes by him. Monroe leaves the tavern and walks behind the young lady.

"It's a beautiful night, isn't it?" He says.

"Just gorgeous," she replies, leaning against the porch column.

Quietly, he introduces himself. "Monroe Wilson, Miss…?"

"Miss Hadley, and it's a pleasure to meet you."

"The pleasure is all mine." He says. "Shall we?" He points in the direction of the tavern.

They walk down the street like a couple, greeting others as they make their way casually to his room, with Elmira not far behind them. When they return to Monroe's room, he opens the door, invites her in, and then sends the young lady over to the mantle on the far wall of his room to pour him a glass of rum. After she fills his glass, she hands it to him by the bed; he takes the glass from her hand, swallows it in one big gulp, and requests a second glass while he gets undressed. She blows the lamplight out and undresses, and then she climbs into bed with him. Elmira goes to the stables and retrieves a tin cup, which she fills with old horse urine from the stall floors. She reappears inside Monroe's room in the dark after he and the young lady have finished frolicking. Monroe slaps the young lady on her backside and orders her to get him another drink, which Elmira knows he will gulp down like the last two she gave him.

"Hand me the glass," she whispers to the young lady.

Elmira startles the young lady, but she keeps her composure when Monroe asks, "What is it?"

She tells him, "I stepped on something. I can't see without the light. I'm getting your drink."

Elmira has already gathered the dress and shoes and taken the money she promised the young lady from Monroe's purse. She gives her everything in the purse, which is all the money he carried on his person, and the dress and shoes. Elmira shrouds the hallway in the darkness and leaves the door open without Monroe or anyone else ever knowing that it was open to allow the young lady to leave without being noticed. The young lady slips out the side door and quickly gets half-dressed while she counts the money. It is more than she could have ever expected. Happy with the results, she returns to where Elmira found her.

Elmira smiles, slowly filling Monroe's glass with urine, and walks to his bed. Monroe grabs Elmira's arm as she hands him the glass of urine. She masks the foul odor of the urine with the smell of rum under his nose, and true to his nature, he takes one big gulp and swallows. Then he gasps, reeling back in the bed and letting go of Elmira's arm, realizing that he has just gulped some kind of foul, thick, putrid liquid. He calls out and swears, gagging and vomiting as he stumbles around the room, looking for the young lady calling for help. Elmira cannot help but laugh at what she is seeing. She is holding her mouth with both hands and watching him stumble around, slipping and sliding on his vomit. She vanishes after a short while but does not leave the room; she watches the whole scene, which is as hilarious as it can be.

Back in her room, she is hysterical with laughter. When Amanda comes to their room, she tells her everything she did.

"Not only will that pompous windbag have syphilis, but he drank a glass of old horse urine I gathered from the stalls. It was so funny watching that jackass stumble all over the room. I can still see the face of the men when they burst into the room with lanterns, only to see a fat old man on his knees in his own filth, with his ass pointed in the air as they rushed in. It was a sight to see."

"Oh, Elmira, you should have let me in on your secret," says Amanda. "I would have loved to have seen that. You had all the fun, and all I had was a seat between two boring men carrying on a boring conversation. I finally had to tell them I was tired and wished to retire to my room. Oh, I wish I could have seen that."

Monroe is sick to his stomach when the men step inside the room. They light the lamp on the mantle and chuckle at the sight of Monroe on his hands and knees. Once he manages to get himself off the floor, he stomps about the room, butt naked and disoriented. He points to the glass on the bed, grabs the linen off the bed, and tells them, "The woman I was with put something in my glass."

One of the men grabs the glass off the bed, and Monroe asks, "What is in the glass?"

The man looks at the remnant of the liquid, a slightly dark yellowish color, and then he smells the glass and quickly pulls it from his face. He holds it under the nose of one of the other men, who then pushes his hand away.

"Well?" Monroe demands.

The man holding the glass snickers and says, "Smells like piss, and from the looks of it, I would say that it's aged horse piss."

Monroe bends over beside the bed and begins to vomit again while the men snicker.

"Sir…" one of the men says, trying to contain his laughter. "I believe your young lady friend you were entertaining probably used the piss to distract you so that she could make her escape with your purse."

"We've already called for the Sheriff, but you had better check your purse and see if she left you a pence." Suggest the other.

He looks up, wipes his mouth, and points to his vest pocket. When the man checks, there is nothing there. Monroe doesn't have a penny. They would have kicked him out if they didn't feel sorry for the man, seeing that he no longer had the money to pay for his room and board.

When Monroe wakes up the next morning, his adventure with the young lady is all the buzz in that part of the city. News of Monroe has already reached the tavern where Elmira and her companions are staying. It is the talk of the town, and it is just as funny hearing what the men saw when they entered the room as it was watching it unfold.

Elmira suggests, "Putting our differences aside, he is from our township. Maybe offering him a ride home would be a good gesture."

"Good show, Ms. Pembroke," Winfred replied. "We'll ride over and offer him a ride home."

When they arrive at the tavern, Monroe is a sad sight to see. He's standing outside the trvern sick, and it shows in his unwashed face and attire. It isn't his usual pompous demeanor to appear in public looking as though a child has dressed him. Winfred gets out of the carriage to offer his colleague a ride, but Monroe is full of pride.

"I'll not ride in the same carriage with the likes of that woman," he says of Elmira.

"As you insist," Winfred replies. He climbs back into the carriage, and they leave Monroe standing penniless in the streets with his bags by his feet. One of his new drinking friends has heard of his demise and offers him the money to hire a coach. His eyes are red and his mouth dry; his hair is swept poorly over the top of his head to one side to cover his bald top; he does not even bother to wear his wig. The man calls for a coach, offers his sympathy, and sends him on his way. When Monroe climbs into the coach, he is the only passenger and is glad for it.

He has enough money for his trip home and more for food and lodging. His ride is hard, and his nights are as sleepless as ever. Over a week into his travel, Monroe notices that he has not only lost all his money, but he has gained something that he cannot wash off or explain to Mrs. Wilson. Thinking only of his reputation, he foolishly believes that his wife would understand if he told her he was dragged off, his money stolen, and that he was forced to drink urine in his most vulnerable state. He drifts in and out of sleep, for every bump in the road awakens him. Because of his illness, it takes him longer to return to the Township. He stays in one tavern for nearly two weeks until he feels better. He cannot find treatment on the road and figures he will get help if he travels to Boston. He knows a doctor in Boston who has treated many patients for syphilis, and Monroe decides he will ask for his help.

After more than a month, he arrives home, he finds the news of his adventures with the young female has spread throughout the township. His wife refuses to meet him upon his return, only to endure his excuses and lies when he arrives at their home. Because of the skin rash on his hands and feet, he stays out of the public's eye. The idea of a plantation is a hard sell for Jameston and Eagleton, with the indiscretion of Monroe still fresh in people's minds. Through it all, they convince many that cotton is the right venture for their town.

Elmira and Winfred call a meeting of the townspeople to inform them of their venture and what they have to offer. They told them they had secured the finances for a mill, spinners, and a sheep farm. They are informed that Elmira will use her farm to grow the flax, and the sheep farm will be located just outside the town past the fork in the road.

Standing on the same platform built for the festival, Winfred does his best to encourage the townsfolk to participate in the growth of their township.

"With your help, we could have the mill ready to run by the time the spinners arrive from Boston." He continues. "Let us build this mill with the pride of knowing we built this township with the labor of our hands and the sweat of our brow. It will not be an easy task; hard work brings about changes. The type of changes that means a better lifestyle for everyone."

Mr. Jameston shouts from behind Winfred on the podium. "Mr. Gaines, where are you getting the lumber to build this mill, and how can this be financed? How, seeing that the town's money has been all but exhausted by the prosperous cotton plantation?"

"Well, Mr. Jameston," Winfred shouts back. "I can assure you and the good Christian people of this township that it will not come from the town's treasury, and it will surely not be misappropriated on harlots and horse urine in New York."

The entire crowd roars with laughter. Jameston takes his seat and says nothing more.

Winfred raises his hands to quiet the crowd. "Mr. Jameston, Mr. Eagleton, and our Mayor, Mr. Monroe Wilson, have underestimated us, just as they underestimate you, the good people of the Williams River Township. Our investors believe in you, and that's why everything you need will fall into place in one week, and we will begin to build our future – a future you can see, a future you can touch, and a future you can believe in."

Everyone applauds and cheers and becomes excited about the good news. Finally, the townspeople can see their future.

Elmira stands and shares her promise for the people and the township.

"I will use my farm to grow the flax needed as the third product of three on our list of raw materials. I promise to give the women and children my full support and care once the mill is running. Everyone working at the mill will be treated with respect, and work will be fair for all."

The women in the crowd cheer and applaud her for promising to stand by them, as they know the work in the mill will be difficult. Even though many in the township believe cotton to be the future crop, they see the mill as their present.

After the townspeople have retired, Jeremiah Jameston and Quincy Eagleton corner Winfred in the courthouse to enquire about his false promises of a mill.

"Gentlemen, you need not concern yourselves with these matters, seeing that you have played the harlot for Monroe and his craftiness," says Winfred. "The mill will be built, and the people will have the work needed to grow this town. For the first time in years, the townspeople are together in high spirits and forgiveness of our past. Now is the time to rally behind the town and think not of the promises of riches the two of you will gain by supporting Monroe Wilson and his never-to-be-seen cotton and tobacco plantation." He wishes them a good day and walks past them out the door.

On Sunday, the church is full, and those attending find comfort in the fact that the Lord has forgiven their sins and blessed their township. Now, they come together as one people working together for the common good of the people. Neither Elmira nor any of the witches participate in church worship, but the townspeople – not knowing their true identity – pray for them in every service.

Six months have passed, the mill is finished, the spinners are delivered, and the women and children are training in the processes for flax and wool. As yet, there is no promise of cotton, and with winter upon them, the town council will wait until spring to address the issue. In the fourth month after planting the flax, the men, women, and children harvest the flax pulling it up by the root from the ground and tying them into stacks to dry. Their first harvest is great; everyone in the township is proud of the bountiful harvest, and the wool on the sheep is thick and full. They use this time to train the workers to thresh, ret, break, scotch, heckle, and finally spin the flax. When the sheering of the sheep is complete, they send the men and boys to the sheep farm to learn the process of wool. The Alexanders have built potash pits like the ones they use in England to degrease the wool before it can be spun. All is going well, and the townspeople could not be happier.

The people built a large mill next to the river, and a sense of pride cultivated a great atmosphere.

Keith is now vice president of the venture, and Charles has taken over as Sheriff. Charles is delighted to be the Sheriff because he can control Trevor better than Keith. Often, he wants to get rid of Trevor, but Keith pleads with him to keep the man on; this is something Charles has a problem understanding. Trevor is more trouble than he is worth, and neither he nor Trevor gets along well.

The town is showing small growth because it is winter. They believe it is only a matter of time before an influx of new people arrives looking for work. Monroe is finally up and about, muttering about the mill much less frequently. Now that the townspeople have trained, they cannot wait to see the outcome of all their work. Monroe approaches Winfred personally to apologize for not backing him and then announces to his colleagues.

"Gentlemen, I have decided that I'm moving my family to the Virginia plantation to run it myself," he announces. "I will continue to allow John Bowe to run as foreman of the estate. I will also promise to ship ten percent of the cotton produced back to the township to support the mill."

Winfred shakes Monroe's hand, thanks him, and wishes him the best.

"Monroe, Your success is our success." He says. "We look forward to the shipments."

Elmira thinks to herself; *it's amazing what syphilis and horse urine can do.* She leaves after hearing the news and goes to Monroe's home while he is still at the courthouse with the men. She does not have to walk up to the door and knock; Agatha Wilson meets her at the gate. Agatha is one of Elmira's trusted friends. The pair grew up together and have always been there for each other over the years.

"Come on in and get out of the cold," Agatha advises.

"Thank you," says Elmira.

"I was expecting you to come by after Monroe left," Agatha said.

"You know me well." Says Elmira.

"We've been friends all our lives," continues Agatha. "I had a feeling you would drop by."

"I just heard you'll be leaving us," Elmira said, concerned.

"Yes, and I don't know how to feel," says Agatha. "This place has been my home all my life. It's all I know." Saddened and looking around the room.

"I understand change can be a very scary thing sometimes." Says Elmira.

"Oh yes, I'm still shaking from the news myself," Agatha said worriedly.

"You listen to me," Elmira goes on. "If you ever need help or want to come back here, you find a way to inform me, and I'll do everything I can to make it happen." Her voice is firm.

"I will, Elmira." She promised.

"I'm serious, Aggie," Elmira said. "You get word to me as fast as you can."

"I will; trust me, Elmira, I will." She said.

"Oh, Aggie, I'll miss you so much." Elmira hugs her dear friend.

"I'll miss you too, Elmira."
They weep a bit, drink toddies, and Elmira says goodbye.

Before she leaves, she looks back and says, "You write me, you hear!" Elmira pleads.

"As often as I can," reply's Agatha.

After Monroe and Agatha have been gone for a week, Winfred approaches Mr. George Thopham, one of the town's most trusted citizens, and asks if he will consider being Mayor. For days George protests, but with the encouragement of his wife and friends, the church, the Sheriff, and most of the townspeople, he accepts the job.

He often thinks about Clarence and Dorothy and their well-being; the night they left, he knew he would never see his friends again. From the darkness of his window, he'd watched them make their silent escape, praying that God would guide them to their destination.

Chapter 8
Out of Sight, But Not Out of Mind

One year after their New York trip, Elmira cannot help but wonder why John Bowe and his two companions have not sent for their wives and children. She also wonders why her childhood friend Agatha has not written. Eagleton visited the plantation, but there was no letter from Agatha. Elmira understands that there would be no houses established for the foreman for the first few months and that it would be hard for a family of five to make it in those living conditions, even though families have been moving into worse conditions for years. But now, she believes John Bowe and his friends used the prospect of the plantation to start a new life without the families they left behind.

The plantation is over a hundred acres and promises to yield a good amount of cotton. They will need more than a hundred slaves, indentured servants, ten work hands, horses, cattle, and much more to start the business. The grand homes on large plantations are a sight to see. Monroe builds his mansion just as elegantly as his neighbors'. After eighteen months, many in the township are weary of how this venture will pay off. Word around the township is that they may never see a single pence from the sale of the cotton. Most of the citizens have their hands full because the wool and flax are genuinely abundant, which keeps the mill busy all day, six days a week. Thanks to the mill, the town sees some growth, and talk of future expansion is also on the table. They have to address the issue of space and housing for the new development they expect.

Life seems good, but Elmira's mind is many miles away. She often thinks, *Is Dorothy and Clarence in Barbados? Has John Bowe started a new family in his new home? Why hasn't Aggie written? And how is Monroe faring now that he's been in Virginia for over a year?*

Elmira has grown to like her town and doesn't want to see it fail. She does not want Unity to be hurt by that idiot husband of hers anymore. Elmira wants to end this once and for all. Unity is sometimes glad that John is out of her life, yet she still wants him. She always did what he asked, no matter what it cost her. Now, with every passing month, she has grown more independent. John left the township four months before Monroe took control of the plantation.

Elmira thinks eighteen months is a long time to be separated from one's husband, and what he's doing is wrong. Unity's children have growing concerns.

"Mother." Gwenavear calls.

"Yes." Unity answers.

"When is father coming back for us?" She asks.

"We must be patient. It takes a while to build a plantation." Unity gives the only answer she knows.

As time passes, she worries more. "Mother, do you think he'll ever come back?" Gwenavear asks.

"I don't know right now. Go to bed. We'll be okay." Unity answers. She believes she and her children will never see him again.

Unity could live without that scoundrel, but she wishes he would return for her children. Elmira suggests she remain patient and wait a little while longer before giving up hope. Elmira cannot believe that she is giving that kind of advice, but supervising the women and children at the mill has made her more of a mother figure, and she is enjoying it for the first time since the death of her son Thomas.

As always, the witches meet at the old settlement two to three times a week, and Elmira has added more women to her fold from other colonies. Most of these women are single, or they are women who had nothing until they started working at the mill, on Elmira's farm, or the sheep farm. Margaret and Premise Jones are sisters who chose witchcraft over prostitution and had no problem deciding to leave the stench of the taverns and the men that inhabit them along the highways. They arrived at the Williams River colony after Dorothy left the township to start a new life elsewhere.

It has been three months since Mr. Eagleton made another trip to the plantation. He returns with news that the plantation is going very well, although the townsfolk meet him with an air of doubt. Overlooking their doubt, Eagleton proudly announces that Monroe and his family are doing well and that things are running smoothly. They've built the main house, and most of the quarters are also ready. Families are moving in and are getting adjusted to their new life. He omits the report of the slaves, and how they've been picked through and purchased. Instead, Eagleton stresses that the cotton is planted, and they can expect a return on their investment. He goes on and on without mentioning John Bowe and the others, nor does he state whether they are ready to move their families in with them. After he concludes, he retires to his home, thinking he has satisfied the naysayers.

The next morning, Elmira drives to the courthouse to see Mr. Eagleton about Mr. Bowes' intentions. She meets him as he prepares to enter the courthouse.

"Morning, Mr. Eagleton."

"A fine morning it is, Ms. Pembroke. I have heard in my absence that the mill has pulled through, and I can see the town is all the bustle about it."

"Thank you, Mr. Eagleton." Elmira takes a deep breath. "May I ask you a question?"

"You may." He answers.

"How is Mr. Bowe doing?" asks Elmira. "Is he the man for the job, or should we be concerned?"

"No concerns at all, Ms. Pembroke," replies Eagleton. "Mr. Wilson has a firm hand on things. He will not tolerate any shenanigans."

"Has Mr. Bowe established his house yet?" She speaks, leaning toward him from her buggy.

Eagleton looks down, trying to think of what to say.

Elmira adds, "It's been about two years, and I'm sure he's eager to be with his family."

"Well, you know things were so busy there that I did not get the chance to talk to him," says Eagleton. "My appointments are reserved for Mr. Wilson and the business, you know." He avoids making eye contact with her.

"I do understand, but we women get a little worried when our men don't come home to their families." There is a new firmness to her voice.

"You're right, but I assure you that Mr. Bowe intends to return to gather his flock and settle there in Virginia. You know he manages those slaves and keeps order there on the plantation. That's a momentous task, and Mr. Wilson assures me that Mr. Bowe is the right man for the job. A little patience, Ms. Pembroke; before you know it, he'll be here for his family. Now, if you will excuse me, I must be about my daily duties."

"A good day to you, Mr. Eagleton," says Elmira. "I have to get to the mill to do the same. Oh, and by the way, you wouldn't happen to have a letter from Mrs. Wilson, would you?"

"Why no. I spoke to her briefly, and she looked to be in good spirits. On my next visit, I'll enquire on your behalf.

"Thanks, and good day." She uses the reins to get the horse to move.

"A good day to you too, Ms. Pembroke."

As Elmira drives her buggy, she knows that it is now time to visit the plantation. She knows Eagleton has lied about not seeing John Bowe, but that does not matter because she will make plans to see the man for herself. At the mill, Elmira talks to Winfred about the plantation.

"Have you heard any news of the plantation other than the old windbag's report?" she asks.

"Fancy, you ask! You're aware of my return from New York last week." Winfred said.

"Yes, I am." She replies.

"Well, I ran into a fellow in New York, and he told me he visited the Windgate Hundred Plantation on a sales call," says Winfred. "He told me that, as far as he could tell, all was going very well. While there, he said he witnessed a whipping, which was a dreadful sight. Not something he was used to, but he said that it may have been necessary to keep order on the plantation. They don't need to experience an uprising as they did in Barbados a few years back. Nevertheless, I don't plan to visit anytime soon, if ever."

"I understand." Elmira nods in agreement. "By the way, where is this Windgate Hundred Plantation? Is it far from the port? And how long will it take for the cotton to get here from there? I've heard talk around town that we will never see the cotton we were promised."

"I'm sure if Mr. Monroe Wilson reneges on the cotton, his actions will have consequences. As for the location of the plantation, I do believe that it is on the south side of the James River, so I would estimate that it could take at least two months to get the cotton to the mill once they've harvested the crop and send it up the river."

Elmira doesn't care about the cotton as much as she cares about Mr. Bowe. Now she'll have to deal with him, although she knows Unity wants to go when they visit the plantation.

That night all the witches are summoned to the old settlement. Elmira has plans to travel to the plantation to see why certain men have chosen to abandon their families. Elmira announces that Amanda, Unity, and Mary will be going with her, while the others will stay behind and wait for their return. Mary looks around at all the witches who have assembled. She is worried, for it seems Elmira is building a small army of witches, and wonders if she plans to fight a war somewhere.

What is Elmira up to? She wonders. *Why such a large congregation of witches?*

Mary counts over thirty witches, and she knows others from other townships are not there. She doubts that Elmira can control them.

Is Elmira getting in over her head? She wonders. *And what would happen if any of them turned against her? Their training is good, and their powers are varied, making them even more dangerous because Elmira does not know their strengths or weaknesses.*

Mary knows Elmira will always support her, but it also seems to her that Elmira treats Amanda and Unity better than she treats her own sister. She senses that Elmira is jealous of her and is limiting her role with the rest of the younger witches. Mary is stronger than Elmira, but she would never reveal this to her. Elmira has a weakness to which Mary is privy, which is her fear of Dorothy. Mary believes they are all destined by fate to meet again. It does not matter what hers is because she just wants to live a life beyond the simple-minded world.

Elmira stands in front of the witches.

"This coming weekend, we will travel to the plantation in Virginia. It would be best to wait a couple of days and venture out on Saturday morning." She explains.

"Where is the plantation?" Amanda asks

"I'm told on the south side of the James River." Elmira answers.

Most of the women there has no idea where the James River is. When the meeting is over, Elmira asks Mary, "Have you flown around or near the plantation?"

"No, I have not, but I have flown over the James River a few times," Mary replies.

"Do you mind leading us to the plantation? Elmira asks.

"It would be my pleasure," says Mary. "It's really beautiful in that part of the country."

Elmira and the others look at one another.

"Mary, we're not going sightseeing," says Elmira sternly. "I just need you to get us there in a hurry. There's no time to look down and admire the view."

"As you wish," says Mary. She turns and walks away.

All the witches assembled at the old settlement at five o'clock on Saturday morning. They are all ready to use the flight as training for longer distances in the future. Mary instructs them to command their brooms to go as fast as lightning, and then they will be there in the blink of an eye.

"Just visualize it, and it will happen," Mary instructs.

Elmira, Mary, Amanda, and Unity ascend slowly over the trees.

Amanda asks, "If we are going that fast, how do we stop?"

"All you have to do is follow me, and I will teach you while we fly," Mary says.

Then she tells them to go as fast as lightning, and the four soar over the James River and look for the plantations. All the witches struggle to catch their breath and get their eyes to adjust.

Mary smiles. "You will get used to it," she says. "You just have to practice as often as possible."

"How many times have you traveled that fast?" Unity asks.

"I've lost count," replies Mary. "I mostly do it to get to the most wonderful places and then enjoy the beautiful land when I get there.

I'll have all day to walk around, pet some of the animals, swim in some of the most beautiful lakes, rivers, and streams; and under the most wonderful waterfalls. You should try it sometime."

"Do you know where we are?" Elmira asks in a harsh tone.

"We're over the James River," says Mary.

"Mary, are we close to the plantation?" Unity asks more mildly.

"I'm not sure. I've never thought about them before," Mary says. "They're a little depressing."

Mary does, however, point out the north and the south sides of the river. They can see plantations all along the river; they know the name of the plantation but not its location. The group decides to go to the harbor, look for someone who might know where it is, and then be on their way. When they arrive at the port, there aren't many people around. Elmira transforms into a man in business attire and asks a fisherman for directions. The fisherman is fussing about his fishing boat.

"My good fellow, could you tell me where I can find the Windgate Hundred Plantation?" she asks.

"I can't rightly say, Governor," he replies. "If you wait about a half hour, this place will be full of gentlemen who do business with the James River plantations."

Elmira nods and leaves the harbor for half an hour. As the fisherman has said, the harbor is busy trading when she returns. Elmira and the others come back as fishermen and ask around for the location of the Windgate Hundred Plantation. After a few minutes, they find out that it is the plantation with the unfinished dock on the south side of the river. They all gather back in the woods, where they vanish and reappear at the unfinished dock. They all saw the dock the first time they flew by but didn't know it was the plantation they were looking for. By the time they arrive, it is nearing six o'clock in the morning, and the plantation is already busy.

They go around into the woods to get a better perspective of the plantation when they hear screaming. The four witches hide behind a house standing near the woods. They look toward the woods on the other side of the plantation and reappear there, where Unity immediately recognizes the man holding the whip. It is none other than her husband, John Bowe. A slave woman is tied to a tree branch above her with her feet barely touching the ground. Mr. Bowe has called all the slaves of the plantation together to make an example of the young slave woman.

He announces, "This is what happens to those who disobey and stir up trouble."

Unity remembers what he told everyone before he left the township: *A few slaves and a good whip, and you can make a fortune.*

"Well," she says aloud. "He finally got what he's always wanted, slaves and a whip."

Unity cringes at the thought of what is about to happen.

John begins to whip the woman, and with every strike of the whip, Unity flinches and hides her face from the others as the young woman screams with every lash. She leans against the side of a tree so no one can see her crying. She knows all about her husband's heavy hand, and it is as though she can feel the crack of the whip against her own flesh. Her flared nostrils, and heavy breathing communicates more than anything Unity can say. Protecting her from the sight of this senseless violence, Mary and Amanda hold Unity.

"What could have been done this early in the morning to merit this?" she sobs.

Before she says anything else, Mary jumps. She bends her knees and looks around like someone has touched her.

"What is it?" asks Elmira.

"We are not alone," whispers Mary. "There's someone here, and they are watching us."

Now all of them are alert.

Elmira asks, "Are you sure?"

"Yes, I'm sure," replies Mary.

"Does anyone else sense this?" asks Elmira.

Unity and Amanda shake their heads. "Are you sure?" they ask Mary.

"Reveal yourself," says Mary, her voice still in a whisper. She raises a cloud of mist around their feet and repeats, "Reveal yourself."

Then, appearing from the mist, the witches find an elderly, frail-looking slave woman. Mary immediately asks, "Who are you, and how did you know we were here?"

"How did you know I was here?" asks the old slave.

"I don't know," replies Mary. "I just sensed your presence."

"And that's how I knew you were here. You have a rare gift, child."

Everyone looks at Mary.

The old woman points at Unity and asks, "What are you going to do, child?"

Unity looks at the old lady and asks, "Why are you asking me?"

"Because you be the man's wife, and I see you have trouble looking when he uses his whip on that poor girl. You be the wife, yes?"

"I am his wife, but why do you ask me what am I going to do?" Unity responds. Elmira stands beside her.

"Do you want to know why he whips that girl?" the old woman asks.

"It's not my business," says Unity. "She was probably out of line."

"No child, he was whipping the woman because she scratched his face while he was raping her early this morning. Him be a bad master, and him forbade the men from sleeping with the women while him and the other white men take advantage of the women anytime they pleased. If one of the slave men is caught sleeping with a woman, they are tied up on the same tree, only worse for the men. This be one of the worst plantations for a slave, man or woman on the whole River.

Your husband and the other two who came with him use that whipping tree almost weekly."

Everyone looks out onto the plantation and then back at the old woman.

"The master of the house be happy with his women who works in the house, so he takes a woman whenever he wants in privacy. His wife never says a thing cause she finds pleasure with one of the young slave bucks. I warn him if he ever caught, both he and that woman be dead. Master's wife or no, they both be dead."

"What makes you think we care?" Elmira says harshly.

"You come a long way for ones that don't care," says the old woman. "These men we see here are the men who left their families for a new life. If you don't care about the slaves, then you must care about each other or this child and her slave-driving husband."

"You didn't answer my sister's question," snaps Elmira. "Who are you?"

"Are you from here?" asks Mary. "You talk differently from the other blacks on this plantation."

The old slave answers, "No, I be from the island of Jamaica. I was born there almost two hundred years ago. I see many of my people die on the island and many more in these colonies. There be many more who die here, away from their motherland. She calls for her children, but only their spirits return to her, not their bodies. Her knows she will lose many more of her children to this and other strange lands, so I be here watching and waiting for their freedom from this slavery, be they dead or alive."

Elmira stares at the old woman for a few seconds and asks, "You seem to know about this place and the people. Tell us about the master and his wife."

"The master of this plantation is a vile and hideous diseased man," explains the slave woman. "He has already sold four of his slave women because they have the disease. Some of the slave men they buried after they are caught sleeping with the masters' slave women, and then those spots tell on them. They get sick, have spots on their body, and are too sick to work. So the other two whip them well, then take them to the swamp and shoot them. As for those women, nobody buys those slave women, so they take them to the swamp and never come back either. The master sends men to the market to buy new slaves."

"What about his wife?" Elmira asks.

"She treated little better than a slave, but she best be warned, her husband hired three men from the Carolinas, and they keep their eye on the wife. She be warned, she be dead if they catch her. The master will kill her for sure."

Elmira looks at the girl hanging on the tree and then at the grand house Monroe is living in. Now everyone is looking at Unity. Elmira takes a deep breath and sighs.

In a whirlwind, the old woman turns into mist. She hovers behind them and asks, "What you going to do?"

Then the mist disappears.

Elmira and the others ask Mary, "Is she still here?"

"No, she's gone."

Elmira is silent for a while; she wants to understand what the old woman is asking them. She wonders why only Mary knew that she was there watching them. *A rare gift indeed,* she thinks. Then she turns her attention to the woman tied to the tree. No one is allowed to cut her down; she is to be left there for the rest of the day or until Monroe demands that she be released.

Unity speaks to break the silence. "I know what I would like to do to that wretch. I'd like to treat him the same way he treated that woman and me."

"We'll have to wait until nightfall and come back," says Elmira. "I think I know what to do, but I'll need all the sisters. If the old woman joins us, we'll take care of all three of these men, and then I'll finish Monroe myself once and for all."

They all vanish from the woods and return to Elmira's farm. After they leave the wooded area of the plantation, the old woman reappears and slithers up to the tree as a serpent. She approaches the poor young woman and whispers to her, "This be the last time you see him; this be the last time." The girl looks up but does not see anyone; she only hears a voice.

Elmira and her sisters gather at the old settlement and wait for the old woman to appear from the plantation. Elmira informs the others of her plan for what she is going to do with John Bowe and his two friends. The wives of the other two are not witches, but their husbands also left their families behind to pursue a new life in Virginia.

On the plantation, the men love life because it is different from life in the small colonial town. They do not have all the religious rules to abide by. Indiscretions are not looked upon as sinful. They have the freedom to do as they please, so they are willing to abandon their families for this taste of freedom they haven't seen in the thirty-plus years of their lives. As long as they keep the slaves working, Monroe allows these men to do as they please. Adam Flynn often goes into the town and finds women to his liking. He does not care to mix with the slave women like John Bowe and Tyler McClann, who do not care one way or the other. Often, all three men travel to the towns of Middle Plantation and Jamestown and indulge in acts that would be considered punishable by whipping or death back in the old colony. They frequented the town of Middle Plantation because it is closer, has fewer mosquitoes and flies, and provides the atmosphere they enjoyed more than traveling to Jamestown. In Middle Plantation, Adam met a woman named Rose in a market.

John Bowe is incensed by the fact that Monroe insists on taking control of the plantation because it was promised to be his from the start. He hates Monroe for this, and he plans to get rid of him somehow and take over the plantation. He would also like to put an end to Mr. Jameston and Mr. Eagleton's visits. This is his plantation, and he has no desire to share any part of it with the old colony. All he needs is a well-laid plan to get rid of Monroe and his wife.

Tyler offers a great idea.

"We can dress up in slaves' clothes and cover ourselves in some kind of tar or mud and disguise ourselves as slaves," He explains. "Then we can break into the mansion and kill Monroe and his wife. I know of at least five troublesome slaves we could blame it on."

"That, Mr. McClann, is such an insane idea," says John, "but I love it." He adds, "I've locked three of them up in the shed, but they've already been there two days." John leans back in his chair and comments. "We could break the slaves out and send them off into the woods to their freedom and then gather a few men and dogs from the other plantations and hunt them down, and they'll take the blame for it all."

"That may actually work," says Tyler.

"When are we going to do this?" Ask Adam. "If we leave them in the shed too long, they'll be too weak to run, and we won't be able to pull this off."

"How about we do it at the end of the week, late at night on Saturday? Let's let them out but keep 'em in shackles all week long. Then, Friday morning, we'll take the shackles off for good behavior." John says.

Tyler laughs. "Good behavior, John?"

They chuckle. "Yes, good behavior. Then we'll lock them back in the shed that night."

"How are we going to get the tar and mud off fast enough to keep the slaves from really escaping?" Adam asks.

"We have the best-hunting dogs this side of the James River. We'll track them down in a matter of hours, and they'll get nowhere," John says.

"I think we'd better use mud because it comes off quicker," Adam suggests.

"Two of us can kill that backstabbing Monroe and that wife of his, and one of us can free the slaves. Then we'll change into our everyday clothing. I'll stay behind while Tyler fetches the neighbors, and then you, Adam, will have enough time to get cleaned up before everybody shows up for the hunt. I'm the foreman, and I'm on the charter, and that means I'll inherit the plantation. Soon it will be back in the hands of its rightful owner."

They all raise their cups and toast, "To Monroe's demise," and they drink themselves to sleep.

While Elmira and the others wait for the elderly witch from the plantation, they talk about their day.

Amanda is describing the plantation.

"The Grand House, you would not believe it," she says. "And the large barns and stables, the cows that roam the land and the many horses, and..."

The old witch shows up in a fiery cloud, which brings Amanda's tales of the plantation to an end. She turns around slowly, taking in all the witches until she's face to face with Elmira.

She smiles at Elmira and says, "This be a good night to plan but a bad night to carry it out."

"And why is that?" Elmira asks in a huff.

The old witch hovers over to Elmira and turns to face the others with a raised voice and an accent that none of the witches understand very well.

"The three men you seek have they own plan, and they will kill the master and his wife. The man who whipped the young girl this morning is angry; he says the master took away his plantation. And they say they not share no part of their plantation with the old colony either. They plan to kill Monroe and his wife late Saturday. They cover themselves with mud and put slave clothes on, and then they go to the master's house and kill him and his wife. They have three slaves locked in the shed they gone release and blame them for the murders." She explains.

"How will they blame them if they run away?" asks one of the witches.

"Like they always do, child," replies the elderly witch. "They hunt them down like animals and kill them."

After listening, they all stare at one another, gesturing and asking what they should do. Unity speaks loudly and looks at the old witch.

"You wanted to know what I was going to do! If they want to be black, then we can make them black. We can cast a spell so that it won't come off when they paint their faces with mud. They'll be as black as you." Unity looks at the old woman. "I mean, no offense to you. What is your name, by the way?"

"My name be Neaira," replies the woman. "My master named me after a Greek slave when I was born. I was born on the island of Jamaica, first of the family of slaves sent to the islands nearly two hundred years ago."

Neaira produces the slave's clothes that the three had set aside as part of their plan.

"You'll need something that the three men own to cast the spell," she says.

Then she ascends into the air above the witches and comes down hard on the ground. Fire swirls around her feet, first ambers and then flames, until the fire has totally engulfed her. Neaira begins to chant. All the witches listen to her spell, although her island language is hard to understand. But Mary understands every word, and all the other witches follow along with Mary. Elmira participates in the enchantment, and it doesn't take long before the entire old settlement joins in. After five minutes, Neaira throws something resembling a ball onto the clothes, and they explode in a large fireball and smoke; then, the wind picks up and extinguishes the fire and settles down as fast as it started.

"It be done," Neaira says. "The spell is set, and now you need to come up with a plan to save the master and his wife. The spell will also keep them from speaking they language, and the language they speak will be the language of my home village in Africa."

"I have a plan that will have Monroe's neighbors on them before they can get up the stairs," says Elmira. "Thank you, Neaira. Now, I need you to get the clothes back to the men before they are missed. Remember, we will meet here on Saturday morning before sunrise." Elmira wants her to know that she is in charge.

Once all the witches have gone home for the night, Elmira and Mary return to the farm. Inside the house, Elmira invites Mary to the table to eat.

As they sit and eat their meal, Elmira says to Mary, "You want to explain yourself."

"I don't know what you mean," Mary replies.

Elmira slams her fist on the table. "Don't play games with me, Mary!" She says. "You know damn well what I mean. You pretended to know when she was in the woods and to understand her language when none of us could."

"It's nothing I can explain, and I was not pretending," Mary says. "I could just sense it. The old witch said it was a rare gift. I'm as confused as you are."

"A rare gift, my ass. You expect me to believe that?" Elmira shouts.

"Yes!" Mary cries. "I've never lied to you, and I don't plan on starting now."

"There's a difference between lies told and lies not told at all, and you're hiding something that you're not telling me," Elmira shouts.

"I'm tired, Elmira," says Mary. "I'm going to bed."

Mary gets up from the table. She walks to her room and closes her door, at which point Amanda appears and sits at the table.

"Rare gift, my ass indeed," says Amanda. "She didn't even know I was standing right behind her."

"Her treachery is going to cost her dearly. Sister or not, I'll kill her like I did all the others in my family. Keep an eye on her, for it seems the beauty of this land isn't the only thing she's been seeing."

Invisible, Mary hovers near the table, where Elmira and Amanda are making plans to kill her as soon as the right time presents itself.

In the morning, both Elmira and Mary prepare to leave for work at the mill. Elmira does not speak to her sister as they leave the house, nor does she say a word on the road to the mill. Elmira no longer trusts Mary; she believes that she poses a threat to her position as leader of the coven.

It was Mary's choice to abdicate the leadership position to Elmira; she wants to tell Elmira everything she has done for her, but she knows that Elmira would take it the wrong way, which would cause an even greater rift between them. Mary loves Elmira, but she knows the time is near for them to separate. Since they may end up on opposite sides, Mary decides to keep all these thoughts to herself and figure out a way to talk to her older sister without angering her.

Before they arrive in town, Mary breaks the silence.

"Elmira, you know all witches have their own strengths and weaknesses, and they all have varying gifts and abilities," says Mary. "You know they can and will use their strengths to their own advantage."

Elmira stops the buggy. "Okay, and what point are you trying to make?"

"I'm trying to say you should learn what makes a witch the way she is. Know her strengths and weaknesses, and use them to strengthen the sisterhood. Witches' different talents and abilities, and even their different weaknesses – you don't want to have someone watching your back if their gifts lie in watching your front. Use these gifts the right way, and you will have an army of witches that cannot be stopped."

Elmira looks at Mary and asks, "Can I trust you to watch my back?"

"That's Amanda's strength," says Mary. "Mine is watching your side."

Elmira screams, "Amanda's place it by my side and not at my back. But thank you, Mary, for letting me know that I cannot trust you to watch my back. I guess you're only good at being a simple-minded retard!"

Mary cries and says, "I'm your sister, and it doesn't matter whether you trust me or not. I'll always watch out for you, and I always will."

"And what the hell is that supposed to mean? You may have forgotten that it was I who watched over you while you drooled all over yourself. I spoon-fed your grown ass like you were a child because you couldn't feed your damn self!" Elmira shouts.

"Elmira, please don't do this," pleads Mary. "I have always been there for you as well, and right now, you are blinded by your power and anger. You were always there for me, but I was also there for you. When Grandma Hadley died..."

Elmira screams and stands over Mary with her hand in her face. Mary leans away from her.

"I don't give a damn. I don't care about when you came to your damn senses, for right now, all I want you to do is do whatever the hell I say without questions." Elmira is enraged.

Mary cries while Elmira screams insensitive and belittling words. Elmira knows she is hurting her sister, but she has no remorse in her heart. After some time, Mary softly fades away and vanishes completely, so Elmira sits back in her seat and slaps the horse on the rump. She drives on, angrily calling her sister a simple-minded idiot.

"Where do you think she went?" asks Amanda as she climbs into the seat Mary has just vacated.

"I don't care," Elmira growls. "She's probably out there talking to some wild animal and telling it about all her troubles."

Amanda laughs. Mocking Mary, she adds, "Or flying over the trees and thinking about how beautiful they look from her broom. Did you notice? She didn't even realize I was behind her again – that's twice! I think she and the old witch are in this together. Can we trust the old witch, do you think?"

"Yes, we can trust her for now," says Elmira. "She wants to get rid of the idiots who have been beating and killing her nigger friends. Yes, we can trust her, but I'm just not sure about my sister. We must keep an eye on little Miss Retard – and the new girls, who may be trying to build their own coven of witches. If she thinks she's going to take over, she's got another thing coming." Elmira whips the horse on the rump to quicken its pace. "I'll take care of her retarded ass like I'm going to take care of that pompous windbag Monroe. She's played the simple-minded idiot with me for the last time."

Elmira is fuming. She gives the horse a swat on the rump again to get him to trot faster as they make their way to the mill. All the while, Mary has been hovering behind them. She knew Amanda was there, and she knew Amanda was in their house before they left. Now her sister has plans to get rid of her because she believes she is trying to overthrow her from her reign.

Mary stops following Elmira and Amanda and goes off to a faraway country for a couple of days, where she can think about everything that has transpired between her and her sister. She realizes that she can never tell Elmira what Mrs. Kirts warned her about; Elmira's life and fate. What she must do is stay away from Elmira and her growing coven.

After much reflection, Mary returns home late. She arrives while Elmira is having conflicting thoughts about her sister. She loves her youngest sister and wishes no harm to her, but at the same time, she will kill anyone who gets in her way or tries to stop her from carrying out her plans. Elmira paces the kitchen floor, waiting for Mary to get home; she wants to know for sure whether her sister is a friend or foe. She sighs heavily and sits down at the table. Mary sits down right beside her, which startles Elmira.

Surprised, Elmira shouts, "You want to warn a person first! And where have you been?"

"I traveled back to the old country, to England. I understand everything now, and I can see what the old fox said about Aunt Agnes was a lie. I went back to the old country and found it far different from our home here. Aunt Agnes is buried in a small town outside of Canterbury, where she lived an impoverished life. She was a prostitute almost all her life, and that's why she was left behind."

Elmira grabs her hand and tells her, "Enough! It does not matter what we were told. We got what we wanted – you, your sanity, and I got the power to do as I damn well please."

Mary tries to speak, but Elmira puts her hand over her mouth and stands over her. "All I want to know is whether I can trust you," she presses.

Freeing her mouth, Mary looks at her sister. "You can always trust me. The question is whether I can trust you and Amanda."

Elmira looks at her sister, covering Mary's mouth once more. Then she turns her face away. Again, Mary removes Elmira's hand from her mouth.

"I'll always love you, and I want to trust you as well, but I can see we are going in different directions," Mary explains. "For this reason, I am leaving here and will never return. I love you, Elmira, but I don't like what you've become. I don't want to fight with you. I want to know you as the loving and caring sister who took the time to wipe the spittle from my mouth without being disgusted by it."

Elmira turns to face her and says, "Actually, it was always pretty disgusting."

They both put their hands to their mouth and laugh. Then Mary jumps up and grabs Elmira; she gives her a tight hug and cries on her shoulder for a moment. When she sits back down, they stare at each other.

"Where are you going?" Elmira asks with genuine concern.

"I'm not sure yet." Mary leans back in her chair. "I found this young man in my dreams, and I just can't get him out of my head, so I thought I would make myself available to him at the right time."

"In your dreams, Mary? In your dreams!" Elmira yells.

"Yes, in my dreams. I saw him as though he were right here right now, a real person. It's not to come right now, but it will eventually. I want to have children, and I want them to be normal."

Elmira stares at her sister. "Children, huh?" she mocks.

"All I wanted was to be normal like everybody else. I didn't know that it would be this way, and right now, I want to get as far away from this as possible." Tears streak Mary's face.

"What makes you think the master will let you leave like this?" Elmira snaps.

Mary looks at her sternly and says, "There really is a God, and he's far greater than that old fox will ever be. He's no master of mine, and he never was. I am going away, and there is nothing anyone can do about it."

Elmira laughs and stands from the table, looking down at Mary. "Are you into the Bible now, Mary?"

"I always was, for it's the only book our mother taught us from. It's all I know, and it should be all you know, but your hatred has consumed you."

Elmira steps forward and leans over Mary with one hand on the table and one hand on the back of Mary's chair, gripping it so hard it creaks.

"Well, let me tell you something," says Elmira. "You're a witch, and that and God don't mix, Missy."

Mary looks at her and says, "I see you forgot the scriptures, which describe how God forgave one of the greatest sinners... King Manasseh."

Elmira narrows her eyes, glaring at her sister. "You'd better be careful about what you say, and I mean very, very careful."

"I'm through with being careful," sighs Mary. "You are the one who needs to be careful, and not I, Elmira Jean Grace-Pembroke."

"I know you didn't just use my whole name," Elmira says, shocked and stepping back.

"And what if I did?" Mary replies.

Staring at her sister, Elmira says, "You look and sound just like somebody I knew a long time ago when I was younger."

"Who?" Mary inquires.

"Never you mind who. You said you're leaving. Are you going back to England? Is that why you were there?"

"Elmira, I just need to get as far from here as possible. I will always remember you, and I will pray for you."

Elmira is seething. Speaking through her teeth, she asks, "When are you leaving?"

"Tomorrow," says Mary. "I'll have Joseph take me to Boston if you don't mind me using your carriage."

"No, I don't mind," Elmira sighs.

"If the people see me leave, they will not be suspicious when they no longer see me. You are sending me to see a specialist, and I'll be there for a while. Everyone will believe that because they all know of my condition."

"Will you tell me where you are going?" Elmira asks.

"It's best that I do not," says Mary.

"Will you at least tell me about Ann Kirts's premonitions? It seems that we are the only two she's spoken this to." Elmira takes her seat.

Mary tells her one of the first parts of the story; she knows that she can never tell Elmira the whole quatrain. She sighs and rests her chin on her clasped hands.

"I try hard not to overthink things, but with my dreams and what she's told me, I'm not entirely sure that it will come to pass."

"Tell me what you know," says Elmira.

"Okay," agrees Mary.

"There will come a light from the womb of darkness," Mary begins.

"And then she held me and kissed me, and then she cried."

"Is that it?" Elmira shouts.

"I'm supposed to be the retarded one, remember? Even I understand what it means." Mary rolls her eyes.

They sit awhile and stare at each other. Mary remembers when she wrote all of Ann Kirts's premonitions that were told to her first and then, in part, to Elmira. All are a curse against Elmira for the murder of her son. She knows Mary is different and only ever desired to be normal like everyone else. She tells Mary three things, the first being:

"There will be a time fulfilled when the winds of time shall carry the innocent to vanquish the wicked."

Ann told Mary she was nothing like her sister or anything like the others. The second thing Ann tells her is a dark story of the *lights' secrete blight:*

"Wisdom is suspended by time till youth becomes of age
Pushing forth from the womb of darkness came a light
Swift as a roe, gifts untold, the light holds no rage
Hidden deep within the light, a dark and secret blight

Time of times shall pass held together by volumes of old
Composed by the ages now made watchers of the night
Long forgotten, long untold, the old fade, the new unfold
Secrets of the blight confuse the light

They come in times of drought, three watchers of the light
Volumes unfold, stories long told, the meek do these times hold
Orphaned is the light, no more secrets of the blight
Humble, mild-mannered, and meek conceal gifts not told

Fury rages, a great quake, and one that will never wake
Times unfold, gifts revealed, fury is put on hold
Flying at night, they carry the light to fury across the lake
The secret of the blight is revealed by the light, fury stone cold."

And the final of the three premonitions Ann Kirts told Mary was of a Dorothy that shall rise after falling unto a strange world.

"There will come a time when a new Dorothy shall be dropped upon a strange world. There she shall rise above her watchers in courage and valor. Beware of the waters of that world, for it will be the fall of the old. Guard well your heart, for the blight will see it part."

Mary remembers these sayings and wrote them down holding them to heart. She breaks the silence. "Elmira, I'm going to have children, and they will not be of a depraved mind," says Mary. She covers her face and cries. "All my life, I've lived in darkness, and now that I am in the light, I will have children who will not be born into that horrible darkness."

Elmira, her face shining like a light, asks, "Are you pregnant and trying not to tell me?"

"No, not yet, at least," Mary says with a shy smile.

Elmira hugs her, and they both cry.

"I'll miss you very much, Mira," Mary says.

Elmira knows now that she will never see her sister again and that she is not the one she was warned about. But if not Mary, then who could it be? Elmira knows she can trust her daughter-in-law.

Mary tells her sister that she is going to bed because she has a long ride ahead of her.

"Oh, Mary, I would really love to travel with you, but I have to be at the plantation on… well, yes," Elmira says with a crooked smile.

Mary looks at her sister, well aware that she is thinking of something devious.

"What are you thinking about, Elmira?" asks Mary. "I know that look!"

"I will accompany you to Boston if you don't mind," says Elmira.

Mary looks at her and utters a slow "Okay." She is hesitant and worried.

"Are you going with us, Amanda?" Mary asks.

Elmira looks at Mary surprisedly and then glances around the room, trying to find where Amanda is standing. Mary points at the fireplace, where Amanda slowly appears. She is standing by the pot of boiling stew that Elmira has been cooking. Her hands rest on her hips.

"So you not only have the gift of knowing that someone is in your presence but also of knowing where they are," Amanda remarks.

Mary looks at the two of them and smiles.

Then Amanda says, "If I'm welcome, yes, I would like to go too."

Amanda turns to Mary, who points to Elmira as if to say, "It's up to her."

"I guess we could have a girls' outing before you leave us forever," Elmira says nervously.

"Okay, I want to do some shopping at the Boston market and enjoy our last days together," Mary adds.

Elmira says excitedly, "It sounds fun; let's do it. It's a trip for the three of us. We'll pack our things and be ready to leave after sunrise."

Mary is still peering strangely at Elmira.

"What?" Elmira asks.

"Don't 'what?' me, Elmira," says Mary. "You still have that look on your face. What are you cooking up now?"

"Stew," Elmira says. "Have some."

Mary shakes her head and tells her that she has already eaten. Amanda claims to have already had some. She walks over to the mantle over the fireplace and retrieves her bowl.

"Tell me, Mary," asks Elmira, "did you know where she was because she was smacking? You do know you smack when you eat, don't you, Amanda?"

Amanda simply turns to look at Elmira scraping the bottom of the bowl. She puts the spoon in her mouth, vanishes, and then takes it, waving it over her shoulder.

In the morning, Thursday, August 2, 1696, they all ride up to the mill in the carriage to inform Keith and Mr. Gaines of their brief departure.

"I'm taking Mary to a specialist in Boston," says Elmira. "I fear she will have to be there for a while and may not be back.

Keith steps into the carriage and gives Mary a warm hug. She was the one who held him close when things were difficult as a child.

"It's best this way. You know that she'll always love you." Elmira said.

"Goodbye, Aunt Mary. I really wish you the best of luck." Keith said sadly.

Mary is wearing a hooded cloak and does not raise her head or even make a sound. Mr. Gaines bids her farewell and wishes her all the best.

"Elmira, if there is anything you need, send me notice," Winfred says.

"I appreciate that, Mr. Gaines, but I'm merely dropping her off," replies Elmira. "Amanda and I will return promptly."

"We'll see you upon your return then," Winfred said.

"Work in the mill is starting; I'll not hold you from your duties, and we'll be on our way." Said Elmira.

As they drive away, Elmira says, "I think that went very well, girls. Now, pray tell, what shall we do when we get to Boston?"

"Well, I know what I'm going to do," says Mary excitedly. "I'm going to buy a wedding dress as close to the one my namesake wore, Queen Mary II of England."

"You are so unfair and awfully wrong for that!" cries Elmira. "Oh... you, Mary, I don't know what to say. We have to be there for your wedding. You can't do me like this, Mary."

"Well, I'll tell you what, as soon as I get the date, I'll send you a personal message, and we'll celebrate. How's that?" Mary offers.

"You promise? I'm serious, Mary," Elmira cries.

"I promise with all my heart. I'll let you know when and where." Mary says excitedly.

Elmira looks at Mary and mouths the words, "You'd better."

Mary is thankful that she is leaving; she does not want to hang around the Williams River Township any longer. Nonetheless, she engages in small talk until they reach Boston.

It's early Saturday morning, around five o'clock, and the witches have gathered behind the plantation for their final briefing. Elmira briefs the others on the roles they will play to get rid of John Bowe and his drunken friends. The woods are full of witches; they go about the plantation from field to field and from one house to another. Mary has no desire to be there, and Elmira does not ask her to follow. They are there to get a full inventory of the plantation. They see the men slaves are separated from the women, just like the old witch said. When they get to the house where John is sleeping, they find him in bed with one of the slave women.

The woman is half-awake and stirring quietly in the bed, trying her best not to wake him. One of the witches who finds him reports the situation to Elmira and Unity, while the other stays behind to keep watch. When Unity arrives, she observes him for a little while, wanting desperately to end his worthless life, but she knows she must wait for their plan to play out. Unity smiles and goes over to the bed, and she just hovers over the young lady face down, displaying only her face. She notices that the young girl's eyes are open to see if John will wake when she moves, but then she closes her eyes. Unity watches her eyes flutter open and closed. Eventually, when the young girl opens her eyes, she screams and awakens John.

He falls out of bed angrily, "What in hell are you screaming about?"

The young slave girl points at the ceiling, trembling, and says, "The spirit of a white woman."

He looks up and raises his fist at her. "Stupid superstitious nigger. I should get the whip to your hide for waking me this way."

She does not seem to hear him, for she is still looking at the ceiling, where she can see Unity looking down at her. John puts his clothes on and storms off. Stretching hard, he is still sleepy, so he returns to his cabin, where Tyler is asleep. He climbs into his bed and falls back to sleep. Adam left the night before to spend time with Rose, the woman he had been seeing for a few weeks now.

"I feel like I'm in love all over again, and I can't wait to see her again," Adam told John and Tyler.

"You'd better not spoil my plans, boy, because if you do, you'd best not come back," John warns.

Meanwhile, Elmira is in the Mansion, and she cannot believe its size. It is grand and far better than any farmhouse she has ever seen. She looks at Amanda in wonder and awe.

"Can you believe this place?" she whispers.

Seeing how Monroe is living makes her think she should let John and his friends go ahead and kill him. She hears some of the slaves already musing about the mansion. They both vanish but remain in the house; then they go upstairs, where Monroe is snoring, and Agatha is sleeping in a separate bed in the same room. Elmira furiously leaves the room and moves through the rest of the mansion, taken by its beauty.

She thinks about Mary, who always talks about how beautiful things are in this world. Then she thinks about how the beautiful and the ugly are all rolled up in one referencing the mansion and Monroe. She wants Monroe dead but does not know what to do with her friend. So, Elmira leaves the mansion and summons all the witches to the back of the plantation. She reminds them of their task and what they will do when the time is right.

"You must follow my plans to the letter," she says. "I'll take some of the men's dirty clothes when they change; this way, they will leave a strong odor for the dogs."

Later that night, they all meet back in the woods, waiting for the three men to change clothes. While John and Tyler change, Premise stands cloaked in the corner of the room, looking on, and waiting for them to leave. Only then can she grab their clothes and take them to Elmira. They are still waiting for Adam while getting dressed and painted up.

Tyler complains, "I knew that yellow-bellied coward would chicken out."

"When I get my hands on him, I'll kill him," says John.

But just then, Adam bursts through the door. John goes up to him and punches him in the mouth, knocking him to the floor and yelling, "Where the hell have you been?"

Adam, wiping his mouth, tells John, "You have no right to do that, you bloody bastard."

"I have every right. You were supposed to have been here over an hour ago," cries John. "You'd better have a damn good excuse."

Adam, picking himself up off the floor, tells John, "I don't have to explain myself to you or anybody else here. You put your hands on me again, and I'll kill you."

Then Adam walks over to his bed and changes his clothes. John and Tyler go over to a bucket where they have mixed mud with a thick black substance. They rub the concoction all over their bodies, covering their faces well. Premise is watching the scene, thinking they might kill each other before they leave the room. Eventually, Adam apologizes for being late.

"Rose would not let me go," he says. "I had to wait until she fell asleep to sneak out. Listen, I got to thinking on my way back about all this. We're not murderers."

John grabs him by the shirt and holds a large blade to his throat.

"The only way you leave will be the same way Monroe is leaving... in a grave," he threatens.

He pushes Adam away and sets the large blade down. The blade is one of the slaves' knives to cut cane and small brush. John turns to

Adam, shakes his fist at him, and then points to the bucket. Tyler walks by and purposely bumps into him.

"You'd better get yourself together. Let's go; you've already cost us valuable time here, and don't forget to wrap your hair in that rag." Tyler warns.

Adam tells them, "I was just thinking, is all. I was just thinking."

Tyler is the first one out the door. Looking around, Tyler thinks all three men should go and free the three slaves.

"We can pretend we are running with them for a little while, just to get a feel for what direction they're running in." Says Tyler.

"Good idea," says Adam.

They turn to go to the shed where they've locked the three slaves. Premise has already taken their clothes to Elmira and told her they are about to kill one another.

"These are the small fish; the big fish have yet to be landed," she says.

Three witches, Hanna, Sarah, and Rebecca, have already transformed into the three slaves that John plans to release. They placed the three slaves in a deep sleep and hid them in the shadow of darkness so they would not be seen. John considers these slaves troublemakers because the three of them attempted to run away once before. This will make it easier to blame them for the murders of Monroe and his wife, Agatha. The three witches act as if they are asleep on the floor when they hear the lock and chains being removed from the door.

Tyler rushes in and beckons for them to follow him out the door. The three witches simply look around the room at each other like they do not know what to do. Tyler goes in and grabs one of them off the floor, and again, he beckons them to follow him outside. This time they get up, look around and see that there are two others. All six start to run, but the three witches get ahead of Tyler, John, and Adam. The three idiots are not in the shape the three slaves are in. Before they know it, they have gone farther than they'd intended. They stop to rest and get their bearings while the slaves run on ahead of them.

John looks around and asks, "Did any of you see where we were going?"

In unison, Adam and Tyler say, "Damn it, we're lost." They turn back when they can no longer see or hear the slaves.

Three other witches, Lucy, Margret, and Ambrose, have transformed into slaves to wreak havoc on Monroe's neighboring plantation. They enter the main house and steal food from the pantry, mostly dry goods. They make enough noise to arouse the attention of the overseers. When confronted, they beat two men with boards and draw musket fire from the others as they run toward the west. The men notice that they are running toward Monroe's plantation and quickly gather themselves to hunt the slaves down before they rob or murder anyone else from the James River plantations.

Elmira helps the three lost idiots find their way out of the woods, at which point they hurry to the back of the mansion and try to ease their way through the kitchen, being careful not to turn anything over. Witches Rose, Unity, and Ella wait until they know the men from the neighboring plantation are close enough to the Windgate Plantation and then set a fire in one of the empty sheds John uses to imprison runaway slaves.

When the men see the fire, they rush to the mansion to warn Monroe of the uprising. They burst through the door when John, Tyler, and Adam are on the stairs. In all the excitement, one of the men fired a shot at the men and missed. Adam runs to the kitchen, thinking he can make it back to the woods, but by this time, Lester Graves, one of the men tasked to help run the plantation, sees the blaze and hears gunfire. He orders four men to rush to the mansion with their muskets. He orders one of the men to run to the slaves' quarters to get them to put the fire out while the other three from the Carolinas tend to the mansion.

Adam's hopes are dashed when he sees his coworkers running at full speed toward the house, so he turns around quickly to hide beneath one of the cabinets in the kitchen. Lester Graves and his men run past him. Adam jumps out from the cabinet, running into a table on his way out the door. One of the men turns, sees him running for the door, and hits him in the back of his head with the butt of the musket.

The man yells out, "I got him! I got one of them murdering niggers."

From the stairway, John rushes down to one of the men, who fires at him and swings the large blade cutting through the side of his skull and into his shoulder; the man screams in pain. John runs and jumps through one of the side windows, and Tyler is not far behind him. In an attempt to break his fall, John fractures his arm when Tyler falls on top of him.

They see horses by the porch the men left behind to rush inside. John and Tyler grab the reins of two of the horses and gallop off. The men fire their muskets through the broken window while others run out on the porch and fire without aiming. They run to their horses to chase after John and Tyler.

"Damn," John says to himself, shocked by what is happening. "We have to reach the shallow point at the bend and cross over from there." To Tyler, he says, "We have to split up. I'll meet you in Jamestown."

They hear the men behind them and push harder to get to the river's shallow point at the bend; when they ride up to the river, they dive in with the horses. John can't hold on because of his broken arm, while Tyler manages to grip onto his horse and swims downriver. John splashes water over his face and arms as best he can, and when he no longer feels the dried mud, he believes his disguise is gone. The horse he was riding turns back to the shore and makes its way toward the plantation. He still does not want to give himself up to the men; in his mind, he could sneak back to the plantation, change his clothes, and send out a party to track down the slaves he freed.

Climbing out of the water, he's met with the butt of the musket in his face. The men who captured him saw him splashing about, thinking he was drowning, and they waited for him to get close enough to the shore to pull him out. Tyler stays in the water with his horse for another half-mile. It takes a long time for him to get to where he feels safe enough to get out of the water. He ties the horse to a small tree and walks up the river bank to the road. He did not see anyone, so he slid down the river bank to his horse.

At the time, the men think Tyler fell off the horse and into the river and possibly drowned. They only check the area where they captured John and search for the others in the woods on both sides of the river. The man then grabs John out of the water, ties a rope around his wrist, and drags him behind his horse back to the plantation. When they arrive at the plantation, they inform Monroe of the situation.

"One of them got away... for now. Come, first light, we'll have that nigger in shackles if he hasn't already drowned; either way, we'll have a body for you."

Monroe wonders where John, Adam, and Tyler are. He asks around, but no one knows of their whereabouts.

A man from the other plantation suggests, "They might have been dragged into the woods and murdered by those heathens. Hell, Mr. Monroe, you might never see them boys again."

He has a hard time grasping this. When the owner of the other plantation finishes his inventory of slaves and property, he determines the runaways have not done any damage to his plantation. He rides to Monroe's porch to see if he can offer more assistance. Monroe thanks him and tells him that the swiftness of his men saved his life. They drag John and Adam out to the front of the mansion.

"Tie them to the tree and let them hang there until the third one is captured and brought back," says Monroe. "These niggers will be whipped and hanged."

Then he calls out to Lester Graves. "I want you to find three good trees on the road where we can hang these ungrateful niggers. And when you're finished, I want you to go out in those woods and see if you can find my boys and bring them back here. It's the least we can do for their poor souls; we'll give them a decent Christian burial."

John looks up at Monroe and tries to talk, but groaning is all he can manage. His entire body is in pain, a kind of pain he has never felt before. Adam is still crying because he cannot understand why none of the men can understand what he is trying to say. When they tie John and Adam up on the tree, it isn't until the early twilight hour of dawn that Adam realizes why no one can understand him.

He sees they are not painted, for their skin has turned black. He cannot comprehend what is going on.

"We're black," he says aloud in horror. "We're…" Adam sees what he thinks is a vision.

John only wishes he were dead and sees Elmira and Unity approach them. They hang from the same tree they tied the slaves to before they whipped them. Adam cannot believe his eyes. John tries to look through his own swollen eyes. He sees Unity as she approaches him from the woods

He speaks, "Unity, my darling, where did you come from?" His voice is weak.

Looking at Elmira, Unity asks, "Did he… just call me darling?"

"Actually, he said 'my darling,'" Elmira replies sarcastically. Laughing, Unity stands with her arms folded. She waves her hands in front of John's eyes.

"Wow, your eyes are really swollen. Can you see me, my love?" she mocks.

"Barely," he replies.

"We missed you so much back home," says Unity, still toying with him.

"I missed you too," he says, wincing in pain. "That damn Monroe wouldn't let me come home to get you and the kids. He keeps me so busy here."

"Oh, does he really?" she asks.

"Listen, I swear I was just telling Monroe that I needed time off to go and get my loving family," John explains.

Unity holds her hand up to his face and looks at him disgustingly. She gazes around the plantation and the mansion and then looks back at him.

"No, I believe you turned your back on your family," Unity says angrily. "But, for all this? I wasn't good enough for you to come back to? Did you enjoy the comforts of your black wenches?"

She takes in a deep breath and grabs him by his privates. Unity squeezes hard. John can't even scream; his eyes roll back into his head, his lips grow tight, he moans, and tears fall from his eyes.

"You are such a liar, John Bowe," she whispers into his ear. "You got what you wanted, 'slaves and a whip,' but now all you're going to get is the whip."

She lets him go, wiping her hands on the grass and then setting her hand ablaze to avoid catching anything from him. Adam watches with disbelief and horror.

"That will be the last time you'll feel my touch," she says. "As soon as they bring Tyler back... all of you will get the whip."

Adam can only stare at her and Elmira in horror.

"What's happening to us?" He asks. "How the hell did this happen? Can you understand me?"

"Absolutely, we understand you very well," says Elmira. "Why do you ask?"

"I think they must have hit me harder than I thought. I look at our bodies, and we look... black." Adam looks around as the morning reveals more of their hopeless situation.

Elmira laughs and grabs Unity by the shoulder. "Oh no, look!" she says, a surprised look on her face. "He's... black."

"Oh no." Unity acts as though she did not notice until now, and she holds her hands over her mouth. "They are black," she said, approaching Adam. "You should have stayed with that Rose whore you were with yesterday!" Then she turns to walk back into the woods.

Elmira looks at Adam and slaps him hard across the face. "To hell with Rose," she says. "You should have returned to Williams River and brought your family here."

Then she takes a couple of steps backward and vanishes. Adam's eyes widen. He looks at John and cries aloud in horror.

"Was all that real?" Adam asks.

"You can ask my privates, but they ain't listening right now," John replies, bewildered and in great pain.

During the night, Tyler is sure no one is following him. He takes the horse's reins and walks him out of the water, checking both the river's north and south sides. He jumps onto his horse and rides on the north side for as long and as hard as possible. Tyler intends to go to the port of Jamestown and stow away on one of the ships. He does not think anyone will believe the story of the three blacks now that things have worsened. In his opinion, he has no choice but to start a new life somewhere else. When he approaches a part of another river that flows into the James River, he must cross. He slowly traverses it thinking it's best to stop in Middle Plantation for the night. His horse is too weak to climb up the river bank, so Tyler leaves the horse and walks for miles until he reaches the town. He has traveled long and hard, and now he must find another horse if he wants to go any farther. In Middle Plantation, he finds some clothes to change into, and that is when he notices that his entire body is black and that the water must not have washed all the mud off.

"What the hell is this?" He asks in a whisper.

He is so perplexed that he just stands examining his body. Breaking into a sprint, he finds a barn where he can hide until he figures out what is happening. For the longest time, he cannot come to terms with the fact that he is now black. He paces back and forth in the barn, rubbing his hair that is no longer long and straight but short and curly, stopping every once in a while to look out of the barn door.

"No, this can't be happening," he says. "This is a dream; I'm in my bed and dreaming."

Alexandra has been following him since he left the plantation and has had enough of his outbursts. She appears from the darkness.

Tyler looks at her in shock and whispers, "Alexandra Schmidt?"

"In the flesh," she replies.

"Now I know I'm dreaming." He says, perplexed.

She reaches out and pinches him on the arm. "No, you're not dreaming."

"What the hell are you doing here?" asks Tyler. "Is this your barn? Do you live here in Middle Plantation now?"

"I'll answer your questions in reverse," says Alexandra. "No, I don't live here in Middle Plantation, and no, this is not my barn. Actually, I'm here to bring you back to the plantation to be whipped and hanged with the other two fools."

"Like hell you are," protests Tyler as he steps back. "You damn well better have someone else outside that door..."

Tyler doesn't see the right-hand punch that knocks him to the floor. He gets up and wipes his mouth. "Oh, little lady, you're going to wish you hadn't done that."

Before he can step forward to throw a punch back, she punches him again with her left hand, knocking him right back to the floor. In an attempt to shake off the first two blows while trying to prop himself up on his elbows, he receives several hard and quick punches to the face.

When he wakes up, he finds himself tied to the tree by his wrists, with his feet barely touching the ground, next to John. John's body is horribly disfigured and swollen from being dragged behind a horse.

When Tyler glances over at Adam on his other side, Adam says, "Thank you, Mr. Great Idea. Our asses are in a bind, thanks to you and this jackass next to me. I hope you can understand me. Did you happen to see… oh, that's right, you probably can't see out of those eyes of yours; they're swollen shut from that ass whipping you got from those Middle Plantation men who found you hiding in the barn. You wouldn't happen to have some kind of great idea to get us out of this, would you?"

Tyler looks at Adam and John's black skin and begins to laugh hysterically. Suddenly, the laughing stops, only to be replaced by a series of screams from the burn of the whip lashing across his back administered by Mr. Andrews. Once they have been whipped, they are taken out to the road and hung by the neck on three separate trees.

Monroe rides by the three men hanging in the trees, pressing a handkerchief to his mouth. When he gets to the stable, he dismounts from the buggy and orders Lester to cut the slaves down.

"The only people these rotting corpses are deterring are the good people of these plantations when they ride past the stench," says Monroe. "I believe three days is enough, don't you?"

"Yes, sir, I agree," Lester says.

Lester tells one of the stable boys to find Mr. Andrews, who will get some of the men from the field to cut the bodies down and bury them somewhere off the plantation.

"Take them to the marsh and toss their bodies there," suggests Monroe, "and let the wild beasts dispose of them."

Then Lester updates Monroe on the search for John, Tyler, and Adam.

"We've been all over these woods and have only found some of their clothes. I think they are dead somewhere; one of those slaves had Mr. Bowe's machete when he killed that fellow from the other plantation."

Monroe asks, "Does anyone know whose slaves they were?"

"No idea," Lester replies. "As far as anybody can tell, they may have come from one of the plantations down in the Carolinas."

"Yes, I believe that as well," says Monroe. "By the by, I do believe John was doing us a disservice by separating the male slaves from their women. Find a way to get them back together, will you? We don't need an uprising of our slaves because of some stupid rule Mr. Bowe made up to keep the women to himself. I think it's counterproductive and breeds insurrection."

"I'll arrange it," Lester agrees.

"You do that, Mr. Graves, and make sure that it happens," Monroe commands as he walks to the mansion.

Chapter 9
Leaving Her Behind

Elmira, Mary, and Amanda continue on their route to Boston for a girl's fortnight in the town. They stay in the same taverns Elmira and Amanda frequented when they last traveled to Boston from New York. When they arrive in Boston, the three enjoy their time around the town. Although they appear to be happy, Mary and Elmira are upset, for they know their relationship is coming to an end. Elmira regrets that she treated Mary so severely.

She wonders, *did Mary hear the two of us talking about killing her?* In the back of Elmira's mind, she still fears Mary, although she cannot put her finger on why. On the other hand, she is very happy for her sister; she could have never known how Mary felt when she was incapable of thinking for herself.

She's a full-grown woman now, both in mind and body, and she no longer wants to have anything to do with our family. Elmira Thinks worriedly.

Elmira is nineteen years older than Mary, and because of her sister's slow wit, she's never really considered her pretty. Now that Mary is leaving, she looks at her differently. Elmira thinks to herself, *Mary is a very attractive and beautiful woman, and as much as I hate to admit it, she's the spitting image of her mother. She has a girlish look about her. Mary was spared the hard work of the family's responsibilities.*

Mary notices Elmira staring at her. "What are you thinking about?" she asks.

"Just lost in thought," says Elmira. "I remembered when you were just a baby, and now look at you, all grown up. Your skin and hands did not suffer from the hardships of life."

When Elmira looks down at her own hands, she sees years of pain and suffering.

"Naturally, my hands are hard and beaten by time," she goes on. "But you... you never had to deal with any of that. I had to take care of you and the family while no one else did a thing. You are lucky you never had to deal with life as I was forced to live."

Mary asks, "How can you say I'm lucky to be retarded? I would never wish that life on anyone."

Then Mary grabs Elmira's hands and holds them in hers.

"These are the hands that once loved many others, and yes, you took care of both Father and Mother when they were sick. You were the only one who cared while all our brothers and sisters lived in their houses and would not burden themselves with me, not even after our parents' death. I did not then, nor do I now, see the hands that you see."

Mary takes her left hand and rests her face in Elmira's right hand.

"I never complained, and I have always been grateful to you. I made it a point to say thank you for all you did, not just for me but for all of us. You cared for us when we were sick, you loved us from your heart, and you hurt for us when we were hurting. That is what you should remember when you look at your hands."

At that moment, Elmira's hands change from old and worn to the hands of her youth. Mary slowly removes her face from Elmira's hand because these are the hands of death.

"I will always remember you for that, Elmira," says Mary.

Amanda sits listening and looking down at her hands, which rest beneath the table in her lap.

"I think we should call it a night," Elmira says. "We'll wake up to a new day and do new things in the morning."

They retreat to their rooms; Mary is boarding separately from Elmira and Amanda. She does not care to know where they are going once they part from one another. When Elmira and Amanda return to their room, Elmira tries to figure out a way to get rid of Monroe without hurting her friend Agatha.

"Women don't run plantations," Elmira says.

So, she has to introduce her to a man she can trust. Jeremiah Jameston has always had an eye for her. Since he reports to Monroe, they might have the needed edge.

"We need to talk to Agatha," Elmira suggests. "She needs to understand her role at the plantation and her responsibility to the township."

"Why didn't we just let John Bowe hack him up when we had the chance?" Amanda asks.

"Time and patience, girl." Replies Elmira. "Three men are gone, and it would not have looked good if they'd killed that pompous twit. Who would have run the plantation for us then? I need to see the books that give us the ten percent Monroe promised the township. We've got to be sure it's there and the townspeople's investment before we do anything."

"You are right," Amanda says.

"This is not going to be as easy as setting up that jackass and his moron friends," Elmira notes. "No, this may take some planning. Let's look at the books and see what's written in the ledger on our behalf."

Mary goes to bed fretting over her dream about the man she will marry and with whom she will have children. She is also a little worried about Mrs. Kirts's prophesy; leaving is the only way she can keep this a secret until her death. If Elmira hears the whole story, she and her witches will surely kill her. Mary knows that she is one of the keys to

Elmira's demise. Elmira is being friendly to her, but she knows she is still looking over her shoulder and will be for as long as she lives. Elmira does not trust Mary, mostly out of jealousy. She can see Mary's powers are greater than her own. Elmira will always keep an eye on Mary, although she realizes she never had control over Mary. Mary does not trust her, nor does she trust Amanda, because Amanda is willing to do whatever Elmira asks of her. Elmira no longer needs her, which makes it easier for her to leave and never return.

Before they depart for the plantation, Elmira and Amanda stay in their room for about two hours. Elmira cannot help but quickly check on her sister before she sets off. She stands in her room for a few seconds to see if she is there. And while staring down at her sister in her cloaked state, she sees that Mary is already asleep. She says "goodnight" to her to see if she answers back, and when she is satisfied, she and Amanda leave for the plantation.

Mary thinks to herself while lying in bed. *This is why I have to go: every night, she and Amanda test me to no end."*

They have been in Boston for almost two weeks, and now it is time for Mary to leave her sister behind. She goes to Elmira's room after she and Amanda have left for the plantation and leaves a simple note:

My dearest sister, the time has come that I must say goodbye. I will always remember the days you expressed your deepest love and care for me. You will always be in my thoughts and in my heart.

Love, Mary

Mary looks about the room closing her eyes, for nothing reminds her of her home or family. There is nothing to look back to, so with tears in her eyes, she whispers to herself, *"Lord be my shelter, my refuge, and my hiding place while I wait for my appointed time."* And then, she leaves the tavern and her sister far behind. She does not want others to watch her leave, so she just vanishes, never to be seen by Elmira or her witches again.

At the plantation, Elmira and Amanda search for signs of change. Even for them, the still night air is alarming. They peer into one house at a time, looking around the plantation grounds. They see that the house they burned down has been repaired and made into one of the overseer's homes. In another house, they find the old witch sitting by a fireplace and boiling meat.

She says in her thick Caribbean accent, "Come in, ladies. I've been waiting for you."

Elmira does not care to talk to the old witch because she believes she has served her purpose. She thinks she should either move on or simply die.

"How are things with you two ladies?" asks the old witch. "You are here to see the mistress of the mansion, no?"

Elmira is cold to the old witch. "I have a feeling you've been watching us," she says.

"Oh no, Elmira, I no watch you," the old witch replies. "I have no reason to. I was just wondering if you've seen your friend with the young blackbuck. She be in the mansion in that upper room, she locks herself into these days."

"What makes you think I care anything about her?" Elmira asks, her tone sharp as a blade.

"Well, if you don't, she be cast off the plantation dead or alive when Monroe returns and finds her still in bed with him. Sure, they do him something really bad, but it may not be any better for her."

Elmira and Amanda look at each other, and Elmira asks, "How do you know they will still be together when he returns?"

"These chicken bones don't lie, child," says the old witch.

Amanda laughs and mocks, "Chicken bones?"

"You have a lot to learn, young witch," the old witch admonishes. "Be careful your mocking."

Then the old witch turns and looks at Elmira. "If you don't do something, she be gone by tomorrow, and then who looks after your investment?" She asks.

"Where's Monroe?" Elmira asks.

"Him be in Middle Plantation on business, the same business Mr. Adam used to go on when him went to the town. There ain't no white women here for them, and him can't find that kind of pleasure on this plantation."

"Hypocrite! Bastard!" Amanda calls him.

Elmira looks down at the old witch with distrust, but she knows she's right. If Agatha is no longer here on the plantation, she'll lose all the control she's been trying to gain. The old witch turns her back to them and stirs the pot of deer meat, humming some tune unknown to them. Elmira and Amanda vanish, but Elmira lingers for a few seconds before she remembers that the old witch and her sister share the same gift. She and Mary can both tell when a witch is in their presence, so Elmira leaves the old witch stirring the pot of meat. Elmira gnashes her teeth and goes to Monroe's room, where Amanda is waiting.

"What did she say?" Amanda asks.

"Nothing more," Elmira whispers. "When I left, she left also. So be alert, you hear me? And listen for any sound that comes toward the door. I have to find Monroe's books, which he is sure to keep near his bed."

Elmira cannot find what she is looking for in his room, so they go downstairs to Monroe's parlor, where he often conducts business. It's a beautifully furnished room, but she can't see him keeping his ledgers there where prying eyes may see his corrupt ways. Then she enters a room where the door is closed and books on the shelves cover nearly every wall. Only one big desk sits in front of a window with a big leather chair, the most comfortable chair Elmira has ever sat on. Two other chairs sit in front of the desk, and a small cabinet in the corner houses two crafts of burgundy and rum. When she looks through the desk for the books, Amanda vanishes.

Meanwhile, Elmira finds several ledgers in one of the locked drawers that she waves her hand over to unlock: The Family, Agriculture, Slaves, Cotton Planting, and Accounts ledgers. She starts reading the Family Ledger, which consists of the work hands and their families. Elmira notes Monroe has entered three of the men with no families listed; the ledger only mentions their dates of birth, colonies, dates of death, plantations, and the reason for their deaths. It says nothing more.

Elmira sighs aloud. She cannot get Mary off her mind. She thinks back to when she cared for Mary and all she had been through.

"What have I done?" She whispers. "Now that I know it was not Mary, then who?"

Elmira turns to face the window to look out. She squints, trying to see through the darkness. Then she looks down at her hands which change to the hands Mary said she'll never forget. Elmira vanishes, leaving the ledger on the desk. She reappears at the edge of the tobacco field and then disappears and appears looking at the cotton field, wondering if she can convince her childhood friend to end her relationship with the slave boy before Monroe puts an end to her life.

"I don't know what to do." She sighs and goes back to the office.

Wingate Hundred Plant

John Bowe, foreman, b. 1656 Willi River Colony, Mass, d. Aug. 4, 1696, Wing Hundred, Virginia, Slave Revolt.

Tyler McClann, Overseer, b. 1655 Williams River Colony, Mass, d. Aug. 4, 1696, Wingate Hundred, Virginia, Slave Revolt.

Adam Flynn, Overseer, b. 1660 Williams River Colony, Mass, d. Aug. 4, 1696, Wingate Hundred, Virginia, Slave Revolt.

Lester Graves, Stables and Livery, b. 1663 Boston, Mass. Married Hanna Winston b. 1670 Newton, Mass, Two boys, Heath and Webb b. 1690 and 1692, Boston, Mass.

William Dane, Overseer, b. Unknown, Came from South Carolina.

Boregard Dane, Overseer, b. Unknown, Came from South Carolina.

David Anderson, Overseer, b. Unknown, Came from South Carolina.

Disgusted, Elmira puts the ledger back and opens another. She reads the ledger but cannot find where Monroe mentions their township getting ten percent of the cotton. Elmira sets this ledger down and contemplates where Monroe might have put the township investments. It seems everyone is being paid but the township. These ledgers do not even mention any of the finances that came from their township in the first place. She sees Monroe's own hand stating whom he received the investments to build the plantation, but nothing on who paid for the land. She takes a deep breath to keep her composure.

"Slow down, Elmira," she says to herself. "There are more books, or maybe I'm just reading too fast and missed it."

She opens the Cotton Planting and Agriculture ledgers and finds nothing. At that time, Amanda reappears, holding her mouth with one hand, and laughing while clutching her stomach with her other hand.

"What exactly do you find so funny?" Elmira asks.

"Mrs. Wilson and her slave boy are up there doing the nasty," giggles Amanda. "Boy, are they ever doing it. She's not acting her age at all."

Elmira stares at Amanda, still holding the books in her hands. She is in no mood to see some sixty-five-year-old woman doing what Amanda considers the nasty with a teenage boy. Amanda stands there, biting her lip and moving both hands to her side, twitching like a six-year-old child. She thinks about what she has seen and almost laughs out loud, but she quickly puts her hand over her mouth, bends over, and vanishes again.

Elmira thinks of Mary. She believes she would have been more mature about this and would have stayed outside, alert and watchful. She sits back in the large chair, takes a deep breath, and returns to the books. She picks up the Accounting ledger again and looks over the payoffs. That's where she sees that Sir Quincy Eagleton and Sir Jeremiah Jameston are also among those who are paid.

Elmira thinks, *"Sir,"... really?* She sits up in a different position in the chair. "I'll 'Sir' them." Whispering through gritted teeth.

"I don't care to look through these books any farther," she says, "Nowhere in these ledgers does it indicate that our township had anything to do with financing this property."

Before she closes the Cotton Planting Ledger, she waves her hand over the book, and there in the book – in Monroe's own handwriting – the document now mentions ten percent of the cotton will go to the Williams River Township. She puts this between the amount owed to

England and the amount owed to the other Massachusetts colonies. Now she wonders if Jeremiah Jameston is the right man to run the plantation once Monroe is dead. The three of them are paying themselves, and not a pence or even one bale of cotton has gone to the colony.

"I'll talk to Mr. Jameston when I get back," she says, "and I'll deal with Monroe in due time."

Elmira puts everything back in the drawer. Then she goes to the room where Amanda is watching Agatha and the slave boy. She stands outside the door and stomps the floor in the hallway. Frightened, Agatha tells the young boy to hide under the bed. She quickly puts on her nightgown and goes to the door. When she opens it, no one is there. She grabs a lamp and walks down the hall. Agatha tries to keep silent in an effort to avoid drawing attention to herself. When she sees no one downstairs, she hurries back to the room and beckons the boy encouraging him to get out and return to his house before anyone sees him.

As he makes his way quietly down the stairs, she rushes back to the room. She can barely see him returning to his house across the field from the window, but she can see him quietly returning. Fortunately, the overseers do not notice him. It is from this room that she summons him. She lights a lantern in the room, quickly extinguishes it, and then waits for his return to the not-so-secret love nest the slaves call it.

Amanda meets Elmira in the hallway.

"They were finished anyway," Amanda says with a smile.

"I'll have to find a way to talk to her somehow. I can only hope she will listen. We'll be back to deal with Monroe later, but for now, I need to stir some people's hearts back at the colony." Says Elmira.

When Elmira and Amanda leave the plantation and return to their room, Elmira notices the letter from Mary on her pillow. She picks it up, reads it, takes a deep breath, and tenses up.

"What is it?" asks Amanda.

Elmira does not answer; she just vanishes and then appears in the room where she last saw her sister. Hovering around the room, she quietly calls Mary's name. Anger consumes her at first, but then tears begin to soften her heart for Mary. She has always been with her and cared for her. Now that she's gone, she approaches the bed, lies down, and rests her head on the pillow where Mary slept. She can still smell the perfume of jasmine and light myrtle that Mary was wearing, which makes her cry aloud. She whispers, "Mary, I'm sorry, I'm so sorry," and then she cries even more. From her open hand, the letter falls to the floor.

Elmira rolls over and hugs the pillow hard; she lays in the bed and curls up for the rest of the night. Amanda, watching her from her cloaked corner, hovers to the spot where the letter fell. She picks it up, reads it, and lets it fall from her hand, mourning for her best friend, who has just lost her sister.

Chapter 10
On Top of the World

Monroe and Agatha may as well be divorced. Since his return from New York, she has had nothing to do with him. After John attempts to murder Monroe, she decides it would be best to have her own room and let Monroe die alone. This gives Monroe the freedom to do as he pleases. Monroe does not care if Agatha knows about the slave women he brings up to his room. He allows her to stay locked up in her room and could care less if she ever comes out. He is busy running the plantation and only invites Agatha to join him when he entertains guests.

Monroe has begun to behave like John Bowe; no one can tell him what to do or say on his plantation. He enjoys the freedom of not having to adhere to the rules of the old township, although those same rules he enforced on others. Living on a plantation in the South is like living in another country. He realizes being a planter means his property is valuable. He knows he cannot keep replacing his domestic workers the way he did when he exposed them to syphilis. He likens himself to the affluent and returns to New York, hoping to find a cure for his disfiguring disease.

He often goes to the larger towns to indulge himself in the provocative lifestyle he believes he deserves. During the day, most of the townspeople avoid him, and because of this, most of his business is carried out by his agent, Mr. Reginald Harper. Monroe covers his face to hide the disease that eats away his nose. Like those in Europe who have contracted syphilis, he purchases powdered wigs to help conceal the scars and the smell of rotting flesh.

Eagleton departed the Williams River Township for Monroe's plantation two days before Elmira's carriage left for Boston. Monroe waits for Eagleton's arrival at the Jamestown Port; he stands outside his new carriage to boast of his notoriety and status among the elite planters. When Eagleton walks across the plank from the ship, he sees Monroe holding the lapels of his vest with both hands and standing on planks to keep his shoes from being muddied. He welcomes Eagleton and shakes his hands. Eagleton wears gloves when he meets and greets Monroe.

"Why, Mr. Wilson, aren't you the fancy of the port?" greets Eagleton. "This beautiful carriage sets you apart from all others."

"Indeed," boasts Monroe. "Shall we be on our way?"

They both climb into the carriage, and Eagleton sits across from Monroe, not wanting to sit directly in front of him. Monroe taps the floor with his cane to let Sam know they are ready to drive on when they are settled in.

"How was the voyage?" Monroe asks.

"Dreadful," complains Eagleton. "But I would wager it's much better than riding along the King's Highway in those dreadful coaches."

"Indeed," mutters Monroe. "By the by, speaking of dreadful, I'm afraid I have some very bad news."

Eagleton turns to Monroe, bracing himself for the bad news. "I'm listening." He says.

"I'm afraid that John Bowe, Adam Flynn, and Tyler McClann are dead," announces Monroe. Without allowing Eagleton to speak, he goes on. "Three runaway slaves raided god knows how many plantations along the James River before they got to the Windgate Hundred, and they dragged our boys somewhere back into the marshes and murdered them. Thank God they were met by men from the Bennington Plantation before they could get up the stairs. They captured one trying to escape through the kitchen, another who nearly drowned trying to cross the river, and the last one who nearly escaped was captured in a barn in Middle Plantation. I'll have you know that I had those scoundrels whipped within an inch of their lives, well... two of them; I spared one of them the whipping they all deserve because when he was captured in the river, the men tied him up behind one of their horses and dragged him over every rock and through every bush. I tell you, he was so disfigured and broken up I had to save something for the hanging."

"Good god, Monroe, I would have never guessed you'd have the stomach for such... um, I can't even think of a word for such heinous atrocities. God, man, when did this happen?"

"About a month ago. And you'd be surprised by what one can stomach when you realize your life could be dashed away at any moment because of these savages. If you think the Indians are bad when they go on a rampage, try being in the middle of a slave insurrection. Dreadful thing — no, I dare say, beyond dreadful. It's absolutely terrifying. Never you worry, for we nipped that in the bud right away. I'm afraid, my good fellow, you'll have to break the bad news to their families back at the old colony."

"I dare say it will break their families' spirits," says Eagleton. "Horrifying, simply horrifying, and tragic news. Now I have the burden of thinking about how I can best deliver this news to their families."

"Well, you are one of the best at comforting bereaved families," says Monroe.

"Why, thank you," Eagleton replies.

"Now that I've gotten the bad news out of the way, I have very important news about that piece of land we spoke of on your last visit."

"Right, how did that go?" Eagleton asks.

"Very well, I'm happy to say. I talked to the investors from the old Virginia Company, and they agreed you are an excellent candidate for that property. They've seen my expertise at work, and I told them that you are a man of elite status. I want you to know that living here is like living in another country; you make the rules and laws that govern your property. You really answer to no one, and I promise you after I introduce you, you'll have to be ready to answer every question. Others have similar interests in the land, so it would be prudent of you to present yourself as the fellow they've heard you to be. Monroe explains.

"I'll be at my best," Eagleton says joyfully.

"I hope you don't mind, but I took the liberty of embellishing your reputation a bit. I think you're the perfect gentleman to purchase this land. The plantation is on the north side of the river, and I'm doing well enough to back you."

"I don't know what to say," says Eagleton.

"I think you should take this opportunity and seize the moment," says Monroe. "It's only going to be offered once, so don't make me a fool after speaking on your behalf. Remember, tobacco and cotton are kings here in these parts, and you have to get in while the getting is good."

"Yes, all this has come very suddenly," explains Eagleton. "I didn't think it would happen so fast. But not to worry, I'll put my best foot forward, and you'll not be disappointed." Clearing his throat, he says, "Not to change the subject, Monroe, but the people there are getting a little worried about their investment. The percentage of cotton you promised has yet to be delivered."

"Oh, let them fiddle and fuddle about that." Monroe waves his hand in the air. "The investment is not even in my books. Let them fight it in the courts; they'll never be able to prove it. The only reason they know anything about the investment is because of Elmira's minion Mr.

Winfred Gaines. He was always suspicious, and I tell you, it's nothing more than that. Not even the great Mr. Gaines can argue with the books."

"You didn't leave any evidence behind when you left the township, did you?" asks Eagleton. His tone is concerned. "I wouldn't want anything to hinder our plans."

Monroe thinks for a second and muddles, "None I'd have to worry about. Has anyone moved into the old Wilson home?"

"No, not yet," replies Eagleton. "That insufferable Elmira hates you so much that she claimed it and will not let anyone move in. She says that no decent person will ever live in that damned home. I think she has plans to tear it down, or I believe she said 'burn it down.'"

"Things will work out for the better if she does." Monroe Sneers. "She has a lot of experience burning things, doesn't she?"

"That she does," Eagleton says with a sigh.

"You just tell them their ten percent of the cotton will be on the next ship out next month. You let me worry about the investment and do what I ask. You'll certainly be rewarded for your trouble."

Monroe reaches into his vest pocket and hands Eagleton a note for forty pounds.

"That new plantation down the road from here has your name on it. Tonight we'll meet at the hall in Middle Plantation with our mutual friends, and they will set this deal, write out the charter, and you'll be back on the boat in a couple of days to report to the old township. Let them know the cotton is on the way and say nothing more."

The next morning, Monroe revisits his books to log the forty pounds he gave to Eagleton. Flipping through the pages, he notices a name he did not ink in, yet it appears in his hand between England and another colony he did ink in. He calls for Mr. Reginald Harper, his bookkeeper and business agent. When he walks in, Monroe tosses the book across the desk at the surprised gentleman.

"What?" Harper asks.

Monroe takes his quill and points to the colony.

"How did that get there, Mr. Harper?" Monroe demands.

"Well, I have no idea," says Mr. Harper. "It seems to be in your hand, and all this was scribed before I took over the books."

"I've been to this page before and never saw this entry." Monroe fumes.

"What do you want me to do?" Harper asks.

"Nothing." Monroe throws the quill at him. "Pick it up and give it to me," he demands.

Harper picks up the quill and hands it back to him with an open hand. Monroe snatches the quill, opens a jar of ink, and dips the tip of the quill into the well. He scratches through the entry Elmira made. When he sees it is still legible, he takes the bottle of ink and pours it onto the entry.

He looks at Mr. Harper and says, "Oops, it seems I've spilled ink in the ledger." Laughing, Monroe continues, "Now, as for the ten percent they are so anxious to receive, we'll send it to them next month. But make sure that it's ten percent of the total tonnage that we sell to the other colonies, excluding what we send to England."

Mr. Harper knows this means he will have to recalculate the twenty-five percent going to the other colonies and send the old colony two and a half percent of that amount.

"Yes, sir, I'll make sure it's adjusted to reflect their ten percent."

At that moment, Mr. Eagleton knocks on the door. Mr. Harper gets up from the desk and walks out at Monroe's request. Monroe pushes the book aside, throwing a pile of fine sawdust on the spilled ink. He places the open book aside, giving the sawdust time to absorb the ink.

"Ah Quincy, I fare you slept well." Monroe greets Eagleton.

"Indeed I did, thank you," Eagleton replied.

"Mr. Harper and I were just reviewing the books to ensure the old township gets their ten percent. I had Sam hitch up the carriage. I see you are refreshed for the meeting this afternoon in Middle Plantation. I was afraid you might not remember after all the rum you consumed last night." Monroe laughs and leans back in his chair.

"I had a terrible headache this morning when I woke, but your Delilah fixed me some kind of concoction I wasn't sure I would live through. Yet here I am, and I would say it worked wonders, although I dare not ask what's in it." Eagleton speaks between a burp and hiccup.

Monroe laughs. "I'm sure you don't want to know." He says. "I dare say those ruffles on your shirt are quite dashing; the shirt goes well with that vest and jacket. Where did you shop for it?"

"Well, I was in New York and found this tailor there," replies Eagleton. "He and his wife have a wonderful shop in the market square. You can't miss it; he's the old French gentleman with the patch on his left eye. Queer, I thought at first, but after his wife finished three of these outfits, I recommended him to many of my acquaintances. I was complimented by a few gentlemen when I wore the blue one to a stage act I attended last month."

"Splendid," says Monroe. "I'll have to venture there on my next trip."

Sam drives up to the front porch and waits for Monroe to board the carriage. Quincy looks out the window and points. "I believe our ride is here," he says. "Shall we go?"

"Not yet. I can't go in this old outfit," protests Monroe. "I'll have Delilah find me a more appropriate attire for the meeting."

Upon Elmira's return, many express their sorrow over her sister's departure.

"We all believe those physicians in Boston have the experience to care for people in Mary's condition." They say, expressing their sympathy.

Elmira has never been without Mary for most all her life, and now that she's gone, she feels she's lost a part of her. She does not leave her farm for a week, for all she can think about is Mary – and what she will do to Monroe when the time comes. She sends two of her witches to the plantation to keep her informed on what Monroe is doing. She tells them to keep an eye on Agatha and if she is entertaining anyone other than the slave boy. Elmira gazes out her kitchen window looking across the flax field at Keith's farm, thinking about Dorothy and Clarence.

She begins to laugh aloud and says, "Dorothy." And then she says her name again, "Dorothy Adams. If you and that scarecrow of an uncle are still alive, I'll get you yet. Don't think for one moment that I've forgotten about you."

Elmira walks to the door In anger, grabs her broom, extends it toward the sky, and screams in bitter anger, "I'll find you, Dorothy Adams, and when I do, I'll make you wish you were never born." Then she flies off in no particular direction at lightning speed, flying in large circles above the woods of the North Country and the Canadian colonies. While flying over both countries, she's reminded of what Mary would always say, "It's so peaceful and so beautiful." Elmira begins to calm down and fly down to the earth. She walks around for a while, seeing what Mary was referring to. She finds herself walking on the earth for hours – even days. She enjoys the freedom away from the township and all the worries and problems. For the moment, she is just happy to get away.

"Oh, Mary," says Elmira, "If I had only taken more time to be with you, we could have seen these things together." She sits on top of a mountain on a large flat boulder eating nuts and berries. She looks across the land and sits there for most of the afternoon. *Where are you, Mary?* She wonders. Reluctantly, she gets up and flies low and slow on her broom across the land until she arrives back at her farm. Amanda is there when she arrives.

"Is everything all right?" Amanda asks.

"Not really, but it's as right as it's going to be," Elmira responds.

"Where did you go?" Amanda asks.

Laughing softly and sitting down in Mary's favorite chair, Elmira says, "Oh, I took one of Mary's tours. Anyway, what do you have for me?"

"Nothing," says Amanda. "I thought I would come over and keep you company. Everyone at the mill wishes you well."

"Have you heard from Hanna or Ambrose? Have they come back from the plantation?" Elmira inquires.

"Not yet, but I don't expect we should hear from them until the week's end."

"Okay," Elmira says.

After a month, bales of cotton finally arrive at the township by wagon. Everyone is excited, and they reassign the workers to rework the cotton to ready it for the spinners. Winfred is there when they unload the cotton, and so is Jeremiah Jameston. Jeremiah isn't too happy because he has heard that Mr. Quincy Eagleton is resigning his post to pursue a cotton plantation in Virginia. He has not bothered to mention it to him. Jameston was never privy to Eagleton's expeditions back and forth to the plantations until they took place; his payments are small and inconsistent from Monroe, and now he feels betrayed.

Two more magistrates must be elected, and he does not know where to turn. He knows that he will report to the governor of the Massachusetts colonies and will have to find the right man for the job. Jeremiah is not an eloquent speaker like Monroe and Eagleton. He has always relied on Eagleton to do all the speaking. Now, faced with being Winfred and Elmira's only opponents, he thinks it is best to patch things up. Everyone has put the witch trials behind them so their town can grow. Jameston does not want to be the only one holding a grudge against Elmira and her family; he wants to let the townspeople know that he is now in full support of the mill and will do everything he can to help make it as successful as possible. He pulls Winfred aside and asks if he can stay a little later that night. He has something to show Winford in the financials.

In the evening, Jameston hands Winfred the Accounting Ledger and asks, "What do you not see?"

Winfred had already looked through the book a couple of years before they took the expedition to New York. He knew then Monroe was ciphering monies from the treasury and keeping it out of the books. Not wanting to play games with Jeremiah, he simply says, "I am already aware of it. Why did you wait two years to confess?"

"Well… I, um…" Jeremiah has no real answer, but he says, "I just wanted you to be informed that we have no real proof that Monroe and Eagleton pilfered monies to secure the land. They had to get funding from the old Virginia Company to secure everything else. They needed the land first or would not have gotten the money needed to start the plantation."

Winfred sits in his chair with his index finger on the side of his nose and his chin resting in his hand. Staring up at Jeremiah, who goes on as though he had nothing to do with Monroe and Quincy, he mocks Jeremiah.

"Poor innocent Jeremiah, left holding a bag of manure, are you?" says Winfred.

"No, not quite so innocent, but I would like to be pardoned of these things," says Jameston. "I would like to support our town, its people, its mill, and the new tavern proposed for next year."

Jameston is one who will side with whoever seems to be carrying the biggest stick. Now fearing he will be the one to face criminal charges, he wants to parley.

"Did you notice the amount of cotton that came in?" Jeremiah asks.

"I did," Winfred replies. "What of it?"

"Well, as you know, I took on the responsibilities for the town, for all things imported from the harbor. I believe I was a great student of the weights and measurements that I've seen shipped in and out of the ports of Boston and New York. I've shipped our raw materials from here to England, and if I should say, I know what ten percent of cotton looks like, and what I saw today wasn't ten percent."

Elmira walks in. "Well, don't stop there," she says. "How much do you estimate we received?"

Both men jump up from their seats.

"My lord, Elmira, must you send us to our graves a little early?" Winfred asks.

"Sorry, gentlemen, since I did not get a chance to talk to you after the cotton arrived today, I thought I would come by and talk to you here," explains Elmira. "I talked to Joan, and she informed me that you were meeting with Mr. Jameston tonight. I wanted to give you a list of women who can start working the cotton and inform you that three more women joined the mill."

"Have a seat, Ms. Pembroke." Winfred motions for Elmira to take a seat. "Thank you for the list. I'll be sure to go over it in the morning."

"You're welcome, Mr. Gaines. And now, Mr. Jameston, about those numbers?" Elmira asks.

"Well, Ms. Pembroke, I'm not sure I should divulge such information to you," says Jameston curtly.

"Oh Jameston, for heaven's sake, she's already heard," scoffs Winfred. "Could you please get on with it?"

Clearing his throat, Jameston says, "Well, according to my estimate… the bales of cotton you received are less than one percent of the gross. Most plantations divide their cotton between England and other colonies and places worldwide. I guess you received about two, maybe three percent of the cargo sent out to the other colonies, excluding what's sent to England or vice versa. I don't know."

He continues, "Now, hear me out here for a second. I'm not sure if Mr. Wilson's statement was for the gross amount or the net. I do remember he said his obligation was to England and the other colonies, so it can be construed as a percentage of what is sent out to the other colonies."

"So what do you think, Mr. Jameston?" Winfred asks.

"Well, it does leave credence to the percentage more than the gross part," Jameston admits.

"I would agree, but I think we'll get started with what we have, and I'll leave all this to the two of you." Elmira excuses herself and leaves the building to retire to her farm.

"I don't think it was wise to divulge that information to her," whines Jameston to Winfred. "If word gets around, it could lead to an investigation."

"Actually, Jameston, an investigation was launched over a year ago," counters Winfred. "It was decided that since the money wasn't logged in the books, it would be hard to prove. A lot of things went on in those days, and now people just want to carry on. The only thing we could get on Monroe is if he defaults on the delivery of the cotton. Well, he delivered, and we have no cause to pursue legal matters. I am glad you came forward on your part in this crime, but you may want to think about resigning your post – turn in your wig, one might say."

"You can't threaten me, Winfred Gaines. You're not as innocent as you play. Everyone knows that you've kept that hussy Elmira's bed mighty warm through many of our cold winters," threatens Jameston.

"In that case, Mr. Jameston, you telling everybody what they already know won't be news at all, now will it?" says Winfred. "Be sure to put out the lamps before you leave, Mr. Jameston. Oil isn't cheap, you know. We'll talk more about your resignation in the morning."

Jameston fumes when he leaves the building, not putting out a single lamp and not bothering to close the door behind him. Elmira watches in the dark as both men exit the building.

"I'm not so sure Mr. Jameston is the best choice to take Monroe's place at the plantation. What do you think, Elmira?" Amanda asks.

"Oh, he'll do well," replies Elmira. "He's a fool, but he's not stupid; he knows which direction the wind is blowing. I'll help him raise the sails and get him turned in the wind as he should." She continues, "I'll suggest it over the next few weeks to stir his heart. We have a lot of leverage with this scared little rabbit. I feel a storm coming over the waters of the James River looming; I hope Monroe's carriage floats and his fat blubbering ass can swim."

Elmira and Amanda put out the lanterns and closed the door before they left.

Monroe is on a roll; he's on top of the world, and no one can tell him what to do. Agatha goes to him and asks for a buggy to ride to Middle Plantation with her friends, but he tells her that it is still being built. It has been a year now, and she still relies on her neighbors to pick her up. When he purchased his new buggy and it arrived, she thought it was the one that she had long been waiting for, only to find it was not; Monroe uses it only when he wants to drive himself to Middle Plantation or Jamestown. Tired of his lies, Agatha marches into his parlor and demands that he have her buggy built or purchased, or she will do it herself.

"If I can't use my own buggy, I will use the carriage when you are using the buggy," says Agatha. "And I will use the buggy when you are using the carriage. You have lied to me for more than a year, and I have not said a word, but now I want what is mine. All I ask for is a buggy, and you have denied me even that."

Monroe gets up from his seat and grabs her by the throat. Throwing her out of the office to the floor, he points his fat finger down at her.

Straddling his wife, and says, "You are never to enter this office again, and if you want a buggy, I'll have Eli the blacksmith and his son build you one from the stables." Monroe pauses. "Hell, woman, go and tell the boy yourself. I'm sure he can use some scrap wood out there."

He turns to Delilah and says, "Go out to the stables and tell them, boys, to build Mrs. Wilson a nice little buggy here."

Delilah simply stands there, not knowing whether Monroe is joking or serious.

But Monroe demands, "Go on and do what I told you to do. Go tell them boys to build her a buggy, and tell them to make sure it has wheels. I wouldn't want her dragging on her ass all the way into town."

Agatha slowly picks herself up off the floor and walks away. Monroe charges after her, grabbing her by her hair with both hands and whispering in her ear. "Never talk to me like that in front of these niggers again, you hear me?" He yanks her head back and forth while she tries to pull away. Then he pushes her away from him, and she yelps.

"All these years, you have never talked to me or treated me this way before," snaps Agatha. "I looked past your indiscretions and gave you everything you wanted. Yet, when I ask you for a buggy, you treat me worse than one of the whores you're sleeping with."

Monroe looks around and sees two of the house servants who are watching, and in his rage, he uses the back of his hand to slap his wife, knocking her back onto the floor. Standing over her, he says,

"The next time, I'll use my whip on your backside. Now get your ass up to your room!"

He turns to the servants and demands that they get back to work. As everyone rushes off, Agatha stands up and wipes the blood from her mouth and nose. She walks back into her room, leaving the door open, and falls face down on her bed. Winnie, one of the house servants, knocks on the door and brings her a wet towel for her tears and a warm towel for her face.

"I so sorry, Miss," says Winnie. "It seems he gets meaner every day. It must be that disease."

Agatha listens to her humming a tune that she often hears around the plantation. All she can do is lie down and cry.

"Miss, can I tell you something?" whispers Winnie.

Agatha looks at the house servant and says, "Sure you can. What is it?"

Winnie bends down close so that no one can hear. "You being watched, Miss," she says. "I think they know about that boy Ben who works with the cows. They know he comes to your room every time Mr. Wilson stays some days into town on business."

Agatha jumps out of bed and walks over to the door, closing it quickly.

"Tell me everything you know," she demands.

"I don't want to get in no trouble, Miss." Winnie's voice is trembling.

"Don't worry," Agatha comforts her. "You won't. What you tell me here stays in this room."

"Well," says Winnie. "We all see the light in this room when it goes out, but Mr. Andrews also saw it one night. He waited for that boy to come out from hidin', and he followed him to the house. I don't know if he told Mr. Wilson or not, but he knows. You best not send for him for a while, for if they catch him and you, they kill him and seeing how Mr. Wilson is treatin' you, he gives you the whip for sho. Back at the plantation I came from; they killed the slave and the woman when they caught them, so you watch yourself."

A knock at the door silences Winnie. Agatha says, "Come in."

Delilah, Winnie's sister, walks in. "I did as the master said," she says. "I tells Eli, and Eli tells me, 'I sho be happy to build her a buggy.'"

"Eli, he be a good man with his hands, ma'am," says Winnie. "He'll go into the town and get what he needs. But it'll have to wait a bit. Eli not due into town for supplies till after Sunday." Delilah says excitedly.

"That's fine, ladies," says Agatha. "I've waited over a year, so what's another week?"

Delilah smiles and asks, "Do you need anything else?"

Agatha rises from the bed and looks out the window.

"No, thank you," she replies. "That will be all."

Winnie and Delilah leave the room, shutting the door behind them.

When Monroe watched Agatha walk slowly up the stairs, he wished he hadn't slapped her the way he did. Although it felt good to him, he now knows he has total control. This makes him wonder whether he could ever use his whip on his wife. After thinking about what she said, he goes to the stables to talk to Sam and Eli, two of the best blacksmiths in the area. Tom, Eli's son, is there as well.

"Morning, Master, Sir."

"Morning, boys," says Monroe. "Listen, I don't want my wife in my carriage or my buggy, you hear me? She comes fussing about wanting to use either of them; you better tell her she can't use them, or you'll get the whip."

"Yes, we be sho to tell her. That Delilah came in telling us you want us to build Miss a buggy. That true, Sir?"

Monroe considers it. "Yes, go ahead." He says, "But it better not interfere with your work. You work on it in your spare time - and boys... I do mean in your spare time."

"Yes, sir, we sho-do understand."

"Eli," Monroe calls. "Have Tom saddle my horse; I'm going to take a ride to the fields."

"Yes, sir."

Agatha watches him from her window as he rides off into the fields. It is a hot summer day, and the heat is bad enough, but the flies and mosquitos worsen it. She had never raised her voice to her husband until she arrived at the plantation, nor had she slept with another man. She misses the affection and the attention he once bestowed upon her, yet she is grateful to him for not giving her that dreadful disease. She thinks to herself, *I'll be sixty-six this fall, and I'm behaving like a child stealing away in the night to meet her secret lover.* Then she thinks about that Mr. Andrews; she's seen him lurking about,

"Why hasn't he told my husband?" she speaks softly to herself. "Maybe he doesn't know the boy is meeting me in this room? Maybe he's waiting to get more evidence. He needs a witness to verify what he believes to be transpiring, and if that's so, he'll get nothing here from me. I'll take heed to Winnie's warnings. I just have to get a message to Ben, or I could have Winnie get it to him for me."

She calls Winnie to her room; Agatha closes the door after she enters.

"Winnie, I want you to tell Ben we are being watched, and we can't be together anymore," says Agatha. "You tell him if he wants to live, he'll understand. You get that message to him right away. You do that for me, okay?"

"Yes, Miss, I'll get him that message as soon as I can." Winnie walks to the door.

"Winnie," Agatha calls.

"Yes?"

"Thank you."

Winnie smiles and replies, "Welcome, Miss." Then she leaves the room.

It's been two weeks, and Agatha walks to the stable to see her new buggy that Sam and Eli have built. Sam went to town to get the metal, wheels, boards, leather for the cover, and the springs he needed under the seat. He and Eli worked on the buggy together; when Eli had spare time, he worked on it, and Sam did the same. Together they finished it in two weeks. Delilah tells Agatha that the work is done, and she accompanies her to the stables.

On their way to the stables, Mr. Andrews walks up to Agatha and grabs her arm.

"Is there something I can do for you, Mr. Andrews?" she asks.

"I know about you and that nigger," he says.

Agatha pulls her arm free. "One, unless you have proof of what you say, I suggest you be very careful what you say, and two, if you ever grab me like that again, I'll have my husband tie you up to that tree over there and whip you within an inch of your life. Now, is there something else you have to say?"

After a moment of silence, Agatha says, "I didn't think so."

With that, she and Delilah walk away from him angrily. He watches her as she continues to the stable. When they walk in, she cannot believe her eyes.

She holds her hands in front of her mouth and says, "It's beautiful, Eli."

Delilah interjects, "I told you he good with his hands. Ain't it beautiful?"

"It's as grand as Mr. Wilson's," admires Agatha. Then she asks, "Has Mr. Wilson seen it?

"Yes'm, he sho did, and he couldn't believe it either," says Eli. "He said we musta gone out and somehow paid for it. Now he wants me and Sam to build him one with two benches, one in the back and one up front. Sadly he tells her. "Master said you have to find a horse for your buggy; he says you can't have none of his."

Agatha drops her arms to her sides. "He wants me to pull it myself, I suppose." She appears disgusted.

"Don't worry, Miss," Sam says, "I'll see if someone has one for sale, and I'll tell Delilah here and…"

Agatha cuts him off. "I don't have any money, Sam, but thanks all the same."

She turns and walks toward the front of the plantation and down the road. Monroe had the slaves build the road out of clay and sand. He had nearly all the slaves walk on it for hours to press it down daily for a week. Agatha pulls her shoes off to feel the warm summer sand beneath her feet. She directs her face to the sun with her eyes closed and continues walking to the end of the road. She leans against the fence post for a moment, walks across the main road, and then through a small patch of weeds, trees, and bushes to the riverbank. She thinks about how tired she is of plantation life and wishes she were back in Massachusetts with all her friends and closer to her family. She finds a large, flat stone to sit on and lets the water cool her feet while she thinks about her new life, or the lack thereof.

Hanna and Ambrose have been walking behind her for a while. At first, they thought she would jump into the river and drown herself, but when they saw that she sat on the stone with her feet in the water, they knew then she just wanted to be alone. They wanted to take Mr. Andrews and beat him with three willow switches, all braided together when he grabbed Agatha, but at this time, they were only there to observe. Now they will have to tell Elmira what he did.

Elmira is already on the warpath back home. She wants to end this, but things with Mr. Jameston are moving a little slower than anticipated. The news hits Elmira hard when they tell her Monroe choked, pulled her hair, and slapped Agatha and that he even wanted to use his horsewhip on her. Elmira does not know how long she has to press Jameston, but his wavering is wearing thin. So far, Jameston has gained Elmira's trust. She helped convince Winfred Gaines to refrain from forcing Jameston out of office. He now talks to her more as a friend than a foe.

Elmira is losing patience with Monroe, although he has been sending more cotton their way. It even seems he's surprised Winfred with the flow of cotton.

That night Agatha waits in the foyer for Monroe to leave the parlor so she can ask if he would please give her a horse or the money to purchase one. He does not offer her any money, and whenever she needs clothes or materials, he sends one of the slaves to the market in Middle Plantation or Jamestown. He controls all aspects of her life, even more than he did back at the colony.

She stands before him and asks, "Will you please give me a horse for the buggy?"

"I'll think about it," he replies.

"No, you're going to tell me now, right here, right now," demands Agatha.

He raises his hand as if to slap her, "I said I'll think about it," he repeats. "Now, out of my way. You're lucky I allowed those boys to build you that damn buggy."

Agatha doesn't think the horse is worth the pain, so she gives way as Monroe walks up to his room. She remembers he brought one of his whores home and had her tied to the bed facedown while he used his strap on her rear end. She's not sure what happened, and she's not going to ask, but Agatha knows he had her removed from the plantation that night.

Agatha has grown tired of hearing what Monroe is doing, especially since her room is direct across the hall from his, so she moves farther from the front of the stairs. Monroe has built a grand mansion with eight bedrooms and a small sewing room upstairs; downstairs is his parlor, his office, a library, a grand dining room, and a smaller dining room he has never used. There is also a food-prepping room and an elaborate kitchen.

Agatha asks herself, "Who is this man? What has become of my husband? This place has changed him, so I no longer know who he is." She watches him walk up the stairs, then she makes her way over to the parlor, to a chair in the corner, and sits in the dark, wishing she had the old Monroe back. Then she wished he were dead because that's what he is to her now.

Time has changed two men, and it is changing another. Elmira's thoughts run free through her mind as she has taken a few of Mary's tours to clear her head. Monroe has got to go, and she has to convince Jameston to take his place after he's gone. With every report from the plantation, If she fails to persuade him, she will have to find someone else she trusts

She whispers, "if I should just," but then a thought comes to mind. *I believe I have my answer.*

She takes a deep breath of fresh air and looks down at the valley below and then up to the sky.

"Thank you, Mary; now I see why you went off to these majestic places for some peace of mind and..." *Wait a minute? She thought,* "Did I just say "majestic"? And then she laughs, "I'm even talking to myself," Elmira laughs some more as she lies in the soft grass on the mountain, looking up toward the sky. She sighs, stands up, and grabs her broom.

"Until next time," she says, flying back to her farm.

Quincy Eagleton and his wife, Rose, aren't as happy as they thought they would be after meeting with Monroe for the third time in the week. Monroe has upset Rose because he said she should have stayed behind, allowing the men to conduct their business properly without the influence of a woman. Quincy and Monroe have not seen eye to eye since their heated argument over Monroe's lack of professional etiquette. Not only is Monroe demanding thirty percent of his cotton and tobacco products, but he is also asking for twenty percent of the gross sales from both. Monroe is furious that Quincy has rejected his proposal.

"You would have never gotten that plantation if it weren't for me," he snapped. "I stood before the investors and gave you credit – credit you didn't deserve. I gave you the money to get started here, and it was I who wasted my time grooming you to become the respectable planter I am today. Quincy, you are a buffoon and an ass. I will ensure you don't get another pence more from the investors, and you'll see how far you get without me."

Quincy bites his lips and keeps quiet.

"I tell you, I will not accept you back here in my home unless you grovel at my feet, kiss my ass, and beg for forgiveness."

Once Monroe completes his rant, Quincy and his wife, Rose, leave the plantation to return to their Massachusetts Township. Quincy apologizes to Rose for Monroe's behavior.

Quincy consoles Rose on their ride back to Middle Plantation.

"I have absolutely no clue what has gotten into that man," he says. "I have no idea who that person is. Six months ago, I was talking to a totally different human being. This evening I was ready to fight our way out of there if I had to, but to be honest, I was terrified and shaken. That man back there is a madman. Absolute power has gripped his soul, and he's oblivious to the world around him. My God, Rose, I could see you were horrified by his demented and delusional state of mind."

Rose is too shocked to speak. She pulls both blankets up to their shoulders, for the late October night air is as cold as it is back home. She kisses Quincy and thanks him for standing up to Monroe. He holds her to his chest as she leans against him in the buggy they borrowed from a business acquaintance who lives in Middle Plantation. When they cross the river on the ferry, Rose looks behind them and utters a sigh of relief.

"The more distance we put between that man and us, the better," she says. "Oh, Quincy, I know I've said thank you, but I do thank you so much for shaking your fist at that tyrant. You were so courageous today."

"Well, if I had to stand there any longer, it would have been very embarrassing and painfully obvious that I had soiled my clothes."

They laugh aloud and ride on to Middle Plantation for a good night's sleep. Both Quincy and Rose look forward to their trip home.

"Well, darling," he says, "I'm afraid I've exhausted all our monies on that damned plantation; we don't have enough to complete the purchase of the things that will make it complete, and I'm not sure how we are going to come up with the rest of the money to do so."

Consoling him, Rose says, "That's okay; I'm sure we'll find a way."

"Well, I guess we can look at it this way," says Quincy. "We won't have to pay all those investors back. In our first meeting, they were like vultures on a dead caucus."

"How dreadful," Rose replies. "Quincy?"

"Yes, dear."

"Do you think we can go to the market tomorrow before we board the ship and buy that hat I saw in the shop? I would hate to return and have nothing to show for this trip."

"Darling?" He calls.

"Yes, dear." She answers.

"Do you think we can afford it?" He asks.

"Oh Quincy, please, it's only one small item." She whines.

"The last time you said that, we left the shop with five boxes." He retorts.

"Just one item," she pleads.

"If you promise only one item, then we'll have a go at it," he says, "but not one box more."

The weather is cold, and the month of November is only a week away. After Mr. Eagleton and Rose return from the plantation, they meet Elmira coming from the new market they built in the town. She was going to pass Mr. Eagleton without speaking, but he stopped her to say thank you, for he heard that she stood up on Jameston's behalf, which would allow him to keep his post and his dignity.

"I would never have believed it, but I thank you for that on his behalf." He says.

"You are welcome, and congratulation on your new venture," she replies.

"Well, I'm not sure if congratulations are in order yet; we still have the matter of raising the money. I'm afraid Monroe has put a damper on things, and he has cut me off from the investors."

"I see," says Elmira. . "I was talking to a few of our friends, and I heard about that and a few other things that madman has done." She looks at Quincy, baiting him for more information.

"Madman is right," says Quincy. "I don't know what has come over that man; you might say his disease has made him a bit bonkers."

"I know what you mean," says Elmira. She had already heard from Hanna on the matter. "But regarding your investment, I was just going to the new tavern to talk with Keith and Mr. Gaines. We may be able to help you, and in return, you can help us acquire more cotton. The mill has grown, and we have more spinners than cotton."

They walk to the tavern and discuss a deal that will work for the township and the new plantation. After two days, they finish negotiating the contract terms that all parties will agree on. Finally, Elmira is ready to wipe Monroe and Mr. Andrews off the face of the earth. They are going to get twenty percent of the gross of the cotton produced, and they are going to be paid back with interest on their investment. She knows with Monroe gone; she can prove he was cheating them on the cotton. She will demand the slaves and send them to the new plantation while it is being built, and with a certificate showing that the property was purchased with funding from the colony, they will demand all the cotton that has not been harvested. Elmira hopes to send Jason to the courts in Middle Plantation or Jamestown to explain their case after she burns Monroe's plantation down.

Earlier at the plantation, Mr. Andrews overhears Monroe's argument with Quincy and decides it may not be the best time to talk. After a month, he believes he has gathered enough information to approach Monroe. He knocks on the open door of the parlor.

"What is it, Mr. Andrews?" Monroe mutters.

"Well, sir, I'm really not sure how to tell you this, but... well, sir, I've been seeing some things going on that I find a bit disturbing." Mr. Andrews speaks in a cowardly manner.

Monroe tells him to walk with him to the office and closes the door. "Now tell me what it is you find so disturbing."

Outside the door, Delilah is listening.

"I believe that your wife and that slave boy Ben have been... you know, doing things when you are out conducting business for this great plantation."

Monroe rises from his chair. "My wife, you say?"

"Now, I know that you require proof or a witness other than me, and I want you to know that I have one. I understand a thing like this is not something you would say about a good Christian woman, but I just couldn't keep silent any longer. It's just not right for her to treat a gentleman like yourself this way. It's just not right." He says.

Monroe is still fuming over Quincy's rejection, and now he's red in the face, sucking air through tight lips, and he's clenched his fist into a ball.

"You better damn well have a good witness because you are one word away from my whipping every inch of skin off your backside," screams Monroe. "How dare you come in here with such accusations?"

Delilah can hear him getting closer to the door, and she dashes to the stairs as fast as she can. Monroe opens the door and calls out, "Delilah!"

"Yes, sir, I'm just coming down the stairs." She hurries to him.

"You go back up those stairs and bring that woman here to me!" He shouts. "Right now, Delilah."

"Yes, sir," Delilah responds.

Monroe looks at Mr. Andrews, then at the stairs, waiting for Agatha to come down. Delilah rushes to Agatha's door and knocks.

"Miss… the master wants you down in the office right away."

Agatha opens the door; Delilah doesn't wait for her to ask why she's being summoned.

"That Mr. Andrews is having a word with yo husband."

Agatha takes a deep breath and asks Delilah to help her get dressed. While she's getting dressed, she whispers, "God save me." Then she begins the long walk down the hall.

Before Delilah goes up the stairs, Mr. Andrews tells Monroe that his witness is being held at the front door. Monroe gives him leave to bring the witness in.

In walks a young slave girl of about twelve years old.

"Now, girl, if you lie to us, you know you'll get the whip, don't you?" Mr. Andrews warns.

She holds her head down and responds, "Yeah, sum."

"You tell Mr. Wilson here what you told me earlier." He presses.

Earlier, Mr. Andrews threatened to sell the young girl and her family to a plantation in South Carolina. He told them they would be sold to different plantations all over the South.

Monroe takes his hand and rests it under the girl's chin so that he can look her in the eyes. He tries to calm himself for a moment. "Go ahead," he prompts her.

But the girl starts crying when she sees Agatha approaching. Monroe peers out the door, and Agatha walks in. He tells the girl, "Tell us what you told Mr. Andrews."

"Yeah, sum," she sobs. And then she tells them. "When you go out and spend the night in town, Miss Lights a lamp in the room. Then it goes out, and that boy comes to huh room."

Agatha's nerves cause her to sweat, but she just stands there idly, listening to the girl. Her eyes, however, are on Mr. Andrews the whole time. Monroe dismisses everyone and walks over to Agatha, punching her right in the face and knocking her to the floor

"Get up and go straight to your room!" he yells to his wife. "Delilah, help her to her room."

"Yes, um, Master."

"Mr. Andrews, go and get Ben and tie him to the tree outside."

Winnie and Delilah help Agatha to her room. Disoriented, she sits silent, knowing she's been condemned to God. She fears that Ben will be whipped and hanged this very day. She cries face down on her bed. Monroe orders two of the men who held the slave girl outside to go up and tie his wife to the bed as they did with the other woman he sent away. When they get to her room, she stands up and tells them to have Monroe do it himself.

Bo, one of the men that came from the Carolinas with Mr. Andrews and his brother William, tells her, "You're in no position to suggest anything." William punches her in the face and knocks her to the floor.

They pick her up off the floor, rip her clothes off, and strap her hands and feet to the bedpost, waiting for Monroe to enter the room. Monroe arrives with the Bible in one hand and John Bowes's whip in the other; he hands Mr. Andrews the whip and tells the others to go and help Mr. Graves with his wife's "nigger lover." Monroe stands behind Agatha, seething over the fact that she has disgraced and defiled herself with a nigger. Agatha pleads with her husband.

"Monroe," she says, bleeding from her nose and mouth, "please, you have to be reasonable. You're not thinking clearly. Please don't do this, Monroe. Listen, if you let me go, I'll leave, and you'll never hear from me again. Let me go, Monroe, please." She begins to scream. "Are you listening to me? Monroe, please, I didn't say anything when you were stealing from the treasury and the townspeople. I didn't say anything when you came back from New York with that horrible disease or when you had those slave girls murdered after you gave them that disease. Oh, Monroe, if you have mercy, the Lord will have mercy on you."

Agatha is crying and shaking with fear. She hears Monroe taking a deep breath and realizes that he's not listening to a word she's saying.

She whispers a short prayer. "Lord, be merciful on my soul. Receive me now, and let my suffering be swift."

Monroe approaches the window and opens it. He says, "I consider myself a good Christian man." He said without looking at his wife, now speaking loud enough for all to hear. "I offered you a life you would never have had in that godless town with that murderous whore Elmira. Deuteronomy 25 states that a guilty person should receive for punishment forty stripes, but in the book of 2 Corinthians 11:24, Paul says he received forty lashes save one. If I remember correctly, your friend condemned her own sister to the same amount, and Mr. Kirts carried out her punishment. You've had your time to pray, woman, and now it's time to pay."

"You're no Christian," she says. "You're a diseased devil."

Without turning around, Monroe points his finger, motioning for Mr. Andrews to proceed.

Agatha holds her breath, pressing her face down onto the bed and biting hard into the sheets. Everyone outside can hear her screaming, along with the whirl and crack of the whip each time it cuts into her flesh. Winnie and Delilah cry as they hide in one of the rooms across the hall, waiting for the whole ordeal to be over and hoping desperately that Agatha will live through it.

Eli, Sam, and Tom sit on their stools crying as well as the slaves and hired hands, for they love Mrs. Wilson. Agatha has always cared for everyone on the plantation. Lester Graves did not want anything to do with it and took his family to their cabin, shut the door, and prayed for Agatha. They know she was treated no better than the slaves, and often worse than they were.

They've all noticed that after six lashes, Agatha stops screaming, but Monroe does not tell Mr. Andrews to stop. Instead, he keeps on whipping Agatha with a heavier hand. In this eerie silence, they can hear the whirl of the whip before it cuts even more flesh from her lifeless body.

Elmira is on one of Mary's tours when Ambrose arrives to tell her that she must get to the plantation as soon as possible.

Ambrose approaches Amanda and asks, "Where's Elmira?"

"I don't know, but I can certainly summon her," Amanda said. Elmira is on her way back to the farm, but she's still hundreds of miles away. When she realizes she is being summoned, she returns at lightning speed.

Ambrose franticly begins to explain what has happened. She says, "Hanna was with Agatha before Monroe started the whipping. That was a few minutes ago, and it's possible that he has already finished by now. The men were waiting on Monroe to finish whipping Agatha before they got started on the boy. William and Bo staked him to the ground face up, beat the boy's face in, cut off his private parts, and then they will whip him face up."

Elmira has already transformed, and her breathing is like the sound of a lioness calling her cubs. She knows it is too late to save her friend and that it is time for her to share her plan with the girls. She does not care if they see her true form. Then Elmira vanishes from their sight. The girls knew Agatha as a soft-spoken woman, so the news of her whipping crushed their spirits. They knew if she was caught, things would go terribly bad for her.

All the witches are at the old settlement grounds, almost all crying for Elmira's friend. When Hanna shows up, she appears to them on her knees and tells them.

"I knew Agatha could not endure the pain and that Monroe had Mr. Andrews beat her harder than they whip most men. So, I held Agatha's head face down on the bed in cloaked form. Then, after the sixth lash, she died." She continues, "Even though she was dead, Monroe gave her all thirty-nine lashes."

"He had no mercy for her," Ambrose spoke, choking and crying.

Hanna continues. "Monroe called Winnie and Delilah into the room and told them to clean up the mess and toss her body deep in the marsh. He said she was not to be buried on his plantation. Winnie and Delilah wrapped her body in the sheets and had Eli and Sam take her to their slave house to be cleaned up for burial. They are going to bury her in the slave graveyard, no matter what Monroe orders them to do. I couldn't stay and see what they would do to that slave boy's body. The two other men had already mutilated him before Mr. Anderson finished."

Elmira's body is totally engulfed in flames; she is so angry that she can hardly get her words out. She walks in circles around the grounds, leaving flames behind her with every step. Clenching her fist and screaming like a banshee, she turns to the girls and shouts.

"Prepare for war!" she cries. Still circling, Elmira continues, "We are going to burn that damn plantation to the ground, and then we are going to rip four men a new ass, but not before we take them away from the plantation. I have something special for Monroe, that self-loathing son-of-a-bitch. Meet me here tomorrow night, and we'll go over what each of you must do. Right now, I want all of you to leave me, and I'll see you tomorrow."

When she has finished speaking, the others stand there in silence. Then Elmira turns her back to them, screaming, and vanishes in a thunderous explosion; the witches are all showered with flames and debris that knock them to the ground from the shockwave.

Unity looks at Amanda. "I think she's really mad."

Amanda replies, "You think?"

Monroe is still angry with Quincy and ensures no investor will touch him in a hundred years. Quincy is in his mid-sixties and thinks he will ask his eldest son Jason to help with the new plantation. He will co-run the daily operations of the business.

Quincy sees the plantation purely as a business venture and will ensure that it is run that way. He thinks of his confrontation with Monroe and knows that he is more afraid of Elmira than Monroe. Monroe's threats will not get in the way of his plans to build the plantation. Quincy has his son, Jason, from his first marriage, go over the charter for the plantation. In the meantime, Elmira needs information proving that Monroe took money from the townspeople.

When Hanna reported to Elmira on the day Agatha was murdered, she told her that the poor woman confessed that Monroe stole from the township before Agatha was whipped.

"How did she know?" asked Elmira. "Was there something that Monroe left behind?"

So, Elmira and ten other women march over to Monroe's old house and tear it apart, looking for something that would indicate his treachery. They want desperately to prove that the plantation is legally theirs. They had to match the amount Monroe paid for the Virginia land before he received the investments to build on the property. Elmira orders the others to search every wall and floorboard. As they storm the house, many of the townspeople stand outside watching. The women even throw furniture out of the house and into the snow-filled yard.

Winfred, Quincy, Jason, and Jeremiah stop by and ask, "What is going on?" Elmira tells them she knows that Monroe was taking money from the treasury and that they are looking for that proof.

"Well, Elmira," Winfred says, "it seems you have the whole town looking. Could you have been a little more discreet?

"I could have, but..."

Before she can finish her sentence, one of the women runs outside with a couple of ledgers she found under the floorboards and hands them to Elmira. Winfred looks at them over Elmira's shoulder.

"I say, do you mind if we take a look?" Winfred asks.

He opens one of the ledgers and finds dates and payments from the treasurer to Monroe.

"My God," Jeremiah says. "Why would the treasurer pay Monroe these sums of money?"

Silently, Quincy thinks back to the day he asked if Monroe left any evidence of the payments behind; now he knows why Monroe hesitated to answer.

"They date back twelve years," Winfred says.

"Mind if I take a look at the other book?" asks Jason.

Jason is a student of law, trained in England at the Inns of the court. As he reads, he walks off, muttering the word "interesting" under his breath.

As the others look on, Winfred calls to him, "I say, young fellow, what is it you find so interesting from that tattered old ledger?"

"Well, this old ledger might answer why Monroe was paid, as it seems, for doing absolutely nothing," Jason replies.

"Would you like to share that with the rest of us?" asks Jameston.

"Sorry old chap, it appears Mr. Monroe Wilson was blackmailing a Mr. Leopold Trenton," explains Jason. "Apparently, he found discrepancies in the accounts. Mr. Trenton was siphoning monies from the till, and this Mr. Wilson fellow profited up until Mr. Trenton passed away about six years ago. From my calculations, he got away with hundreds in change."

"Why, that's enough to purchase and build more than five plantations. Quincy states.

"Can we prove any of that money paid for the Virginia land?" Winfred inquires.

"Well, we'll have to find in one or both of these ledgers some sort of reference to such matters," says Jason.

Winfred hands him the other book, and they all walk back to the courthouse, debating the reasoning and gall of both men. Before Winfred leaves, he thanks Elmira.

"Well done," he says. "Once again, you've come through for the townspeople. I hate to muddle with such a great moment of triumph, but do you think your girls can tidy up before they return to the mill?"

Elmira smiles and says, "I'll do better than that."

Winfred walks away, looking back, for he is not quite sure what Elmira's intentions are. Elmira calls the girls together and asks them if they can return the next day. She encourages them to bring their husbands and young ones and tools for woodworking. She thanks them and asks them to go back to the mill.

About thirty people show up the next day at the old Wilson house. Elmira is waiting inside when they arrive.

"Good morning, everyone." She says. "I'm so happy you showed up in such great numbers. I will ask the young boys to take all the furniture to the mill so the carpenters can restore the pieces. As far as this house goes, I want it torn down piece by piece and take the lumber to the mill to be available for those who need to build a new house or barn. All the ladies, including myself, will cook and set up tables under the trees."

It isn't long before the whole place is abuzz with talk and noise of tearing down the old house and stables. By noon, there is nothing left of the house or stable on Monroe's property. Now Elmira turns the land over to the courthouse to be put up for sale, giving up her ownership, so there is nothing left to remind her of that old windbag.

Chapter 11
Monroe's Last Stand

After two days of researching the books in the warmth of the courthouse, they find links between the plantation and the money pilfered from the Williams River Township's treasury. All the men get together to discuss a strategy to carry out the next phase of their plan. They know they will have to appear at the Jamestown courthouse because the charter for the plantation would have been issued there. They inform the township of Monroe's treachery and will be traveling to Virginia to see if they can have the township recompensed for the monies they believe were taken by Monroe while he was mayor of the Williams River Township. Once they have properly examined their options, Jameston, Quincy, Winfred, and Jason leave the township to travel to Jamestown, Virginia, and to the site of the new plantation. Their expedition will take them to the Jamestown courthouse to look at the charter and determine how they should proceed with their claim on behalf of the Williams River Township. Then, the four of them will invite Monroe to Jamestown to view the books, defend himself in the courts, and then pay restitution to the township. After that, they will secure the lumber, workers, and slaves to build the new plantation with the monies they acquire from the settlement.

It has been two weeks since the men left the township for Virginia, and Elmira gathers all the girls together at the old settlement and informs them of her plans.

"I have waited far too long, and because of my delay, I have lost a dear friend," she says. "I am told that Monroe is in the town of Middle Plantation and will be back at his plantation in two days. Ladies, that fat bastard will never cross that river again, and we will burn that plantation to the ground."

"It's about time," said Joan James, whispering, one of Agatha's friends.

"When I get word that he has left Middle Plantation, I promise the skies will bear a storm never before seen in Virginia. It will pour freezing rain on that fat bastard Monroe as no one has ever seen before. A little rain will drive them to the ferry, and at that point, it will be too late to return to the town. We'll wait until they are in the middle of the river, and then we'll bring the heavens down on Monroe. When he gets on the ferry, we will make the waters too rough to move forward and too rough to go back; that's when I'll bring that windbag down to his knees."

The old settlement roars with the howl of the witches.

Elmira continues. "The rain and lighting will start a fire in the two houses closest to the mansion. That will force the slaves and the workers to leave their homes, and I want one fire to ignite another. I don't want the rain to extinguish the fire, so once everyone is out of the houses, I want one of you inside each home to set the structures ablaze from the inside. I want three of you inside the mansion and every room to be set on fire, one at a time. Spare no room inside that damned mansion!"

The witches listen without speaking a word.

"Then I want four of you to transform yourselves as help from the other plantation to keep the slaves from running away. No cotton or tobacco is to be touched, nor are any slaves. I want them alive, and I will personally deal with the four men myself; David Andrews, the two idiot brothers William and Bo Dain, and Monroe. Bring them to the place I told you about – and I want them in good health. I want them all stripped of their clothing and shoes, and I want you to bind their ankles with a strong rope and stake them to the ground. Then we'll deal with them all at daybreak."

Monroe is returning to the plantation in the late evening, just before nightfall. Sam notices the wind is picking up, and the waters are getting a little choppy. Rain begins to fall, which makes Sam wonder whether he should stop the coach and let Monroe know the river may very well be rougher by the time they arrive at the ferry.

George tells him, "Unless you wants the whip, you might wait for the right time, and that be at the ferry."

"You right, we can always turn back and go back from there," says Sam. "The only ones get rained on be us. I'm already cold, can't rightly feel my toes and fingers now.

"Mine too," agrees George. "Cold is bad, and now we get rained on too."

"Better the cold and rain than his whip," says Sam.

They haven't gone a mile when the rain begins to fall a little heavier. Sam stops the coach, gets down, and knocks on the coach's door.

"Master, you think we should turn back?" he asks Monroe. "We still have some miles fo' we get to the ferry, and that water looks a little rough for crossing," Sam said.

"Sam, you'd best let me worry about the weather, and you worry about all those damned holes you drive through," says Monroe. "Get back up there, and get us back to the plantation before I tan your hide."

It has been a long time since Monroe was last with a woman. They all fear catching his disease.

"Yes'um, Master," Sam responds.

He climbs back up to his seat, and George remarks, "Boy, don't you knows you too old to be getting whipped?"

"You just fetch yonder in that there box and get us mo' blankets," says Sam. "No time for funning; we catch our death a cold on this here, coach."

"That there water pretty rough," George says.

Monroe rides in the new coach, as he has Sam and George drive on. By Monroe's side is a young woman he has been seeing for the past few days in Middle Plantation, where he was on business. He thinks it is a good time to impress her by giving her a tour of his plantation and showing off the grandeur of his mansion. By the time they arrive at the ferry, some men are in a hurry to escape the freezing rain; their horses are in full gallop coming off the ferry. The ferryman, drenched and freezing, tell them it will be a rough ride, and he will need them to help pull the ferry across the river.

Sam says, "If'n it gets us across faster, I'll pull like five men."

He drives the coach onto the ferry. The horses are spooked by the lightning and the swaying of the ferry.

"You make sure you hold them horses steady, boy," the ferryman tells George. "I've never lost a customer, and I don't plan on losing none today."

Sam wants to tell Monroe that it will be a rough ride and that he may want to hold on as they cross the river. Inside the coach, Monroe is cursing the ferry for it's a very rough ride inside the coach. Elmira and Amanda are watching, hovering in the dark sky above, waiting for the ferry to get closer to the middle of the river. When they reach the point where she expects them to be, Anne and Sarah are upstream of the river waiting on Elmira's signal. They will then uproot two of the largest trees and send them downstream with the root base in front. When Elmira's hand flames up, they send the trees down the river.

It is hard for the ferryman and Sam to pull the ferry across the river, and George has a hard time keeping the horses steady. By the time they pull the ferry to the middle of the river, the rain is pouring down so hard they cannot see the bank of the south side; their hands are frozen, and their backs are aching so badly they can hardly pull, but they have hope they will make it to the other side. The ferryman asks Sam to hold on to the rope and not let go of it to rest for a couple of seconds while he warms his hands by cupping them together and blowing into them. When he looks up, he sees two huge trees about to ram the ferry. Before he can say anything, the first tree rams into the front of the ferry, sending Sam and the ferryman over the edge on the right side and knocking George to the floor. The second tree hits the ferry from the back while George is trying to stand and knocks him overboard on the other side. Sam and the ferryman manage to grab ahold of the branches of the first tree as it swings sideways and gets tangled in the rope.

George is struggling in the water, disappearing beneath the ferry. The rope breaks and both trees swing sideways, turning the ferry; then George pops up in front of the ferry, still struggling to stay afloat. One of the horses remains onboard the ferry, lying on its side and trying to get to its feet, while the other is in the water, kicking about in an attempt to escape the coach. George grabs ahold of the branches from the first tree, and they all wash down the river ahead of the ferry.

Elmira and Amanda jump from their brooms and come down so hard on the front of the ferry's deck that it shatters, freeing the horses and catapulting the coach into the air above their heads. Elmira and Amanda ascend quickly above the coach, and when the coach hits the water, they both come back down as hard as they did on the ferry, destroying the coach. Amanda grabs the woman and tosses her to the south side of the river, while Elmira grabs Monroe and tosses him to the north side of the river on the shoreline. Both Monroe and the woman are unconscious.

"Leave the woman; someone will find her later. Go to the plantation and help the girls, and when you finished, I want all of you to meet me at the appointed place." Elmira instructs Amanda.

At the plantation, the mansion has already ablaze. The ferryman, Sam, and George manage to let go of the tree they were using to float down the river and grab ahold of some of the other smaller trees at the edge of the river bank. Rebecca, Lucy, Margaret, and Premise have taken the image of four men from one of the nearby plantations arriving at the river where the ferryman, Sam, and George are holding onto the trees. They are too exhausted to climb out of the water and too afraid to let go of the trees. When they are helped out of the river, the men thank the disguised witches repeatedly.

"While we were crossing the river, we could not go any farther than the middle of it. It was raining so hard we couldn't see the rope in front of the ferry. I looked up, and two large trees rammed into the ferry, knocking us into the water." The ferryman informs them.

Lightning flashes all around them, and when they are less than half a mile from the plantation, they can see the flames rising high above the trees. Sam and George realize it is their home plantation.

"Sir," Sam calls out as they are closer to their home. "Me and George here is from that there burning plantation."

"And that is where we will turn you two over." One of the men says.

"Sir." Our master was in that coach on that ferry; we ain't to sho what happened to Mr. Wilson and his lady friend after we were thrown from the ferry."

"Mr. Wilson's a very big man around these parts. We'll search for them in the morning." Says another man.

After pulling the men out of the water, they lifted the ferryman up on one of the horses and made Sam and George run behind them until they reached the burning plantation. Sam and George are told to join the other slaves at the edge of the plantation property, where they collapse and lie on the ground, too tired to speak.

The blaze of the burning building is a welcome source of heat, and they are glad for it. They see the slaves gathering in one place with the men and their families in the pouring rain. Each time the lightning flashes and the thunder rolls, the women and children scream and cry.

The four men ask if they know if anyone is missing.

"There may be a couple of slaves and a few men who worked on the plantation that are unaccounted for. Other than that, I believe everyone is here." Lester Graves informs them.

As more men from other plantations rush in to help, they bring buggies, carts, and wagons.

"Do you men mind if the women and children can be taken to the nearest plantation to escape the rain? A couple of our men will accompany you if that is okay?" Lester asks

"Sure, let's get them on the wagons."

Once the workers' families are on board, the slave women and children climb onto separate wagons and are taken to the nearest plantation.

Lester asks Sam and George about Monroe.

"We got caught on the river when the ferry was torn apart by two large trees," Sam explains, shivering. "We got knocked off the ferry with the ferryman over yonder, and Mr. Wilson and his lady friend were still inside the coach. Don't rightly know what happened after that; we too busy try'n to hold on to them trees afore that water kills us." Sam states.

"I do thank you for rescuing these men. They mean a lot to us.

"We just happen to see the three of them holding on for dear life at the river's edge. We're glad to help." The man says.

"You didn't see the coach that was on the ferry, did you?" Lester asks.

"Mister, there was no ferry, let alone a coach; we only saw the three men we brought here."

More men arrive from the same plantation the witches took the horses. They found the young lady Amanda left on the riverbank, picked her up, and carried her to their plantation. The girls turn the horses around to leave; as they ride off, they vanish when they can't be seen from the plantation. The horses run free before being picked up by the men arriving to help at the Windgate Hundred. When they arrive, Lester lets them know the women and children were taken to neighboring plantations. None of the men were allowed to leave because they were there to try and save what they could. All night the men battle the flames that have consumed much of the plantation mansion. When the roof collapses into the mansion, they determine it is a total loss and decide to let the remains burn. Exhausted, the men fall back just far enough from the burning mansion to use as a source of heat they quietly enjoy for the rest of the night.

When the other girls arrive with the three dazed men, Elmira has the girls strip them of their clothes and bind their ankles. They stake the men to the ground, encircle them, and wait until morning. Elmira and her witches are all in black hooded cloaks and on their knees, resting and sitting on their legs with their hands clasped in their sleeves while surrounding the four men. The men sit in the sand, dazed and unsure of what is happening or even where they are. It is late December, and the sun has not yet risen over the mountains.

The air is frigid, and the men's wet bodies cause them to shiver violently. The men cannot figure out what surrounds them because the women's heads are covered and facing the ground. One of the men counts over forty of them.

William yells, "Hey, you there!" But he receives no answer.

By this time, all the men are awake, but only three are trying to get the attention of the strange figures silhouetted against the night sky.

When the men stand, they notice their ankles are tied with rope and staked to the ground. They try desperately to remove the stakes and untie their feet, and they are spaced too far from each other to touch the other.

Monroe speaks in a hoarse and tired voice. "It won't do you any good," he says.

"What?" William asks. "Who are you, people?"

"Who are you?" says Monroe.

"William, is that you?" Bo calls out.

"Yes," replies William. "Is that you, Bo?"

"Yeah, it's me. What the hell's going on, big brother?"

"Don't rightly know, but you give me a little time, and I'll find out. Who's that next to ya, Bo?" William asks.

"It's me, David."

"Was that you mumbling something earlier?" asks William.

"No, it seems there's somebody on the ground next to me," David responds. "You two boys are staked to the ground like wild hogs."

"Yeah, and I ain't liking it a bit," Bo says.

"That makes three of us, or maybe even four." Says William.

"Mister, you wouldn't happen to know what's going on, would you?" asks William.

"Hey!" Williams shouts. "Who the hell are you, and how do you know pulling on these confounded stakes won't do us any good?" Throwing sand in Monroe's direction.

"First and foremost, William," Monroe says in a sarcastic tone. "I've tried and gave up trying long before you three idiots came along. Only one of these figures was out here when I first awoke, but now I fear we are surrounded by many. I fell asleep from exhaustion trying to free myself, and when I awoke, you were here."

"Idiots, huh?" William storms. "If I could reach you, I'd wring your damn neck."

He laughs and says, "My guess is that we are still waiting on more to show up before we find out what these strange shapes have in store for us. I threw a rock, and it rolled to the side. I didn't have the strength to hit one, but it didn't move when I threw the rock; it just stayed there.

The men are looking at the women as Monroe speaks.

"Strange, though, they are all the same. None of them are moving! I'm sure you've noticed by now that you are without clothes and that we're sitting in the sand," Monroe informs them.

"I'm cold," says Bo.

"Roll around in the sand," says Monroe. "It'll dry you off, and I suggest you get some sleep and wait until morning. I'm sure your questions will be answered then."

"I don't know who you are, mister, but by morning we won't be here." Says William.

Monroe laughs and lies back down. He tries to sleep his fears and worries away.

"Come on, guys, let's see if we can escape and leave our mystery friend here in the sand." David encourages.

Tired, Bo rests on his back and looks up. Then he says, "Look at them stars. I ain't never seen them like that before."

"There ain't no trees to block them," William explains.

"You two horse thieves going to talk about the stars and trees, or are you going get out of here? David says. "Find a rock and try cutting these damn ropes."

They all try to escape but find it impossible to free themselves. William is so angry that he uses a hand-sized rock, franticly cutting at the ropes. He screams and then throws it in the direction of the strange figures; He throws it as hard as he can, and it hits one of the figures, but the rock glances off into the distance.

William screams until he is too tired to do so. He lies down, defeated.

The sun rises, and all the men awaken to see it rising above the mountains. They gaze at their surroundings and see that they are in a desert valley. They can see the strange figures are covered in black hooded cloaks. They sit, waiting to see what will happen next. After an hour, the men observe the front of the hoods rising from a bowed position. Still, the openings of the hoods reveal no faces, just a series of dark voids. The figures all seem to rise from a kneeling position and hover high above the ground. All but one are levitating in the air. These are tall figures, and none of the men can believe what they see.

"Hey, William."

"Shut up, Bo."

"William," Bo calls again.

"I said shut up, didn't I?"

"I don't think it was smart, hitting one of those things with that rock last night." Bo states.

William shakes his fist at Bo. "I ain't telling you to shut your trap again, boy."

They are all perplexed by the flying cloaks that seem to float above them. Monroe is covered in so much sand that none of the men recognize him. While they are all looking up, they do not notice Elmira until she gets their attention.

"Gentlemen," she says in a growling voice. They stare into the distance, wondering who has spoken. The figure is long and thin, between six and seven feet tall, and the voice is raspy and coarse. Then one of the others hovering over them comes down and pauses in front of William. William takes a step back, leaning back and looking at the others, who are waiting to see what happens next. They all wonder what is going on. Without warning, the figure punches him in the face and knocks him on his back to the ground.

The second figure hovers before Elmira and says, "He hit me in the head with a rock last night."

William struggles to pick himself up off the ground. He spits out a couple of teeth, stumbling to his hands and knees while Bo watches his brother moan in pain.

"Will, you all right?" Bo asks.

William looks up at Bo, grabs a handful of sand, and tosses it his way.

"I told you to shut up," William complains.

"Yeah, and I told you that wasn't a good thing to do," Bo said.

William stands up and wipes his mouth. He spits and then fingers his gums where his teeth used to be.

"That damn thing knocked my teeth out," cries William.

The figure on the ground walks toward them. As it approaches the men, it gets shorter; it walks within ten feet of David Andrews and stops. Then its hands appear and pull the hood back. When Monroe sees who it is, his eyes widen, and fear runs through his body; he wipes the sand off his face to reassure himself, and then he clutches his chest and falls to his knees.

"It can't be," he moans.

The men finally understand what is going on, but they say nothing. Andrews takes his gaze off Elmira and turns his head slightly to Monroe.

"Is there something we should know, old man?" He asks.

Monroe takes a deep breath, collects himself as a gentleman, raises his head, turns his nose up, and stands.

"You've been waiting for this day for a long time, haven't you, Mrs. Elmira Pembroke?" He says. "Gentlemen, I present to you the witch of the Williams River Colony."

"A witch!" Bo and Williams shout. "Did he just say a witch?"

"What the hell, old man?" David asks. "You telling us that you know these witches?"

"I know her as an irritating old hag." Says Monroe. "And I know her murderous son, the Sheriff. As for her being a witch, I have always suspected it, but I was never able to prove it. I only knew of her true identity when she pulled back her hood and revealed that ridiculous thing she calls a face."

"Mr. Wilson," Elmira says, pausing for a second as she hovers in his direction, dragging her cloak across the sand. "I was happy when you left the township. You could have lived the rest of your life on that plantation as the diseased bastard you are. You should have let Agatha go, but the fool you are, you listened to this idiot and murdered my friend. Of course, I'm not here to waste your time with talk, so I'll say what I have to say and get on with this. As for this pitiful wretch and his two puppets, they really ought to have stayed in South Carolina."

"It appears, woman – or witch, or whatever the hell you are –you seem to know more about us than we know about you. We haven't been properly introduced," David says.

Monroe snaps, "Don't play games with her, you damned fool."

David smiles. "First of all, old man, I don't know if you noticed or not, but we ain't at the plantation. And as far as I can see, you ain't in charge." Directing his attention at Elmira. "Boys, I ain't afraid of no damn witch. A woman is a woman, and I ain't never met one I can't beat down, and I don't give a rat's ass about her or her cheap magic tricks."

"You tell her, David," Bo shouts encouragingly.

With confidence, David continues. "If your witch friend cuts me loose, I swear I will put her in her place. We burn witches where we come from."

Bo laughs.

"Stop laughing, you fool," says William. "I done told you a hundred times to shut your bear trap. I've been in a lot of fights, and no man has ever hit me that hard." Then he turns to Elmira. "Whatever you're going to do, get it over with." He demands.

Eight of the witches come down from behind the men and kneel down at the stakes.

"Mr. Andrews, Mrs. Wilson was a very dear friend of mine." Expresses Elmira. "You should have left her alone and minded your own damn business."

"Your friend was a nigger's whore, and…"

Before he can say another word, all four men are snatched up into the air. Wiggling and trying to see what is holding them up, David is still cussing and asking the witches to let him go, and he'll show them who they are messing with while Monroe begs for his life.

"Ms. Pembroke, I will make sure that your secret will never be known," Monroe begs. "Who could I tell? We're in the middle of some godforsaken place, right? Please, let me go. You know that I'm an old man who doesn't have long to live. That disease has…"

Elmira pulls her hood over her head, and in her rage, she changes back to her true form and roars.

"Silence, you ignorant fool; how many times did she beg you to let her go while you stupidly read biblical scriptures to her?"

She hovers around to face him now that he is upside down and facing the other direction. Grabbing his face with her talons, revealing her face, and says.

"Neither one of you idiots will die today; maybe you'll live until tomorrow, but I promise, every day you live, you'll wish you were dead." She scratches Monroe across his diseased nose with her talon.

Bo begins to laugh again while William manages to catch Elmira's attention.

"Witch, you are a coward," Williams says. "Let me down, and I'll kick your ass."

Because they are now facing the opposite direction, they do not see Premise – the witch William hit with the rock – has descended into one of the cactus groves. Pulling her hood off her head, she picks up a rock and uses it to clear the spines off the bottom of two cactus plants that look like paddles; she then tosses sand on them, chants, and they become stiff as planks of wood.

When she's finished, she breaks them off so she can hold them like paddles without hurting herself.

Still talking to Elmira, William says, "The boys and I have dealt with pretty little women like you before, and I can tell you they ain't so pretty anymore."

"Give her hell, Will!" shouts Bo.

William looks over at Bo and winks.

"I'm going to get me a rock and rearrange your face like I've done on many occasions," William threatens.

Now, in a jerking frenzy, all three men are trying to pull down on the ropes that are tied around their ankles. Monroe knows that the end of his life is near, and he can only continue to beg Elmira for mercy and cry, hoping he will be spared and left to fend for himself in the desert.

"Quit your babbling, you old fool," David demands. "Real men don't give women the satisfaction of seeing them cry. After all, that's what this is all about, to make us beg them to let us loose. Your witch whore already done told us they ain't gonna kill us. You have to call a woman's bluff." He laughs and continues, "Honey, you cut me loose, and I promise I'll have a little mercy and pull a few of my punches." Then David boasts, "I ain't been to no place that can kill Ol' Dave, and this patch of dirt ain't no different."

Premise is now standing behind William with the two paddle-like cacti hidden inside the wide sleeves of her cloak. She and her sister knew the likes of these men when they worked in the taverns. It was the reason they left that kind of profession because the men often beat the women after sleeping with them and then paid only half the price, for they complained they got only half the pleasure. Men like William, David, and Bo disfigured the faces of many women.

Premise motions for Elmira to let William down. Then Elmira tells Rebecca and Lucy to lower him back to the ground so he can stand on his feet. Premise takes a few steps back as William stands up with a big grin on his face.

"You would have made a good bed warmer, little lady. I tell you what, witch." William looks at Elmira and says, "I beat this little wench of yours to the ground, and you cut us loose. I don't care what you do with the old man; hell, you can do what you like with him. Now, if I lose…" William grunts, lifting his shoulders and then dropping them. "That'll never happen, and we'll leave you and that fat old man here in this desert." Then he bows down to her.

Bo and David try to turn their bodies to see William, who is now facing Premise.

Bo laughs and says to William, "Kick her ass, Will, kick her ass."

William pivots his body and pretends he's not watching, although he is waiting for Premise to take a swing so that he can catch her arm and punch her as hard as he can.

"You know, Bo, this one's as pretty as that little wench we left on the side of the road in South Carolina."

Bo, still laughing, tells him, "Save enough for me, Will."

Premise takes a swing with her right arm. William, however, anticipates the swing and turns to catch her fist. Premise has seen this done before in the taverns, so she brings the cactus down short on his hand, and instead of grabbing her arm, William catches a handful of spine needles. He screams and clutches his left wrist, bending over slightly, and then Premise brings the cactus paddle down on his right shoulder with her left hand. In his anger and pain, he tries to charge, but she puts her left hand up with the cactus in his face, which causes him to hesitate for a second. She spins both cacti in her hands to expose the spines on the other side of the paddles. Then, taking a step forward, she swings her right hand upward to hit him between his legs. Now on his knees and fuming in anguish, William groans and spits on Premise's cloak. Premise takes a step back and drops the paddle from her right hand in front of his knees.

"This is for the little girl you say you left on the side of the road, you heartless bastard." She says.

Before he can move, Premise slaps him in the face with the cactus in her left hand. She drops it, pulls her hood back over her head, and then levitates back to the others.

Elmira tells the girls, "Introduce them to the desert girls. Fly, fly, fly!"

The men's legs are spread apart, and the witches fly off in four different directions, dropping the men to the desert floor and dragging each one of them on their backs through the rocks and cacti plants that grow in the valley. Then the witches ascend, lifting the men off the ground and switching places in the air, changing the direction of the men and turning them, so they are now face down on the ground. They drag them on their stomachs through more rocks and cacti plants, keeping their legs spread the whole time. All the men are screaming; the thorns and three-inch spines burrow deep into their flesh, and even those who soil themselves find it excruciating. There is nothing they can do to help protect the most sensitive parts of their bodies. Long thorns and small spines offer no mercy for their bodies. The witches drag them through the rugged terrain twice on their backs and twice on their stomachs before they bring them back to where they started. They hold the men high above the ground and drop them back down on their heads.

Elmira shouts over the cries of the tortured men. "The sun is going to get hotter, and the nights will bring out desert creatures that none of you fools could have ever imagined. Stand on your feet and try walking… that is, if you can. You three fools can thank Mr. Monroe Wilson, who should have let his wife go when she begged him to do so."

Monroe, still screaming, yells at Elmira through gritted teeth, for thorns have pierced through his chin and lips. "Go to hell," he mumbles.

Elmira looks down at him in disgust and says, "You go first."

None of the men are able to sit, stand, or rest on any part of their bodies; the way they were dropped is the way they will stay. The ropes burn away from their ankles. The witches watch for a few seconds as the men whimper like Monroe. The witches surround the men as they did the night before, in kneeling positions, and then they vanish.

After the storm, everyone returns to the plantation, wondering what will happen next. There isn't enough cotton or tobacco left on the property to build a new plantation, and the boss is presumed to have drowned in the river. Jason and the others hear about what happened the night before and take a trip to see what remains. When they arrive at the plantation, they find it a total disaster. Quincy asks of Monroe and Mrs. Wilson.

Lester says, "Monroe drowned trying to cross the river in the storm, and… well, as for Mrs. Wilson…" He looks around at the others.

"Did she die in the fire?" asks Winfred. "If so, I can understand your hesitation. It's a horrible way to die."

"No, sir, she did not die in the fire or the storm. She was dead long before that," Lester replies.

"My God, man, say whatever you have to say, and stop leading us on," Winfred says in a frustrated tone.

"Mr. Monroe had her whipped to death," Lester said in a low hesitant tone.

Winfred grabs his chest and winces at the thought, remembering over fifty years earlier. He has to be helped back to the coach.

"Are you okay?" Jason asks.

"Yes," Winfred reassures them that he is okay. In his rage, he walks back over to Lester and grabs him by the collar. "Why would Monroe do such a damnable and ghastly thing?" Winfred asks, infuriated.

They have to pull him off of Lester and restrain him.

"Well?" Quincy asks. "Why would he do that?"

Lester looks around for someone else to explain what happened. "First of all, sirs, none of us had anything to do with it."

"And not one of you tried to stop him, either," Winfred counters.

"Say on, man, and waste no more of our time," says Quincy.

"She was accused by three of the new overseers of having an unhealthy relationship with one of the slaves."

It remains quiet for about ten minutes; the men mill around the coach without uttering a word.

Jason takes a deep breath and says, "There's not much we can do. Monroe is dead, and so is his wife. Gentlemen, I believe we have a business to attend to here, and I think the inventory is what we ought to discuss right now. I'm terribly sorry about Mrs. Wilson, but we must carry on."

"You're right, young Jason, we must," agrees Quincy.

Winfred stays in the coach with his face in his hands. Quincy approaches him and tells him that he and Jason can handle the business.

"It looks as though all the houses burned down. So rather than simply go around aimlessly trying to piece together what we can, why don't we get organized?" Jason suggests.

They both walk back to Lester and the others. Jason speaks to Lester and Mr. Reginald Harper, who kept the books for Monroe. Quincy only met him briefly, as Monroe never meant for them to meet.

After all, Monroe said, "The books should never be called into question."

Quincy says, "We of the Williams River Township have the rights to all slaves and everything on the land except the cotton and tobacco. We have agreed with the other investors that they can have the cotton, tobacco, and land, and we can take the slaves and any other remaining property."

The investors considered the structures a total loss and believed they could recover any monies by hiring someone to manage the property. Quincy points out the direction of the new plantation that is on the north side of the James River, where they will travel six miles west after crossing the river to get to the new plantation site.

Lester tells Eagleton, "The ferry that used to cross the river near here was lost in the storm. We cannot get anything across the river, let alone all of us and our women and children."

"Yes, I understand," says Quincy. "We were told we must cross farther down the river, closer to Middle plantation."

Jason looks around at the lumber that did not burn completely. A great deal of lumber and large beams escaped the fire with very little damage.

"Could we get the men and women of the plantation to gather the lumber and separate it into usable heaps? One heap for the lumber the fire did little damage to, and all the heavy beams needed to be taken to the river road, and they can use it to rebuild the new ferry onsite. We can build it bigger and better. That way, the ferry can carry twice the load." Jason suggests.

When the men inspect the property, they find one buggy that survived the fire.

"A fine buggy this is," declares Eagleton.

"Yes, sir, it was built by Sam and Eli for Mrs. Wilson; God rest her soul. She never had a chance to drive it," says Lester.

Jason looks around and states, "There's a lot of lumber here that seems to have escaped the raging fires, so let's get started on that, and let's get the people moving again. Can we do that, Mr. Lester?

"Yes, sir, we sure can," Lester replied.

"Why don't we use the talents of Sam and Eli to build a new ferry?" Jason suggests.

"Sounds like a good idea," Mr. Lester replies. "I'll have them find some tools, and we'll get started right away."

"Jason, I can see that you are going to be a great asset to the new plantation. You're showing wonderful promise." Says Quincy.

"Thank you," says Jason. "Father, I can assure you I'll do my best."

Jason, his father, Mr. Gaines, Mr. Jameston, Mr. Lester, and Mr. Harper then travel back to Jamestown to inform the magistrates of what they have witnessed at the plantation. All parties agree the land must go to the investors and the slaves to the Williams River Township. The men who worked for Monroe are all too happy to know they will still have a place to call home. The slaves desperately hoped their new owners would treat them better than Monroe and the three men who rode in from South Carolina. After a week of working in the bitter cold all day every day, the new ferry is complete, and it is far better than the last; it is five feet wider and ten feet longer, and there are rails on the sides, making it much sturdier than the old structure. The ferryman is pleased with his new ferry and offers to ferry them for free over the next month while they travel between both plantations.

After finishing, they load the remaining usable lumber and beams onto wagons and deliver them to the new plantation on the north side of the James River. They moved the livestock after they completed the fence around the plantation. They bring the material in along with Mrs. Wilson's buggy. They gave the buggy to Mrs. Rose Eagleton, seeing that they were longtime childhood friends. The new mansion is designed by the same architect as Monroe's old mansion. The slaves' houses are built facing east; they are located two acre behind the mansion along a narrow road that the slaves built for themselves after they finished the main road on the plantation. The mansion has a large porch with ten columns, looking out onto cotton fields on the left and tobacco fields on the right. The new plantation is built on two hundred acres of land, and twenty percent of the cotton grown and harvested will be sent to the Williams River Township to be spun into yarn and sold on the market. The rest of the cotton and all the tobacco are sold directly to England and other markets.

Monroe and William remain in the same position in the desert where they were dropped. Bo and David held their hands in a fist, keeping them from much of the damage while doing their best to protect their privates. They were able to pick the thorns and spines from their feet and faces after many excruciating hours. By the time they picked out enough to walk, William had already died from a spine that pierced an artery in his neck.

"You did this to us, you fat bastard!" Bo shouted at Monroe, who lay motionless in the sand.

"I'm going to find that witch and butcher her like a pig," David said. "Leave them; they're dead. Get over here, and we can pick these damn thorns off each other." He demanded.

Throughout the next few days, David and Bo remove spines and thorns from one another. Bo hears a rattling sound and sees a Black-Tailed Rattlesnake under one of the cacti. He looks around and picks up a stick, and uses it to shovel it over to Monroe.

"Say hello to little William, you son of a bitch," Bo says.

"You name the damn thing?" David laughs.

He looks over at William's body, "this is for you, big brother." Then he kicks sand in Monroe's face.

Monroe flinches, and the snake strikes him in the arm and hand.

"Now you're dead," Bo says and walks away.

"Which way?" Bo asks David.

"East." And he points east.

"How do you know which way is east."

"Damn, Horse thief." Looking at Bo. "It's where the sun rose, you fool."

After walking for hours into the night, they walk into an area with tall grass and can hear what sounds like flowing water. They walk until they are standing at the bank of a river. They both run and dive in with swollen feet, legs, faces, and parched lips. They stay there in that area of the desert for a couple of weeks while they heal, removing the remaining spines and thorns from their bodies as they stand in the water, which seems to help as they pull out their unwelcomed guest.

"That witch is going to wish she had killed us when I catch up with her. I told that bitch there ain't no place that can kill me, and this one no different," David bragged.

Bo laughs as he finishes off a fish they caught earlier. "Yeah, and that little wench that crippled William, she gone wish she never was bone."

"What was the name of that place that fat bastard said she was from?" Ask David.

"Can't rightly remember, something about some river." Said Bo.

"Ah, yes, I remember the witch of the Williams River Colony." David says as he pulls a one-inch spine from under the skin of his shoulder."

"I'm kind of thinking, why don't we just go somewhere else? I ain't never seen nothing of the likes of them witches, and I ain't in no hurry to see them again. If'n you don't mind, I'm going my own way in the morn." Bo states.

"Let's get some sleep. We have a long walk ahead of us. We'll follow this here river as far east as it will take us. And your dumb ass won't last a day without me." David says as he spits, ignoring Bo's suggestion.

"Maybe not, but if you do manage to come across them witches, whatcha gone do? Throw rocks at'um. You ain't got no weapons." Bo says.

Bo doesn't trust David, so he waits until he's sure he's asleep and leaves him by walking in the river's shallows and then crossing it to the other side, remaining in the shallow river. It's what he and his brother William did to throw off their pursuers after stealing horses.

The next morning David is livid and curses the day Bo was born.

"That yellow-bellied coward up and left me here alone." *I'll track that horse thief down, and then I'll deal with those witches.* David thought to himself.

David walks back and forth on the river's edge and screams because he can't pick up Bo's tracks. With his hands on his hip, he thinks about what Bo said the night before, "whatcha gone do? throw rocks at'um." In his frustration, he continues to walk with the river until the river turns north. In the falling light, all he can see is the desert beyond the grass. Then he thinks, *I can make this place my home. I have fish in the river, rabbits, and other critters to eat.* He shakes his head, agreeing with himself, "Yeah, that's what I'll do. Do you hear that witch? I'll make this place my home!" David shouts.

Laughing, he finds a place to sleep for the night.

In the morning, David awakens to find himself staked to the ground by his hands and feet. He realizes he's back in the place with a dead Monroe and William, whose bodies have been ravaged by animals.

"You got to be kidding me," David said.

Looking around, he knows he is all alone. He yanks and twists for a couple of minutes and realizes his situation. He screams for a while until he hears coyotes in the distance. He looks to his right, sees nothing, and then to his left. Far off into the distance, something appears over the rocks, going from right to left as if they are searching for something.

"You just remain still and silent, and maybe they'll pass on by," David said to himself.

After the sun rises high into the sky, David believes he is safe for the moment. Then he tries desperately to free himself. Then one stake came free, and he used his free hand to pull the other arm free. He sits up to pull up the stake holding his right foot, and then stands to pull the stake from his left foot. While pulling on the stake, he hears growling behind him.

"You clever witch held me down just long enough for them to find me," David says.

David shouts and screams at the pack of coyote as they approach, growling and gnashing and drooling at the mouth. He grabs two of the stakes and holds them like knives.

"Come on!" David shouts

The pack is hungry, and they attack. David screams as one of them bites into the back of his leg. When he goes down, they tear him apart. Before he dies, he watches as one of the coyotes transforms into a hooded witch, and then she disappears.

Months later, they find a humbled Bo living among the natives that are dwelling on the cliffs of the mountains.

Chapter 12
Love and Hidden Secrets

It has been two years since Uncle and I left the old township and all the hardships behind. I try to write in my journal daily, which helps keep my sanity.

We never had plans to go to New York. Our journey took us to Boston, where we took everything we had with us on the buggy. Sadly we sold the old mare, Sam, the buggy, boarded a ship and headed for the Carolina Province. The boat ride made the two of us sick, but it was faster than the horses and buggy on the King's Highway. On the ship, I tried to eat as little as possible, for I found I would make fewer trips to the side of the ship that way."

On one occasion, I heard a voice behind me while holding my hair back and leaning over the side.

"You keep that up, and they'll have to repaint the side of the bloody ship."

I did not look up immediately, but when I did, I stared at him for a moment.

He continued, "I think you're depriving the fish of all their supper," he signaled with his hand that I needed to wipe my chin.

"John Westley." He removed his hat and introduced himself.

I wiped my chin and told him, "You're a funny guy; you should hold a puppet show for the children."

And then I walked past him.

He watched me walk away and said to himself, "Way to charm her, John." He waited for the next time to run into me and hoped he would make a better impression. He saw my Uncle and me on deck and waited until we came near. He introduced himself to Uncle, and then Uncle introduced himself to John.

"I'm headed to the Carolinas to grow tobacco," John explained. "Where in the Carolinas are you going?"

"The northernmost part holds the most promise for us, but we'll see what awaits us when we arrive," Clarence stated.

I tried to avoid eye contact by going over to the ship's side and pretending to notice something in the ocean. When they walked over to the side of the ship, John asked, "Who's this dashing young lady?"

"This is my niece, Dorothy Adams," Uncle said.

Once again, I gave him a look and continued to peer over the side of the ship.

John then asks. "If I may ask, what are you looking for in the Carolinas?"

I turned to him and said, "My uncle and I will know that when we get there."

"What are the two of you going to do there? I apologize; please excuse my absent-mindedness. What did you say your name was?" inquired John.

Uncle says again, "Her name is Dorothy, and she's my niece."

"Well, Dorothy," continued John. "Where do you think it's best to grow a good tobacco crop?"

"If you are asking me, then maybe you should not be wasting your time," I snapped.

"You will have to excuse my niece; she gets her strong will from her mother – and my dear wife, I'm afraid," Uncle apologized.

"Quite all right, my good man," replied John. "I'm learning to get used to it."

Uncle Clarence laughed as they walked the length of the ship and talked.

"My niece and I ran a small business of cured meats, and everyone in town loved it, so we plan to do the same when we get to the Carolinas," Clarence stated.

"Carolina and cured meats, you say. So tell me, why did you leave home if everyone loved it so much?" John asked.

"For a change of venue," Clarence explained.

"Do tell, I'm doing the same thing," John said.

As the days passed, we became closer as friends. John and I spend more and more time on the deck talking.

"Do you think your uncle's cured meats will sell as well in the Carolinas as they did in Massachusetts?" He asked.

"I sure hope so," replies Dorothy. "They're all we have left. Looking at my uncle, you will see a very frail man. I don't think he could have taken any more of those Massachusetts winters. To be honest, I'm not sure how many winters he has left in him at all."

"He does look a bit worn, doesn't he?" John observed.

"You know a little more about us than we know of you. How about you? Are you one of the newcomers?" She asks.

"Not really," explained John. "I was born in the small fishing village of Woodbridge in England. My father was a soldier, and when I was old enough to join, I joined the British army under King William III. I was wounded in the Siege of Namur and released from duty. When I was able, I left and sailed to Boston two years ago. I've been working for merchants trading goods for the West Indies Company ever since.

Well, I thought I'd try my hand at growing tobacco, so I saved my money, and here I am. Over the years, I have heard the Carolinas have good fertile ground for growing crops."

"We've heard the same," says Dorothy, "that's why we are moving there. The game there should provide us with plenty of meat to cure. I hear the deer and fowl are so plentiful that everywhere you shoot, you are sure to hit something."

"If that's true, then we should never starve," he joked.

"Mr. Westley, why don't you consider growing tobacco in the northern province of the Carolinas? I hear many are already farming tobacco there. I'm sure you've been in the merchant business long enough to know of this already."

"Yes, I have," he replied, "but I just thought it would be better farther south. You know they say it's harder to get to the port in the north. We would have to disembark from one ship and board a smaller vessel that would take us up the Albemarle Sound to the port in the town on Queen Anne's Creek.

"Would you reconsider?" asked Dorothy. "My uncle and I would find it terribly hard to get started on our own, and I believe the work alone will kill him. You do know he has taken a liking to you, right? That's not something that often happens, especially since my aunt passed away."

"Is he the only one who has taken a liking to me?" John asked, looking her straight in the eyes.

I rolled my eyes and stared at him.

"Well," he said, gazing off in another direction. "It does give me something to consider. Tobacco will grow well in both locations." John walked away from Dorothy but hesitated, hoping she would follow him. Instead, Dorothy turned her back and began to walk in the other direction.

Clever girl, he thought, and then he turned around to catch up with her.

Uncle and I reached the end of an era in our lives and began a new era that summer, in the year of our Lord, 1694, when we landed at a port in the Towne on Queen Anne's Creek. Of course, John had made up his mind long before I poured my heart out to him to settle in the northern area of the Carolinas. It was warmer than the old township, and I watched the sweat build up in Uncle's shirt as I had never seen before.

I worried that Uncle would not make it through the summer. It was awfully humid, and the flies at the port weren't helping much. I didn't mind the heat and flies as much as I was glad we got away from Elmira and her witches. Uncle Clarence, John, and I looked around the area to buy a buggy and a couple of horses to pull it. The stables weren't in the best condition, and the horses looked as though they needed a little more care than they were getting. We did not have much money, and neither did John. We all prayed that the Lord would give us the desperately needed essentials. The three of us purchased an old wagon and a couple of horses. John said he could fix the wagon, and we hoped we could nurse the horses back to better health. Uncle Clarence, John, and I set off in the direction with some older man riding ahead of us to a plot of property he said he could offer at the price that Uncle and John negotiated. They agreed to purchase it only if they liked what they saw.

Before we set off into the unknown, John purchased some corn, rice, and beans from the merchant in the town and loaded the wagon up for the trip. Uncle also purchased some dried herring and cheese. Uncle believed the meat could have been better and the cheese a little fresher. If this is what they had to offer, we would do very well with our cured meats and could make goat's cheese ourselves.

The pickings were sparse, but we saw something in the old farm as we drove up, even though the place was quite rundown. The owner sold us one hundred acres for the price of fifty. Looking at the property's condition, it was all overgrown and had a lot of rubbish that looked as though the owner used it to dump all the unwanted rubbish from the port. There was an old house leaning to one side, and it made sense that he was having problems getting rid of it. John talked him down to a better price and signed the papers. When he drove off, he had the biggest smile on his face and whipped his horse to get away before we changed our minds. John and Uncle said it would be best if we also rushed back to the town to register the papers before we staked our claim and started building. When we arrived back at the farm, we were all too tired to do anything, and it was getting dark. None of us wanted to sleep on the ground because we were too afraid that something would crawl out from under the piles of stuff and make a quick meal of us.

John made a cover for the wagon with a canvas he purchased in Boston. We slept in the wagon, and when we awoke, we could not enjoy the fact that the farm was ours, all because of the hard and raggedy wagon, the moans and groans, and the sight of the ugliest and nastiest-looking farm this side of the Carolinas.

Uncle looked at the meats and cheese again and thought it would be better to lay hands over it and pray before we venture any farther; the products did not look their best, but we ate them for breakfast nonetheless, hoping no one would get sick. Before work began, Uncle blessed the property and thanked the Lord for bringing us this far and for John, and he asked God to keep us from harm as we began to clear the land for the living. John opened his cedar chest and pulled out a short-handled ax and two flintlock pistols; he loaded both pistols and hung the ax on one side of his belt, with one pistol in his belt in front and the other on his hip.

There were quite a few old wagons and wagon wheels, rusted chains and pulleys, long beams that looked like they came from the roof of some building in the town, large pieces of lumber that could be used to build the house, and an unfinished barn. There was so much wood and metal that none of us could guess how long it would take before it could be cleared.

John woke up each morning mumbling the same thing: "Time to clear the bloody rubbish heap."

I refused to help because of the snakes, lizards, and rats as big as cats and other things that scurried about the heaps of junk. It was so funny watching John firing his pistols and quickly reloading as he did not know what would crawl out next. He left the musket with me, but I was too far away from the men to be of any help.

John and Uncle loaded the old chains and wheels onto the wagon, and we took it all back to town to a blacksmith to see if he could repair them as spares for our own wagon. We had twelve extra wheels and sold them for a good price, and we took the profits and bought the supplies we needed to build our home. I wanted a home with plenty of rooms inside, but John thought otherwise.

"That kind of home will have to come later," said John. "We'll have to add to the existing home as we sell our goods."

They melted some metals into the tools we needed on the farm, and we kept the large beams. There was nothing we could do for some of the broken wheels and rotted wood, so we heaped them in a pile to be burned. After three weeks, things were looking better. I dragged everything into one big pile to burned.

After a couple of months, it was a great feeling being able to walk around the property without stepping on old junk and without me running from some critters that scattered from under the junk heaps. John thought it would be good to bring in some goats to help clear the land of weeds. Of course, the fence needed repair, just like everything else. John had to melted down plenty of lead to mold balls for his muskets. He traded a couple of axes he had the blacksmith make from the metal found on the property for another long rifle-musket. Once the land was cleared, we began to make the house sturdy. It took a week for John and Uncle to steady the old house, which they had to do before they could begin to repair it. Most of the timber had to be replaced, and John repaired the roof with the timber we found on the land. Some of our neighbors were kind enough to help build the house.

After five months, John and Uncle Clarence added three rooms to the house, and the goats got to work on the weeds and everything else on the land. John is a good man, twelve years my senior and over six feet tall with brownish hair, dark eyes, and a scruffy beard. He seemed to have lost over thirty pounds by the time they finished the house.

In the sixth month after our arrival in the Carolinas, John talked to Uncle about asking for my hand in marriage. Uncle, of course, was overjoyed, and to be honest, I had fallen in love with John the second time I saw him on the ship. At the time, I was too sick and embarrassed to admit it, and I had not appreciated John's humor the first time he'd tried to introduce himself.

We were married two months later and had a simple wedding with only a couple of neighbors in attendance. After another six months, John and Uncle began to salt meats that John hunted and trapped. They traded beaver, gray fox, and black bearskins. The business and farm were going very well, and we began growing corn, a few vegetables, and beans on one side of the barn. The goats cleared about fifty acres that John needed to grow tobacco. John purchased an ox to pull the plow in the field and is excited about getting started. Uncle seemed to be doing very well in this new land, and his health had improved better than expected. John took Uncle to the doctor, and as I suspected, his ribs were broken. They had begun to mend, but because they'd gone so long without care, they caused him great pain. When they returned, John had many questions he demanded someone answer.

He asks, "Why is your uncle walking around with broken ribs? When were they broken? And who had broken them?"

Later that night, after supper, I asked John to sit down and poured him a cup of tea. I sat beside him and started from the beginning. When

I told him all that had happened, I wasn't sure whether he was angry or wanted to cry, or maybe both. He had even expressed some fear.

"I've fought men in battle with swords, axes, lances, and muskets; I've even resorted to throwing stones," John said. "But what do you do to fight witchcraft?"

I grabbed his hands and cupped them into mine.

"You fight it the same way we've always fought evil, and that's with prayer, God's mercy, and being smarter than the enemy," I explained. "God has brought us here together, and he will take care of us. I have been closer to a witch and have smelled her stink breath; let me tell you, she's no beauty in her true form. She's strong and has skin like a lizard, claws like an eagle's talons, teeth that can shred leather, and screams that sound like a woman and a panther mixed together. If you want to know what evil is, she's that and a whole lot more." Dorothy laid her head on the table, resting it on her folded arms. Looking up, "Oh John, I'm sorry I got you mixed up in all this, but if I told you we were running from witches, would you have still come here? Would you have married me still?"

With a serious look on his face, John pulled back and said, "Why darling, certainly not." He laughed as he spoke. "Really darling, it would not have changed a thing. I fell in love with you the first time I laid eyes on you, feeding the fish from aboard the ship. I would still have married you even if the king himself was after you."

"Yes, well, this thing can kill the king and his army if it wants to," Dorothy explained.

"Yes, about that, let's just omit the part where I was in the king's army," said John. "Besides, we're hundreds of miles from there, so what's to worry about? I'll just put up a leather barrier, and that'll give us the time to run like the devil while she chews her way through it."

"I won't be running too fast these days, being with child, you know," Dorothy said.

"Then I'll carry you with one arm and fight your witch with the other," John replied, gesturing wildly with his arms.

Dorothy just looked at him and smiled. She said, "I hope it will never come to that."

I closed that chapter in my journal and began to live our lives together.

The year is 1705, and Dorothy and John have three children and another on the way. Things are faring well for them. They live miles away from the town, but they make their way to the port twice a month to sell their cured meats, trade furs, and sell tobacco. It's good to get away from the farm every once in a while. It's even harder now with the three children; Johnny is nine, Elizabeth just turned eight, and Anne is four. And, of course, Dorothy is seven months pregnant.

She and John have hired servants to help out on the farm. The children love to sell their products while watching the merchant ships sail in and out of the port. At the end of the day, it's all they talk about before they fall asleep on the trip home. Dorothy worries about her uncle because it seems his health has turned for the worse. John hates to leave him alone in the house, but one of their neighbors goes in to check on him.

She's an old widow with a young granddaughter who helps her with their small plot of land. Samantha is a common-looking young lady of about thirteen years of age, and she fancies Johnny. She tries to hide it, but Dorothy notices her interest when Samantha, Elizabeth, and Johnny play together. When Dorothy looks at her, she thinks of her aunt Liz and what she was like when she and her mother were young. Dorothy's mother was the wild one, while her aunt Liz was the serious one. Samantha is more serious and mature than other girls her age. Dorothy assumes that growing up in her grandmother's home has made her this way. It wasn't until her aunt Liz died that Dorothy became serious and truly understood the nature of hard work.

Her aunt Liz was right; Dorothy had to grow up and take on the responsibilities of a wife and mother. She cries as she peers out the window and watches her children. Dorothy remembers her aunt telling her that she wanted grandchildren, and now she has three and one on the way, only she's not here to enjoy them. Yet, Dorothy is so thankful that her uncle is around; he tells her that her mother and Aunt Liz would be very proud and that he, too, is happy.

He often thanks the Lord for giving Dorothy the vision and desire to come to the Carolinas. He gives her hugs and kisses on the forehead every day, then he walks out to the porch, sits in his favorite chair that John made for him, and watches the children run around the farm. It reminded him of Dorothy when she was their age.

The next morning, Dorothy gets up to start her day, and she recites her daily prayer:

"May the Lord watch over us as we journey through the day, may the Lord cover us in his bosom and hide us from the evils of the wicked, and may he be our strength, our sword, and shield. I ask this in Jesus' name, amen."

She watches her husband from the house while he chops wood or when he's felling a tree. Then there are times when she knows he sees her watching; she knows because he takes a harder swing at the log to split it and steps back as though he's admiring his handiwork. One evening, Dorothy goes out and pours him a cool cup of water from the well. John carries the ax over his shoulder, drinks from the cup, and then pours the last of it over his head. Dorothy takes the ax and holds it with both hands.

"This ax is heavier than the one we used when I was on our farm in the township," she says. She tries to cut one of the logs John has piled up next to the cutting stump. His modified ax is bigger than a typical ax. It has a wider blade than the others. Carefully, Dorothy pretends to chop the log as though she has never done so before. She listens to her husband's remarks and laughter.

"I want you to teach me to use the ax as you do," says Dorothy.

"Now Dorothy," he replies.

"No, John, what if you are off in the field, or you and Johnny are at the port selling goods, and a bear came by? If I could defend myself and the girls, I would have a better chance."

"You already know how to chop wood, and you do a good job," says John. "And if a bear comes by, you shoot the bloody bugger, and if the ball bounces off, you run like the wind."

"Come on, John, I'm talking about really using it," she pleads, "and the sword too."

"You plan on joining the militia?" He asks.

"No, John, but I want to learn how to defend myself and the girls when you are out," explains Dorothy. "Now that Uncle's health is failing, he couldn't get up fast enough to throw a rock, let alone try to defend us. There's no one here but us. How can you look into these beautiful eyes and not say yes?" Dorothy turns, looking over her shoulder, and blinks rapidly.

John sits on the ground against the stump, staring at Dorothy for a long while, to the point where it becomes uncomfortable.

"Teach me, John, please," she pouts. "Don't just stare at me like I've asked you for the moon."

"Training to fight with a weapon takes time, Dorothy," says John. "We have the tobacco to cut and dry, meats to salt, hunt for furs, milk the cows, and gather the eggs. There's wood to chop, and we are educating the children..."

As he speaks, Dorothy walks away and returns to the house without a word. She looks at John with a serious expression he's seen before.

He yells out from the cutting stump, "Oh, come on, ol' girl! Where will we find the time?"

"Humph," Dorothy says, raising one brow. "I'll remember that when you're tapping me on the shoulder tonight."

She closes the door behind her. Dinner that night is quiet from his end. The children are all chatterboxes, so Dorothy only responds to the children's queries. And John only receives cold looks from his wife.

The winter months are upon them, and now they have another child, Clarence Westley, and they are preparing for the cold. None of the children like the cold, and neither does Dorothy, as far as that matters. Getting up in the cold mornings makes them all slow to move about. Johnny rushes to bring the wood inside, and John ensures the fireplace has what looks like half a tree inside. The fireplace is broad and deep. John likes to keep at least two large logs on the fire all day.

The fireplace served as the house's primary heat source and cooking pit until John decided to add a stone pit on the other side of the room. It holds wood underneath for fire and two large cast-iron plates that John made from some of the old metal on the property, a small cabinet where Dorothy stores the pots and pans for cooking, and a new chimney which makes the situation better for two reasons: First, the fireplace is so hot that Dorothy often burns herself while cooking, so having the cooking pit is a really good fix for her, and second having it on one side of the room and the fireplace on the other keeps the home warmer.

In the winter, the boys travel into town only once every two months. Johnny always complains before he goes to town because it's too cold, and he has the same complaints when he arrives home from the port. He swears he will not go with John on the next trip, but he really has no choice. If the girls mock him, I will make them go out into the cold the next morning and chop wood. This way, the next time he complains after a trip from town, they will be a little more compassionate, and maybe they'll bring the boys a blanket to warm themselves as they sit in front of the fireplace.

It never takes either of them long to fall asleep. The following month, John and Johnny come home from selling goods, and John walks in carrying a large item over his shoulder wrapped in cloth. Dorothy notices that it is about two feet long, narrow at one end and wide at the other. Dorothy lifts the wide end and finds that it is heavy, but the other end is light. Then John walks into the bedroom, goes to his cedar chest, and pulls out another item he's wrapped and tied in a cloth. Dorothy knows what it is because she has been secretly practicing with his sword for the past three months. Since John would not train her, she thought it would be best to train herself. He walks back to the table.

"This, dear, is a hanger sword, but of course, you know that already."

Johnny's eyes are wide and glaring, and his mouth is open even wider with excitement. He grabs the sword, but John restrains him.

"You must be careful, young Johnny, when you handle bladed weapons."

"Yes, sir," Johnny replies with great joy. "Mother, we have a gift for you; please open it."

Dorothy walks to the table and looks at John.

"Go ahead, open it." John encouraged.

She closed her eyes and began slowly unwrapping it, not knowing what to expect.

"It's a two-bladed ax," exclaims Dorothy. "Oh, John, does this mean you'll train me?"

"I thought it would be a good time to tutor my best pupil. While I was in the king's army, I met a Scottish chap who carried this strange type of ax. It had two heads, and he used it with great efficiency. Like you, I asked him to teach me to use the bloody thing, and he just stared at me. The lessons were hard, and he hardly gave me rest. I practiced as often as I could and watched him use it in battle. Magnificent bloke, he was, weeks later the old chap died in battle, I took up the cross, so to say, and I carried that ax with me until the day I was wounded. I guess someone decided they needed it more than I did because when I woke, it was gone, and I had no ax. Nevertheless, I drew up a plan and had the blacksmith forge this for me. The blades are curved just right to give a really nasty cut. I say… Training early Monday morning?"

Dorothy jumps into her husband's arms and says, "I'll be the best student you ever had."

"Well, you're my only pupil, and you may be singing a different tune before the day is over." Says John. He turns to the children. "Okay little whippersnappers, off to bed with you now."

"Ah, we're not tired yet," they groan.

Not to my surprise, John knows how to use the sword and ax very well and has a long staff. He informs her, "To be in the British army, you had better be a fast learner and take advantage of your time to learn such skills during breaks between battles. Of course, I kept up the practice even after I arrived here in the colonies; all I could think of was having my own place to come home to, a wife, and little children to love. Everything I ever wanted, I now have with you."

I did not want to wait too long to train because I believed it would not be long before that witch and her watchers found us. I told Elmira that when the day came, I would be ready and far less weak than I was then. As I lay awake at night, I think about how I believe my uncle Clarence knew of Ms. Pembroke and hiding a lot more than Thomas's death from me; just as I hid the fact that I had seen a side of Ms. Pembroke I believe no one has ever seen – or maybe they did, and they suffered for it. Whatever Uncle is hiding, he takes to his grave.

He does not make it through winter; he takes to a cold and never recovers. The doctor said it was pneumonia, and it was only a matter of days before he succumbed to it. Old Mrs. Nobles and her granddaughter Samantha are there at the burial. I can tell the old woman liked Uncle, but he was still mourning my Aunt Elizabeth and could not return her affection. Instead, he talked to her about the olden days whenever she stopped by.

Now, I want to learn more than just sword and ax play; since John was in the army, I need to know tactics. I know how to use the woods to my advantage, for I now know these woods just like I knew the woods behind the old farm.

At the time of Uncle's death, he warned me to 'be watchful, and not to trust strangers, because they may not be who or what they appear to be.' I have been watchful and know what I saw in the woods on my way home from watching aunt Liz was no animal. What they were doing in the woods that night remains a mystery to this day. Thinking back, I remember the creature did not move like a man running but more like a man standing upright on his buggy. *Was it possible that they could float in the air? What did Uncle know? And what did he mean when he said people might not be who or what they appear to be? Maybe he confided in John because he knew John would protect the children and me. How powerful is their magic? When John talks about having spies in the camps of their enemies, he says it helped them learn their enemies' strengths, weapons, and strategies in battle.* Dorothy struggled to find sleep.

This enemy watches them at every turn, and after being confronted by Elmira, Dorothy understands how they knew when she was in the woods. She knew there was no one there but herself. People say that witches use stones and pools of water to see what they want to see. This frightens Dorothy to pray.

"Oh Lord, I pray that you hide and train us to be ready to fight this battle against our enemy." She prays. "Hide us from any way the wicked uses to see what they see. Please, Lord, be our strength, sword, and shield in these times of need. Help me, Lord, to know what Uncle hid from me all these years. I ask this in Jesus' name, amen."

I train every day when I have time. After a year, I have become proficient enough not to need much of John's time. He is amazed at how quickly I have picked up the skills. He no longer wants to use the sword with me; he says it is because he has chores to do. I have started Johnny and the girls' training with the staff. At ten, Johnny is learning to chop wood with the two-bladed ax. This is good for John because now he has someone to help with the workload. It is good for me because I can see he's able to defend himself with the sword, ax, and staff. John trains Johnny, Lizzy, and Anne at the week's end, and I train them during the week and the girls when the boys go off to sell goods in town.

Time has passed, and I don't know where it all went. Johnny has taken to the young girl Samantha Worthington, who is now sixteen. Johnny is twelve, Lizzy is eleven, Anne is nine, and Clarence is now four and training.

I believe perhaps John was right when he said, "The witches are hundreds of miles away. What do we have to worry about?" Our children are secretly training to fight off an enemy they do not know exists. I often wonder when I should tell them of the witches. Johnny has turned into a great swordsman, and so have the girls. They are good with the ax but look at it as a tool for work; of course, they would rather avoid anything they might consider "hard labor." I see it as the best weapon a person can have, and if you learn to use it the right way, it can become "an extension of your arm, which is what John says."

Business is going so well that John has decided to build a small store at the front gate of their property. Our customers loves cured meats and tobacco. John lets Johnny hunt and trap for furs while we run the store. There are many farms around, and they love the convenience of not having to go into town or to the harbor for these types of products. The boys still go into town to sell goods; the extra money between the visits helps.

At thirty-two, Dorothy finds she doesn't have the strength or energy she did when she was twenty. She teaches them to use the woods to hide and how to use a bow and arrow because it's quieter than the musket. The children find it more of a challenge while hunting rabbits or other small game. They find ways of making different types of arrowheads, and they have the blacksmith fashion their weapons for them. They have arrowheads for small, medium, and large game. Dorothy is so proud of her children; they have grown up to be great frontiersmen. She thinks back to the days when she believed she would be a great Warrior Princess and laughs; she is neither a warrior nor a princess, and she sure doesn't see either one when she looks at herself in the mirror.

In the late evening, John and Dorothy are at the store, taking account of the goods before they end their night.

"John," Dorothy calls.

"Yes." He says lazily.

"Did you and Uncle ever talk about anything that he did not want me to know?" Dorothy asks.

Puzzled, John inquires, "Why do you ask?"

"Because I need to know if he knew anything that would help me understand all this madness," says Dorothy. "Maybe he knew how to defeat those witches. I don't know anymore. I lay awake most nights thinking of the day Aunt Liz died and of that witch Elmira. I think of the townspeople and how the whole lot of them allowed her to do as she pleased. I think of the night before my aunt died and how there was something in the woods with me. I wondered if they could see me when I hid in the woods in the late evenings, and I wonder if they can see us now."

Dorothy screams in frustration. John walks to her, holding her shoulders firmly in an effort to calm her down.

"Uncle often said things that made me feel as though he knew something he believed I could not handle," Dorothy continues. "He and Aunt Liz would often talk about things amongst themselves, and when I walked into the room, he and Aunt Liz would change the subject. I also walked into the room when you and Uncle were talking, and the two of you did the same thing. He told you something, John Westley, and I'm asking you to tell me what he said. Trust me, don't just keep it to yourself. Please tell me what it is."

"Why don't we go back to the house?" suggests John. "I'll pour us a cup of tea and tell all."

They close the store and return to the house.

"You know, Dorothy, he never asked me to swear not to tell you." Says John. "He just said the time will come when you are ready to know the truth."

After they enter the house, they find Lizzy and Anne playing games, and of course, Johnny has his sword and is shadow-playing while his brother Clarence watches. John approaches the stone pit and pours hot water into two cups from the kettle he purchased from a merchant.

"Okay, kids, it's time to put away your things now and get to bed," Dorothy says.

After the children have gone to bed, John readies himself to tell Dorothy all he knows. He sits down and looks Dorothy in the eyes.

"I hope you are ready for this, old girl. It may sting a bit."

Dorothy takes a deep breath and says, "Okay."

"Before your uncle died, he told me he had a secret he could not bring himself to tell you. He wasn't sure if you would be terribly upset with him if he told you this, so I presume he put that burden on my shoulders. Anyway, the old chap said every day he looked at you, he counted it as a blessing, and every day he looked at..." He hesitates and takes a sip of tea. "Every day he looked at your brother, he saw it as a curse on the family."

"My brother?" asks Dorothy. "I have no brothers or sisters. I'm an only child. My parents died when I was just four years old."

"Dorothy, calm down. I can only tell you what I was told. Shall I go on?"

She sighs and gestures that he should continue.

"He said your father was eight years your mother's senior. Before he married your mother, he and some other women had a secret courtship; she was older than him. Her parents would not allow them to be married because they didn't think he could provide for their daughter. Her family had a substantial amount of wealth, while his family, of course, was as poor as rocky soil, good for nothing but the ground they tread on. So she married some other chap named Gregory Pembroke. She was already four months pregnant with Avery Adams's son by this time. Keith, I think his name is."

"Keith!" Dorothy screams. "Did you say, Keith?"

"I do believe I did," John replies.

"Oh my God," shrieks Dorothy. She stands up from the table, walking in circles with her hands covering her face.

"Are you okay?" he asks.

"No, not in the least," she says angrily.

"Shall I go on?" He asks.

Dorothy sits down at the table in tears, with her hand covering her face.

"Well, this Gregory chap loved this Elmira woman so much that he didn't care if she was pregnant; he married her anyway and raised Keith as his own. Bad luck struck Elmira's family, and her father made some bad investments with some merchants who never made good on their promises. Needless to say, Elmira and her family fell into despair. They lost the family farm, and Gregory's money fell short trying to assist Nigel Grace, Elmira's father, in keeping the family status. Eleven people living in one small house made for a lot of mouths to feed, and it was hard on them all. Things did not get any better when Keith was born."

Dorothy rests her head on the table.

"In the meantime, your father worked for a merchant and did very well for himself. Some say he disappeared off the face of the earth, and no one knew where he was for quite some time. And then he returned out of nowhere, that's when he married your mother, and you were born a year later." John sighs. "Oh, the irony of it all, quite the story, actually. It's believed that Keith had the fever as a young lad, and they later found he had polio, or so they said – some didn't believe it for one reason or another. They were already prepared for his funeral when the young lad pulled through."

"You sound as though Uncle doubted his bad leg was from his illness." Says Dorothy.

"I said the same thing." Says John. "He only said the doctor knew differently, for he was too afraid to say otherwise. Anyway, the family was miserable, and none of them liked Keith very much. Some years later, Elmira had the young lad Thomas, and he became the center of her life. It seemed she believed she had been redeemed and that things would finally be okay for both the Pembroke and the Grace families. A couple of years after Thomas was born, Gregory was able to secure a small house, and they moved out of her family's home. Everyone was happy for her; her spirits were lifted, and your uncle said she was happy again – that is, until the day of Thomas's death. Your uncle did not know that Elmira was a witch, or at least he did not tell me. But having that wretch for a brother is something else entirely." John puts his hand on his chin and thinks aloud, "Kind of makes you wonder if that clever chap knew that you and he are half-siblings?"

Then Dorothy says, "I guess it makes more sense now. It may be the reason they were so hell-bent on taking all those farms and homes. I guess they felt it was owed them. That is why he took our family farm

– his inheritance. I thought Uncle had told you something about those witches. They seemed to congregate somewhere in the woods behind our farm."

"Well," said John, "I did tell you he did not know that Elmira was a witch, but I didn't say he did not have his suspicions about witches in the colony. The townspeople were very suspicious of Gregory's wife after her son's death. There was a time when Sheriff Williams, whom your uncle admired very much, suspected Elmira of dabbling in the craft. He said something about a mist that surrounded only their house early one morning. He may have questioned her husband about it, and her husband then told her. After that, they built a farm not far from the town. And it wasn't long after that when the Sheriff fell very ill and passed away. No one attended the funeral because they all feared he'd died of some plague.

The funny thing is that no one else got the sickness, not even his wife. I guess that's why they were suspicious of Elmira. Anyway, I digres. But then Undersheriff James Whiley took his position as Sheriff. Your uncle said that he often felt sorry for Keith. His mother was so angry that she would openly vent her frustrations on the young lad. The only child who could play with him was a young lad named Charles Langram. Your uncle remembered while this witch Elmira lived with her family, her father and siblings often beat her during her pregnancy with Keith. And whenever Gregory was out trying to secure a proper living for his family, they would beat her again. You would think she would take it out on her family, not yours. A woman scorned, for sure. She was also suspected of having something to do with her siblings and husband's deaths, but some witnesses say they saw him fall from his horse."

"Witnesses?" Dorothy asks. "Who, her witch sisters?"

John continues, "Clarence did not say whom. He only said that Whiley was not as strong as Sheriff Williams and that Whiley fellow was a good friend of the Pembrokes. As Keith got older, he stayed away from the farm; I guess it was his way to escape the beatings. At sixteen, he became one of the Sheriff's deputies. He adapted to having just one good leg, and he learned to ride the horse very well, he and Charles both. The two of them were inseparable. It wasn't long after that the Sheriff mysteriously died in a freak storm like the one that took your parents. Keith took his position as Sheriff and Charles as his Undersheriff. And Clarence emphasized *took*."

"I don't get it," Dorothy cries. "Why am I hearing this from you?"

"Well, they say that wisdom and maturity come with time, and I believe that your uncle Clarence was afraid you would respond the way you are now. He loved you very much, but he may have felt you would think of him as weak."

"I never thought that of him." She says.

"Well, after your aunt's death, he didn't want you to hate him for not telling you that the man who burned your aunt at the stake is also your brother. Half-brother, I mean, but nevertheless, your brother. I guess he would have rather lived with your love and die with his secrets."

Dorothy sighs, whispering, "Oh Uncle, I loved you so much, and even in your weakness, you showed strength. I could never think of you as anything less than a good man."

John comforts her. "I believe he meant it to be this way, Dorothy; he wanted you to know after he had gone. He knew one day you would ask, and that's why he told me these stories over the years. He told me these stories many times over and over and over." John says as he slowly rears his head back to the back of the chair and then pretends to snore.

"I get it, John," Dorothy staring at him and then covering his mouth.

"He just wanted to keep his promise to his wife, which was to get you out of that town. He hoped he would be able to see you with your own children before he died. He kept his promise to his wife and saw you a very happy mother with a very handsome, daring, and dashing husband."

She laughs and takes their empty cups, refilling them with more tea. Dorothy sits down and waits for John to continue.

"Clarence said that strangers would visit the town, and when they left, no one ever saw them again or even knew if they'd ever left at all. At first, I believed he was just a superstitious old fool, but I remembered you told me she was transformed right before you. It makes sense now that they believe those who showed up in town always did so right before a death or disappearance occurred. Many of them believe that it was Elmira or her daughter-in-law. Amanda, Keith's wife, who is very close to Elmira. There was a time Clarence said he felt sorry for Elmira's simple-minded sister Mary; he said she was retarded. He said Mary was the only one who was there for her through those bad times, so Elmira was very protective of her, and they lived together after Elmira's husband died." John sits back in his chair.

"In England, the superstitious believe in vampires and werewolves. They believe they can take any human or animal form, so no one really knows who to trust. They call them changelings or shapeshifters. I'm getting goosebumps just thinking about it all." John shivers and hunches his shoulders. "Makes for a good old-fashioned scary bedtime story, wouldn't you say?"

"It would if only I had not been up close and personal with the real thing," Dorothy thinks aloud. "That may be the reason why they never found that traveler they called a warlock. He was neither a traveler nor did he ever leave. But I can't see her or Amanda posing as a male traveler. There must be a man in league with them, and if that's so, who is he?" She continues, "Now that's become a well-kept secret. Who's the male warlock among them? The woman does all the work and takes all the blame, while the alpha male grows stronger and stronger while practicing his craft in secret. The real question is, why in the woods? And why in the back of our family farm?"

"I don't know," says John. "He never said if there was a hive of witches in the back of the family farm, but he did say that there was something that often made the old mare uneasy. He said it might have had something to do with the old colony that failed around 1650 or so he said. Maybe they used the old settlement to congregate. They would be far away enough not to arouse attention, and maybe it was for that reason they wanted your family's farm. How far did you venture back into those woods? It was a shortcut to the town you mentioned before, so you would have to have passed it on your way to the town, right?"

"No, no, you wouldn't," says Dorothy. "To get to the town, you had to travel northeast going across our neighbors' farm. Their farm was on the other side of the road, and if you ran back there, it led to the west side of the town. Now, if you went northwest... I was not allowed to play there because it was behind Old Man Kirts's farm and off-limits. Old Man Kirts would always get on me for climbing over his fence and crossing his farm. I was too fast for him to catch me. He was a fat, mean old man who looked about a hundred years old. He was really mean." Dorothy laughs as she remembers him from when she was a little girl.

"He would see me and take about five steps, huffing and shaking his fist at me as I ran across his farm, but he died when I was young. I don't remember Mrs. Kirts that much. We hardly ever saw her in church service or on their farm. She never spoke to anyone, and she always kept to herself. They had the largest farm in our colony. The Kirts family was one of four large families of farmers who were there when they first started our town.

"Ah, pioneers." He interjects.

"Uncle said they came from a failed colony that the natives attacked; three of his sons and two of his daughters were killed in the attack. Two of their children survived the attack, one son and one daughter. Avery Kirts was born after they built the new colony. Uncle said the older son and daughter moved back to England, and the old man died in his misery. I remember his son and his son's wife; Mr. Avery was nothing like his father, he was nice, but they kept to themselves. No one knew when or where he buried his mother died."

"Interesting, you mentioning that." John interrupted.

"Yes, Uncle said Mr. Avery took her to the old colony to be buried with her children and friends. There were times when Mr. Avery saw me running across the field and waved at me, and I would wave back but keep running. The town's history tells that Mr. Randolph Williams was the man who founded the old colony, so after they built the new colony, they named it after him. Everyone at the time knew who came from the old colony, but they never knew where it was. I just ran across Mr. Kirts's farm to annoy him."

"I can believe that to be true," John interrupts.

Dorothy dips her finger into her cup and flicks a few drops of tea onto her husband. She continues, "It couldn't have been too close. If the natives attacked them, then why would they start a new colony so close to the old one?"

"I don't think they would," John interjects. "They would move miles away. During the Indian wars, many of the tribes were defeated, and the natives were forced to move on; even if that were the case, they would build the new colony a safe distance away from the old one. You did say there is a lake and a river near the town?"

"Yes," says Dorothy. "It ran behind the farms and around the town. The old colony ruins may have been no more than a few miles or so away.

"I would wager if you followed the river to the west, you would find the old colony. And if the old geezer was one of the founders, he probably built his farm not too far away from there. Perhaps he thought the natives no longer posed a threat. So, it wasn't in the back of your farm but to the west of old Man Kirts's farm." John said.

Dorothy looks up at the ceiling. "Ugh," she grimaces. "I'm going in circles."

"Well, isn't that what happens when you speculate and assume?" Asks John. "It's like being lost in the woods; you have no clue where you are and often find yourself going around in circles. I'm terribly afraid we're no farther than where we started, old girl."
Dorothy raises her head from the table and gives him a hard stare, "Not really, *ol' boy*, now I know why they were in the woods. Uncle used to tell me that Mr. Kirts and the others from the old settlement told stories that the old settlement was cursed. You know, they'd talk about how most of the old colonies were built like forts, so they had walls, and walls hide a lot of secrets. If you want to hide your secrets, then make up stories and tell them to a bunch of superstitious people."

"You've deduced that very well. You'd make a great constable." John says.

"Don't patronize me," Dorothy scolds, "I'm serious."

"I'm not patronizing you," John says, "for you can't find answers if you don't ask questions. Well done, Dorothy, but it gets stranger and spookier. You said you hadn't seen this Mrs. Kirts much, right?"

She looks at him and agrees, and then she asks, "What of her?"

"Well, your uncle stated that he once shot a deer somewhere behind the Kirts's farm, and it ran deeper to the other side of the Kirts's farm. When he caught up with it, he saw… well, he saw Mrs. Kirts hovering off the ground, but not too far off the ground. The old man said he soiled himself when she passed by him in the woods. He was hunting about two miles west of the Kirts's farm. He said he did not make a move or a sound when he saw her. He took his time leaving the woods that night and never returned. So, now you know why you were not allowed to venture in that direction when you lived on your farm."

Dorothy stares at the table with a puzzled look on her face. "Mrs. Kirts?" she whispers. "She must have been a hundred years old."

"Your uncle stated that he could only guess, but he believed that she grieved as much as Elmira did when she lost her child. He thought she might have made a deal with the devil after her loss. I guess Old Man Kirts wasn't the only one who was bitter about the loss of his children; Mrs. Kirts was just a little quieter than her husband."

John takes the last sip of tea from his cup. "I'm afraid it's rather late, and we have a store to open in the morning." He says. "We'll continue this another time. Wow, I find this more refreshing than just lending an ear and popping off to sleep in the middle of the story. Maybe that's why Clarence told me so many times over the years."

"Maybe," Dorothy says, "But I wish he had trusted me more and told me first."

They get up from the table and walk to their room, unaware that their son overheard their entire conversation, with great attention and anticipation to hear more. Johnny slips back into bed, thinking of all the stories that were told that evening, and like his father, he thought this was far better than listening to the stories of his late great uncle. Until now, he simply thought they were just stories told to his father, but now, he has a more sinister view of things.

"Witches and warlocks," Johnny whispers to himself. "Is this why mother has us training so hard?"

At the back of the house, a tree branch scratches against his window and frightens him; it makes him jump up in the darkness of his room. Johnny sits quietly, watching Clarence in his bed and listening to him snore. He peers at the window again and sees the tree branch that scratched against his window, pulls the covers over his head, and does his best to fall asleep. In the other bedroom, Lizzy is just as afraid after listening to their parents tell tells of witches from the old township of her mother.

Chapter 13
The Darkest Hour

Johnny and Lizzy have grown old enough to help train the two youngest using carved wood. They carve wood into a sword, an ax, and a staff. Samantha shows no interest in what they are doing, but she helps John and Dorothy run the store, and she is a great help when the boys go into town to sell and trade goods. Both Anne and Clarence had just walked away for a break in training.

"I could not sleep last night," Johnny said.

"Yes," Lizzy said, "I, too, was scared, and any noise kept me awake."

He asks her, "Why were you still awake?"

"Why were you still awake?" she replies.

"I asked you first," says Johnny

"We'll say it together at the count of three." Says Lizzy.

"Okay," agrees Johnny. He starts counting, "One, two, three…"

"I overheard Mother and Father talking," they say together.

"Oh my God, Johnny, I had to pray to get a little sleep." She says.

"Do you think these witches are real?" asks Johnny.

"I used to listen in on some of Uncle Clarence and Father's conversations, and I thought they were stories." Says Lizzy.

"You too? I thought I was the only one who heard them talking." Johnny presses his hand to his forehead and turns in a circle. "Oh my God. I find this to be so incredible and so exciting at the same time. I can't believe this is real."

"I first thought, wow, my mother is being hunted by witches, but the more I listened to her, the more I became afraid for our family," Lizzy said, holding her hand to her heart.

"Yes, I felt the same way," Johnny said.

"I think we have to really train harder just in case those witches come here. Do you think they can be killed?" Lizzy asks.

"I don't know, Lizzy," Johnny replied. "But the only way to find out is to be ready. I've been practicing with the sword and dagger together."

"I think I'm going to practice with the ax and dagger together, too," adds Lizzy.

"I'll work with you on it; that way, we'll defeat those witches," says Johnny.

"Hey Johnny, do you think they ride on brooms as people say during All Hallows' Eve?" She asks.

"I don't know; we'll have to wait and see." He said.

They discuss how they can train with different weapons simultaneously for the rest of the day. They talk about using old native tricks to lure the enemy into traps they've set and springing on them.

Over the next two years, John and Dorothy watch their two eldest children train with various weapons simultaneously. They work on timing as they fight an imaginary enemy with their backs to each other.

"I've never seen this before," says Dorothy. "What's gotten into those two?"

John says, "Don't look at me. I didn't have anything to do with that. I've been in here with you most of the time, remember? I would have probably cut meself in the unmentionables if I tried some of the things they're doing. I do think it's time we ask them what they are up to."

"I agree." Said Dorothy.

"But look at them... magnificent blokes, they are; I'm in awe just watching them work together. This is a proud time for us old girl, and now we know they can protect themselves and us when we are too old to fight for ourselves."

Samantha admires Johnny's fighting skills, but she does not think it is proper for his sister to indulge in such an act, so she keeps to herself and stays busy at the store. Even Anne is trying to do the same with the sticks she uses to train. That evening at supper, John lets the children know how proud they are of them.

"We've been watching you train from the store." He says. "Your mother and I want to know more about the change in training."
Johnny and Lizzy simply look at each other.

John says, "Oh, come now, no secrets."

Johnny asks, "Can Lizzy and I stay up later and tell you?"

"I think it's about those witches," Anne blurts out.

Clarence kicks her from beneath the table, "Hey!" Anne yelps, and she kicks him back, which causes a kicking frenzy under the table.

"Okay, enough!" Dorothy shouts.

"He kicked me first!" Anne retorts as she slaps him across the head.

"Hey." Clarence jumps from his chair to attack Anne.

John whistles and calls for a truce. He looks at Dorothy and asks Anne, "What do you know about the witches?"

"Only what Johnny and Lizzy say. Clarence and I heard them talking about it after training a while ago." Anne answers.

"Okay, Johnny, you want to enlighten us?" John asks.

"I... Lizzy and I only know what you and Mother were saying a couple of years ago about how she and Uncle Clarence's experience with witches back in Massachusetts," Johnny replies.

"Well, if there was a better time to drop the rock and surrender, this would be it," John says.

He and Dorothy agree to tell the children all they know so that there will not be any misunderstanding between them. They tell the kids that it is possible they could be talking to a witch or warlock and not know it, and that goes for the workers on the farm, so they will have to be careful about whom they talk to.

"At least we know you four can infiltrate the enemy's camp and listen without being seen or heard," John says.

"Well, you said we have to be able to strike at the enemy without being seen. Right, Father?" asks Johnny.

"That's how the Indians fight their battles. If they had our weapons, they would have been an even greater formidable force to be reckoned with. Your mother believes these witches are stronger than the strongest man, so don't let them get their hands on you, so use your arrows to keep them at bay. You've heard your mother describe them: longer arms and hands, fingers like an eagle's talons, and... really sharp teeth that can chew through wood." John holds his hands up and opens his mouth to show his teeth. The kids laugh.

"Must you make a joke about everything?" Dorothy groans.

"I'm just trying to lighten the mood with a little levity, ol' girl. By the way, if she can take on the form of a witch and keep the form of her old self, you young ones have to be careful around strangers. I doubt she'll introduce herself as the lean, mean, green-chomping thing." And John wiggles his fingers in the direction of the two youngest just to hear them scream. They hold their arms up to keep him at bay. They all laugh, but at the same time, they take what their father is saying very seriously.

"Really, John, I think we are past that, don't you?" says Dorothy.

"Anyway, we were going to tell you youngsters all this sooner or later, but it appears, old boy, that you've had the drop on us all along. Your mother and I are very impressed with your training and cunning moves. You'll have to show me how you do it. Of course, I'll have to use the training sticks. I wouldn't want to mortally wound myself trying some of those jumping and turning moves the four of you make."

The children laugh at John's humor.

"Just watching you young whippersnappers tiers me out," John says with a big smile.

"Right now, we all need our sleep, and we have our chores to do in the morning. Pop off to bed with you now," says Dorothy. "We'll revisit this again sometime soon."

More years have passed, and things have settled down with the children concerning the witches. Each year, Dorothy sees the children growing up like weeds. She can see that Johnny is showing a true liking for Samantha. He is ever more like his father, even in his jokes and wit. Dorothy stands at the counter in the store and watches Samantha watching Johnny as he trains. And she can see that he notices her watching him from the window, and he does his jumping, turning, sliding, and spinning to impress her. Then Dorothy looks at John, whose chest is out; his chin is up, and she sees the biggest smile on his face. Dorothy, too is very proud of her family, the fellowship of their friends, and how well all four children have turned out. She gives the Holy Father all the glory.

Meanwhile, Johnny has started picking Samantha up in the mornings and taking her home in the evenings. Dorothy and John both agree on how good they look together. That night, Johnny walks in before they close after hitching the buggy. Samantha is waiting near the door, Anne is sweeping the floor, Lizzy is re-stacking the material, and Clarence… well, he's pretending to be doing something. When Johnny and Samantha leave, Lizzy, Anne, John, and Dorothy watch the two of them.

"Okay, let's finish and close the store," says Dorothy.

"You smell that?" John asks.

"Smell what?" she says.

"Baby poop," John says. "I can see it now, my son, the father, starving for sleep in the early mornings."

The children laugh.

"That's gross," remarks Clarence. "Johnny will have to clean after his baby poop because I'm not going to.

"Dark rings under their eyes," John adds.

"Shoes on the wrong feet," Lizzy says.

"And their hair looks like a bird's nest," Anne says, with one hand holding the broom and the other on her hip.

"Him running out of the house, glad to go to work," says John. Dorothy turns and looks at her husband sternly.

"What?" John reveals a crooked smile.

"Is that what you were doing?" she asks.

"Well, not exactly running." He protests.

"Uh-huh," says Dorothy, her hands on her hips. "Finish up, all of you. And remember your words, young ladies. They have a way of coming back at you."

One night after closing the store, Johnny drove Samantha home and returned. He has just walked into his room, and the rest of the family is getting ready for bed. Dorothy does not feel right; she feels the way she did on the night she walked to the old farm. Strange, like someone is watching her. She sits down at the table.

"Mother," Lizzy calls. "Are you okay?"

"I feel a little dizzy." She explains.

"Maybe it wasn't Johnny and Samantha's baby's poop I was smelling," says John.

"You would think that, wouldn't you?" Dorothy says, looking up at her husband.

"Let me get you some tea." John turns to the kettle, not wanting to look at his wife.

"I'll be okay, and you can stop pretending to pour tea," she says. "I know the kettle is empty."

"Really, I just noticed that," John said, shying away and pointing at the kettle.

She stands up, and they hear the horses fussing about in the stable. They initially think it's the cantankerous old bear that comes around sometimes, or perhaps a mountain lion.

"If it's that old bear, I'm going to shoot it in the mouth, and then I'll have his skin on my bed to keep me warm," shouts Clarence.

"You should be in bed, young man, and that goes for the rest of you, too," John says.

John takes his loaded musket and his lamp and steps outside. Dorothy watches him scout the area carefully from the porch holding the lamp as high as he can to give some light to the night. He steps out into the night; when he reaches the back of the stable, he screams and fires his musket. As soon as Dorothy hears her husband's scream, she runs as fast as she can to help. When she gets around the backside of the stable, John is lying on his back. His lamp is out, and she bends down to him to comfort him and help him up. She is trying to comfort him and keep him from talking. The bear has ripped his shirt with its claws.

But when she tries to help him up, John pushes her away and says, "Not the…," he gasps. "Not an animal."

As soon as Dorothy thinks of the children alone in the house, she shouts, "Get up, John!" As she shows the strength that lifts him up from the ground.

John puts his arm around her neck, and they both walk back to the house as fast as they can. Dorothy does not want to leave her husband lying there, but she cannot leave the children either. With the lamp in one hand, Johnny stands at the door and asks, "Mother was it that old bear?"

"Get back in the house!" Dorothy orders, "And close the door."

Lizzy closes the door behind them.

"Johnny, help me carry your father to the bed." She commands.

Then Dorothy runs back to the kitchen and grabs the ax and sword, and John writhes in pain from his wounds. Dorothy runs to the porch and screams at the shadows of the night.

"Come on. I told you I'd be waiting! Come on!" She screams into the darkness.

She stands poised for only a moment, then runs back into the house and waits for whatever Ms. Pembroke throws her way. The children are frightened by her screams, but Dorothy just tells them to get back and blow out the lamps. Johnny takes his sword in one hand and his ax in the other, guarding the closed door while Anne runs out of her room with her sword. Lizzy stands next to her mother, poised to defend their home at any cost. Neither of them knows what has happened.

They ask quietly, "Is it the old bear?"

Lizzy returns and stays by her father's side, tending to his wounds.

"Help me get some water and heat it on the cooking pit," says Dorothy. "We need to tend to your father's wounds."

Her eyes are full of tears as she watches her husband's blood fill the bed. She bends over and kisses him.

"I'm sorry, John, I'm so sorry," cries Dorothy. "Oh my God, I'm sorry I got you into this."

He looks up and whispers to his wife. "I wouldn't change a thing," he says weakly. "I loved you from the first day I watched you feed the fish from the ship."

Then he looks around Dorothy to see the children.

"Be ever watchful, one second they are there, and the next they are gone," he says. "Take care of your mother."

"What is he saying, Mother?" Lizzy asks, frightened.

John extends his hand out toward Johnny. "I'm very proud of the man you've become," he says. "I'm very proud of all of you, and I love you all so very much." He pulls his hand back in pain. "Now, if you young whippersnappers don't mind, it's been a long day. I'm going to pop off for a wee nap."

He closed his eyes, and they all watched him, crying aloud as his breathing became shallow.

"It's the witches, isn't it?" asks Johnny while turning to leave the room.

"You stay right where you are, young man," says Dorothy. "You can't defeat the one alone, let alone the many."

At first sight of sunrise, they cannot see anything or anyone. Johnny runs to the stable, jumps on his unsaddled horse, and rides past the store, riding hard to Doc Chandler's farm about a mile down the road. When he arrives, he beats on the door desperately until Doc appears. He is a little upset, for he was still in bed until Johnny arrived.

"What in blazes is going on here?" Doc asks.

"My father needs your help urgently. We think he was attacked by a bear last night," Johnny says franticly.

"Hurry back, son, and I'll be right behind you. Tell your mother to boil lots of water and get as many rags as she can," orders Doc.

"I'll get the cloth from the store," says Johnny. "Will that be enough?"

"Don't waste time talking, son; just hurry and get going!" Doc shouts.

Johnny rides back home as fast as he can. He darts inside the store and grabs rolls of material. Then, leaving his horse behind, he runs back to the house.

"Where's Doc Chandler?" Dorothy screams.

"He's coming," explains Johnny. "He told me to gather as many rags as I can." Running back to the door, he announces he can see him riding up the road. "Mother, may I go and get Samantha? She may be worried because I have not picked her up yet."

"Yes, but hurry and get back here." She demands.

On his way back to the store to fetch his horse, Johnny sees Samantha climbing down from the buggy. Doc rides right past them to the house.

"Johnny, what's going on?" Samantha asks.

"I need to get more material from the store." He runs inside and grabs two more rolls of material, loading them onto the buggy and telling Samantha to climb back up.

"Johnny, what's going on?" She demands.

"Father was attacked by a bear last night." He says.

"Oh my God," Samantha gasps.

Johnny takes her to the house and tells her to help his mother and sisters. He grabs as many pots and pans as possible and fills them with water from the well. Samantha runs into the bedroom, where Doc Chandler has already taken charge.

"What do you want me to do?" Samantha asks.

"We need more water, and I need you, ladies, to make rags of that material," Doc commands. "He's lost a lot of blood, so just help where you can."

"I don't want the young ones in here seeing their father this way," says Dorothy. "Could you watch them until Johnny gets here with the water?"

Samantha grabs the two youngest and takes them to Johnny's room, which is the farthest from their parent's room. Johnny is getting more water and putting it on the cooking pit while Lizzy takes the pots of water warmed earlier to the bedroom. They take blankets and wrap John in them to help keep him warm. Doc spends hours stitching his wounds closed; the house is abuzz now that more of the neighbors have been alerted of the attack. Most of the women are helping as much as they can, keeping Johnny and Clarence out of the house.

"Now, Dorothy, you'll have to make sure he's not disturbed and doesn't move around. He's got some deep wounds that have caused him to lose a lot of blood." Doc sighs and leans back into the chair that one of the women had placed next to the bed for him. "I've never seen wounds like this before. Was it more than one bear?"

"I don't know," Dorothy says through her tears.

"Johnny!" Doc calls him in from the porch.

"Is he going to be all right?" Johnny asks as he rushes into the room.

"Well, that's why I called you in. You will have to be strong and the man of the house for a while. Your father won't be able to help you, and now everything will fall on your shoulders. When he recovers, he wouldn't have any use of his left arm. The cuts are just too deep. I want you to be strong for these young lads and your mother; they'll need you, do you understand?" Doc asks.

"Yes, sir, I understand," Johnny replies.

"Good, continue to be prayerful." Doc rises from the chair. "I'll be back tomorrow morning to check on him." Then he gathers his things and walks out the door. Johnny follows him and approaches the buggy.

"You know, Doc, I think I can take it," says Johnny. "Tell me the truth. Will my father recover?"

"He's pretty bad off, son," Doc replies. "Only time will tell. You may want to hunt those bears down, though. Once they attack like that, they'll do it again."

"Are you saying there's more than one?"

"Son, I have treated many of whom bears have attacked, and I have never seen these types of wounds before. Whatever did this; you'd better hunt it down because they will return," Doc said.

"You better believe I will," replies Johnny. "They are as good as dead."

"Good luck, Johnny, and good hunting," says Doc.

Johnny acknowledges Doc once more, and then he sets off.

"It or them?" asks Lizzy, who has just approached her brother after overhearing what Doc. Chandler said.

"Yes, I think the training is over," says Johnny. "As Doc said, they will return."

Lizzy looks in the direction of the barn. "Let's see what the ground tells us."

They walk to the other side of the stable to see if they can find any bear tracks. When they get around to the side of the barn, they only see their father's blood where flies are gathered, and his lamp remains where it fell. Johnny picks up the lamp and motions for Lizzy to walk back to the house.

"There's nothing here, no tracks at all," Johnny says.

"Weird," says Lizzy, "so they do fly above the ground. Remember what mother said when she was in the woods? It was like it hovered as it passed her."

Johnny looks back as they step onto the porch. "Yes, and remember what father said of Mrs. Kirts; she floated just above the ground."

"Do you think they are still here watching us right now?" Lizzy asks.

"Not sure," says Johnny. "Not sure at all."

Most of their neighbors leave and offer their condolences and well wishes as they walk out. When everyone is gone, the family gathers in the bedroom. Samantha's grandmother and the other women have already cooked food and cleaned up all the bloody rags; they've also washed the floors of blood. The house is clean, and the food is ready to serve, but no one leaves the room. Samantha's grandmother, Ms. Nobles (*Grandma Nobles*, Clarence calls her), suggests that they all get something to eat.

"You must eat so you will have the strength to carry on. Samantha, help me get the food on the table." She directs.

"Yes, ma'am." Replies Samantha.

"I'll help, too," Lizzy suggests.

"Sure, child, you do good to do something else." Says Grandma Nobles.

Lizzy nods.

"How do you feel, child?" Grandma Nobles asks Dorothy.

"Angry that I can't do anything to help," says Dorothy. "I feel so helpless in this state."

"Be strong, Dorothy," encourages Ms. Nobles. "Johnny needs you to be strong."

"I feel so sad for Mr. Westley," Samantha says, holding her hand over her face.

"As do I," Grandma Nobles agrees. "Wipe your tears, set the table, and I'll help Dorothy."

"Yes, ma'am." Says Samantha.

Grandma Nobles encourages the others to eat and let John rest. Samantha does not have a hard time keeping Anne and Clarence from fighting at the table for the first time. The room is as quiet as a church in silent prayer. Lizzy and Samantha stand and clear the dishes. Then Samantha walks into Johnny's room with Clarence.

"I don't want to sleep by myself tonight," Clarence says.

Samantha sits on the edge of the bed and cries with him in her arms. When Johnny walks into the room, he finds the two of them crying. Samantha stands from the bed, and Johnny takes her in his arms and pulls her close.

"Everything is going to be all right." He says. "I'll hunt that bear down and kill it if it's the last thing I do."

"Please tell me you will be careful." She pleads.

"I've killed a lot of bears, and even though this one has escaped my father and me for years, it will not escape this time."

"Oh, do be careful," pleads Samantha. "Anger and revenge have a way of clouding our better judgment."

Samantha turns into his arms and rests her head on Johnny's shoulder.

"I changed my mind. I'll sleep in my own room," Clarence pouts. "All alone and by myself in the scary darkness..."

"All right, you can stay," Johnny says.

"Does she have to stay? It's too mushy when she's here." Clarence pouts.

Samantha leaves the room, shaking her fist at Clarence.

Everyone but not all believes it was a bear; they tell everyone it was a bear because they do not know what else to believe. John is too weak to survive the attack; they waited too long because they were afraid to go out at night and ride to Doc Chandler's farm. John lost so much blood that he lived only a couple of days after the attack. The children are devastated by their loss. It is the spring of 1715 when they bury John beside Clarence. A week goes by, and no one has done any of the chores around the house. Grandma Nobles fusses about the house, demanding the children do their chores.

Many of the neighbors come by to comfort the Westley's and offer their condolences. Most of the neighbors also offer to help with some of the chores. After a couple of weeks, Dorothy and her children begin to pick up around the house and try to start over. As time passes, Dorothy watches her boy grow into a handsome man at nineteen. He is taller than his father and has a well-built body, with long dark hair and dark eyes. Johnny is now the man of the house and has asked for Samantha's hand in marriage. It seems he has grown up too fast. Dorothy watches him cut wood like his father. Every once in a while, he takes a break swinging the ax like a weapon against an unseen enemy.

One morning he walks into the house with that devilish look on his face, a look that his father often had.

"Mother, when Samantha and I are married, I want you to know that I will always take care of you," he says.

"Thank you, son," says Dorothy. "And I want you to know I will take care of you for as long as possible."

"I see Father was looking into the future when we added the other rooms to the house. It seems our family is about to get bigger."

"Your father was a wise man," says Dorothy. "He was a very good man."

Two years earlier, Johnny and his father tore down the girls' room that was between their bedroom and the boys' room to build four more rooms in the house. They built a hallway where the girls' room was to make the two rooms in the front larger, and they made the other rooms down the hall the same size. Anne and Clarence are happy because now they have their own rooms.

"Mother, how did you feel when you got married?" Johnny asks.

"I was really nervous," she reminisces. "Your father was the most handsome man on that ship, and I knew if he'd asked me to marry him, I would be crazy to say no."

"My friends say I'm getting married too young," he continues. "Do you think that I'm too young?"

"No, I think you are more mature than most of your friends. The question is, do you think that you are too young?"

"No way," Johnny says, his voice excited. "Even though she's four years older, I fell in love with Samantha when I was twelve. I feel that I am the luckiest man alive. I'm glad she didn't tell me to bugger off like she told some of the other guys. She said she loved me the day she saw me when I was, as she calls it, 'playing with those dangerous toys.'"

"Oh yes," Dorothy responds, "those dangerous toys. I watched your father with that ax and just daydreamed about him. Of course, I found out I was pregnant not long after whenever I finished daydreaming."

They both laugh.

"How's Samantha's grandmother?" Dorothy asks, "Will she be able to come to the wedding? Samantha told me she's been sick and bedridden."

"I think she'll be there. She is pretty old, you know," adds Johnny.

"I think I'll make some stew, and you can take me over there." Suggest Dorothy. "Which will give you an excuse to talk to Samantha."

"Mother, I see her every day at the store," says Johnny, holding both hands over his head.

"Oh, son, that's work talk," says Dorothy. "You need that alone talk so she can admire you more."

Johnny blushes and tells her, "I think I have some wood to chop or something."

Walking out the door, he waves at Clarence and tells him to come with him and help him look over the beaver skins to ensure they are drying. Lizzy and Anne talk to their mother about the wedding while the boys check up on the skins. They talk about the material they want to use and the patterns they will need to sew it all together. Dorothy has added a sewing and spinning area to her room. Lizzy rolls over on her back, gazing into the air and flopping down onto her mother's bed.

"There is not a boy here who is good enough for me," she says. "I can outrun them and outfight them all…"

Anne blurts out, "That's not true. I saw you and that David boy from the cotton plantation down the road holding hands behind the store."

Lizzy jumps up from the bed and punches her on the arm. "Why, you little spy!"

Anne laughs and runs to the other side of the bed. She asks, "What's the name of that plantation?"

Lizzy grits her teeth and shakes her fist. "I'll get you later for that." Outside, Clarence is bugging Johnny about not being the best man.

"In three months, you'll be married." He whines.

"Two months. July is only two months away, Clarence, remember?" Johnny corrects him.

"I should be the best man, not that bumpy-faced Nathan Winslow." Clarence stomps his foot. "I've known you all my life, and he's just known you for a few years. What's more, a whole life or a few years? I don't get it."

"Clarence, don't start that again. No matter how many times I explain it, you still don't get it. I've known him for more years than you've been living. Besides, you have the most important job of them all." Johnny pauses and smiles. "You must hold the ring for Samantha; you lose that ring, and there will be no wedding."

"Well, I can hold rocks in my pockets for days, so I think I can hold one stinking ring for a few minutes."

"Okay, get on with your chores and go practice holding my ring." Johnny leans against the post, trying not to overthink his wedding, while Dorothy and the girls are now at the table looking over what kind of shoes will go best with their dresses. Samantha is at home, a little nervous about the wedding herself. She has already purchased everything she needs for the ceremony.

"Do you think this color goes well with my skin?" she asks, standing before the mirror in her grandmother's room. "Do you think he will be happy with me?"

"Child, that young man thinks the world of you." She says. "If you went out in your bedgown, he would be floating in the air for you."

"I have waited so long for this, and now that it's so near, my nerves are driving me batty," explains Samantha. "I lie awake at night hoping I won't faint. How embarrassing that would be."

"You think you worry now, child, wait until you have children of your own," Grandma Nobles says. "You talk about not getting any sleep. Just wait until the baby is born. As they get older, you'll have no problem going to sleep; it's waking up you'll have problems with. You need to get your sleep and be off to bed. You have to be at the store early in the morning, so go ahead and get your rest. You'll understand that a tired man makes more noise when he's asleep than he does when he's awake. Get your sleep while you can, child."

Six weeks later, at the end of the evening, Johnny and Clarence finish their work and go inside. Clarence is still complaining about not being the best man at Johnny's wedding.

Johnny tells him, "Go to your own room and complain."

Johnny walks into his room and closes the door, lying awake and thinking of Samantha.

Dorothy got the same feeling she had when John was attacked. It's as if she is being watched.

"Mom," Lizzy calls. "You're looking the same way you did when…"

Before she's finished talking, Elmira's voice comes through the door like she is standing over the table where they are sitting. Dorothy stands up and takes the ax that leans against the leg of the chair. Anne screams while Johnny jumps up from his bed and blows out the lantern. He grabs his bow and quiver of arrows beside his bed, stopping Clarence from leaving his room and signaling to him to get his bow and arrows and blow out the lantern. Johnny and Clarence quietly step out into the shadows of the hallway, standing back with their bows partically drawn. Clarence kneels in front of Johnny with his bow, keeping as quiet as possible. Lizzy grabs her sword and a dagger, while Anne panics and grabs her sword that fell to the floor.

"Get behind me, girls," Dorothy shouts.

Elmira appears out of nowhere from a cloud of heavy gray mist. They stare at each other without saying a word. Dorothy thinks she must be in her mid-eighties or maybe nineties, so why does she appear to be as young, if not younger, than Samantha?

Elmira breaks the silence. "I warned you that you can't hide from me, Dorothy Adams, or should I say Dorothy Westley. I've been watching you and your children and the task you have taken upon yourselves. I'm impressed. I've always believed that there was something special about you. I haven't figured it out yet, but none of that matters now that I've found you. I'm here to finish what your family started and to make sure that neither you nor any of these children see their future..."

"Get out of my house!" screams Dorothy. "Get out!"

Elmira laughs and looks at Dorothy's daughters.

"Your mother never told you about me, did she?"

"She told us enough," Lizzy replies coldly, rocking from side to side. She is poised to fight.

"Oh, but I bet she left out the bad thing she did to my son, and she thought running away would make me forget. Not something a mother would ever forget or forgive," Elmira sneers.

At that moment, Amanda and Unity appear. The witch Alexandra speaks before she appears out of the gray cloud.

"It was so easy to tear through your husband's flesh." She brags. Lucy appears between Dorothy and Elmira.

"He screamed like a woman in..." Lucy said before being cut off.

Before she can say another word, Dorothy takes a step forward, starting her swing with the ax from behind her to swing upwards to split the witch in two, starting between her legs. Dorothy lets the momentum carry the heavy ax up above her head, lifting her feet off the floor, and with all her might, she brings the ax down heavily upon Lucy's head. She swings the ax so hard that it splits the floor and gets stuck. It feels as though time has slowed.

"Was it as easy as that?" Dorothy shouts.

It happens so fast it catches everyone in the room by surprise. Johnny lets his arrow fly, which catches Alexandra in the neck, and Clarence releases his, impelling her in the ribs in her side. Lizzy swings her sword down at Sarah; Sarah grabs the sword, but she doesn't see the dagger until Lizzy sets it twice in her side with her left hand, pulling the sword from Sarah's hand, cutting her, and twisting it through her midsection. She pulls it out and kicks the witch in the stomach, throwing her dying body across the room. They are all screaming; the witches, Dorothy, and the children are screaming. And as fast as the witches appeared, they vanished. The only thing left are pools of blood where the witches fell. When the screaming dies down, Dorothy and her children stand there, ready for them to return. Johnny and Clarence have already drawn their bows with another arrow. Finally, after about fifteen minutes, they convince themselves they are gone.

"It is doubtful they will return, at least not this evening." Says Dorothy.

Clarence and Anne say, "Whoa, did you see Mother cut that lady in half?"

"Yes," says Lizzy. "But where did they all go?"

"Witches, honest to God, real witches," Johnny remarks. "Oh my God... wow!"

"At least now we know we can kill them," Lizzy says.

"That witch Elmira came here herself, just as she said she would," Dorothy whispers. "Oh my God, this is worse than I thought it would be."

"She and those other women made some real deal with the devil they did," Anne says.

"That's one powerful witch to just drop in without notice," Lizzy states. "You didn't say that they could do that."

"I didn't know myself until now." Dorothy sits down at the table, her entire body shaking.

"I don't even want to think of what else they can do. How long have they been watching us? Why now, for Christ's sake?" Lizzy wonders.

"They may be using a tactic the Indians use: harassment," notes Johnny. "They attacked us two months ago, and now they are back."

"Oh, my head is spinning out of control," Dorothy complains. "Oh Lord, I have all kinds of questions that need to be answered. I honestly don't know what to do next."

Anne and Clarence hug Dorothy.

"Elmira has got to be really pissed off right now. She just lost three of her witches, and I guarantee she will hunt us down no matter where we go. You just don't kill one of hers without her coming back and murdering every one of yours." Dorothy summarizes.

"I can't believe we just killed those ladies," Anne remarks.

"Oh baby, those weren't ladies anymore," says Dorothy. "If they had come here in their true form, I think the sight of them would have given them the edge. It's a very frightful and dreadful thing to witness."

"Wow," Clarence says.

"We're not leaving our home, and we're not going to run," Dorothy decides. "We know we can kill them and when they will appear. They all appeared in a gray cloud of mist. When we see it again, we'll attack."

"It's what Father said before he died," explains Johnny. "They appear one second, and the next, they are gone. No matter what they look like, Mother, we'll fight them to the end."

"Thank you, Johnny. I'd like to thank all of you," Dorothy says. "Your father would be as proud of you as I am right now."
She grabs them all as they stand at the table, hugging one another.

"We are going to fight for our home, and we will train, and yes, you will tell your children and their children's children the whole story," Dorothy says.

"Mother, Elmira has to be an old lady... She didn't look old. She was very pretty," says Lizzy.

"They were all very pretty," Dorothy replies. "They are all older than I am, but they appear as young as Samantha. Apparently, they are as vain as they are arrogant. Now, I believe they are capable of taking the shape of anyone or anything they want. I now understand Uncle's warning about strangers."

"Mother?" Lizzy calls.

"Lizzy, what is it, baby?" she answers.

"You," Lizzy replies.

"What about me?" Dorothy looks puzzled.

"Yes, what about Mother?" Johnny asks.

"Mother, this is the second time you felt dizzy right before they showed. You did the same thing before…"

"Before your father was attacked." Dorothy finishes Lizzy's sentence with a puzzled look.

"Is that what that nasty witch meant when she said 'there is something special about you?" Lizzy asks.

"Mother, you were warned before the witches appeared. How can that be?" Anne asks.

"And you all but carried father in when they attacked the first time. You are stronger than most women. Said Anne.

"I don't know, child. I just don't know," Dorothy says, getting up and walking to her room.

Everyone just stares at her and feels so sorry for her. Clarence runs to her room and climbs into her bed, holding his mother as they both cry. Then Johnny, Lizzy, and Anne join them, and they all cry together. No one sleeps that night, for all they can think about is how the witches appeared out of nowhere in a gray cloud. In the morning, they try to settle down. Johnny goes to the store carrying his father's flintlock pistols in his belt. He wears his buckskin jacket, trousers, leather boots, and a tricorne hat.

Johnny meets Samantha at the store. "Why are you carrying those pistols?" She asks.

"Just in case we have an unexpected guest." He replies.

"Are we expecting trouble?" She asks.

"No, but I'm doing my best to impress you." Smiles Johnny. "All the frontiersmen carry their pistols and knives on them at all times." He tells her as he leans against the counter. "You know, you never can tell when you'll have to wrestle with a bear or something like that."

She bursts out laughing, holding her hand over her mouth and leaning against the counter. He walks over to her, holding her waist with both hands, and then Anne and Clarence walk in.

"Ewe!" shouts Clarence. "I'm going to tell Mother." Then he smiles at Johnny and says, "I won't tell if you make me your best man."

"Bribery, huh? How about I let you fire both pistols instead?" Johnny haggles with Clarence.

"Hmm… I'll have to think about that." He tilts his head to one side and rubs his chin.

"It's quite common for people in love to hold each other close. One day I'll be held in the arms of a dashing young prince," says Anne, turning in circles with her eyes closed.

"A prince only holds princesses in their arms, not dreaming frogs like you, Anne. I'm going to be a soldier, and I'm going to wear a red coat like Father did when he was in the British Army."

"Okay, enough," commands Samantha. "The customers will be coming soon, so Clarence, behave yourself. You hear me?"

"I will if Johnny gives me one of those pistols, just in case another witch decides to drop by," Clarence exclaims.

Shocked, Anne and Johnny peer at Clarence. Then Anne runs over and punches him in the arm hard, so Clarence turns and storms out of the store, screaming as if someone has shot him. Johnny looks back at Samantha to see her reaction. She walks up to him and pinches him on the arm.

"Witches?" She whispers.

"He's just joshing, right?" Johnny replies, looking at Anne.

"Yes, he'll say anything to be Johnny's best man," Anne says nervously.

"He also knows Mother doesn't like it when anyone talks about those superstitious things. You know how religious she is. Witches, warlocks, vampires, werewolves, and all those old wives' tales." Johnny says nervously.

Mrs. Gilford and her daughter walk up to the store for material while her son goes straight for the sweets jar.

"How's your mother doing?" she asks.

"She's doing well, thank you, she will probably be here at the store later this afternoon," Johnny replies.

"Well," whispers Samantha, "I'm going to see your mother and take her the material for Anne's dress. She wants it to be a surprise. It's almost finished, but she has to sew the lace on the neck and sleeve."

"I'll walk you to the house," says Johnny.

"No." She holds her hand out to stop him. "There might be a surprise there for someone else, and we wouldn't want to spoil it, would we?"

"I guess not," he replies.

"Anyway, Anna may need a strong frontiersman to protect her from wrestling bears," continues Samantha. "And besides, you forgot to sweep the floor last night before we closed."

She hands Johnny the broom.

Dorothy is afraid because the wedding is so close to Elmira and her witches' visit. They all spent most of that night cleaning the blood off the floors, walls, and ceiling. Now, she wonders if the witches will wait until the day of the wedding to return. There are so many things to worry about. While sitting at the table, Dorothy can hear Clarence screaming all the way from the store. She and Lizzy look out of the window and know right away that it is just another fight between him and Anne. Lizzy walks to her room, uninterested in the latest battle.

Clarence runs into the house, exaggerating his crying to get his sister in more trouble for punching him. He holds his arm like it is broken.

"What in the world could have happened that would cause you to scream like you were mortally wounded?" Dorothy asks.

"Anne hit me in the arm as hard as she could." He cries.

"Now, why did she do that?" Dorothy asks, her arms folded across her chest while leaning against the doorway to her room.

"I don't know." He whines. "She just hit me because she's mean."

Then Samantha walks in and hands Dorothy the lace.

"Do you know what the latest battle is between the youngest?" Dorothy asks, fatigued.

"Yes, ma'am," reports Samantha. "He said something to her, and she hit him. I don't know why he's all upset. I've seen her hit him harder than that before."

"Well, young lady, there are times they both want the other to be in trouble with the judge; you do know that's what they call me when they don't think I'm listening. Something you'll get used to in due time." Says Dorothy as they walk to her room.

She looks in the mirror and sighs. "There was a time when I put my hands on my hips, and my aunt would call it, putting my hands on my imagination," Dorothy sighs. "Now look at me. Four children and thirty pounds have been added to my imagination alone. It seems like yesterday I was just hopping over fences and running through the woods as free as a deer."

"Oh, Mother Westley, you look great," Samantha says. She walks over to Dorothy and hugs her.

"You're a convincing fibber, Samantha, and I love you too. Now tell me more."

They laugh, and then Lizzy runs in from her room. She is wearing her new dress. She twirls in it and stands before the mirror.

"Samantha, isn't it the best?" she asks. "I love it so."

Lizzy grabs Samantha's hands and twirls her around like her dancing partner will be doing in a week. Dorothy and Samantha examine the dress to make sure that it's ready. The excitement of the wedding is rather exhausting for Dorothy, and even more so because of Elmira, but she wants her family to dress well for the wedding.

"Will you be getting dressed here, Samantha?" Asks Lizzy.

"Yes, but we have to keep others' prying eyes from seeing it." Samantha grabs a ball of yarn and throws it at Clarence for peeking into the room.

Lizzy yells at him, "Go back to the store, you little weasel, and help out. Leave Anne alone if you know what's good for you."

"Samantha," Lizzy calls, "Come see Mother's dress. It came in last week. When Anne saw it, she wanted more lace on the collar and sleeves of her own dress; Mother told her no at first, but she's going to sew it on today as a surprise."

Dorothy tells Lizzy, "Go and take that dress off, and help the others at the store, please."

Lizzy agrees, and then she goes to her room, humming to herself and holding her dress with one hand and her arm in the position of her invisible partner.

"I don't know if she's practicing for you and Johnny's wedding or her own," Dorothy sighs.

"I think both," Samantha replies.

"Come look here; I've finished Johnny's father's red coat. It's really beautiful," says Dorothy. "I can only imagine what his father must have looked like when he wore it."

"I'm sure he looked very handsome in it," Samantha says.

Dorothy lays the coat on the bed and gives Samantha a big hug. She tells her she's proud to have such a warm and caring daughter-in-law.

And then she says, "I have to get back to work on Anne's dress, or I'll never finish it."

It is now only two days before Johnny and Samantha are to wed. The last thing any of them want is for Elmira and her army of witches to show up at the wedding. Since Johnny and his friends are part of the militia, Johnny thinks it will be good to wear his father's sword by his side. Besides, he says it makes him look more debonair. Clarence declares that if Johnny can wear his sword, then he can too. Dorothy, Lizzy, and Anne decide to wear daggers strapped to both thighs. They want to be ready for whatever Elmira throws at them. The wedding is to be held on their farm, so they hide weapons in strategic places around the property. Johnny will pick up Samantha and her grandmother that evening, so he and Clarence will sleep in the store. That evening, Nathanial Winslow, Thomas Hadley, Abraham Benders, and Andrew Wilson come by the store with their knapsacks, ready to camp out. When they walk in, Clarence walks over to Johnny and punches him in the arm.

"What are they doing here?" He whispers. "Does Mother know?"

With his arms folded across his chest, Clarence pouts and walks over to the aisle, standing in the way as they walk in. Andrew walks right by him and musses his hair, and then they all leave him standing there alone. The five of them start a conversation about the girls they would like to marry.

Clarence pouts, "I don't want to be a part of your old conversation anyway. Besides, that Betsy girl likes that Theodore James boy from the farm down the road off the river, so you're the last boy, she'll want to marry."

Nat throws a shirt at Clarence. "Go stuff your face with a sweet stick."

Clarence goes to the door, closes it, locks it, and then walks over to the counter and grabs a handful of candy. He would eat sweets all night if Johnny did not take all the jars of sweets off the counter. A heavy knock on the door scares all the guys, and they jump up to see who it is. Dorothy and Samantha are there, carrying stew, bread, and water for all the men. Nat and Thomas clear one of the tables while Abraham and Johnny take the food. Andrew grabs the wooden bowls and spoons and sets them down on the table. With his arms folded, Clarence pushes his way through to the table, grabbing a bowl and spoon.

Dorothy, ignoring his ill manners, warns him, "Clarence, the sweets jar is off limits! Do you hear me?"

"He had a couple of sticks of sweets before I took all the jars off the counter," says Johnny.

Samantha pours Clarence some stew and breaks off a piece of bread, allowing him to eat first. He sticks his tongue out at all the guys and goes back behind the counter. Johnny wants to walk walk his mother and Samantha back to the house before it gets too dark, but Samantha forbids it.

"It's your last night with the boys, and I want you to enjoy it," she whispers.

When Dorothy and Samantha walk back to the house, Johnny's friends chide him over the remarks.

"It's your last night with the boys," they say, laughing.

"That's the thing about marriage; the woman takes all the freedom from the man," Thomas complains.

"Yes," agrees Andrew, "I see my father hiding in the barn sometimes with a jar of rum in one hand and a tobacco pipe in the other. He looks much more relaxed in the barn than when he's in the house with my mother."

"Speaking of tobacco pipes, look at what I have," Nat says. He pulls out a clay pipe and tobacco pouch.

"I was going to give it to you tomorrow, but I thought tonight was the best time to do so. I know you don't smoke now, but the way things are looking, man, it may not be long before you use it."

They pass it around. Seeing the pipe draws Clarence from his corner.

"Can I hold it?" He asks. But Johnny keeps it away from him.

"Only if you promise not to break it," Johnny warns.

"I promise, cross my heart," pledges Clarence. "Wow."

"This is the way Doc Chandler holds his pipe." He demonstrates. "He holds it in the corner of his mouth so that he can still talk." Then Clarence tries to imitate Doc Chandler. "Mrs. Westley, could you be so kind as to get me a bushel of that dried herring? The missus would be a little cross if I came home without it. Ha, ha, ha."

Then they all try their hand at imitating someone they know. Clarence forgets that he is supposed to stay mad at Nat until after the wedding.

Meanwhile, the women are enjoying a night of Fox and Geese while Lizzy and Anne play Cup and Ball. Samantha pulls out her pennywhistle and begins to make music that they all dance and clap to. It is a time of great enjoyment. Soon Lizzy drifts off into a daydream, imagining her own special day.

"Mother, will you make my wedding gown?" she asks. "I want lots of lace on it."

"I'll do my best," Dorothy replies.

Their conversations are mostly about weddings and how many children they would like to have.

Anne says, "I do not want to have any boys because they may turn out like Clarence, and I would have to strap them something awful."

When they retreat for the night, they fall asleep immediately to help make the morning arrive all the faster.

The morning starts out fair but uneasy for the family. Dorothy, Lizzy, and Anne have already gotten dressed, and they hurry to help Samantha put on her beautiful wedding gown. The gown has a golden petticoat, and a red overdress, with ruffles on the sleeve and neck. It is held on both sides by golden ribbons from her high waist to her hips. Samantha excitedly holds her hands to her mouth, not wanting to spoil the moment with words. Soon she and Lizzy are dancing barefoot across the room, and she and Anne do the same. Dorothy stands with her arms folded and with the biggest smile on her face until all three girls grab her by the hands and invite her to join in the dance. After a mild protest, Dorothy dances around like a little girl. She begins to relax and enjoy her time with all her girls. Samantha's grandmother sits in her chair, clapping her hands and making merry of the time they are sharing together. Samantha has not finished dressing yet, so she suggests that they help her with her stay. Holding her hand on her abdomen, she happily draws in her breath as Lizzy pulls the cord.

"Not too tight, Lizzy! I do need to breathe, you know. I want to walk out and not lose consciousness before we recite our vows," Samantha lightly complains.

"I'm not pulling too hard," Lizzy replies.

Dorothy moves in. "Let me do it. I don't see why it's even needed; you're as thin as a board."

Anne and Lizzy help Samantha step into her petticoat, and then they slip her gown over her head. After buttoning her buttons, they smooth and fluff her skirt. Dorothy straightens the sleeves and adjusts the fabric over her shoulders.

"You look so stunning and lovely today," Dorothy says with tears in her eyes.

Samantha smiles and runs her hands over the textured bodice and down the silk skirt.

"This is the happiest day of my life." She bends down and gives her grandmother the biggest hug. "I love you," she says. "I mean that with all my heart. I love all of you so much."

Johnny is dressed in his father's long red coat that was part of his British army uniform and in white trousers that go to his knees. He is also wearing white stockings with black shoes. Dorothy finds a costume that fits Clarence, so his attire is as close to Johnny's as possible. The wedding goes on without a hitch. Johnny and Samantha are now husband and wife, and Dorothy finally understands what her aunt Liz was requesting of her: grandchildren. Samantha's grandmother has already given Samantha her home and land as a gift, and soon she will move into Dorothy's home with her and the children. Johnny has been working on their property with the hope of getting a good price for it. All they have to do now is wait for it to sell.

When they are before Reverend Hale, everyone stands to sing a hymn. Then Reverend Hale reads a Bible verse from Proverbs 31: 10-31 concerning the virtuous woman. Samantha and Johnny exchange vows, and then he asks for the ring. Clarence acts as though he cannot find the ring, but then he sees Dorothy getting up from her seat. He quickly gives Johnny the ring, peering back and sticking his tongue out at Anne, who shakes her fist at him. After the vows are read and pronounced husband and wife, Johnny kisses Samantha, and then they walk through the gauntlet of grain throwers. There is plenty to eat, and music fills the air around the farm for hours. Clarence avoids Anne all day because she tells him he is going to get it for misbehaving with the ring. As the day turns into night, Dorothy and the rest are so happy that the ceremony comes to pass without a single event, including anything between Anne and Clarence.

Samantha's grandmother helps out a lot around the house, as much as Dorothy and Samantha allow her to work. Dorothy and the girls go to the store while the boys tend to the farm. Johnny stops growing tobacco because he has always seen it as a temporary crop; he makes a deal with one of the tobacco plantations to purchase a certain amount of harvested tobacco, which he and Clarence will dry, cut, and then sell in their store. He continues to use his uncle's recipe for drying meats, for he cures deer, fish, rabbit, and other wild game that he hunts for his family while purchasing more cattle for the farm. Samantha's grandmother dies months after the wedding of pneumonia; Doc Chandler figured she would not survive another winter, and Grandma Nobles dies two weeks before Christmas. She was a sweet old lady who did everything she could to raise her granddaughter; she just never got to see any of her great-grandchildren.

Dorothy knows this all too well, having been raised by her Aunt Elizabeth and Uncle Clarence. She continues to write in her journal, dating it from the early months of 1692 to the present time, documenting the witch hunts and the attacks on her family, including the storm that killed her parents.

It's late February 1716, and Dorothy calls a family meeting late one night and tells them of her journal and how important it is that Samantha know and understand the truth. After Samantha hears the whole story of how Elmira appeared twice at the farm, she cries. Samantha expresses how sorry she is for all the things that have befallen them. She cannot believe what has happened around her, nor can she believe that she was totally unaware of it all.

"It's for this reason that we have trained for all these years," Dorothy explains. "We did not know when they would come or from where. Elmira's revenge and hatred for my family have deeply impacted many's lives for more years than I know."

"I hate Elmira for the senseless murder of the innocent," cries Samantha. "I pray she will never come this way again as long as we live."

"Well, from the looks of it, she'll most likely live for an eternity," says Johnny.

"Yeah, like a million, thousand years," adds Clarence.

"Oh, I don't think so, Clarence," Samantha says quietly. "Everyone has their appointed time to die, and I'm sure her day is coming."

"That's right, little brother, everyone," says Anne looking at Clarence with her hands on her hips.

Everyone remains silent as Dorothy reads more from her journal. Samantha, Lizzy, and Anne cry when she tells them of her aunt Liz and how brave she was when she was jailed, dragged, tied to a post, and burned to death. Johnny sits at the table, listening with his face in his hands, trying to hide his emotions, while Clarence stands beside Dorothy.

"I will protect you, Mother." Says Clarence.

"I know you will, my son," Dorothy says as she comforts him.

They all make a pact to become watchers of the night. They pledge to be prepared forever, and they decide to train their children and their children to fight the witches of the Williams River Colony. The journals will show them how to train and describe which weapons to use and how the witches are able to appear and disappear. The journals instruct them on how the witches have the power to change into any form they wish. Every known description of the witches is detailed in the journals. Dorothy left nothing out in her descriptions and details concerning the names of known witches. She warns them to report every appearance the witches make and what they can do. Johnny, Samantha, Lizzy, Anne, and Clarence pledge that they will be the book's keepers and the Knights of the watch. They will pass this down from generation to generation, no matter how far down the line. No matter what, they will protect their family.

"Mother, have you thought about what Elmira said about you?" Lizzy asks.

"What did she say?" says Samantha.

"She said that there was something special about her," Lizzy replies.

"I really don't know," says Dorothy. "I have thought about that ever since she said it. I can only say that the God we serve is greater than the devil they serve, and how he is strong in our family."

"Mother gets dizzy right before they show up," Anne explains.

"Do you sense their presence?" Samantha is curious.

"I don't really know, and I can't explain the strange feeling I get. It's like…"

"Someone is watching you," Samantha says, her voice quiet. "Did you know your mother?"

"Not really," Dorothy explains. "My parents died when I was three or four years old."

"They say that a mother passes things down to her children." Said Samantha.

"I didn't get it passed down to me!" shouts all of Dorothy's children.

"Maybe there is something that is inherited in one or all of you," says Samantha. "One or all of you may be special in some other way, and we should protect all the children until they are old enough to protect themselves." She clutches her stomach. "Do you think she may know that you or one of us holds the key to her last day as a witch? If she's as old as you say, then she has time on her side."

"Right," Anne agrees. "She could wait until we are really old or until after we are dead, and she could come after our children."

"How will we know if one or all of our children are special?" Johnny asks.

"We use the journal, and we write down everything the child does that is out of the ordinary," Dorothy exclaims.

"Like Mother's headaches, she gets right before the witches appear. Things like that need to be in the journal. When anything happens, we will protect that child from one generation to the next." Lizzy says.

"And don't forget she's stronger than the average person as well," Johnny adds.

"We are the Watchers, and we will watch until the day we die," Dorothy says sternly. "Elmira has an appointment, and we will make sure she keeps it, no matter how long it takes. Elmira's day is coming."

"We promise." They all say.

"When I am gone or too old to keep them, the journals will become the responsibility of Johnny first, and then they will be passed down to the next generation. If there are no heirs, then it goes to Lizzy and her children, and so on, until that wicked witch is dead," Dorothy explains.

She takes Samantha by the arms and holds her firmly.

"You, Samantha Westley, are now part of the family, and you must train for the battles ahead, just as Johnny, Elizabeth, Anne, Clarence, and I have been doing all these years."

Samantha pledges that she will do all she can to protect them and their children's children. She also knows how important it is that she tells the story in the journal that was told to her. It is an important part of who they all are now—Knights of the Watch.

Chapter 14
Time is on My Side

It shocked Elmira and the witches when Dorothy and her children killed Lucy, Alexandra, and Sarah.

"Tools of men fought with children and a madwoman," Elmira sneers.

She looks at Alexandra's mutilated body and at the dead bodies of Lucy and Sarah. Until now, the witches thought they were invincible and could not die. Now Elmira is worried. She's worried about the warning, which rings louder and louder in her head. *Beware, Elmira, beware…* Now they are all aware that all the power in the world does not give them immortality.

"We're not immortals," Amanda whispers.

They can still appear and disappear as they please, but now they must proceed cautiously.

"We must be ready when the clouds clear, and we cannot be caught off guard as we were tonight," Amanda says.

"Dorothy Adams, you'll pay for this for sure," Elmira says as she walks in circles. "Damn!" She screams.

She screams with all her might, and with her fist so tight, she rips the palms of her hands with her talons, and then she screams louder and longer. "Can somebody tell me how this whore keep escaping me time after time? I want her dead – why isn't she dead? What does a witch have to do to kill one person?"

Elmira is enraged, turning and walking in circles crouching and holding her arms up close to her body like she is in great pain. She shouts, "Dorothy, I'll hunt you down from generation to generation until I kill you and everyone and everything you care about." In her true form, Elmira hunches over with her fingers motioning like spiders' legs; she looks from left to right, mumbling to herself with her eyes drawn wide. She looks at the corpses of Alexandra and the others and orders the surviving witches to throw their remains into the fire.

She warns them, "We must cover each other's backs, sides, and fronts." Still mumbling, she adds, "I have to think things over. Dorothy is far stronger and faster than I imagined."

Elmira thinks, *if only I had appeared in my true form, maybe that would have scared Dorothy enough for my girls to get the upper hand on them.*

"A lesson learned tonight, ladies," reasons Elmira. "We strike first and talk after. Too much talking let them know where we were before we appeared."

The witches are mourning the lives of their sisters when Elmira says, "Calm yourselves, ladies. We shall prevail. This is but a minor setback, for there is more than one way to kill this slippery ell."

She continues to whisper. "We can make storms of rain, snow, lightning, and hail, but one thing we lack are the tools of man. Our enemy is strong, and her daughter is as strong as a man and able to get close enough to kill Sarah. She's not only strong but cunning. Soldiers they be, and now we – like them – will ready ourselves for this war."

Everyone's eyes are on Elmira as she circles the area.

"We have an enemy to vanquish, ladies. No matter how long it takes, time is on our side. We'll meet again tomorrow night, and I'll figure something out to give us back the advantage in this war. Now leave me."

The witches return to their homes, but Amanda and Unity stay behind and watch Elmira. She looks back at them.

"I'm all right; I just need time to think." And then she vanishes.

Unity looks at Amanda and says, "Mary's tour?"

"No," replies Amanda, "this is something else. Let's go home. When she wants us, she'll summon us."

In the days to come, Elmira and some of her girls appear as men and others as the three fallen witches, so there will be no suspicion from the goody-goody Sheriff and his men. They carry on this charade for over a month, and then they have them all leave so that Charles and his men will see that Alexandra Schmidt, Lucy Waynes, and Sarah Kane are now the objects of envy from many young women in the township.

"We've lost three women from the mill," Elmira tells Winfred. "I'll have to find replacements for them."

"Be patient. Many are leaving for bigger cities; nevertheless, some are looking to get away from the big cities and relocate to smaller townships like ours," Winfred advises

Elmira does not want to invite any other women into the sisterhood right now. She remembers Mary noticed before she left; there were over thirty women in the sisterhood at that time, now, there are close to fifty, and not all of them are from the Williams River Township. She warned Elmira about having all those witches, warning her that they may not see everything her way. Elmira has a lot to think about, but now what she wants most is the heads of Dorothy and her children in her hands.

Lost in thought, Elmira is startled when Winfred breaks the silence.

"Occasionally, I promote our township in Boston and New York..." As he babbles on, Elmira pays no attention to him; his words are like dull sounds from far away. She hardly ever comes into town anymore; she sends her servants for the things she needs on the farm. Alexandra

Schmidt, Lucy Waynes, and Sarah Kane are the new reason for Elmira's rage. Elmira makes an announcement at the mill stating Amanda will be the new manager and supervisor for the ladies. She states that she will no longer make it out to the mill because of her age and declining health.

Everything is going Elmira's way once again; she has successfully hidden the deaths of Alexandra and the others, and now she and the witches practice their craft while she continues to put a plan together, calculating how to deal with that 'madwoman and those damn children.' She believes time is on her side and that she can reach Dorothy and her family later, when she's older and weaker and when Dorothy will least expect her. After everyone has turned in for the night, the witches meet at the old settlement. Elmira needs time to plan and does not want to rush things; she does not want to risk showing up at Dorothy's house and being killed by an ax-wielding madwoman.

Keith is now into politics and desires to be among the social elite. He loves being a big wig like the others. He often goes on expeditions to Boston, New York, and Virginia with Gaines. Jameston passed away seven years earlier and Eagleton a year before that. They were always looking for ways to build their town into a larger metropolis, and now the area has grown and can no longer be considered a mere township.

With Eagleton's son Jason and his family running their plantation, Keith believes it is now his responsibility as Magistrate to build the township into the future. It has been twenty years, and he's at the top of his game. Keith and Charles are better friends now that Charles is Sheriff. Once a week, Keith rides from the edge of the woods just beyond Elmira's farm to the fork in the road by the sheep farm. They use this time to talk about ideas that Keith will discuss back at the town hall and imply the ideas as his own. Charles doesn't care because he is in control of the law and manages to put Trevor on as one of the volunteers he will never call upon for duty.

Trevor hates the way Charles treats him, for he had more freedom when Keith was in charge, and now he spends much of his time drinking and speaking ill against the Sherriff and Keith. His boasting of how he could be a better Sheriff is now in the open among the townspeople. It is for this reason that he was placed as a volunteer.

"He's insubordinate in everything he does," says Charles as he and Keith ride through town.

All the Sheriff's men are volunteers for the township's militia, except for Trevor, and they are currently being trained by the new Undersheriff, who arrived from England eight years prior. Mr. Gregory Ford was a Lieutenant in the British Army, and he believed he could whip the men into shape. While riding patrol, Gregory tells Charles and Keith, "I referred to these men as a ruddy lot, not fit for militia duty."

"My mother would agree with you wholeheartedly," Keith says, readjusting in his saddle. "Of course, she refers to them as a band of bumbling idiots."

They all have a good laugh as they trot past the sheep farm on their patrol of the area. On their way back to town, Keith tells them he will embark on another expedition to the west of New York, and he bids them a good day as they continue on their patrol past the courthouse. Winfred Gaines used this time to travel between the townships and the Eagleton Hundred Plantation as a delegate for the township.

These days Elmira keeps a watchful eye on Winthrop Trevor. She doesn't want Rose, one of her favorite witches, to be blamed for what she says, 'that idiot's death.' Since Trevor has been sacked, he has been angry and abusive toward her even more than before. Rose is weary of it all and wants to end it as soon as possible. She understands she has the power and the strength to put him out of his misery, and she often confides in Elmira.

"I'm too old for this," says Rose. "The children are grown, and this is the time I should be living a happy life as a grandmother. Instead, my husband is a drunk, and when he is not beating me, he tries to take advantage of me. The sad thing is he's not often up to the challenge. You should see him, limp as a wet rag."

They all get a good laugh at his expense.

Amanda asks Elmira, "Is that what Monroe looked like when he was slipping and sliding on the floor of his room with his ass on the high end?"

The room erupts with laughter.

"Oh, Elmira, just one punch will be all that is needed," Rose tells her. "Just one punch and I don't want him drunk when I do it, either." She begins to cry. "Even though I protect myself by transforming my body when he's punching me, sometimes he gets me when I'm not expecting it, and it hurts badly." Wiping the tears from her face and holding her head up, she says, "I don't know what to do, and since he's home most of the time, it's hard to get away."

"I'm sure there is something we can do to help," Amanda tries to comfort her.

Still wiping the tears, she says, "Everyone at the mill can see how he treats me. He accuses me of being with one of the younger men, and then he comes by and pulls me from the mill."

Elmira reassures Rose that she will inform Keith to talk to Charles and see what can be done about it. The following week, Charles arrives at the mill when Trevor comes by to drag Rose outside.

"Go home, Trevor; you're drunk," Charles says calmly.

"Kiss my ass and go to hell," Trevor replies.

Raising his voice, Mr. Gregory Ford demands, "Please remove yourself from the mill, Sir."

Trevor then spits at him and takes a drunken swing at Ford. He misses, but Ford promptly returns the swing and knocks Trevor to the ground. They drag him to the jail, where the pillory stands. When they lift him up on his feet, they place Trevor's hands and neck between the cutouts and close the top over his hands and neck. Then they nail both his ears to the board. Trevor has to stand there while the townspeople throw fruit and vegetables at him. Some of the townspeople he's offended throw stones his way. Trevor stays there from morning until the evening and is only released to go home shortly before nightfall. Rose stays at Elmira's and does not leave until the next morning.

When she gets home, there he is, drunk and passed out on the floor. She considers placing a spell on him but decides he should live as a miserable drunk for the rest of his life. She gathers a few of her things and asks Mr. Thopham if it is okay if she moves into the house Clarence and Dorothy left behind more than twenty years earlier. New tenants have moved in and out of the house, but it is vacant for the time being.

"It's all but a rundown shack." He reminds her, then shows her the inside. "I have not let anyone move in since the last tenants moved out, but for you, I'll give it to you. It's yours."

He has some of the men from the mill help move her furniture in and make it more livable, leaving Trevor to sleep on the floor.

Mr. Thopham is no longer the Mayor of the township, but everyone there treats him with great respect. Now over eighty years old and nearly deaf, he can only wonder what has happened to his good friend and his niece, who left more than twenty years ago. His wife died five years back, and his children no longer visit the old township. He thinks now is a good time to go on a personal quest to find Clarence and Dorothy. Over the years, he has gathered enough information to know that they are somewhere in the Province of Carolina. He often talks to Winfred, asking him if he would accompany him as far as Harvard, which is on the way to Boston.

"Neither of my children comes here anymore, winter will be upon us soon, and I want to visit them before I die," George tells Winfred. "I'm a lonely old man, and this expedition will cheer me up a bit."

Winfred agrees. "Be all the ready by next week. Keith and I will leave on Monday morning, and we'll pick you up on our way out."

"I'll be packed and waiting for you," George replies with a big smile on his face.

George has sent a message to Harvard, where he has a longtime friend.

He says, "I will do a little traveling, and if you would be so kind, could you help me get to the Carolinas?"

His friend replies and lets him know it would be a grand experience for the both of them.

He does not want Elmira to know what he is doing because he does not want her to follow him to Dorothy and Clarence. He has no idea that Elmira and her witches have already made their presence known twice on Dorothy's farm, nor does he know they murdered Dorothy's husband.

Chapter 15
Band of Bumbling Idiots

It's November, the nights are cold, and Elmira's frustrations have overcome her. She has allowed her enemy to live far too long and wants Dorothy dead immediately. Elmira summons all her sisters to the old settlement and tells them that she is going to gather the winds from the four corners of the earth and bring them down onto Dorothy and her family in the Carolinas. She sends Unity to see if they are still living on the farm.

"Go to them and see if they are still living on their farm, or perhaps they ran like rats after our last visit," Elmira commands.

As soon as Unity appears on the farm, she gets so sick that she can only stand off the road a good distance from the farm, and then she can only stand for a few seconds before she returns to Elmira

"I believe they are still there, but I could not get close enough to find out for sure." She explains. "As soon as I got close to the farm, I got really sick for some reason, to the point where I cannot stand up straight or breathe."

Next, Elmira sends Premise and Joan to the farm, and they report back that they could not get too close because they fell ill trying to do so.

"What in the world is going on here?" Elmira fumes and screams aloud.

She turns and rubs her chin with her talons, trying to figure out if something is in the air or if something or someone is protecting the family after their last attack.

Amanda asks, "Could it be the old witch?"

Elmira turns to Amanda and points at her.

"I was thinking of that, but then I asked myself why, and what connection is there between them? Why would a witch protect them?" She reasons.

"Does Dorothy have black servants? Do you think the old witch found them and started working for her? She could have fallen in love with the way she treats them. Maybe she fell in love with the uncle?" Premise speculates.

"That old weasel died before I could get to him!" Elmira yelled.

Everyone looks at Premise and laughs.

"There was nothing left of that old man when they fled," Amanda states. "What Trevor didn't beat out of him, sorrow for his wife did."

"True," Elmira acknolodges. "But there might be something to what she said."

Elmira walks in circles, hunched over with her hands slightly below her chin. She wiggles her fingers, trying to figure these things out. Then she turns and asks the girls.

"Is the enemy of my enemy a friend of my enemy?" She turns, holding up her finger. "When I could think of nothing more, I figured it may be someone or something we know."

"So, the old witch?" Amanda asks.

"Not sure which witch it is, but a witch indeed. It's times like this when I wish my Mary were here with us," says Elmira. "She and I could go there, and she would tell me if there be a witch or not."

"I, for one, am happy for her. She left to live her life free from your hatred." Unity whispers as she stands away from the others.

Most of them agree with Elmira, and then Amanda asks, "What can we do? Dorothy does have servants, one among them could be a witch. Maybe not the old one, but a witch indeed."

"Just like the old witch who was once a slave herself, this one must also be." Elmira thinks about the warning to beware. "We have to make sure that they are there, and we need to find out who is protecting them. We need to find a way to get them to reveal themselves." Joan adds.

"Without Mary, how do we do that?" asks Unity. "She was the only one among us who could sense the presence of another witch."

"You're right, but never mind all that," says Elmira. "I have something else in mind that will destroy all that in one night, witch or no witch. Amanda and I will go there and see what we can see from all sides of their farm. We'll meet here again tomorrow night; sooner or later, I'll concoct the storm of the century, and then I'll have my revenge." Elmira rages.

Elmira and Amanda leave for Dorothy's farm, trying not to get too close. They fly in large circles around the farm, closing the circle tighter as they go. They are soon overcome by the same illness but can see Dorothy and three young ladies entering the store that morning. They return to the Williams River Township and determine a powerful witch is protecting them.

"Are you okay?" Elmira asks Amanda.

"I'm feeling much better now that we are away from that place." She answers.

"I have no doubt a witch is protecting her and those tramps she was with. None of that matters now, for they will all suffer the same fate."

Monroe Wilson's words ring loud in the memory of his speech,

"Big cities, big problems."

The township has grown over the years and has spread well past the fork in the road. Charles remembers Monroe's words. 'Big cities, big problems.' Most of the children who grew up there now have children of their own, and all Charles can think about is the safety of his children and grandchildren. The Sheriff and his men are having difficulty tracking a man stealing and butchering sheep. They often meet to discuss the best way to capture the thief. They know the culprit is using the woods around the township to get in and out of the area. They first search the roads leading away from the town from the fork in the road, but to no avail. They searched the lake and the river, but they could not see any reason the thief would be there to go from one end of the town and walk back with an armful of sheep. It was really puzzling, and the townsfolk had no clue how to hunt him or them down.

"Gents, I believe if you want to catch a fox, you use foxhounds," says Mr. Gregory Ford. "These chaps are clever and know how to cover their tracks. We must be just as clever and set a clever trap for a clever chap." They just stare at him. "A what?" he laughs, delighted with what he considers his clever play on words. Of course, no one else thinks it's funny at all.

"Anyway, my good men." He continues after clearing his throat. "It seems you gentlemen are in no mood for levity, so we'll carry on. The next time these thieves come into town to lighten us of the burden of our livestock, we should have a well-laid plan."

"Well, I sure hope it's soon," Keith says. "We can't afford another loss."

Since the first reported theft and killings of the sheep two weeks earlier, the men were given wooden rattles to alarm others if they saw the thieves. When an alarm sounds, the others hearing it will run to assist them.

When Charles and Mr. Ford leave the courthouse trying to figure out a way to catch the thief, Charles wants to know just how hard can it be when he or they is packing sheep in his ruddy arms.

"I don't get it. Today it's stealing and crudely butchering sheep; tomorrow, it could be even worse. We have to get a handle on this, and it has to be soon." He demands.

Charles looks at Ford. "We must step up our watch in patrolling the township." He sighs. "It's the best we can do right now. So, pick one of the deputies, and he'll take the first watch and get the volunteers to help him."

Ford agrees. "I'll use three of our men with the volunteers in three different groups. We can cover more ground that way."

"Make it so by tonight," Charles demands. "Oh, and by the way." Charles stops in the street and turns to Ford. "Tell whoever it is walking their patrol and using their rattle like a toy to cut it out, or he'll spend time with his head in the pillory."

"I'll talk to them all about it," Ford replies.

That following Saturday night, there's a cold chill in the air. Charles, Ford, and all the deputies are patrolling the area looking to capture the sheep thief; they want badly to put the sheep-killing business to rest. It's late evening, and Charles, Ford, and Keith are on their evening patrol when they hear shouting and frantic rattling. They pull the reins of their horses and head back into the town from the fork in the road. Deputies James and Greene are chasing someone toward the woods headed in the direction of the old farms.

Ford calls out to James, "Fetch the hounds."

As they wait for the dogs, Keith asks Greene, "Did you see the perpetrator?"

"I didn't, but I believe Douglass may be able to identify him. He was slashed with a knife by the man when they struggled, and that's when we started after him." Greene reports.

"Where is Douglass now?" Charles asks.

"Thomas Gilliam took him to Doc's house to get that cut tended to. It was pretty deep," explains Greene. "I believe that's him running back now."

Now there are more than ten other men who have joined the hunt.

"Mr. Gilliam," Ford called out.

"Yes, Sir," Thomas answered.

"Did Mr. Douglass see this villain?"

"I don't think so. The man turned pretty quick and slashed him badly." Said Thomas.

"Whoever he is, he's using the woods on the east end of the town for cover. He knows these woods pretty well," Charles announces. "It's just as I suspected; he's a local. He knows these woods too well to be a stranger."

The dogs are excited and ready for the hunt.

"Take them over to the area where the two men fought," Ford orders.

After scurrying about in circles, the dogs catch the right scent and set off running and barking on the hunt with five men running behind.

"You may want to stay behind," Charles advises Keith.

"I haven't had this kind of excitement in a long time," says Keith. "Surely you won't deprive me of the chase?" He turns to Deputy James. "Lend me one of your pistols, my good man."

"This one belongs to Douglass," says Deputy James. "Here are all his artifacts, and the pistol is loaded."

"It seems he is headed toward the farms," Charles observes. "We can cover more ground if we split up. James, you take four men and cut through the wood behind the first group just in case he doubles back. We'll take the road and wait for him, for at some point, he will have to cross the road at the back of the farms. When he does, we'll be waiting for him there."

"Good show, Charles!" Ford shouts. "Now, we must cut to the chase."

They all split up, some covering the woods with the dogs to drive him while the others wait for the suspect at the farms.

At the old settlement, the witches encircle the fire pit, chanting. Elmira is in the midst of them, conjuring up a large storm to teleport it to the Carolinas to destroy Dorothy and her family. More than forty witches are flying in a double circle around Elmira, for they have been waiting for this great storm of Elmira's for over an hour. They are growing tired of chanting and have begun to lose faith in Elmira's ability to conjure up this superstorm. As they chant, many witches grow weary of the show and vanish back to their homes. Most of these witches are from other townships as far as Boston. Elmira notices this and fumes, but she knows Dorothy is more important than insubordinate witches.

Elmira thinks to herself. *I'll find those witches and put an end to their miserable lives when this is over.* She notices those that remain are getting restless, but she has to stay focused on making this happen. Flames shoot from her mouth and hands, and then she begins to twirl in a circle, making a twister of flames until she stops midair. Nothing happens for a few seconds, but then the wind picks up from the east, and the witches stop chanting. Another gust comes in from the west and clashes with the wind from the east. The wind rushes in from the south, warmer than the east and west, and finally, a cooler breeze flows from the north. None of the witches can see the eyes that narrows and pierces the darkness from the trees outside the old settlement. The storm gathers dust from the Earth, drawing it up within itself. The breeze slowly turns as the four winds come together. As fast as it started, it seemed to fall off just as fast. Elmira starts chanting again, prompting the others to continue as they did before. Elmira stops spinning and chants louder, and as the wind picks up again, the witches get more into it. Now they are beginning to see the results of their long and laborious work.

Fog and mist fill the air as the cold wind picks up more than before. They go on through the night with the wind getting stronger around them. The wind blows and howls, turning and twisting to the point where the witches have difficulty controlling their levitation. They see the fog and mist being pulled into the rotating void, frightening most of them. As they go on, they believe they will be sucked inside the huge, twisting storm if it gains any more strength. More witches vanish for fear for their lives which fuels Elmira's rage.

At the farms, Charles, Ford, and Keith hurry to the front of the woods behind the property closest to the road, hoping the dogs will drive the thief their way. When they arrive, they notice the wind in the area has picked up around the farm, yet it remains calm in the town.

"I sure hope they hurry." Ford expresses with worry. "There seems to be a storm headed our way."

They hear the dogs barking and the men rattling and shouting in the woods, but when the thief is preparing to exit the woods, he sees men waiting on horses. He turns and hurries back into the woods, going north before they see him. The deputies and their dogs exit the woods just at the street. Deputy Winston James is holding the dogs back with ropes tied around their necks. Ford is furious when he sees the hounds being held back.

"Let the bloody hounds run free!" He cries. "How do you expect them to corner the thief if you hold them back?"

They untie the hounds, and they sniff around for a second and then head north into the woods barking after the thief.

"Come on, men!" Keith yells.

They head deeper into the woods, going north, where the river cuts through the hunting grounds.

"He's headed towards the river!" shouts Charles. "We have to cut him off before he gets there."

When they arrive at the river, they notice he is using the river's edge to throw the dogs off. They can hear the dogs hot on his trail, and then they hear a shot and one of the two dogs yelps. They hurry on, using the river as a guide. The men on the horses arrive and find one of the dogs on the ground. He's been shot in the underside of his chest.

"He must have tried to jump on the man when he shot him." Keith states.

"Well, we have to find this murderous villain," says Charles. "We can't let him go. We're closer now than we've ever been before."

They want to ride harder to catch up with the other dog, but they notice the barking has stopped.

"What in bloody hell is going on here?" Ford asks. Their horses are very nervous, and the wind is getting stronger on and off. "Where's the other hound?"

James and the other men catch up with the group at the river, glad for the chance to stop and rest.

"We can't sit down now," says Ford. "He could be right behind you, waiting to strike you in the back of your head."

"Oh, that's good to hear," James sneers. "Why don't you get your carcass off that horse and let us ride, and you run through these woods on foot?"

"Cut the chatter," Charles demands. "Quiet."

"You think he killed the other dog?" Keith asks.

"No," says Charles. "I think I know who's behind this treachery, and the only reason the dog is no longer barking is that he knows the man he's been chasing."

Charles gets off his horse and walks to the river's edge, where he sees it has not been disturbed. There are no footprints in the soft mud. "He's back in the woods." He whispers.

He walks to the edge of the woods and sees broken branches; it is clear they did not break naturally. The thatch on the ground has been kicked up, and now he knows his direction.

"We can go through here." Charles charges. "We'll need every man we can get if we are going to catch this thief."

"Who is it?" asks Ford.

"Yes, Charles, who are we chasing?" Keith begs.

"Our old friend and nemeses… Winthrop Trevor. And he's as tired as you are, so let's get going. By the way, he knows how to use his knife, and he's had plenty of time to reload that pistol of his, so let's be careful. We can drive him just as hard as he can drive us, but it's different when you are the hunted. Even if he does know these woods, the fear of being caught will keep him confused."

"There's fourteen of us, and this Trevor fellow has outwitted the whole lot of us. Let's end this," Ford shouts.

"He's probably drunk!" James shouts, and the others agree.

"Then you ought to be extremely careful," Charles warns. "If he's drunk and eluding us, just think of what he'll do when he's sober."

"That man is about as sober as we are," Gilliam exclaims.

They drive Trevor farther into the woods for about an hour. Then Charles begins to whistle.

"What in blue blazes are you doing?" Ford asks.

"If he's as tired as I am, I doubt if he can't keep that hound from giving up his position."

"Hell, why didn't you say that earlier, Charles? He'll only come by my whistle," James says.

"Rubbish," scoffs Greene. "You don't know those hounds as well as you've been bragging."

"Enough, you two!" Ford shouts.

"James, give it your whistle when I tell you, but it has to be loud," Charles explains. "This infernal wind is getting louder as we get farther into these woods."

"Right, I will, and you'll see." James boast.

They venture deeper into the woods for another hour, and then Charles gives James the go-ahead. James whistles as loud as he can, and the dog comes running by and jumps into James's arms. A shot is fired not far from their position, but no one goes down. They see Trevor, who turns and runs as fast as he can, but the mist is getting thicker, making it harder to see. They all chase him until they run right through the gate into the witch's haven. Charles chases down Trevor and tackles him, but he is surprised by what he sees.

The witches stop flying, and Elmira looks down at the men as they look up at her.

"What are you fools doing here?" explodes the voice of a strange being in the midst of a large fire, surrounded by a group of hooded flying creatures. Suddenly, the wind surrounding the settlement has grown stronger. A dog runs past the other dog from the woods, and they immediately run away.

"You fools, what have you done?" The strange figure screams. "Fools, fools!"

The storm begins to move to the east, and none of the witches can control it. The men try to hold onto the trees, but being on foot amid a three-hour chase has tired them out, and none of them has the strength to hold on for long. The hooded creatures are being sucked into the storm, screaming, and Elmira follows close behind them. When the men can no longer hold on, they, too, are sucked into the storm that seems to be picking up speed and strength as it moves across the land. All kinds of debris flow across the storm's edge. Gilliam is struck by a large branch and thrown from the fort by strong winds. One at a time, the witches and the men are plastered against the inner edge of the storm's wall. None of them could move, and then they all began to get sick and vomit from the twisting and turning of the storm. The men are the first to blackout, and then the women follow.

A strange figure steps out of the woods from the old settlement, controlling the storm. Her head bowed down, her eyes closed, and her arms outstretched in front of her. She lifted her head and began to roar like a lion. Flames in a whirlwind engulf her body, and then she roars even louder, and the storm seems to burst into flames, and lightning flashes inside and outside the twisting storm. She drives the storm as it widens and strengthens, pushing through the woods. Her fury and rage push it on as she roars.

"You wanted a storm, Elmira? I'll show you what a real storm looks like. You and your witches will pay for your arrogance, and your colony will pay with their lives."

Then she spreads her arms out to her sides, and the storm widens to three times its width, pulling up trees and soil as deep as a hound's legs. When the storm is well away from the settlement, one of the hounds returns to her side, and she calms down as she takes deep breaths to silence the storm within.

"Good boy." she praises, bending down to pat it. "You did well."

Then the hound transforms into a man.

"This is only half it. I'll finish this in the morning." She says. They walk back into the woods behind the old settlement and disappear.

Chapter 16
The Witches Storm

The townspeople awake to the aftermath in the morning to see the damage caused by the storm.

"Lord have mercy," says Reverend Prather as he looks out the church's window at the destruction while it is still in the twilight hours. Half the town is missing, and a huge path that seems as wide as a river flows through it, meandering through the woods like a giant serpent. Many of the townspeople cry because they have lost friends and family. The storm's violence has left nothing behind except rubble. The storm's path was more than three hundred meters wide, uprooting trees and laying waste to more than half the town. They look around, and none can tell where the mill is anymore. After an hour of searching for survivors, the men think of the farms and families. They climb on the horses they've managed to round up and follow the path to where the farms should be on their buggies. Once there, they find no houses or stables, fences or crops, only a wide-open space with one huge path plowing right through them. They notice the storm's path has come in from the west of the farms. Richard Douglass, one of the new men in the town, is one of the volunteers who stayed behind when Trevor sliced his arm in the struggle. He suggests that they follow the path.

"I advise you to stay, Mr. Douglass; the travel may worsen your wound." Advises Mr. Thopham.

"Well, George, old boy, how about an adventure before you go off on your own adventure?"

George Thopham points westward. As they ride off on the path the storm left behind, they notice there are no trees, and the storm has plowed down into the earth.

"This is the deepest I've been in these woods in a long time," Winfred remarks.

"It's the deepest many has ever been," says George. "Maybe we should tell the others we're turning back. This is getting a little too spooky for me."

"Where's your adventurous nature, George?" asks Winfred. "You're not getting soft in our old age, are you?"

"That adventurous nature went in the opposite direction, and I'm serious about turning back." George expresses fear.

They follow the path for over five miles and end up at the gate to the old settlement.

George is about to protest more when they enter the gate.

"Oh, Lord, have mercy on us," George cries. None of the men notice the angry eyes watching from the trees. These eyes are narrow and inflamed, and fury rages as the storm within is rekindled by the sight of two intruders of a time long past.

"So, back to the old settlement," George and Winfred say simultaneously.

"Hold your tongue, old friend," says Winfred.

"Why," George replies. "Everyone who knew us then is either dead or moved on."

Winfred stands up in the buggy and looks around. Then he and George glance at each other, wondering if they should get off the buggy.

"Maybe we shouldn't be here," George says in a frightened tone. "I have a bad feeling about this place and don't like it one bit."

Winfred calls out to the men who have already dismounted. They start to walk around the old place.

"Maybe we should leave now," Winfred says. "There's nothing here, so let's go back. We do have a long ride back to the town."

None of them has seen it before, and now some men have an eerie feeling.

"So, this is where it all started, right here at the old settlement," says John Tensely.

"I hear tell of our founder Mr. Williams's daughter and some Indian. They say they were lovers." Mentions one of the men

"And one of the men shot the Indian in the back," Amos Dryers adds.

"I heard the same thing," Adam Tonstall speaks out. "You two older gents must know whether it's true."

"Well, is it true?" Eckerd Hess asks.

"We should leave the past in the past, young man," states George. "There's nothing here, and we should leave now."

"They say this place is cursed. I think we should do as he said and leave," another man shouts.

Winfred starts to turn his buggy around.

"This place gives me the shivers." George worries.

"I'm with you, old man. I'm out of here." Eckerd shouts.

A strong warm breeze sweeps through the old settlement from the south, and a cold breeze from the north blasts across the old settlement without moving any of the trees. The men just stand as though someone has told them to freeze. George and Winfred look at each other without saying a word. The horses rear up on their hind legs and run towards the gate. Winfred tries to hold his horse steady and head back out the gate while some of the horses run back onto the path. Winfred regains control of his horse and buggy and heads back to the storm's path in the direction of their town. Another strong gust of wind comes in from the east and another from the west. They struggle to ride out of the gate through which they come. On the other side of the gate, the horses settle down. Some of the men curse at them as they run after them on foot.

"Maybe I should have listened to you, old friend," says Winfred. "This doesn't seem to be going well at all."

The men retrieve the horses that ran from the settlement, and the men mount up and try to get the horses to gallop, but instead, they move as though they are heavily-burdened mules. George looks back and is frightened by what he thinks is a woman in a pale blue dress with a white jacket and mob cap. She is moving just above the ground. Then George sees a tall and pale man walking behind her; the man transforms into a wolf-like creature and runs into the woods. Winfred looks at his friend as he turns slowly in his seat, wondering what seems to have frightened him.

"You've turned frightfully pale, George." He says. "Are you all right? You look as though you've just seen a ghost."

George does not say a word; he wants to get as far away from the old settlement as possible. His thoughts take him back to Clarence as they sit in his home and spoke of a time Clarence was out looking for the deer he shot in the woods. He recalls Clarence had seen a woman hovering above the ground in the distance. He said it frightened him so badly that he soiled himself and was unable to move for what seemed like hours. Just the thought of it brought goosebumps and chills all over his body, and what he had just witnessed was more frightening as — surely even more frightening than what Clarence saw over forty-five years ago.

How can this be? Frets George. *She's been dead for more than sixty-five years, and that man that turned into that creature... Lord be merciful.* Then he thinks that if he took one look back and saw nothing, he could blame it on his nerves, so he turns around slowly, looking back at the old settlement. She's still there, only now she is hovering past the gate and seems to be following them with her arms out, elbows bent, and her fist closed as if she is holding something back. George closes his eyes tight and pivots around in the seat as slowly as he does when he looks back. The horses start running out of control, and then they stop. This time Winfred looks at George, whose eyes are shut as tight as those of a child who believes he has seen a specter in the dark of the night. Winfred turns to look in the direction that made his riding companion so afraid. He sees the woman, and the two of them stare at each other for a few seconds. She drops her arms, with flames in her eyes, and screams his name. Only he can hear her.

"Winfred Albert Gains!" She screams. "Elmira's whore."

She transforms into a large serpent dragon that is just above the buggy and inhales deeply. Winfred can't move and just stares up at the beast. Then she exhales, and fire bellows from her mouth, and his head bursts into flames, but George doesn't see it.

"Winfred, Winfred." George call.

The flames take Winfred's breath right from his lungs, and he makes a gurgling sound. Winfred grabs his chest; his face is blood red, and he falls over into George's lap. George calls out for help to those who are trying to get their horses to move ahead of them, and then he takes the reins of the buggy.

A couple of the men stop and ask, "What happened?"

George can only say, "He grabbed his chest and fell over in my lap."

They check to see if he is still alive. "He's burning up and barely breathing." They noticed. "You'd better get him to Doc Hadley's in a hurry."

He raises the straps and brings them down on the horse, which begins to gallop faster as he drives on.

The young men shout, "Get these damn horses moving!"

The majority of the men are in agreement. They all know of the witch hunts, and they are thinking of how eerie it felt right before the winds blew into the settlement and how the winds blew only in the settlement and not outside of it. They look at the settlement and watch an ever-growing storm twisting inside the old settlement, and now Winfred Gaines is dead.

They all shout irrationally. "The witches are punishing the town!"

The men drive through the trail as fast as their horses can travel. With tears in his eyes and fear in his heart, George slaps his horse to get his friend out as fast as the horses can run. This time he swears he will not look back. He thinks of Mrs. Kirts's son Adam and his wife, Clarence and Elizabeth Lester, Dorothy, and then he thought of that hellish night more than sixty-five years ago. His thoughts take him all over the path. Fear drives him; fear drives all the men already out of sight on the path.

"Don't look back." He tells himself. He repeats this all the way back to town. The trip seems to take hours, as if time has slowed. When he drives into the town, he finds total chaos; no one listens to anyone. The winds have already caught up with him. George takes Winfred to Doc Hadley for help, and they get other men to help get him out of the buggy. Doc. determines that Winfred has most likely suffered a heart attack.

"Unfortunately, Winfred did not survive the trip back." Doc told George."
George, in turn, does not want to spend another minute in town after seeing the woman and whatever it was that followed them before she vanished.

"Mr. Hadley, I'm a rational man with modest beliefs," George says. "I can't tell you exactly what I saw at the old settlement, but it might be best that you pack up and take your family and get as far away from here as possible. I believe the storm that destroyed half the town last night was the work of a very angry witch, and I don't believe she's finished yet."
He looks at Doc Hadley with a stern face.

"Leave now, leave this town as fast as he can. He turns to leave the house, and he finds that someone has taken his buggy. He looks back at Doc, who appears bewildered, and says with deep concern and tears falling from his face.

"Leave now, man." He warns. "For God's sake, leave now."

A limb hits the side of the house, and when he looks past the house, there it is, the wolf, dark gray, just staring up at him; then it transforms into a man, a man he once knew, a man he helped bury. Without a word, he turns and walks away as fast as possible. George runs to his home and grabs the only bags he considers important. The wind is cold and picking up fast, so George finds the first family on the road and asks if he can ride with them as far as they are going.

"We are returning to Newton, a small town outside of Boston."

"Know it well, young man. Let's ride then talk." Says George quickly. "I will pay for my voyage and travel with you there."

He plans to leave from Boston in the hopes of finding his old friends in the Province of Carolina. It has been over twenty years since Clarence and Dorothy left quietly in the night from the Williams River Township. He often thinks of the place where Dorothy had always wanted to move. This, he thinks, will be a great place to start. The trip takes only a few weeks; it is a hard journey, but it is far better than the nightmare back in the Williams River Township. When they reach Newton, George thanks the family and pays them well for their kindness, he has his sights set on the Boston harbor.

"Mr. Thopham." The man calls.

"Yes, my son?" He replies.

"Please be so kind not to mention anything that has happened, and not to mention that we helped you leave that place?" asks the family. "We wouldn't want these people to think we are bringing that curse here with us."

"My good man," George says. "What we saw when we ran from that place will go with me to my grave. And If I find the courage to tell anyone, I promise not to tell them your names, only that we escaped with our lives."

"I wish you safe travels, kind sir," they reply, smiling. "I hope you find your family."

"I wish you and your family the same." He says, walking away swiftly.

In Boston, George finds a ship sailing to the Province of Carolina. During his journey, he finds out that the Province of Carolina was divided in 1712, and now there is a North Carolina and a South Carolina. He isn't sure whether this will make it harder to find Clarence and Dorothy, but he still wants to carry on. This is his expedition and perhaps his last adventure. George hopes they aren't too far from the harbor because he isn't sure how long he has left to live; most of the men his age are either dead or, like himself, dying of old age. George promises never to look back because he does not want to see her face or that wolf creature ever again. After a seemingly endless voyage, he arrives in the new Province of North Carolina. George disembarks from the ship only to board another smaller ship traveling to the port of the old Towne on Queen Anne's Creek, later to be renamed Edenton. He sets his heart on finding his old friends. After asking around for hours, he grows tired and weary and begins to lose hope, so he decides to ask one last person before returning to a tavern for some rest.

"I say, young man." He asks. "Would you know of Clarence Lester and Dorothy Adams? I have traveled far and pray it has not been in vain."

"I'm sorry, but those names are not familiar." replies the young man. "Where did you come from?"

George is not sure whether he should tell the young man. "My travels bring me from Boston."

"Well, sir, if I hear of anything, I will let you know. Where are you lodging?"

"I'm not sure yet," George admits. "I have been trying to find my friends for hours, and I have not had time to find a proper place to rest my head. If you hear of anything, you will find me there when I find a place to let."

"If I find these friends of yours, whom should I say is looking?" asks the young man.

"Quite right, my name is George Thopham," George says. "I was a friend and business partner of the family."

"Well, sir, I think I can help you with a place to stay." The stranger replies. "There's a place my father and I often spent nights when travel was impossible or when it was too late to set off for home."

The young man takes him to a store belonging to a friend of the family.

"Good afternoon, Mr. Kinsley."

"Afternoon, young Johnny. How can we help you today?"

"This gentleman has traveled here from Boston, and I am assisting him in locating friends of his," Johnny explains. "Could I trouble you and ask if you will allow him to stay here until I bring him word?"

"It's no trouble at all." Said Mrs. Kinsley.

"I will stay only if I am allowed to pay for my lodging." States George.

Johnny shrugs his shoulders, Mr. Kinsley agrees, and Mrs. Kinsley shows him to his room. It is a small corner room off the main part of the store, just big enough for a cot and table against the wall. George is tired and takes no food. He lays his bags down, pushes them under the cot, and soon falls asleep. When Johnny arrives home that night, he talks about his day.

"Mother, do you know a man named… George Thopham?" He asks.

She looks at him in fear, approaches her son, and grabs his arms.

"Where did you hear that name?" She demands.

Her reaction shocks the others at the table. Samantha stands up next to Johnny.

"I'm sure he's going to tell us," Samantha suggests. "Why don't I fix us all a cup of tea?" She takes Dorothy by the arms and gently sits her back down in her seat. "Sit here, Mother Westley, and I'll get you a cup of tea." She looks at Johnny. "Well, tell her."

"Okay, I was outside the harbor store when I heard this old gentleman asking about Clarence Lester and you, only using the name Dorothy Adams," Johnny explains. "I thought it best to make myself available to him to end his search asking about you and Uncle Clarence. I told him I did not know who you were, but I would try and find out for him. I was relieved he told me that he was looking for Clarence and you, and he was a friend of the family, so I took him to the Kinsley's store for the night."

Dorothy shakes her head because she is sure by now that he is dead, yet here he is, right in the Carolinas.

"Well." She says. "I want you to take me there to meet with him first thing in the morning, and if it is him, we'll bring him here, and he can stay with us. He was a good friend of Uncle Clarence and his partner in the salted meat business."

"Surely, I will be going as well. I want to see Mother Westley's old friend," Samantha declares.

"We'll leave early in the morning," Dorothy suggests. "Lizzy, Anne, and Clarence will run the store while we're out. It's late now, and I think I'll go to bed and see you in the morning."

"I don't think I've ever heard her or Uncle Clarence speak of this man before," Johnny remarks.

"Nor I. She said Uncle Clarence ran a small business salting meats," Lizzy says.

"Well, we'll know soon enough." Says Samantha.

"What did he look like?" asks Anne.

"Just a really old man, and he doesn't hear very well," Johnny explains. "I had to keep telling him the same thing over and over again the whole way to the store. He was pleasant enough, but he seemed afraid of something. I did ask him if he had any other bags and pointed to the wharf, but he did not want to look. He pressed right past me like he was running from something."

"Hard of hearing like Clarence!" Remarks Anne.

"Hey, I hear very well, thank you." Blurts Clarence, folding his arms.

"We'll remember that when it's time for you to do your chores," Lizzy says.

Clarence sticks his tongue out at Anne. He walks away with his arms still crossed. "Tattletale." He calls Anne.

The morning is cool, and the wind only stirs a little. Johnny goes out to the barn and prepares the two-bench buggy for the trip. Clarence follows his brother outside.

"Can I go?" He asks, kicking the dirt on the floor of the barn. "Anne and Lizzy are mean to me. I hate them."

"You will do no such thing Clarence," Warns Johnny. "And if you do what you are told, they won't beat up on you so much."

"Yes, they will." He replies. "No matter what I do, they always pick on me." Climbing into the back of the buggy and raising the blanket over his head, he curls up, trying to convince Johnny to let him go. "I can hide under this blanket in the back. They'll never know I'm here if you don't tell anybody."

Johnny laughs. "No, Clarence, you can't keep your mouth closed long enough to stay hidden. You tell us where you're hiding all the time."

"But I do that because it takes you too long to find me!" He pouts.

With a sigh, Johnny rubs the top of his brother's head. "Just do what Mother tells you to do." He suggests. "When you're in the store, sweep the floors, clean the counters, and clean the windows inside and out. Above all, stay out of the sweets jar."

After hitching the horses to the buggy, he and Clarence ride up to the house. Johnny climbs down to help his mother and Samantha.

Dorothy looks back and sees Clarence. "Get out." She tells him. "You have to help the girls at the store."

"I'm just riding to the store." He says.

"Your father always said you were a crafty little bugger." laughs Dorothy. "Now, you make sure you get off at the store."

"Yes, ma'am." He obeys, pulling the blanket off his head. "Mother?"

"What is it, Clarence?" Dorothy asks.

"What does crafty mean?" He asks.

Samantha sounds off with a list. "Underhanded, a little schemer, and cunning," she says. "Need I say more?"

"What's a schemer?" Clarence asks.

"Oh my God, Clarence," Dorothy shouts. "You'd better keep your mouth shut, or I'm going to pound you worse than Anne does." She pulls the blanket back and angrily points her finger at him, shouting at him. "Hush, and don't say another word! Do you understand me?"

"Yes." He says, folding his arms. He presses his lips tightly together and bows his head.

Lizzy and Anne are standing in the window at the store when they see Clarence waving at them from the back of the buggy. Anne shakes her fist at him and goes to the door to complain, for it appears Clarence will be going, and they have made to stay. The buggy stops at the front of the store, and Dorothy makes Clarence get out of the buggy.

"You'd better behave yourself and do your chores," Dorothy warns.

Anne stands in front of Clarence as he reluctantly climbs out of the buggy.

"Don't worry, Mother." Says Lizzy. "He will do what he is supposed to do."

"Anne is being crafty and won't let me by," Clarence complains.

"Don't start, Clarence." admonishes Dorothy.

"Are you going to ride off and let her beat me up as soon as you're out of sight?" He whines.

"No, she will do no such thing." She says, looking at Anne. "She'll do her chores, and you'll do yours. Lizzy, you keep the two of them separated, and don't let them tear up the store."

Lizzy agrees.

Johnny drives off, shaking his head and looking up at the sky while the others see them off. Before they ride around the corner, Dorothy and Samantha look back to see Anne and Clarence swinging at each other.

With a loud sigh, Dorothy looks up, pushes her hair back, and closes her eyes. "I have no clue what I'm going to do with those two."

Johnny jokes, "Put them in the privy and make them clean it every time they fight?"

Samantha and Dorothy turned and gave him a cold look.

"Where do you get these crazy ideas?" Asks Samantha.

"Oh, he's just getting started." Says Dorothy, rearing her head. "His father was full of those crazy ideas, so I'll apologize. You'll have to deal with it for the rest of your life."

After a few minutes, Dorothy says, "Oh my God, am I dreaming? Listen, can you hear that?"

"What?" Johnny and Samantha say, bewildered.

"No Clarence, and no Anne." Smiles Dorothy. "Just the birds singing. Between the two and their constant battles, I almost forgot what it's like to have peace and quiet."

Dorothy takes a deep breath and relaxes on the backbench with her eyes closed. Johnny raises the reins to bring them down to the horses' rumps to get them to move faster so that it won't take them all morning to reach the harbor. Dorothy thinks back to when the only people she and Uncle could depend on were the Thophams. She is so excited to go to the harbor to see Mr. Thopham, if he is who he says he is. She remembers her uncle's warning, "There may be those who are not whom you think they are."

They are prepared for the worst but hope for the best. Nonetheless, Samantha and Dorothy have strapped daggers under their dresses, and Johnny wears his pistols on his side and a knife in his boot. A cool breeze fills the air, making for a nerve-easing conversation to the harbor. Dorothy is nervous because she really wants to see her uncle's old friend, and most importantly, she wants to find out why he is there. She cannot wait to see him after all these years. The ride seems longer than it really is, and they ride most of the way, talking about the old township and how Dorothy used to run through Old Man Kirts's farm.

"Uncle and Aunt Liz would warn me about running through his farm, but I didn't like him, so I did it out of spite."

Neither Johnny nor Samantha has ever heard Dorothy talk this much.

"Now we can see where Anne and Clarence get it from," remarks Johnny. "That girl even talks when she's asleep."

Dorothy pops him on the back of the head and laughs.

"You could be right." She says. "I just hope I wasn't as much trouble as those two."

When they reach the harbor and turn down the harbor's main street into town, Johnny sees Mr. Thopham sitting on a stool outside the store with his bag in his hand. They stop the buggy short of the store, and Dorothy climbs down and slowly approaches her old friend, looking back at Johnny, who walks up to the store on the other side of the street. Johnny is carrying his pistol under his arm, ready to fire. Samantha stays on the buggy, watching to see if anyone else is with Mr. Thopham.

"Mr. Thopham?" Dorothy calls out three times. "Is that you?"

"Oh, merciful heaven!" He cries. Then he stands up from the stool, gives Dorothy a big bear hug, and kisses her on the cheek.

"Look at you, all grown up." He says. "I've missed you and Clarence so much in the passing years. I wasn't sure I would find you, but here you are." Johnny approaches them from across the street.

"Young man, I have much to thank you for." Says Mr. Thopham. He reaches into his purse to pay him, thanking Johnny and shaking his hand.

"I don't have much, I'm afraid." He says. "How can I ever repay you, my son?"

Johnny refuses the money and tells him that payment will not be necessary.

"Sir, I believe it would be better if we got out of the street and returned to the house."

"Mr. Thopham, I want you to meet Johnny, my eldest son." Dorothy proudly points out.

"Well, I'll be." Says Mr. Thopham. "The Lord works in mysterious ways. "Your son, you say?"

Johnny signals for Samantha to bring the buggy.

"Yes, and this young lady on the buggy is his wife, Samantha."

Johnny helps Mr. Thopham and Dorothy up onto the buggy. Dorothy tells her old friend that she will explain everything on their way back to the farm.

"I'll put my trust in your capable hands." He says.

On their way back to the farm, Dorothy asks, "What brings you to the Carolinas? Why not Florida or some other place?"

"You, Dorothy." Replies Mr. Thopham. "Remember? It was all you would talk about."

Dorothy sits quietly for a moment.

"What made you seek us out?" She asks.

"Long story, young Dorothy, and I'm afraid I have bad news about our old township." He warns.

"How bad?" She asks.

"Disastrously bad." Replies Mr. Thopham. "I have never heard or seen the likes of it before. So many are missing, and even more are dead." Then he whispers, "Never look back."

At that, George bursts into tears. Dorothy and Samantha do as well, for they wonder what all this really means; even Johnny wipes the tears from his eyes. The ride back to the farm is quiet. Johnny drives the buggy up to the front of the house, and then he helps Mr. Thopham and the ladies down so they can show their guests to his room.

"Thank you," whispers Mr. Thopham, and then he cries himself to sleep once in bed.

Leaving the room and shutting the door behind them, Dorothy says, "I guess we'll have to wait to hear what the bad news is when he awakes."

"I'm not sure I want to know." Samantha states. "All I can think of is how so many are missing and even more dead. It's a vision that disturbs me to no end. What does it mean?"

Dorothy reaches out to her and hugs her close as she weeps. "We can only wait until he wakes."

Johnny walks into the room. "What did he say?" He asks.

"Nothing, he just cried himself to sleep." Dorothy states.

"I'll go to the store and help the girls with Clarence." He offers.

"That will be a great help for them," Dorothy says thankfully.

Samantha wipes away her tears. "You mean a great relief." She says concerning Clarence and Anne. They laugh as Johnny walks to the store.

The next morning, everyone in the house is anxious to hear the news from the Williams River Township. Mr. Thopham is a little slow to rise, but when he does, he finds an audience waiting for him at the table. Dorothy, Samantha, and Lizzy have made a warm breakfast of oatmeal porridge and fresh-baked biscuits. Thopham insists on blessing the meal and the family when all the food is on the table.

"Holy Father, we are thankful for your love, mercy, and grace that you have bestowed upon us." He prays. "I thank you for this family and pray for your blessing on each member and upon this house. Merciful Father, let their winters be warm, their summers cool, and their families large; bless this food and all that is, and shall be set before you on this table. We thank you in the name of your son Jesus, amen."

Everyone at the table says, "Amen." And they begin to serve the food. The meal is quiet.

Clarence asks, "Mr. Thopham, is that your name?"

Anne kicks him and gives him a stern look.

"Yes, young man, that is my name." Mr. Thopham replies. "What is your name?"

"My name is Clarence." He boasts.

"Oh…" George looks at Dorothy.

"He's named after Uncle, and this young man who found you at the harbor and drove us home is my eldest son, John Westley II, and this is his wife, Samantha." Dorothy points to Lizzy. "This is Elizabeth, my eldest daughter, and my younger daughter Anne."

"Well, it's a pleasure meeting all of you." Replies Mr. Thopham.

"Mr. Thopham…" calls Clarence. Before he can say another word, Anne puts her hand over his mouth. He pulls her hand away. "Mom, can I talk?"

"Why don't we hear what our friend has to tell us? If you can remember your question, you can ask later."

"Oh, I don't think he'll forget," Johnny declares.

Clarence sticks his tongue out at Anne, and she pops him in the mouth. Dorothy grabs Anne quickly and exchanges her seat with her.

"Honestly, I don't know why I ever let the two of you sit next to each other. I apologize, Mr. Thopham. This is something that never ends."

Thopham laughs. "I've been there myself." He says. "My son and daughter are a little closer in age than these two, but they fought each other like bitter rivals. They grew out of it eventually."

"That'll only happen when I'm married and in my own house," replies Anne.

"Well." He says, smiling, "I guess you're waiting to hear what I have to say. It's early and Sunday, so I guess we have time. I hope what I have to say doesn't scare the young ones or any of you. I'm an old man and don't have long to live, but I have to tell you these things before I die. I can't keep this secret any longer." He said wearily.

"Lizzy, run, and get our journal." Then Dorothy tells Mr. Thopham, "I have a journal and will write down what you have to say."

"Well, I speak slowly, so it won't be hard to keep up," laughs Mr. Thopham. "Before I get started, would you mind if I troubled young Johnny here to bring me my bag?"

"Sure, he'll be glad to." Answers Dorothy.

Lizzy brings Dorothy the journal and a graphite stick for writing.

"Okay, I'm ready when you are." She says to her guest.

At that moment, Johnny walks in with the bag and hands it to Mr. Thopham.

"Thank you, young man." Says Thopham. "Now, before I start, I'm going to give you these." He reaches into his bag and pulls out three large old bound journals. "Everything you need to know about the

Williams River Colony, the old settlement, and the new colony is in these journals. This one contains everything you need to know about the Williams River Colony from after you and Clarence left the township."

Everyone pulls from the stack and reads on their own. Every important date and event is written in the journals.

"Now, if you don't mind, I'll start from the beginning." Mr. Thopham states. "There are a lot of secrets in the Williams River Colony. When your uncle Clarence and I would talk, I always listened to his tales of witches and Elmira. But I often encouraged him to change the subject because I knew many of us already knew the dirty secrets. For decades, we were too afraid to talk about it for fear of our families. Clarence and Elizabeth's family came west from New York and arrived after a young lady's death, which seemed to be the beginning of many things in the colony. What I am going to tell you happened right after they built the New Williams River Colony.

Everyone listens without a word. Dorothy puts her finger to Clarence's lips to keep quiet.

"It was around 1650 when the Indians attacked and destroyed the old settlement because of men like Mr. Randolph Williams, Mr. Abraham Kirts, Mr. David Gaines, and yes, my own father, Mr. Andrew Thopham, and there were a few others as well. Their arrogance and stupidity got a lot of people killed."

Mr. Thopham clears his throat and continues. "Most of the people knew about Mr. Williams's daughter Rachel and the young Indian."

"I was told about that," Dorothy said, sitting up in her seat.

"Well, what you don't know is that Mr. Kirts shot that young Indian boy in the back and said he was trying to escape. He wasn't trying to escape; they left the gate open and told him he could leave. When he turned to leave and made his way toward the gate, he started running because his friends were waiting on a hill on the other side, and that's when Mr. Kirts shot him. His friends ran off into the woods, and the rest of the men shot at them as well. The Chief came to the colony and demanded to know why his son was shot in the back. He called Mr. Kirts a coward, and when he said that, the whole colony turned against the Indians; they kicked them out and told them never to return.

They took the boy's body and waited three days before they attacked us. We never had a chance; on the third night, they attacked the colony, and all hell broke loose. More than half the colony died in one night. The rest of us were left to defend those who remained. It was more than three days after the attack before we could bury our dead, and it wasn't until the end of the week that we felt safe enough to move what was left of our families."

"You mean to tell me you knew where the settlement was all along?" Dorothy Snaps. "You're one of the original survivors?"

"Yes, I am," Mr. Thopham acknowledges. "The horrible ugliness and secrets did not come until after the arrival of Nigel Grace and his family." Samantha looks at Mr. Thopham and turns her head to hide her concern. "He arrived with two beautiful young daughters, one twelve years of age and the other eleven. The trouble started when Elmira was seventeen and her sister Victoria was sixteen."

"Wait." Asks Dorothy, "I've never heard of Victoria. Did she move away or something?'

"Or something..." Mr. Thopham responds cryptically.

Everybody looks at one another.

"Or something?" Samantha asks in an angry tone. "What do you mean by that?"

"Well, I'm about to get to that." Continues Thopham. "Elmira and Victoria were much like these two, always fighting but more serious than anyone could imagine. They both fell in love with the same young man, and their father hated the man because he believed him incapable of supporting his daughters."

"My father?" Dorothy interrupts.

"No, not your father, but a man we knew very well." Says Mr. Thopham. "Mr. Winfred Gaines."

Dorothy stares at him in shock, and her mouth opens.

"He and young Joan Ladette were already promised to wed." Says Thopham. "For a long time, his family were considered indigents because they had no money and moved from colony to colony like gypsies until they found the old settlement and helped build the Williams River Colony. His father did whatever had to be done to support the family. One late evening, Victoria and Winfred were caught behind the barn of his father's house by Elmira and her friend Abigail Pembroke. They dragged the two to Mr. Williams and Mr. Kirts, who was then appointed the colony's magistrates. The trial was very short because they'd been caught in the act. They tied the two of them to the whipping post facing each other, and Mr. Kirts had the pleasure – and I do mean pleasure – of whipping the two of them so they could see each other's pain and hear each other's screams. Mr. Kirts was one who did not spare the whip, not even with his own children."

"That's why his children ran away and returned to England." Says Dorothy.

"Exactly." Says Thopham. "They were tried for sexual depravity, and at that time, it was considered a serious offense, so the townsfolk felt they had to issue serious consequences. Winfred was seventeen at the time, and Victoria was sixteen; later that year, it was found out that Victoria was pregnant, and it seemed to her that her punishment would never end. About the next year she gave birth, she was accused again of being with another man, Avery Adams, your father, Dorothy. Elmira hated Victoria, for she was a much prettier young lady, and it seemed that whomever Victoria liked, Elmira would set her eyes on the same man. Again, the services of Mr. Kirts were used to execute the sentence for sexual depravity. This time Elmira supplied as much evidence as she could against her younger sister. For some strange reason, Avery Adams, age fifteen at the time, was never tried for the crime, only Victoria, and he was held down to watch as Mr. Kirts administered the lashes. Victoria screamed and screamed…"

Mr. Thopham cries again, tears streaming down his face at the table. He sobs aloud until his voice cracks. They waited until he was able to calm himself to continue.

"The poor girl hung there like she was an animal being skinned alive by that monster Mr. Kirts. When he finished, she whispered something about her baby and then gathered enough strength to take a deep breath yelled. 'I will get all of you for this. You will all pay for this, the entire township will pay.' She screamed at Elmira, cursing her to hell, and then Mr. Kirts shouted 'Blasphemy!' and began whipping her again until there was no more life in her. It took Mr. Williams and two others to grab the whip and force him to stop. That was the last time he was called upon to administer whippings. About a month later, he found the courage to leave the farm and come back into the town. After that, no one saw much of him or his family."

"He murdered her?" Shouts Samantha.

"Yes." Replies Mr. Thopham. "In his anger, he would not stop whipping her until Mr. Williams interjected, grabbing his arm and pushing him away. Then they realized she was dead. You would think Elmira would have remorse for her sister's death, but it seemed to us that she had Mr. Kirts do her dirty work for her. She sentenced her own sister to death."

"What happened to her child?" asks Lizzy.

"The baby Victoria left behind was born retarded; they knew this because she didn't develop when all the other children were developing and doing well. Victoria's child remained unresponsive and required lots of care."

"What was the child's name?" Samantha asks.

"Mary." He replies.

"What?" Dorothy asks.

"After you and Clarence left, Elmira sent her to an asylum in New York. I guess she got tired of taking care of her."

"Why didn't Victoria run away?" Clarence shouts. He jumps up from the table and swings in the air. "I would be fighting and beating up that old Mr. Kirts man."

Anne jumps up and pops him on the top of his head. "You're dead." She says.

Clarence falls to the floor as if he were dead, with his tongue hanging out of his mouth. Everyone laughs at him.

"Clarence, get up off the floor and behave," Dorothy demands.

Mr. Thopham laughs at Clarence's innocence.

"Well, son, she had no place to go. There were many occasions when Elmira and Victoria were seen fighting in the open, but they always seemed to blame Victoria. So when Elmira found out that Victoria and Avery Adams were talking, she put an end to her sister's life. Elmira was mean and hot-tempered, and no one wanted to deal with her. The only one who had the courage to fight back was Victoria."

"Victoria had a retarded daughter?" Asks Dorothy. "Are you saying Mary Grace isn't Elmira's sister but her niece?"

"Yes, the illegitimate daughter of Winfred Gaines. After that, Mrs. Grace took care of Mary until the day she died, and then Elmira took care of her after that. Elmira took care of her father until the day he died as well. Not really sure if he died of natural causes, no one knows for sure. Elmira was in full charge after that, and it seemed that way until now. Her fury was in full rage when her secret affair with Avery Adams ended, which occurred when he left for work in Boston, and she was pregnant with Keith. It seemed her sister Victoria was willing to be with Avery even though her father treated him the same as he did Winfred. Avery loved Victoria more than life, and it did not matter that

Mr. Grace thought of his family as nothing less than the dirt they trod upon. Out of spite of her sister Victoria, Elmira had an affair with Avery Adams, no one really knew how long the relationship lasted, but everyone knew when it ended. Her family treated her horribly, and the only one who seemed to cling to her was Mary, her niece. So when Avery returned out of the blue after nearly ten years, it seemed that his financial status was better than the Graces' and the Pembrokes.'"

Mr. Thopham turns to Dorothy once more. "And that's when he fell in love with your mother, Beatrice Arnold. Keith was a cripple, and Elmira's husband was a failure in her eyes. They lived in a small house not far from the pond where Thomas and Nathan James drowned. She was a scorned woman who saw the father of her son married to some wild woods-running, fence-jumping, simple-looking trash, as Elmira often referred to her.

"Oh, did she?" Dorothy protested.

"Shortly after your mother and father were married, Elmira's sisters and brothers ran into a bit of bad luck; one by one, they got sick and died, and those who didn't die left. Everyone suspected that Elmira was getting them back for the harsh way they treated her around the time she had Keith. The only family Elmira had left was Gregory Pembroke's family. When she had Thomas, it seemed the entire town breathed a sigh of relief. She was the happiest person in town... that is, until the death of Thomas.

That was when the nightmares of the Williams River Township started all over again. One by one, people began to die, and Elmira appeared responsible. But, like the night Victoria died, the townspeople did nothing to stop it. We were all afraid to do anything, including our founder Mr. Randolph Williams and his family. Not long after they built the new colony, his daughter ran off one night deep into the wilderness, and they never saw her again; they suspect she took her own life, but they never found her body.

"What did they think happened to her?" Lizzy asks.

"Well, many thought she ran back to the Indian tribe who accepted her as part of their family." He says.

"What about you?" Samantha asks.

He hesitates before he answers. Then he looks up and sighs.

He wipes the tears from his eyes. "I was there when they punished her for being with the young Indian boy, and when it was over, she cursed the colony's men to hell. Her father beat her again for cursing the man and forbade her from leaving their cabin. As some of them believed then, I believe she's still with them today."

"Are you saying she's a witch as well?" Dorothy asks.

"I'm just saying after what I saw may not have been the work of one alone." He says with his head lowered.

Everyone at the table looks at each other.

"So this Elmira was getting even with everyone in the colony?" Johnny asks.

"Well, Mr. William's wife died in their barn while milking the cow; they say that it must have kicked her to death. And as for Mr. Williams, he died in the woods while he was hunting. They found his body lying near a fallen tree stump, and they said he must have tripped and hit his head. And then his son Lester, whom we all respected as Sheriff, mysteriously died shortly after little Thomas drowned. Lester would have never let Keith take his position as Sheriff. Everyone was nervous for years after his death, especially after your mother and father were found in that storm that took their lives. When the trials started, we feared the worst and believed it was better we carry on as privately as we could manage. Of course, I don't have to tell you more about that. You lived through those hellish days. May the Good Lord rest aunt's soul.

"Hold on..." Samantha is upset now. "How old was Mary when Keith was born?"

"It's recorded in that journal there." Dorothy opens it and searches for Keith's date of birth.

"It says here that Victoria Grace gives birth to a daughter Mary Grace out of wedlock June, 15 in the year of our Lord 1656." Dorothy scans down and turns the page and finds that Elmira Grace-Pembroke gave birth to an illegitimate son Keith Grace October 31 in the year of our Lord 1665. When she turns the page and finds that Beatrice Adams gives birth to a daughter, Dorothy Adams November 5, in the year of our Lord 1674, she holds her mouth. Tears fall from her face, and Dorothy apologizes for her reaction.

Johnny asks Samantha, "Why are you so upset, and why do you want to know about the year Keith was born?"

"I'm trying to get a better understanding of it all." She says. "If Keith is the son of Avery Adams, and Dorothy is his daughter, then that makes him her brother."

"Yes." She says quietly. "Surely not a very nice one at that. My own brother murdered my aunt." Dorothy rubs Samantha's back. "I only found out we were siblings a few years ago. It's hard to believe that he would do the things he did knowing we were family."

The table remains quiet for a moment.

"Like his murderous mother," Samantha whispers. "Oh, Mother Westley, I'm so sorry. It's so upsetting hearing all of this."

"Well, I'm afraid it doesn't get any better." Mr. Thopham takes a deep breath and continues. "About two months ago, the town had a bit of trouble with a thief or a gang of thieves butchering and carrying off our sheep from the sheep farm. We weren't sure if they would ever catch the culprit until about four weeks ago. We were all awakened by those infernal rattles the Sheriff's men and volunteers used as alarms. They must have found the thief and chased him through the woods, and we waited hours for the men to return with him, but they were so long in the chase that we were told to go back to our homes and wait until the morning. We were sure they would return with him victoriously. After I went to bed for the night, the wind picked up, and after more than three hours had passed, there was the most horrifying sound I had ever heard before. This storm went through the backside of town with a vengeance, and I had never been more afraid in my life. It wasn't until we woke up the next morning that we saw the damage it had done. More than half the town had no houses, barns, mills, or markets. And they were building a second tavern, but all that was gone. This storm left a path of no less than three hundred meters wide and no more than four to six miles long.

"Wow!" Clarence exclaims. "One time, the wind here got so strong I jumped in the air, and it made me fly!"

"Impetuous boy, please," Dorothy demands.

Samantha takes Clarence in her arms and holds him tight as she wipes away her tears.

"We thought it would be good to go out to the farms and see if there was anything we could do, but when we got there, the storm had wiped away all evidence that any farm ever existed there. Then we foolishly followed the path."

"Foolishly?" Anne interrupts.

"Yes, we followed it all the way to the old settlement, where the storm seemed to have originated." Samantha takes a deep quiet breath at the mention of the old settlement.

"I wanted to turn around, but Winfred decided to continue despite my protests. My heart nearly failed me when I saw our old home. When we drove through the gate, it was like we were in a glass jar. We could see the trees swaying in the wind around us, but no wind was swaying in the old settlement. A warm blast of air blew from the south, and we noticed the trees weren't swaying outside the settlement. A cold blast of wind air blew from the north, and again, none of the trees swayed on the outside. When the wind blew in again from the east and the west, it seemed that it was all starting over again as it had the night before. Winfred tried to turn the buggy around, but all the horses began to behave strangely, and we had trouble getting them to turn and leave. We got out as fast as we could, but the horses didn't run. It was like something was holding them back."

"Elmira?" Johnny asks.

"No." Thopham shakes his head. "As far as we figured, she was wiped out with the storm, and the same with every man who went out to capture the thief. When we left the settlement, the horses were back to normal. We all stopped just outside the settlement to retrieve the horses that had run out earlier."

Mr. Thopham leans over and rests his head in his hands on the table.

"Lord help us." He cries. "Please, Lord, have mercy on us." Soon he begins to sob. Lizzy tries to comfort him, but she finds that she cannot.

Dorothy suggests that they stop and talk about it another day.

"Just a little more time that I may finish." He pleads. He composes himself. "We were getting on our way, and I just happened to turn and look back at the old settlement, and that's when I saw her." He sobs aloud again, taking a deep breath to hold back his tears. His body is as tense as it was when he turned around the first time; his fist is tight, and his eyes are closed. "Never look back," He says again, just like he did on that fateful day.

"You did not look back. I asked if you left your bags on the wharf, and you walked by me like something was after you?" Johnny asks.

"That's right." He replies.

They sit there looking at him, and then Samantha shakes him.

"Mr. Thopham, you're safe here with us." She says. "It's okay."

Dorothy asks, "Who did you see when you looked back?"

Mr. Thopham sits there, his body tense, and he shakes his head. He prays for mercy.

"We just stood there and watched her get beaten to death." He cries. "We just stood there and did nothing."

"Victoria!" shouts Lizzy.

He takes in another deep breath. "A blue and white dress and no shoes on her feet. They buried her in the same clothes she died in, with no shoes. I knew I shouldn't have looked back, and I thought she would be gone if I looked back again, but that wasn't the case. She was still there, her feet not touching the ground, and she followed us out of the settlement. A man I thought I knew walked up behind her and changed into a wolf, and then he ran into the woods. The woman that followed us was Victoria. I know it sounds crazy, but I really did see her and that other thing. I really did. I did."

"We believe you," Dorothy says. "We've seen some things too. I've seen Elmira change into something so horrible I couldn't believe it when I first saw it."

Still sobbing, Mr. Thopham wipes his eyes and blows his nose. "Your uncle feared you saw something when you went back to the farm. So you saw her change to her true form, did you?"

"Yes, and apparently, so did you." She says.

"No, but Mrs. LeAnne Hempstead did. She told her husband about it, and he asked your uncle and me for advice. We were too afraid to help, and then they stoned her to death at the steps of the courthouse."

They all remain silent for a moment, thinking of LeAnne Hempstead.

"We were all just too afraid of Elmira." Continues Mr. Thopham. "But now I fear her sister is far greater than she. She's more powerful than Elmira. She always was. Elmira feared her sister more than she was jealous of her. Their family descended from a clan of gypsies out of Ireland known as the Pavee. Then they moved to England and then to Holland until they took passage here. She feared her sister because she believed she was casting a spell on men, and that's why Elmira did all she could to take from her sister everything she had, including her life and her daughter Mary."

"No," Dorothy says before Clarence can jump from Samatha's arms.

Thopham continues. "Anyway, I looked around and saw the man that turned into a wolf. Winfred turned and saw her, and he fell over in my lap. There was nothing I could do. I tried to get him back to Doc Hadley's, but he died before we returned to town. The whole town was in chaos, and I could see the wind was picking up again, so I warned the Doc to get him and his family out. I warned him, I did. I would have used the buggy we rode back into the township on, but someone had taken it. Then, while I was warning the Doc, the wolf appeared outside his house; it was staring at me, just staring at me. I was so afraid I jumped on the first wagon out of the colony because I knew that she was coming and bringing the storm of death with her. She promised before she died that she was going to get us all. It would be only a matter of time before she finished what she started the night before."

"Are you saying the storm killed Elmira and all her witches?" asks Dorothy, looking at Johnny and everyone else at the table with wonder and grabbing her children's hands.

"I'm saying that God did not make that storm any more than He did the one that killed your parents and others who died over the years."

"So she could still be out there somewhere?" Johnny asks.

"You need to see what we saw," says Mr. Thopham. "Much of the earth seemed plowed under, with no trees, no houses, and no rain. That was the strangest part. There was no warning, and it was like nothing was ever there."

"No, thank you," replies Dorothy. "I pray we never see anything like that here. We've seen enough here already."

"I didn't want to wait around to see what Victoria was going to do to the rest of the town, so I ran. I got out of that place as fast as I could. We tried to get those horses moving, but the wagon was full. We could hear the wind and see the trees bending, and we could only pray that we could get as far from there as possible. You could hear the screams even when we were past the fork in the road. We could see the storm, the sky was as dark as night, and then it seemed as though the storm was on fire. The lightning struck trees and the ground. It filled the air, and the thunder frightened us all as we ran. And that sound, I'll never forget the noise the storm made as it ripped up the earth.

"Are you sure you want to keep going?" Lizzy asks.

'Yes, I have to." He continues. "She was so angry when I looked back from the buggy at the old settlement, and she was saying something that I could not hear. I could only see her mouth moving and the rage on her face. I knew then we were in big trouble. Only a few of us were able to leave, and those behind us feared it would overtake us.

All those with lighter wagons passed us by. Some even felt the slower-moving cow-pulled wagons, like the one I was in, didn't go fast enough, so they jumped off and ran on foot. They kept telling me to look, but I was too afraid, and when I did, it was the worst thing I had ever seen. It reached to the clouds and tossed the trees like they were mere sticks; most of us believed that she was throwing the trees, lumber, wagons, animals, and... the bodies of some of the townspeople at us, all because we had escaped her fury." He puts his hands over his ears. "The screams and the sound of the storm, I can still hear them. Deaf as I am, she made sure I could hear them."

Everyone at the table tries to calm him down and let him know that he's okay. Samantha sits down, unsure of whether to cry or scream. She often left the table to breathe, trying to take everything in. Johnny tries to comfort her, but she cannot be comforted and begins to shake.

"It's so hard for me to believe that Mother Westley was in such grave danger… until now. I went along with the stories but was unsure of all of this. Elmira is a seriously evil woman. I don't believe for one moment she is dead, but someday she will die."

Samantha becomes feverish and retreats to bed for the day. Mr. Thopham is given a hot toddy and laid down to rest for a while. Dorothy tells him that she'll read the rest and will not ask him to talk about it anymore. Dorothy's thoughts take her back to the day of her dream before they murdered her aunt and the thought of that old play she swore she would never allow her children to read. Mr. William Shakespeare's play, *Macbeth,* speaks of the witch's part that reads, *"By the pricking of my thumbs, something wicked this way comes."* Dorothy knows she can't outrun it, so she and her family choose to stand and fight the evil when it comes their way again.

Mr. Thopham doesn't talk anymore after that; he just sits in uncle Clarence's chair, watching Johnny and Clarence work on the farm. He greets Dorothy and her children with a nod as they walk to and from the store. He never told them whom the man was that transformed into the wolf he helped bury – Avery Adams, the man Victoria loved more than any man on earth. He realizes now that Avery's leaving and reappearance was the work of Victoria. Victoria wanted to get back at Elmira by having her mage Avery marry and sire his child. A child that is the daughter of a warlock, with power unrealized and an enemy of her enemy. *Sad,* he thought, *the only one that died in that storm was Dorothy's mother*. Little did he know, it was the beginning of a plan laid out when Victoria rose from her grave.

These days it is much like watching Uncle after Aunt Liz died; Uncle let himself waste away for a year before he and Mr. Thopham started the meat salting business. Dorothy encourages Mr. Thopham to help Johnny with the salting, but he never does; he just sits in the chair every day from sun up to sundown. Only the Lord knows what he is going through.

It was a humid Friday morning on September 18, 1716. Dorothy and her family bury Uncle's old friend next to John at the family gravesite. Samantha seems too weak to do much for the next three weeks, and she apologizes and cries herself to sleep almost every night. Dorothy and Johnny continue checking on her, thinking the Williams River Colony and Elmira stories are too much for her.

Samantha lies awake wondering what her life would have been like if she had not been born retarded, and if her mother had raised her like Dorothy raised her children. Mr. Thophams news today only strengthens the vow she made years earlier. She vows never to use the powers that have changed her into what she is, but only to use them to conceal her true identity; she lies awake thinking and trying to contain her anger toward Elmira, her wicked and evil aunt. Lying next to Johnny, a thought comes to mind... *Maybe I've already met my mother, and maybe it was she who gave Mrs. Kirts prophesy of Elmira and myself? Maybe it was she who combed my hair all those months at the grave of the old settlement taking the image of Grandmother Hadley, which made me feel pretty. A mother never forgets her child; maybe she did love me enough to change me. And then there's the future of Elmira. Elmira, you took my mother away from me. Is that why you mistreated me, because I was more like my mother... the sister you hated to death? You deserve whatever is in store for you when the time comes.*

Samantha knows now that she is the beginning of the new Dorothy that is to come. She also knows that much like her, but not knowing the power within her, either Dorothy's mother or father wasn't who everyone thought they were. Dorothy and Samantha share the same special gift, which means both of Dorothy's daughters have hidden gifts as well. If Elmira and her witches are still alive, then Victoria used the storm Elmira brewed with her army of witches and vanquished them to a faraway land, where the new Dorothy and Elmira will meet sometime in the future.

Samantha's grandmother, the old slave witch, put a spell over the farm for when Elmira and her witches return, they will fall ill and die if they visit the farm staying too long. She secretly pledged to be a watcher, protecting Dorothy and her family.

There is much on Mary's mind as she lies awake. *Did Mother wait until she knew I was safe to get her revenge on the township? Did she kill Mr. Gaines, my father, because she knew he and Elmira had been secretly meeting all those years? All those innocent people had to die for something they had nothing to do with!*

Samantha thinks about all these things and prays.

"Oh Lord, be merciful on your handmaiden. I pray you will continue to hide me until the day you bring me home. I love you and thank you with all my heart, and I thank you in Jesus' name, amen."

Then she wonders when she should tell Johnny and her family about the new life growing inside of her.

"I can feel as each day passes, I am getting weaker as the baby in me grows stronger." She whispers. "I believe Dorothy knows already but is waiting for me to say something. The baby will carry both our family's secret in its body and pass it on to each female born from generation to generation." Then she thinks, *if either of Dorothy's parents is a witch, then this child will be far stronger than us all, and so will each generation as time passes.*

Then Samantha thinks about the story of the light…

Hidden deep within the light, a dark and secret blight.

She falls asleep thinking about how she never got the chance to love her mother, Victoria Grace.

Chapter 17
What a World, What a Rush

Picking themselves out of the grayish mire, the men wonder what happened. They are alive and relieved for that, but now they are trying to overcome the sickness of spinning from the storm, which seems to have dropped them off in the middle of nowhere. The air is warm, thick, and humid, the mosquitoes fly in mass swarms and biting mad, and the musty smell of the air they breathe only worsens their recovery. Most of the men cannot stand; they simply roll over on their backs, swatting blindly with their eyes closed.

Elmira's anger subsides until she regains her balance while stumbling and falling face-first into the mire. She struggles to sit, using her elbows to support herself. While on her elbows and knees, she laughs aloud and thinks of what Monroe looked like in the tavern. She looks back to see how high her butt is above her head and laughs even more. Some of the girls attempt to fly, providing a bit of amusement for Elmira and the others; they fly about three feet off the ground and crash back down head first, tumbling like desert bushes blown by the wind. After a few minutes, most of them have shaken off the sickness, and all the witches stand on their feet. They look around and notice it is already morning, or at least it seems to be morning, with a heavy mist and cloud cover. They pull the hoods over their heads and protect themselves from the swarms of mosquitoes, levitating just above the ground; Elmira, one of the last witches to get up, pulls her cape off that's caked with mud and slime from the mire. She gets on her feet and begins to fly around in circles.

"Idiots!" She shouts. "You bumbling Idiots, look at what you've done."

The men begin to come to their senses. They hear Elmira shouting something but have not gained the full function of their minds and are dull of hearing. She has transformed, but Keith knows those words all too well as his mother screams with anger and frustration. For the first time, Keith sees his mother's true form as a witch.

"Get up, you bunch of stupid idiots." Elmira's features changed before any of the men could regain their senses.

"Get up!" she shouts loud and long, "I should kill all of you."

"Now that's the Elmira I know," whispers Keith. "Now she's showing her true nature."

Looking around, Keith tries to get a count of the men who survived.

Fourteen of us started out after Trevor. He thinks. Then he noticed that one was missing, Gilliam. He counts again.

"Oh, that's just peachy, the lucky number 13." He whispered.

Elmira is waiting impatiently for the men to pick themselves up off the ground. Bracing his hands on his knees, he looks away from his mother.

"The mighty Elmira has arrived at last," he whispers.

Watching her fly around the marsh screaming, he thinks, *this is not good; this is not happening. I've danced to this song before, only now I have plenty of company to share this ass-whipping we're about to get.* He looks around in a slight daze at the men with him, trying to reason how to get out of this. The beatings he received as a child are the reason he's crippled. In one of Elmira's rages, she nearly beat him to death with a board when he was only four years old. It was Mary who saved him from her, lying over his body to protect him as he lay unconscious. Elmira was enraged and broke his hip and arm in several places for wetting the bed. The doctor said that it was polio for fear of his life, and they kept Keith out of sight for more than six months until he healed. His leg never grew right after that, which explains his limp.

Keith stands upright, thinking, *There is nothing that can be compared to what it seems we are about to get from this angry troll of a woman.* Then he finds a bit of humor in what he has just thought. "The angry troll," He repeats to himself in a low voice. He has not used that term to describe his mother since he was a child.

The men look down at their hands and rub their faces in shock at what they see. Elmira levitates just above the ground as she begins to move about the men, giving them a vivid view of her face. Her face is as green as a scaled lizard, her teeth are sharp, and her eyes are no longer blue and pearly white. They have become black and red. Elmira's hands are elongated, and her fingers are like an eagle's talons. Even her body has changed. She is taller and more slender, and her arms are thin and muscular. In one of her hands, there is a red glow as if a flame is trying to burst through. All the men can do is stare until she passes their way, at which point they hold their heads down so as not to look into her eyes. Now she moves about and circles the area, trying to understand what has happened and where in the world they are. Elmira takes wider circles through the dead trees and sees they are in a large marsh. As far as she can see, it is not like the woods they left behind. By this time, Keith notice who is among the witches. Elmira, in her rage, is the only one that has transformed. Those who have cloaked their heads have not fully covered their faces. He notices the mosquitoes swarming around them, but none light on their cloaks. Keith is the first to notice his wife, Amanda; he taps Ford's arm and lazily points to his wife. For now, all the men are astonished at whom the witches are.

All the witches are levitating above the ground. Elmira speaks in a raspy voice, and then she stops and faces the men in front of her girls.

"Ladies, unveil yourselves and show these fools who really kept the order in the township." She looks down at Keith. "You didn't think you incompetent idiots ran that town on your own, did you?"

Elmira laughs aloud with her hands on her hips.

This makes Keith angry, and it shows on his face. Amanda moves quietly over the ground to Keith and caresses his face with her hand. She kisses him on the lips and says, "Remember this, for it may be the last kiss and the last time you'll touch this body for a while." Then she and the other witches begin to change into their youthful selves.

Their husbands and the other men can only watch and wipe the drool from their mouths. The witches are beautiful, absolutely beautiful. Twenty-four witches survived the storm, not including Elmira. None of the men had seen them look this way since before they were married. Then Elmira begins to transform to a time from before Keith was born. Keith cannot believe that the woman he sees is his mother. She's in her mid-eighties, but she looks like a young nineteen-year-old.

Incredible. The men think.

In his usual temperament, Winthrop Trevor looks up at Rose and calls her out.

"You bitch!" He yells, pointing at her.

Before he can say another word, Rose flies down to him ferociously without stopping and slaps him backhandedly, reaching down and swatting upward as hard as she can, lifting him backward from the mire and into a dead tree across the marsh. Many times Rose has been slapped backhanded by Winthrop for one reason or another. Now she lifts her head and sighs as if the whole world has been lifted off her shoulders.

"Now that felt good!" She sighs loudly. "That felt damn good." She says, wiping her hands on her cloak.

At that point, all the witches except Amanda and Unity begin to move toward the men to do the same. Seeing this, the men scramble to protect themselves.

Elmira shouts. "Girls!"

She calls the others back, preventing them from beating the mire off the men. The witches are a little miffed after being called off and look back at the men angrily. The men cannot believe the strength of the witches. They all look back at Winthrop Trevor and cannot believe how far he sailed across the marsh when Rose hit him.

Charles is leaning against a tree away from the others.

He thinks. *If he had any teeth left in his mouth, they're all gone now.* None of the men think to go over and help Winthrop back on his feet, for they believe it would be best for him to get himself up and fight back. They are all waiting on him to charge at her and get slapped back into another tree. He can only hold himself up on his hands and knees in the thick mire in great pain. He stays a while, trying to breathe, for the air was knocked out of his lungs when she hit him and when he hit the tree.

"Sheriff," Elmira shouts. "Get your band of idiots together. We need to talk." Charles stays back as they slowly walk and stumble to stand in front of Elmira.

"I said all of your men, Sheriff, and that includes you too." Elmira points.

Keith looks back at Charles and whispers to him, "This is not the time." Then he extends his hand out to his friend and says, "Charles, join us, please."

Elmira says, "You can obey or die. It's your choice. You will all bow down to me and do as you are told or else."

The men turn to one another. "What choice do we have?" They say.

Charles leans against the tree and lifts his feet from the mire. He feels a little sick and off-balance.

"I can't do that." He says. "You want us to bow down and pledge our souls to you. Is that right, Elmira?"

"Charles, you fool," Keith calls out. "This is not the time."

"I'll not bow down to any witch, devil, or anyone of his demons. I don't know where we are. We may have been blown to some murky part of the colony. I don't know, but I will not follow that thing." He says, pointing to Elmira.

Elmira shouts. "Silence, you insolent fool."

He stares up at her. "Following you doesn't exactly sit right with me."

He yanks his pistol from his belt, pulls the hammer back, and points it at Elmira.

"I serve God and not the devil." He says. "Go to hell, witch."

Before he can pull the trigger, a loud thundering sound seems to echo across the wasteland, and then a searing pain in the right side of his chest. Charles looks down at his chest and then up at Keith.

"I guess that makes two brothers you've murdered." He says.

And then he falls backward into the mire as everyone looks on. Keith puts his pistol back into his belt and orders Trevor, who is still collecting his wits near where Charles fell, to retrieve Charles's pistols and sword.

"We may need them later." He states.

Still hurting from his wife's blow, Trevor crawls over to Charles, bleeding from his eyes, nose, and mouth, believing his jaw to be broken. He spits in Charles's face while he takes his weapons.

"You won't need these anymore." Trevor sneers in pain.

He then collects himself, stands up over him, and gives him a hard kick in the ribs. Elmira smiles and repeats her order to the men.

"If you want to live, you will serve and submit yourselves to me. If you do, I will show you, idiots, how to survive as my apprentices." She gloats at the thought that she can now train men as wizards. "I will make wizards of you all, real mages you'll be. I will give you powers and riches untold. Give yourselves to me, and I will give you more."

Her promises please most of the men, hearing of the powers and riches they stand to gain.

Trevor stumbles back with his head down, smiling. But Keith takes Greene's pistol and puts it in Trevor's face.

"Give me his things." He orders through gritted teeth. Keith snatches both pistols, the powder horn and lead ball sack, and the sword from Trevor.

"I didn't tell you to spit on him or kick him, you bloody boozer," Keith yells angrily.

When Keith pushes him away, Trevor stumbles and falls back into the mire. He looks up at Keith smiling and shaking his head. Trevor slowly rolls over to stand, staggering farther away from the group and falling to his knees. This is an image they are accustomed to seeing. Often he traveled through the township stumbling around in a drunken stupor. Keith knows better than to confront his mother. He will wait until the time is right, and that time is not now.

He looks back at Charles and wishes he hadn't shot him. He lowers his head, and he and the rest of the men pledge themselves to Elmira. They are all looking forward to the day they will be trained in the craft. Thoughts of riches untold please them more than the idea of power. As they bow down to serve her, Charles lies bleeding in the mire listening to them sell their souls to Elmira, the devil's daughter.

Elmira transformed into her youthful self, not wanting to be outdone by the other girls. She looks down at Winthrop Trevor and then at Keith.

"What were you and that band of idiots doing chasing this uncontrollable jackass?" She demands.

"Well," Keith Starts. "It appears that Trevor here is the thief who was stealing and slaughtering the sheep. We were trying to apprehend him, but he managed to give us the slip in the woods. Charles was able to reacquire his whereabouts, and he ran farther into the woods, trying to evade us. That's when we ended up at the old settlement."

Elmira is livid when she hears that Trevor is responsible for the slaughter of the sheep and the storm she could not control that brought them to this strange land. The storm did not accomplish what Elmira intended, which was to destroy everything Dorothy has and cares about. With every word of Keith's story about Trevor's stupidity, Elmira's breathing grows heavier, and she begins to exhale with a loud hiss. She reveals her teeth and transforms again, only this time into a serpent dragon, as she roars with her head towards the misty sky. She lifts herself up from the mire, slithering and crawling with her powerful arms, and positions herself in front of Trevor. Her large head with mane, sharp teeth, large arms and clawed hands, and serpent body is immense and powerful, spreading fear and panic into everyone present, causing them to fear for their lives.

"Oh shit, what the hell is this?" Says Keith as he makes a path far away from Trevor.

"Bloody hell!" Says Ford as the men begin to back farther away.

"Oh shit, this is new!" Says Amanda as she and the others levitate away from Elmira.

"God help us all," Charles whispers as he lies motionless, held captive by the suction of the mire.

Elmira lifts herself from the mire rising more than twenty feet above Trevor. Trevor has a smirk on his face. He has neither shaven nor bathed in months, and his drinking has made him a foul-smelling town's fool.

"All of you can kiss my ass." He sneers as he watches everyone back away.

"I'm going to slap that unkempt drunken face off your head if you don't wipe that smirk off your face." She warns.

Nervously, he stares up at her and the serpent down at him. He looks down at his ragged clothes and at the blood flowing from his mouth. Then he turns to look at Charles, who's staring back at him and trying his best to shake his head. He tries to warn him not to do whatever it is he is thinking of doing. Then Trevor stands up off his knees and slurs with his broken jaw.

"I have no wife, and my children don't bother to visit me no more." He moans. "I ain't no sheriff and lost everything I ever had. I did everything you told me to do. I murdered innocent people and watched you take everything they had. I may be unkempt, but I'm not drunk." He stands tall with his chin up as he pulls his shirt down around his waist to present himself before her.

He closes his eyes. "I pray now that the Lord forgive me for all I have done in your name all those years." Then he looks at all the men, all the witches, and his wife. "Please, God, forgive me." He whispers, bowing his head to pray. Then he looks up and points to Elmira, hesitating while trying to steady himself standing in attention.

"So, you can kiss my ass; you foul green murderous scaly dragon bitch."

Elmira does not hesitate; she roars and brings her claws down hard on his face, cutting through his skull and chest like soft cheese. His body drops to the ground like a sock doll on his knees, then folds backward in the mire. Elmira then inhales, taking a deep breath, with her head tilted back, and she looks down at Trevor and exhales flames from her mouth. These flames consume his entire body. The men run to protect themselves from the flames that seem to hit the ground and fan out towards them, and the witches drawback as far as they can. Looking on in horror, Charles cannot move, and he hopes that Elmira won't come to him to finish what Keith started. As Trevor's body burns, she screams with her head toward the sky and levitates higher and higher, slowly spinning as she ascends. The flames spiral engulfing her body, and then Elmira explodes in an inferno of fire that seems to spread across a large area of the marsh. The witches cover themselves with their cloaks, and the men jump into the marsh face-first. The heat from the flames burns their flesh, and all they can do is roll over onto their backs to let the wet marsh provide cooling relief from the heat.

Charles closes his eyes and drapes his left arm over his face. He can smell the burning hair and flesh on his face and body, and the exposed scalp that is above the mire burns away as he moans in pain. When Elmira vanishes from the flames, the men slowly rise from the mire, and the witches remove their hoods and wonder whether she is dead this time. While everyone slowly comes together, the witches notice the men's clothes are burned away by the flames. The witches laugh at the exposed backsides of the men as they crawl in the mire.

"At least she rid us of those infernal mosquitoes," Keith remarks, wincing from his burns.

Amanda prepares to speak when Elmira reappears in front of the men.

"I will not have this type of insolence from any of you!" She shouts. "If you do not follow me, then you are against me. And if you are against me, I will destroy your very souls. Am I making myself clear to all of you?" She turns to face the witches.

No one says a word; they all just bow to her. It is then Elmira notices the men's burned flesh.

"Stupid, weak fools." She mutters. "I don't even know why I bother."

She waves her arms, sweeping them around from left to right, and a heavy mist covers them all. Charles welcomes the cooling of his burning face and body, for the mist heals his and the others' burns. With a collective sigh of relief, the men stand on their feet. Charles can only lie in the mire with an open wound that seems to be slowly healing. He thanked God for the cooling mist, not noticing that his face, hair, and body were slowly recovering. Unity begins to wish she had faked an illness and not shown up at the old settlement; she wonders if she will ever see her children again, and she desperately wants to be with them and her grandchildren. With their heads bowed low, the witches begin to wipe tears from their faces.

"Let's get the hell out of this swamp and find a dry place," Elmira demands.

When they have finished, Charles watches the witches slowly maneuver through the dead trees as they levitate above the ground. The men stumble, running behind them on foot like the devil's imps. Charles's sight is blurred, and his thoughts and hopes are that he will not become food for some wild beast. He prays he will be dead before some bear or wolf begins tearing him apart, fighting over his body, and devouring him.

He feels exhausted and thinks if he could just get up, he could probably crawl out and look for help. He finds his body very heavy and immobile in the mire. Externally his body is healing faster than his body is internally while the ball in his chest slowly dissolves. The blood and fluids are building up in his chest and throat, and he struggles to spit it out. He closes his eyes and thinks of his wife and children; *he thinks of his children's laughter and teaching his son how to hunt when he was a young child. He thinks of spending time with his daughter, and then the thought of never seeing them again flashes before him. Charles thinks of his wife's love and kindness, her soft caresses, and her cold hands and feet as she climbs into bed, seeking warmth from his body.* All this makes him smile through the tears that flow from his eyes.

His thoughts end when a sharp, piercing tug on his ailing shoulder causes great pain. Charles screams a blood-curdling scream that causes both the witches and the men to stop in their tracks.

"It sounds like Charles has become food for the beast," Elmira says. The thought passes Keith's mind that he shot him and left him there without any way to defend himself, and his heart drops.

"His sacrifice will give us the time to find a way out of here." Says Elmira emotionally. Outwardly she did not like him, but inwardly she loved him, for he was the son she wished she had.

She orders Unity, Anne, and Rebecca to fly ahead and find out how far they must go to escape the marsh. Charles's screams frighten the men as much as the women, for no one knows what is attacking him. The men look at each other briefly, and with heavy feet, they push their way past the witches. The witches follow the men, amused, for they have never seen them run this fast before and never with their backsides exposed.

No one looks back for what follows from the marsh.

More books by J. Lew

Rock, Paper, Scissors – *Reflections of Life*
Red Beans and Rice with Cornbread

Coming Soon
The Witches and Wizards of Ozz – Kingdoms Divided
Sepulcher – *The Devil's Den*

We would like to hear from you
———————————————————————

Visit our website at:
www.jlew-books.com